AND YET IT MOVES

Galileo and the Price of Genius

Matthew Minson

TLOEDPRESS

AND YET IT MOVES

FOR INFORMATION CONTACT :
WWW.WRITERMINSON.COM
TLOED PRESS
24230 KUYKENDAHL ROAD
SUITE 310 PMB 131
TOMBALL, TEXAS 77375

BOOK AND COVER DESIGN BY MINKE RANSIHOFF
PRINT ISBN: 97989854717-2-4
EBOOK ISBN: 97989854717-5-5

FIRST EDITION: SEPTEMBER 2022

10 9 8 7 6 5 4 3 2 1

Library of Congress Cataloguing-in-Publication Data available on file

"No man's life can be encompassed in one telling. There is no way to give each year its allotted weight, to include each event, each person who helped to shape a lifetime. What can be done is to be faithful in spirit to the record, and to try to find one's way to the heart of the man..."

from Gandhi by John Briley

In this dramatization of the life, struggles and triumphs of Galileo Galilei, certain situations have required creative license. While acknowledging the historical record as it is known and debated, where documentation is lacking, details have been referred to the spirit of the subject.

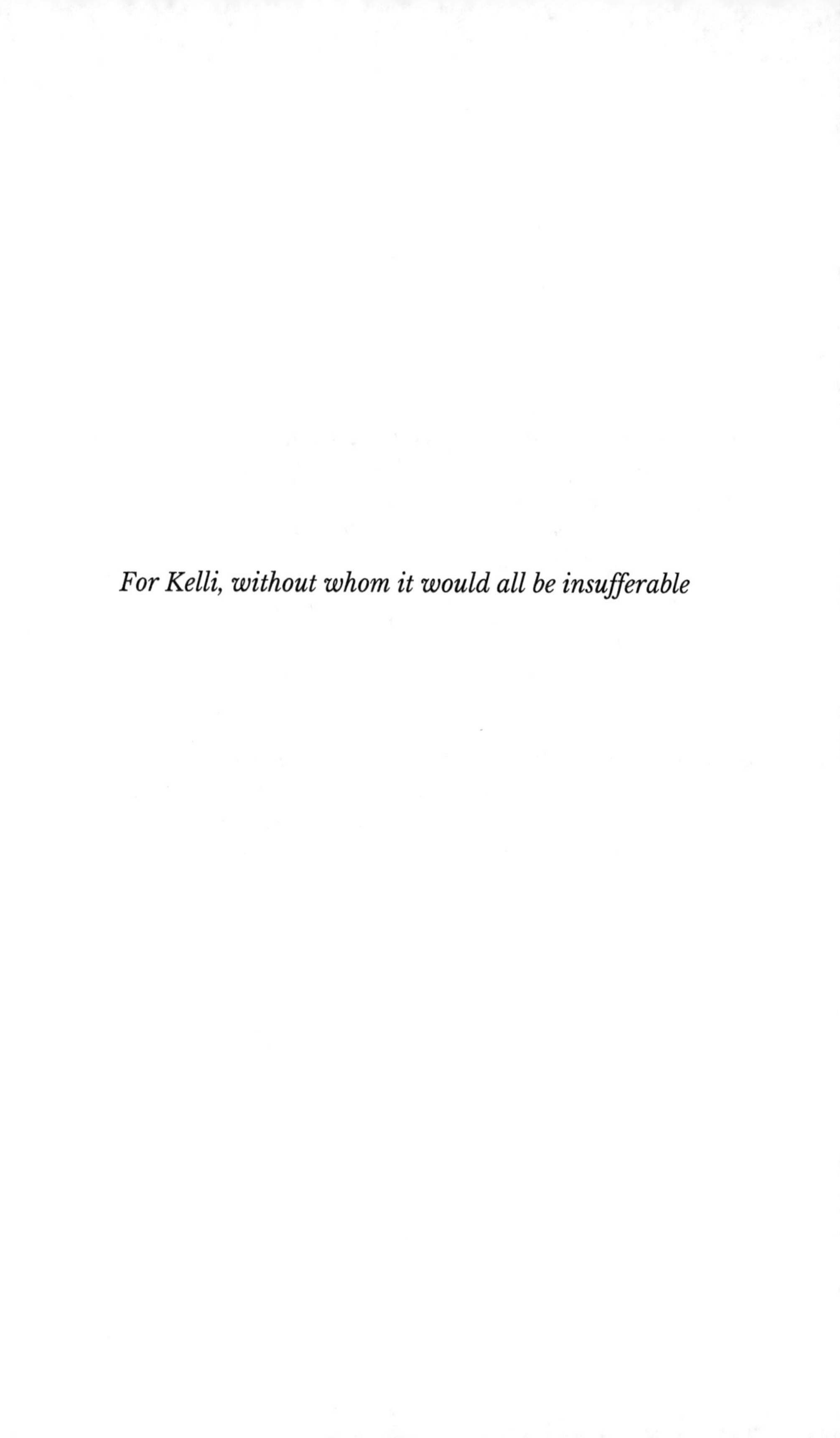

For Kelli, without whom it would all be insufferable

Also by Matthew Minson:

Fiction:

Sun City, A Hilariously Addictive Story of Rebellion

Stories Through the Ages

Non-Fiction

Prepare to Defend Yourself: How to Navigate the Healthcare System and Escape with Your Life

Prepare to Defend Yourself: How to Age Gracefully and Escape with Your Life

"All truths are easy to understand once they are discovered; the point is to discover them."- Galileo Galilei

Image by kind permission of the Master and Fellows of Trinity College, Cambridge.

AND YET IT MOVES

CHAPTER ONE

One look at the three imposing clergymen marching up the ancient cobblestone street, and everyone they passed could tell, a Holy War was coming.

The year was 1632, and for some time the Inquisition and the Renaissance had been in conflict. Despite the promise of progressive enlightenment, the world was still in the grip of superstition shrouded in religious fervor. In the highest offices of the Church, the threats of independent thought and science were more than unpopular. For the most brilliant, they were a crime. Now, even with the warm sunlight bathing the city of Florence in its peaceful, golden hue, the mighty hand of the Holy Roman Church was about to strike. Keeping a deferential step behind Father Vincenzo Maculani, church scholars, Lodovico Delle Colombe and Vincenzo Cremonini, stared intently ahead at the forbidding stone garrison. The academics knew they were the reason the Pope had signed the writ of arrest for Galileo Galilei, but the power in its execution was unmistakably Maculani's. Even before the lesser official for whom it was intended saw the papal seal or Urban VIII's signature, the appearance of the tall Inquisitor would demand his compliance. From the intense expression of his deep-set eyes and black beard trimmed to a spear-like point, to the dark flowing robes bearing the official mark of the Inquisition, Maculani was the very personification of the wrath of God. The timing was perfect. They entered the garrison just as *Comandante* Carlo Gregano was about to start his lunch.

Until that moment, the meal had promised to be a good one.

His wife had mixed the spices in the meat and onions just right, and the soup and bread paired with the hearty red wine were going to be the perfect gustatory highlight of his otherwise slow day. Food was important to Faustino Gregano, as evidenced by the immense girth that now made his once roomy chair a tight fit. It didn't really matter, though. His job was an easy one. Not much happened in the small Florentine section of Arcetri. The people were generally affluent and well-behaved enough that on most days, he could take long lunches and even get in a post-prandial nap. Today, however, was not most days. He was just raising a first spoonful to his lips when Maculani's intrusion put an intimidating stop to it all. At the sight of the Inquisitor's heavy gold cross that looked more like a badge of enforcement than a symbol of God's grace, Gregano's spoon plopped into the bowl with a soft splash. He struggled up from the chair and crossed himself. The subservient gesture was a perfect accompaniment to the intimidated look on his porcine face and Cremonini and Colombe didn't even try to suppress their derisive smiles at the social dynamic.

"*Comandante*," barked Maculani.

"Yes, Father?" choked out Gregano.

"I have a papal warrant."

He didn't even have to show it. Gregano was already lumbering to the door of the garrison barracks.

"*Attenzione*," he yelled. "*Attenzione*!"

The sudden stumbling and shuffling of armor-clad bodies inside indicated that the panicked urgency of his voice was something new for his troops and a contagious impetus for them to act. In the barracks, helmets were pulled on hurriedly as steel-tipped pikes were dragged from their racks. A moment later, the troops rushed out and assembled into formation.

For Cremonini and Colombe the display of force triggered an even greater vicarious surge of empowerment than they had so far experienced riding on Maculani's coattails. This was earthly physical might, a war machine, the kind that could force an opponent into humiliating subjugation, and they puffed as if it was an extension of their own ego and strength.

Gregano drew his sword and gave the order, "March!"

As they started on their way, the synchronized stamp of boots echoed menacingly on the narrow street, and the impact on the civilian population as they approached made the two Church scholars' experience even headier. For men who spent their lives poring over texts and arguing vigorously with other spindly, bookish creatures about the nuance in a scriptural verse, this was a real taste of power, and they liked it. After years of intellectual humiliation, they were finally going to see the egotistical Galileo brought to heel. In their minds it was too long in coming. They smiled, remembering the day they brought the heretical text to the Pope. When His Holiness had not been appropriately offended, when he had actually seemed amused by Galileo's satirical representation of the characters arguing the blasphemous concepts, they had been the ones to point out the critical passage that kindled his fury.

They had done that, and now with the massive force presence marching ahead, they were going to teach the offender an overdue lesson.

•

The cluttered table where Galileo scribbled feverishly on his new work was a true representation of order among chaos. Though Sister Maria Celeste, who really ran the house, felt compelled to begin cleaning around him, she knew better than to do so without caution. To say that her father could be temperamental was a sympathetic assessment worthy of a saint.

Even at her arrogant worst, Sister Maria Celeste, or Virginia, the birth name that her father still sometimes accidentally called her, would never have considered herself a saint. Now she moved around him carefully, plucking up wadded bits of editorially discarded parchment, empty inkwells, a plate leftover from his lunch, and an empty wine bottle next to a glass with barely one sip remaining. Throughout her cleaning, Galileo hadn't looked up once. Such was his focus, his obsession with getting what was in his head onto the page intact. She knew why. If he were disrupted, even for a moment, the string of words issuing from his brain would break and be gone like a ribbon slipping from his grasp in a high wind. Interruption when he was like this was the intellectual version of an unforgivable sin.

Silently, she leaned in, balancing the collection of crockery and trash on one crooked arm, and reached for the wine glass. She was just about to grasp it, when without looking up or slowing his scratching pen a whit, he extended a cautionary hand. With his ink-stained fingertips spread wide, he grasped the glass. Without pausing in the slightest, he brought it around to his lips and drained it before holding it back out for her to take. It was the only sign that he was aware of the existence of anything other than the parchment in front of him at all.

It might have been truly infuriating, but she loved him. She knew too well that these sorts of moments were the trade-offs of living with genius. Despite her irritation, she couldn't help but react with a smile. She took a quick look at the other items in the room that attested to what that great gray head was capable of producing. There was the telescope, aimed at the window, where later the night sky would reveal its wonders, and above it and closer to the wall, the large uniform weight suspended by a spring from a beam in the ceiling. On a shelf, next to his precious books, some by his own authorship, was the famous Galilean thermometer, a fluid-filled, glass cylinder containing colored, weighted globes that suspended quantifiably in concert with the temperature. Spread out on the walls where any other fashionable home would have had tapestries of rich color and material, her father had attached maps representing the phases of the moon and correlated tables of high and low tide. Alongside, was a hand-drawn representation of the lunar surface and the world-famous sketch of the starbursts composing Orion's belt. Lastly, on the opposite wall, but not in opposition, was a large wooden crucifix.

"Thank you, Papa," she said and took the glass before turning and heading toward the door.

Behind her, Galileo stopped writing for a moment. He paused, working something out, and thoughtfully stroked his long beard with an ink-stained thumb. When he had his conclusion, he went back to writing. The gesture left a thin dark trail from his mouth down his silver facial hair, then the ensuing loud scratch of his pen on the paper indicated the intensity of the captured thought. It was always that way. The more difficult the question, the more effort it took to arrive at the solution, the harder he bore down with his pen. As a result, the tip of the quill dug into the paper a little more forcefully, and the script stood out in a darker fashion than the rest of the text.

"Involuntary emphasis." That was what Maria Celeste called it whenever she read his work and saw the incidentally bolded passage. Now, however, her attention was focused on the dirty dishes that she set on the shelf in the kitchen. There was some comfort for her in that simple task and not just because it was helping him. It represented that no matter how great his intellect, just like the rest of them, the man had to eat. And, she thought, looking at the empty bottle and wine glass, he definitely has to drink.

•

Back on the Florentine thoroughfare, the militant, staccato trudge of the armored men's feet echoed off the narrow stone walls framing the street. It was an impressive and formidable sound and told anyone who heard them approach that someone somewhere was in trouble. Most reacted with fear, even if they didn't have a reason that would make them the unfortunate candidate.

A simple vendor with his wares on display began grabbing his belongings to haul them away. A merchant closed his doors and shuttered his shop windows. Beggars with no possessions to protect, but mindful of the potential end to their freedom, scurried away at the sound of the approaching footfalls.

Behind the intimidating processional, Father Maculani and the two malevolent scholars followed like royalty behind a battlefield cohort.

"Strength and justification," mumbled Cremonini.

"On earth as it is in heaven," added Colombe.

Maculani, of course, said nothing. There was no need. He was used to this. An Inquisitor inspired fear wherever he went, even without an armed retinue.

They had gone about a quarter of a mile when they rounded a corner to a row of houses. While not of an overtly affluent style, they were nonetheless, the sort that indicated the occupants were of the newly expanding bourgeois as the French were calling them. These fledgling owners of modest wealth that even the commoners could accumulate if they had an idea, product or willingness to exert themselves were an exciting hallmark of the Renaissance. Appropriately enough, Florence had emerged as the very cradle of the movement. Free thought, within reason, and a new valuation of personhood that included a departure from the social permanence of birth class, was a unique phenomenon, and everyone that lived there felt fortunate to be a part of it.

Of course, "within reason" was a tricky, paranoia-inducing qualifier, and it was just that which led to the worried expressions on the faces peering from the row of windows as the platoon came to a halt in front of the Galileo home. Inside, Maria Celeste looked out curiously and frowned as *Comandante* Gregano withdrew his sword and pointed it authoritatively at the front door.

"*Immettere*," he ordered, and immediately the front row of armed men charged forward. They shouldered in against the door, knocking it open and poured into the house as if they were breaching an enemy fortress. Unfortunately for them, once inside they didn't appear to have any idea what to do next. Nothing about the place seemed remotely out of the ordinary or nefarious. There was no apparent opposition or felony underway. Confronted with only an elderly nun emerging from the kitchen, they lowered their pikes and looked at each other with conflicted, uncertain expressions.

"Wh...what is it?" asked Maria Celeste.

Silence followed. The troopers couldn't answer at first and a couple even looked away with embarrassment. Maculani, however, was at no such loss for words.

"The will of God...Sister," he said sweeping into the house.

He held up the opened writ so that she could see the declaration and the ornate papal seal at the bottom.

The use of her title was intentional, a tactic to remind her of their respective stations and rank in the Church. At the same time polite in language and forceful in tone, it made her step back involuntarily. His penetrating stare fixed on her expectantly as he snatched the writ away and rolled it up. Lowering her head submissively, she crossed herself. Behind him, Cremonini and Colombe smirked delightedly.

Despite the civil authority of the armed men, it was clear to everyone that Maculani was in charge now. He looked at the door to the study.

"In there." He pointed.

Without hesitation, the troop charged the door and knocked it open where, despite the ruckus and noise, Galileo was still feverishly working at his desk. He didn't look up. Not even as the armed men invaded. Not even as they halted and looked around in awe at the veritable museum that was manifested in the different apparatuses, inventions, charts and drawings. Not even when Maculani stormed in, glowered at them and gave the order to seize him.

At no point did Galileo look up.

"Please," gasped Maria Celeste. "He is an old man."

They weren't listening.

It wasn't until two of the guardsmen had grabbed Galileo's arms and pulled him away, mid-sentence, that he turned his face toward them with a startled look of surprise. The pen tumbled from his grasp and landed on the document with an inky splash. Drawn by the absorption of the dry paper, the rest of the retained ink in the quill's tip bled out in a wide, black pattern that eventually swallowed up and obscured the last unfinished word.

Galileo didn't see any of that. He was too busy being dragged away. It didn't matter though. He was so old and thin and frail that the two strong *Conestabile* easily lifted him, and there was no chance he would fall. He craned his neck to get a look at his study, disturbed by the breakage he now heard. Cremonini and Colombe walked presumptively past him and looked around the room with an indulgent hatred that only emboldened when Maculani expressed his own estimation of the study with a look of disgust. They had the upper hand now, and Cremonini in particular couldn't contain himself.

"Destroy these abominations," he commanded.

A momentary silence followed as all eyes turned toward him. None had more of a quelling effect than Maculani's. His stare bored into the presumptive church scholar with an expression of offense and surprise. Colombe looked at his colleague as though he thought he might really be in danger from the Inquisitor. Cremonini all but withered.

"Apologies," he said looking down.

That satisfied Maculani. With an encompassing sweep of his arm, he gave the reinforcing order, "Destroy it."

Galileo didn't show any emotion at all now. He just looked on calmly as the troop began a wholesale smashing of his life's work. One of the guardsmen slammed his pike against the glass cylinder of his thermometer, shattering it into a cascade of distilled water and jagged shards. The suspended globes inside spilled out in a chromatic avalanche of wet breakage that landed musically on the stone floor.

Another pike swept upward knocking his military compass, a brass instrument that looked something like a cross between a masonic square and nautical sextant, off its hook. It fell clattering, and even before it stopped bouncing, another steel-edged blade slammed down breaking it in half. Other hands grabbed charts and drawings, ripping them from the wall.

Then they came to the telescope.

At that moment, Maculani stepped in front of the stoic Galileo. With his view blocked, the only evidence of what was happening was the distinct sound of metal giving way and the sharp brisance of the thick lenses cracking. It seemed to Galileo remarkably like the sound of a cut stone being freed. Then more glass broke, and he heard a splash. Mercifully, he couldn't see the explosion of smashed inkwells with the dark droplets landing on the wall like intellectual blood splatter.

His eyes were fixed on Maculani, who unfurled his writ and started to read.

"Galileo Galilei, you are charged with the crime of heresy and will be jailed until such time as you may be judged, and the proper course for the reclamation of your soul, determined."

Maculani looked up and rerolled the document.

"Surely it is harmful to the soul to make it a heresy to believe what is proved," answered Galileo.

It was unemotional, professorial, defiant. For a moment, Maculani stared at him with those keen, piercing, black eyes. The light in them was almost eager. Clear to all observing, the battle of wits was on now, and it was one that could very easily lead to death.

"Take him to prison," said Maculani without breaking eye contact.

The strong hands grabbed his shoulders and hoisted Galileo backward. As he was whisked through the doorway, Maria Celeste reached out in desperation, but Galileo didn't see. His attention was focused on the carnage and destruction of his telescope. Cremonini and Colombe watched with complete satisfaction as the instrument that inspired Galileo's offending documentation was reduced to ruin.

As the two *Conestabile* dragged him across the threshold to the street, Galileo glanced back at his daughter.

"I will bring food to you in the prison," she promised.

He smiled wryly.

"Just don't forget the wine."

She didn't quite manage a smile, but nodded vigorously, willing back her tears.

Inside the study, the victorious invaders were now pawing through Galileo's remaining belongings with a voyeuristic relish. While Maculani was infinitely more vicious, his interest was purer, a pursuit of evidence. For the church scholars, it was an odd form of intellectual prurience, an unsavory voyeuristic peek into the mind of their academic better. They greedily perused the papers, the charts, the scraps of paper bearing only a few phrases or in some instances, a single word. In other cases, the hen scratch was just the germ of an idea. The naked, exposed process of what they could never hope to emulate, and it was all defiled now. Cremonini and Colombe leered at it with an unprofessional glee while the armed men continued with the wreckage. Colombe rummaged through the rubble on the desk. Among the pieces of collapsed bookshelf and volumes scattered about, he spotted something.

"Wait," he said.

The activity in the room came to a stop and every head turned. Colombe swept away some loose sheets to uncover a text. *The Dialogue Concerning the Two Chief World Systems*. He picked it up and with a triumphant look held it above his head. Then he stepped toward Maculani to hand it over.

"Ah, the book," said the Inquisitor.

"His fate," affirmed Colombe with a self-righteous tone.

This was what they had come for. Evidence of the offending text. It was probably the original draft of the work that had led the Pope to consign his former friend, Galileo, to the tender mercies of the Inquisition. Now there would be no way that he could offer the argument that someone else had used his name. Not that any of them thought he would opt for that. Galileo was notoriously defiant, even in the face of scrutiny and criticism, but he had already been brought up on charges years before and warned, so this time a judgment would carry real punishment.

Maculani looked at the book. It wasn't just an original text. It was bound by a uniform woven thread, meticulously stitched. It was almost perfect, the work of a real craftsman. Maculani ran his thumb across it. That was not one of the *Professore's* competencies and with the papal prohibition against such a publication, whomever had done the work had committed a crime as well. He filed that away for later use.

On the floor, Cremonini pawed through the fallen books from the shelf, tucking selected volumes under his arm. When he had what he was after, he stood up. Maculani, Colombe and he walked out the door.

Just before they exited, Gregano asked, "What about the rest of it?"

His statement and tone indicated the final stage in a complete abdication of authority. Maculani paused and looked back.

"Destroy everything," he said. Then he spotted the crucifix. Pointing his finger at it, he added, "Except for that."

•

Despite the heavy traffic over the years, the steep road to the hilltop prison had somehow never worn smooth. Perhaps it was all the large rocks or some inherent quality of the hard soil that stubbornly defied the processional of boots, hooves and wheels that had borne the numerous condemned to their fate. Whatever the reason, it made the harsh interior of the prison wagon that now carried Galileo even more of a punitive ordeal as it jostled and bounced him on the rough wooden seat. With each rise and fall, the chains that linked him to the floorboard clinked a reminder of his current state as did the metal cuffs that scraped and cut at his ankles. Each sharp jolt was a painful offense to his ancient, skinny hips, and in an attempt at distraction, he stared through the bars at the growing, gawking, hostile public that seemed to relish his predicament.

Apparently, some charges triggered a special kind of public fury. For Galileo, there was no logic to the different responses of a society and its quick mass judgment of a crime. An act of treason or offense to God generated a much greater and disproportionate reaction than did, say, the taking of a human life. It was curious to him as he watched the mob along the road, how the charge against him provided a convenient outlet for such a broad range of hysterics. The unhealthy, ugly, festering boils of emotional reaction arising from their lifetimes of humiliation, poverty, and cumulative rage were giving out now in a cathartic release. To Galileo, observing from within the relative safety of the wagon, it was a disturbing, alarming, and tremendously fascinating phenomenon.

A toothless old man shook his bony fist furiously but impotently in the air.

"Heretic!" he squawked with a yodeling lilt.

An ambient chorus of aggrieved shrieks rose behind him in agreement. From the look on his face, it was easily one of the most validating moments in his life and his lips peeled back in a horribly gummy smile.

A filthy old hag, wrapped in rags, reeking with an unwashed stench, limped up next to the road and spat viciously. Next to her, an emaciated, wild-eyed woman made an obscene gesture.

"Blasphemer!" she shrieked.

The undaunted Galileo looked back through the bars with a neutrally fascinated expression. Then he raised his manacled hands and gave a simple wave like a dignitary acknowledging an adoring parade crowd. The gesture was like dousing turpentine on an open flame, and the reaction of the mob became even more violently agitated. Galileo didn't notice though. He was already looking above them, toward the distance where the high tower of the prison loomed ominously.

His expression sobered, though it was not fearful at all. His eyes were considered, fierce and conveyed the grim visage of a general, anticipating an impending military campaign.

•

Upon receiving the news of Galileo's arrest and the Pope's appointment of him for the defense, Cardinal Roberto Bellarmine had left immediately for the prison. Although he viewed Galileo with high esteem and even some affection, he knew that the man's arrogance and radical scientific views would require powerful advocacy if he were to escape the Inquisition's punishment.

"I hear *Doctore* Galilei is clever," said his young assistant, Father Leonardo Ferrero.

Cardinal Bellarmine paused on the steps inside the prison tower and looked back at him. The aspiring Jesuit hadn't been entirely eager to join his mentor to defend the accused, and so far, the experience at the prison wasn't changing his mind.

"Yes," panted the plump Bellarmine, putting a steadying hand against the damp stone wall. "Sometimes too clever, by far."

Ferrero looked at his struggling superior with genuine concern. He loved the man. Bellarmine had been his mentor for over a year now, ever since he heard the old Cardinal speak during a symposium of the *Collegio Romano*. His eloquence and brilliance made it no surprise when Ferrero later learned that he had been a lifelong friend of the controversial genius Galileo, but this new duty put the young clergyman in a conflicted state of mind. He had read Galileo's other great work, the infamous and popular *Sidereus Nuncius*, and like many other scholars, especially among the Jesuits, he recognized that the work in "The Starry Messenger" was sound and accurate.

But the charges and coming trial weren't about that work.

This new hearing was political and personal, and it carried with it the formal charge of heresy. Galileo had angered and alienated powerful people, and they were bent on retribution. If he had tried to select his enemies purely for their ability to do him harm, he couldn't have organized a more devastating group. But Ferrero wasn't thinking about that now.

He frowned and placed a concerned hand on the bent back of the old winded Cardinal.

"So many stairs. Eminence, are you sure you should be doing this?" he asked.

Bellarmine glanced back at him. His face was sanguine now, almost scarlet. The question was a little impertinent, but seeing Ferrero's genuine worry, he couldn't take offense. He nodded an assurance. A moment later, the distressed flush had stopped its spread and the color of his face began to return to normal. He took a restorative breath and straightened up.

"Yes," he finally said and slowly resumed the climb.

Fortunately, they had only a short way to go before the stairwell opened onto a wide hall. Standing before a closed door was a cretinous, paunchy guard whose badging indicated some moderate seniority. He hadn't been waiting long for the churchmen, but even the brief exertion of standing at attention constituted a strain and he looked at Bellarmine and Ferrero with an expression of happy relief.

"Eminence," he said opening the door.

Inside was a spare, stone room with a single large table and chairs. Bowl-shaped sconces of lamp oil jutted from the walls, and small flames flickered just above the rims. Between their soft illumination and the ambient light from the single narrow window, the forbidding details of the room stood out in their austerity. That was the point, though. It was the interrogation room of a prison, after all.

"My son," answered Bellarmine as he walked in and sat down heavily on one side of the table. Ferrero went to the far end and unshouldered the bag he had been carrying. He started unloading the contents – paper, ink and a large number of books. The guard watched suspiciously, lingering a little longer than was necessary. Bellarmine looked at him, piqued immediately by the questionable interest. The man was a spy, and Bellarmine could guess for whom.

"How long have *Professore*s Cremonini and Colombe been here today?" he asked.

The first reaction of the cretinous guard was obviously to lie, that much was evident, but one sharp look from the Cardinal and the guard knew he was too smart for a clumsy attempt at deception. The doughy man faltered, stammered, and then swallowed hard. Finally, unable to come up with something better, he defaulted to telling the truth.

"Uh, they, uh, have been here all morning, Eminence. With the large crowds, they've had to arrive early every day."

He had said too much. He stopped, looking uncertain and horrified, like he had lost control of some embarrassing bodily function. Once open, it seemed, the floodgates of truth had been impossible to close, and he flailed a bit now, bewildered and appalled at his involuntary issue of candor. Bellarmine almost took pity on him, but he knew that this man was not an ally, so he said nothing and kept the stern glare on until the cretinous guard turned and walked uncomfortably from the room. As the door closed, Ferrero looked up.

"He is no friend, that one. Be careful what you say in his presence," warned Bellarmine flatly.

Ferrero looked back down at the line of books on the table.

"But Galileo is a friend of yours."

It sounded like both an analysis and an open-ended question. Bellarmine smiled. A sense of real affection for the young Jesuit washed over him. He knew his acolyte wasn't in agreement with Galileo's most recent actions, and was greatly offended by the new book, but he had come along with Bellarmine, nonetheless. Now Bellarmine felt he owed him an explanation.

"We were students together." He smiled at the memory. "He was always a much better student than I."

Ferrero sat down, ready to listen as the Cardinal began his story.

"Like myself he came from an accomplished family. His father, Vincenzo Galilei was a virtuoso with the lute. A member of the Holy Academy, in fact. Because of that, it was a given that his son would follow suit. That is what you did in those days." His smile broadened. "But they had no idea. Even then Galileo had a mind of his own."

"Willful," said Ferrero tersely.

"Mmmm." Bellarmine made a laughing sound that was partly scoffing. "If you wish. He was ten. His father was giving a recital, and young Galileo was watching him play, very closely. Everyone there thought he was entranced by the music." Bellarmine shook his head before continuing. "It wasn't that. He was watching his father's foot. The tapping was a perfect mathematical timing of the music. From the way he told it later, I'm not sure he was even aware a song was being played."

Bellarmine paused, indulging his amusement at the memory. Then he glanced at Ferrero. The young priest's face showed he wasn't nearly as charmed by the anecdote.

"He sees the world in ways that not everyone else can. I've always thought that such an intellectual gift forgave many of his minor sins... and a few of the major ones as well," he offered as an explanation.

Ferrero didn't look swayed.

"It was the same many years later when we met at the University. Galileo was there to study medicine. That was the compromise he made with his father. If he were allowed to do something other than music, then he had to choose a lucrative course of study. So, he was going to be a physician." Bellarmine looked off thoughtfully and smiled. "I can still recall the details of that first day. *Professore* Antonelli was our teacher, the leading medical scholar in the whole of Italy." He paused a moment before adding ironically, "He was certainly the oldest. We used to joke that if a patient were in real pain, all that was required to alleviate their suffering was to force them to listen to one of his lectures, and within minutes they would be anesthetized."

Ferrero smiled. He had heard of the legendarily boring *Doctore* Antonelli.

"He had constructed a wooden homunculus, representing every aspect of our knowledge of pathology at the time."

"A homunculus?" asked Ferrero.

"It's an exaggerated alchemical form of a human body in diagram, disproportionately presented to emphasize which held the most importance anatomically. A large head, hands, things like that," he said. "In this case it also had the seasonal landscapes that governed the different systems of the human body and the manner in which they manifested as a disease, all arrayed next to it."

He suddenly took on a raspy, nasal tone and began imitating the late *Professore* Antonelli.

"As all educated people know, illness occurs when sin causes an imbalance in the natural alignment of the humors established by God the Father, and He shows us that autumn is associated with an overabundance of black bile. Spring is blood. Winter, phlegm, and summer, of course is yellow bile."

Bellarmine chuckled, shaking his head.

"It sounds awful," said Ferrero.

Bellarmine looked upward to heaven. "Forgive me Father, for speaking so disrespectfully of the dead." Looking at Ferrero with another slight, mirthful sparkle, he added, "Of course those lectures killed my interest in medicine so—"

"Is that why Galileo didn't pursue it too?"

Bellarmine's smile widened.

"No. With him it was different. One day while I was attempting to take notes and stay awake, I looked over and saw Galileo staring up at the ceiling. I knew how smart he was, but to not to have to take even a single note, well, I was a little resentful. I remember challenging him on that. He just kept looking up. Then he placed his hand over his heart. You know what he said to me?"

"What?" asked Ferrero.

"He said, 'Why should I? The answers are always the same. Drink Holy Water. Cut holes in the skull to let out the evil thoughts. Bleed them white to expunge the sin...and always...always...pray, pray, pray.' He was very disdainful. But he was also right."

Ferrero smiled. From what he knew of medicine, Galileo had a point.

"The whole time, he was looking up with his hand over his heart. So, I looked up, but all I saw was the chandelier swaying slightly with the breeze. I had no idea what had him so fascinated."

"What did he see?" asked Ferrero. He sounded interested. Bellarmine liked that.

"I didn't know until a month later. He had stopped coming to classes and there was word that they were going to expel him, and then... one day, out of the blue, he walked in with his first breakthrough."

"His twin pendulums," affirmed Ferrero.

Bellarmine gave him an appreciative look. He was hooked, just as Bellarmine had been that day.

"Yes. The pendula. Twins but for their corresponding size, mass and length of the lever arms. He set them on a table in front of the whole of the faculty, with that look on his face. You know, the one that told everyone in observance that he knew something more than the rest of them. Then he set the apparatus in motion. They swung in perfect unison. Identical arcs." Bellarmine leaned forward toward Ferrero for emphasis and added with a delighted energy, "That was what the observation of the chandelier had inspired. With his demonstration he had proven the mathematical theory that 'like' objects in motion are equal to each other, regardless of their size." Bellarmine looked energized. "This was groundbreaking. There was a democracy in the inanimate, and he had shown it with his simple elegant experiment. It advanced on every conventional academic theory and made him at once controversial and celebrated."

Bellarmine sat back chuckling, savoring the reminiscence.

"All the mathematicians' squabblings were resolved right there in front of them as the pendula continued their irrefutable synchrony." Bellarmine's eyebrows went up. "It very nearly set off a riot."

For a moment he could see it all again. The triumphantly exulting scholars, celebrating as their theories were confirmed. Then when one of the intellectually vanquished could take it no longer, a desk was overturned, and two scrawny octogenarians began trading blows as the rest of the college attempted to separate them. Galileo was paying no mind, however. He was busy unrolling a large scroll of parchment upon which he had diagrammed the calculations and formula that supported the demonstration. When it was fully open, the furor in the room quelled, and soon even those who were still stinging from their error were congratulating him.

Bellarmine grinned at Ferrero.

"He was soon appointed the youngest *Professore* at the *Accademia del Pisa* where he was free to pursue the *Disegno* philosophy."

Ferrero looked impressed. "I did not know that."

"The institution dedicated to raising science to an art," affirmed Bellarmine.

Ferrero mulled that.

"You wonder why I am here?" reiterated Bellarmine. "Because he sees what no one else can see. He measures"—Bellarmine searched for the exact words— "the immeasurable."

Ferrero smiled politely. He understood, but it was also clear to Bellarmine, he did not yet completely agree.

•

In another part of the prison tower, Cremonini sat on the edge of a high window and watched the courtyard below as if waiting for a sign. Seated at a table in the room, Maculani was working his way through the documents stolen from Galileo's home while Colombe, at the other end of the table taking notes. From the look on the Inquisitor's face, it was apparent that he was getting what he needed from the material.

Just then, a movement below caught Cremonini's attention.

Sister Maria Celeste was leaving, an empty basket in her hand. He had to admire her dedication to her father. Family members of prisoners were notorious for early enthusiasm in supplying an incarcerated loved one with food and comfort, only to exhaust quickly. The long trip, the unpleasant setting and procedures wore them out in short order, which was, of course, the intent. The eventual privation and hunger were as much a part of weakening an accused's resistance as any legal tactic of the system. The sustained visits over the last month, however, had made it clear that the nun was not about to let that happen.

Every day, she had come, carrying enough provisions that except for the harshness of his cell, Galileo was living fairly well. In her own way, she was as obstinate as her father, but more importantly, she was predictable. Given Galileo's fascination with the mechanics of time, it shouldn't have been a surprise. Regardless, Cremonini was grateful for it and turned back toward the other two as she swept out through the prison gates with her habit flapping like the wings of a blackbird. Colombe was holding up a worn copy of *The Works of Copernicus*. Given on his expression, he could have been a sleuth brandishing a newly discovered murder weapon.

"The root of his heresy," he said trying to sound wise. Then he picked up the copy of Galileo's infamous document, the *Sidereus Nuncius* or Starry Messenger. "And the leaf," he continued, referencing it.

Maculani barely looked up from the newly printed copy of *The Dialogue Concerning the Two Chief World Systems*.

"This then would be the flower?" he asked. He looked at the two church scholars. "Have you read them?" He sounded distant, neutral, despite the severity in his eyes.

Cremonini and Colombe shot each other a quick look. They had, but the direct manner of the question by the Inquisitor gave them both pause.

Seeing the reaction, Maculani stifled a smile and said, "It is not a sin to be informed."

"A necessary evil, I'm afraid," agreed Cremonini.

"Forgive us, Father," piled on Colombe.

A wrinkle of irritation at the unctuousness formed around Maculani's eyes. Generally, he liked men with a little more spine. Mostly though, it was the context of the confessional tone and the term *Father* that bothered him. He had been a lot more than a lowly priest for some time now, and the reference and reminder landed wrong, angering him just a bit.

"I gave up a country priesthood for the Inquisition, in no small part, so that I wouldn't have to listen to inane confessions." The intrusion of the distasteful memory showed powerfully. "You've no idea how wearisome the daily disclosures of country boys buggering cattle can be."

For a moment, silence held the room. Cremonini and Colombe just stared, uncertain how to respond at first. Finally, Cremonini remembered what he had intended to say when he left his perch on the windowsill.

"The, uh, Sister, she's gone."

Before either one could respond, a knock sounded at the door.

"Come in," said Maculani.

It opened and the cretinous guard entered dutifully.

"You wanted a report on the *Professore*," he said.

"You made sure the Sister didn't bring him anything with which to write?" said Maculani with a slight edge to his voice.

"No, Father, it was just food and wine."

Maculani and the others didn't say anything at first. The guard looked from face to face. Eventually, he couldn't stand the silence.

"It was a very good wine," he added clumsily. "*Doctore* Galilei is partial to good wine."

He hesitated, at a loss, and stood there like a giant infant.

"Has he asked for pen and paper?" said Maculani impatiently.

The guard shifted his stance uncomfortably. "Oh, uh, no, Father. He asked for a knife."

Maculani's eyebrows went up. Colombe and Cremonini looked at each other in silent speculation and then back to the guard.

"Did you give him one?" asked Maculani.

The cretinous guard smiled and straightened with a look of self-congratulation. Then with a note of braggadocio he added, "We gave him a spoon."

The churchmen chuckled.

•

The inadequate light from the tall slit window in the prison cell was just enough to make the otherwise overwhelming darkness seem even more sensorially deprived. Against one wall, a rough cot was positioned with a small table next to it. Alongside a bottle of wine, the single flickering candle in its center cast a strangely variable illumination onto Galileo's back as he knelt and worked at the stones on the far wall. From beneath his body, a scraping sound could be heard in sync with his movement, and a small cascade of dust and occasionally coarser sand spilled down onto his robes and the floor. He paused and flexed his hands, spreading and clenching his fingers to work the circulation back into them. This kind of work was a lot more demanding than scratching an inky trail on a sheet of parchment, and on top of that, he was an old man. Nevertheless, he was committed to the task and once the ache subsided, he gripped the handle of the spoon to resume carving the letters into permanence.

When he had finished, Galileo ran his finger along the grooves of each letter. Then he blew away the remaining dust. He was just taking stock of his work when the sound of heavy approaching footsteps made him alert. He tucked the spoon away and brushed the dust off his robes hastily. Then he stood up and hurried back across the room to sit down on the cot. He looked at his work on the other side of the cell. Standing out, a foot high, in the candlelight were the etched letters of his defiant manifesto. The heavy tread outside was almost to the door and Galileo reached out to pull the small table with the flickering candle a little closer. As he did, the soft illumination of the words disappeared into darkness. It didn't matter that his captors weren't confronted with it immediately. In fact, that was preferable. What mattered was that he knew they were there, and darkness or not, like the truth behind them, they had been commemorated.

The guard's key rasped harshly as it turned in the lock and the hinges whined as the door to the cell swung open. The cretinous guard stepped in and looked at Galileo. The old scholar stared back with a look that wasn't like what a prisoner normally showed. In most instances resignation and even outright fear occupied the face of anyone who had been in the dungeon room for even a short period of time, but Galileo did not show any of that. He almost looked at ease. One edge of his mouth was turned up in a kind of mirthful defiance, and the look in his eye as he estimated his brutal captor, was nothing short of amused. It was the opposite of what the guard expected, and he suddenly looked as confused as he had when Maculani asked about Galileo's supply delivery from Maria Celeste earlier. All else failing, he opted for an abrupt directive.

"On your feet. You've been summoned," he said.

Galileo didn't move. He simply held up a finger for a minor indulgence of time and then reached down to retrieve a half-empty glass of wine. Tilting his head back, he drained it as the guard watched. When he set it down, he had a sudden look of sensitized awareness at the heavy man's interest. Smiling generously, he stood up and handed the wine bottle to the guard. At first the heavy jailer looked delighted, then he frowned. It felt empty. He shook it, only to find not even the slightest drop remaining. With a resentful grimace, he tossed it away angrily and followed Galileo out.

•

Bellarmine didn't need to read the texts on the table. He'd been privy to most of the work when it was composed. Now he was far more intrigued with Ferrero's reaction as he digested the content. He smiled at his protégé's concentration. There was hope for the young man. Certainly, he possessed all of the absolutes of youth, the certain disdain for the archaic traditions and nonsense from the previous generation. He also had a hubris brought on by the circumscribed awareness of one's own experiences in that absence of historical context, but even as much as he had not wanted to assist with the defense of Galileo, he tempered his instinct with thoughtful consideration.

Yes, thought Bellarmine, there is hope.

Something in one of the passages had triggered a question, and Ferrero frowned and lowered the book.

"He can't help himself, can he?"

"Galileo? No. He cannot," said Bellarmine. "You'll see when you speak with him. His conclusions are unbroken horses he simply can't bridle."

Ferrero nodded his understanding if not his agreement. "So, it all started when you were friends at the University?"

That made sense to him. The Cardinal was being loyal, if not to the ideas, then surely to his friend. Bellarmine considered Ferrero's words a moment.

"I don't know," he said a little sadly. "I think some men are just born to an incongruence with the world, but the university is certainly where the open conflicts began. Genius by its very presence draws fire. It was when he put his theories down on paper that he really began the great battle that defined his life."

The conflict on Ferrero's face deepened. "And that could end it."

They both sobered at that.

"I am curious," started Ferrero before hesitating.

"Yes?"

"Well, why did he choose to write in Italian? It would seem an educated man, one who knew Latin, who could record in a scholarly way, would not have used the common language."

He looked like he didn't want to continue, but Bellarmine could tell that there was more.

"Go on."

"Well, did he refuse to do it because it was the language of the Church, was he trying to oppose...God?"

Bellarmine looked at his young colleague and smiled gently. "No, he wanted the truths of God's works known to all men, not just the select few. In many ways, he was the Greek ideal of scholarship right down to the very principle of the *Demokratus*, accessibility of the idea to all."

"You admire him still," said Ferrero.

Bellarmine shrugged.

"It is a noble philosophy, and that is hard not to admire." He considered something and continued with, "Not that the *Doctore* was completely impractical. For example, when he told his father he was giving up medicine for mathematics..." He chuckled. "Well, he very nearly disowned Galileo. Then he challenged him. Told his son, he would change his opinion if, and only if, he could make a financial success of it."

Bellarmine shrugged and smiled, savoring the recollection.

"It seemed impossible," he continued. "Then again, it probably would have been for anyone else."

Bellarmine paused and stared into space as if seeing some long past event. He was remembering that day when a young Galileo had taken his first steps toward the prison cell he occupied today. It had been an extraordinary moment in the lives of both men.

CHAPTER TWO

The energy in the main hall of the *Accadémia dei Lincei* was a combination of excitement, incredulity and begrudging respect emanating from the mix of scholars, military men and church officers in attendance. Having heard that a demonstration by the young *Professore* Galilei was in the offing, they knew it could not be missed, no matter how incredible the rumors might seem. His most recent invention, even if it only delivered half its claims, would have not just scientific, but political implications as well.

No one that had been invited dared to decline.

Seated in the back, the young clerical scholar Bellarmine waited for his friend to arrive. No matter what anyone thought about Galileo, he knew the presentation certainly wasn't going to be anything near normal.

At one end of the hall, a large, hay-stuffed target had been set up facing the front. At the other end, a light swivel gun was aimed at it. The dramatic arrangement promised that unlike most dry academic presentations, what they were about to see would at least be distinguished by smoke and loud noises. Despite his being an extremely young professor with just a year's teaching experience, Galileo was already becoming known as one who could shake up the academic world in a very non-traditional fashion. Even so, the audience had been waiting for some time and were now starting to look a little impatient. Just when they seemed at their limit, he swept into the room with his latest device.

At first glance it wasn't all that impressive.

In his hands were two long cubic rectangles of wood inscribed with markings, similar to those found on a ruler and joined by a circular brass hinge. That was it. The faces in the audience showed that they were clearly underwhelmed. Brows knitted with confusion. Heads shook, and more than a few shoulders shrugged. Bellarmine, however, simply smiled. He was watching Galileo, who took no notice of the tepid response.

He was too focused on setting up the device next to the swivel gun. He spread the two pieces of wood to an angle of 45 degrees, and reaching to his pocket, retrieved a U-shaped brace of metal, which he attached to each respective leg by a small pin. From there, he stood the device up and attached a clamp that steadied it on the table. Then he tethered a small cord with a weight at one end and suspended it from the center of the hinge so that it hung straight down. To all watching, the fully assembled apparatus resembled something like a strange naval sextant crossed with a T-square. Happy with the result, Galileo looked at the target.

"How far is it?" he asked.

"Thirty-five strides, *Doctore*," answered an assistant in the back of the room.

Galileo thought for a moment, then adjusted the device. He scribbled some notes, computed, and then looked at the audience.

"In the past, artillery accuracy required three shots. One for distant range, or to overshoot. One to undershoot. And a third intended to hit the target," he said.

The military men in the room nodded their agreement.

"That means three cannonballs, which do not come cheaply. It also means three discharges of powder, which come at a dear cost, and it means an opportunity for the enemy to strike first, which measures its cost in human life."

It was obvious now from the expressions on their faces that he had them.

"Now," he continued, "Using my compass, it will only take one shot to hit the enemy."

A rumbling dubious murmur of disdain and incredulity answered the assertion, but Galileo wasn't listening. He was measuring a small charge of powder. The amount was so small that one Vatican Guard General in the back couldn't contain himself.

"That is not enough. It won't carry the ball near the target."

Other heads around him nodded their agreement, but again, Galileo wasn't listening. He handed the powder to an assistant who loaded it into the barrel and added wadding. Galileo calculated some more and then weighed out a small iron ball that he then handed to the assistant. Finally, he adjusted the elevation of the tiny cannon's barrel and confirmed the angle by his new compass.

He paused and looked at the crowd haughtily.

"And now you shall see," he said.

He nodded at the assistant who picked up a smoldering wick and touched it to the gun's fire pan.

Even in the closed room, the *pop* and cloud of smoke exploding from the barrel was substantially less than what most had anticipated. Sure, it was still enough that they felt the percussion of overpressure in their ears and teeth, but that was nothing compared to what a standard cannon loading would have caused. They all turned and looked as the projected missile tore through the target with a harsh ripping sound of canvas. When the smoke finally cleared, the looks of astonishment had spread across every face but one.

The hole was dead center, right in the middle of the bullseye.

A plump general in the crowd crossed himself as if he had just witnessed a miracle of artillery. Young Bellarmine looked over at his friend. Galileo was smiling.

•

In the interrogation room, the much older Cardinal Bellarmine wore a similar smile at the memory.

"As a mathematician, Galileo was extraordinary, but as an inventor, the world hadn't seen his like."

"Not since da Vinci," said Ferrero with a gentle smile.

Bellarmine looked back at him and grinned.

"Perhaps, but good company, that."

A sudden boom of a cannon sounded in the distance. Ferrero got up and went to window. In the courtyard below, a billowing cloud of smoke rose above the single twenty-pounder flanked by an artillery squad.

"The noon-day signal," said Ferrero.

"And thematically, how timely," said Bellarmine with a certain ironic lilt.

"You were saying," said Ferrero returning to the table.

"The Galileo artillery compass could calculate a trajectory with deadly accuracy. It made him a very wealthy man and given the advantage it gave the papal armies and the other principalities in battle, brought him even to the attention of the Pope. The word was out, and soon he was a Medici favorite and a rising star. Famous."

"So, he was given free rein to study what he liked," said Ferrero.

"Yes," said Bellarmine. "He was indulged, and for a time...ungoverned." He paused, as if the next thought was difficult to properly convey. "It was his understanding of optics, though, the compounding of lenses, that ultimately led him to his most impressive, and ultimately damnable discovery." He shook his head again before continuing, "He had read about the Dutch and what they were doing with the magnificent tool that unlocked insight into the heavens—"

"The telescope," interrupted Ferrero.

"Yes, but it was much more than just the instrument. What he had discovered, working alone in his study, was that stacking the lenses could magnify his observation, providing much greater detail and insight than ever before."

Bellarmine looked at Ferrero like a man about to share a dangerous imputation.

"Copernicus," said Ferrero, as if reading his master's mind.

"Yes," said Bellarmine. "He proved Copernicus."

"His book, the *Sidereus Nuncius*."

Bellarmine nodded. "One might say the condemnation of it is hypocrisy. There are a number in the Church, in your own order especially, that didn't find a whit of heresy in the concept that the earth is not stationary."

Ferrero didn't say a word. He couldn't. It was true, the Jesuits had long since realized that the scientific postulates of Copernicus were undeniable. They even discussed them, albeit only within the confines of their order or the canonical school. Beyond that it was forbidden. Some members of the more conservative, less intellectually driven orders, the Franciscans and Benedictines, held fast to the idea that the words of Copernicus were an anathema to those of God. For the common parishioners, who struggled with the simpler accommodations of sin and the struggle for daily bread, witnessing such dissension within the clerical ranks would have been a disaster, and the Pope knew it. Like it or not, the head of the Church was a king, with all the politics that entailed. It wouldn't do to weaken the faithful's popular support, and so Pope Paul V had made it clear that Copernicus could only be discussed in theoretical and philosophical terms, not as scientific fact.

What Galileo wrote in the *Sidereus* text definitively and scientifically proved Copernicus' theory that the sun stood still and the planets, including Earth, revolved around it. He had, with the enhanced magnification of his telescope, mapped the movement of the heavens.

From his study he had followed the positional phases of the moon, and more importantly, the satellite bodies of the distant planet Jupiter. He established to even the least educationally sophisticated eye that, in fact, it was the Earth that moved. As is often the case with an inconvenient truth when the facts are irrefutable, the opposition chose to attack the messenger. *Ad hominum* was the term in Latin, the language of the educated, and it had been enacted completely and with full fury against Galileo.

"You know, he called the bodies, the little whirling moons surrounding Jupiter, the Medicean stars," said Bellarmine. "Forget the advancement of science. Forget the discovery. That might have been the smartest thing he did."

"Medici," said an impressed Ferrero. The utterance was accompanied by an unmistakable tone of respect.

"Yes. He allied himself with the era's greatest combined political and intellectual power, Cossimo Medici, Grand Duke of all Tuscany. The highest civilian authority, who in terms of influence was exceeded only by His Holiness, and then only in the realm of the spiritual. He had a fortune equal to the Holy Mother Church, the political acumen of Machiavelli, and should that fail, a powerful army. On that front, he had already been an early subscriber to Galileo's artillery compass for its improvement of accuracy and what it saved him financially in terms of powder and iron. So, when Galileo presented him with a beautifully drawn map of the heavens including the newly dedicated Medicean stars, well, Medici was sold. Along with the soft consent of half the intellectual clergy, Galileo was saved."

"So, no real punishment then," said Ferrero. "A slap on the hand. He was ordered to stop writing and lecturing about it."

"Yes."

"But he couldn't."

"No."

"That's why he is in trouble now."

Bellarmine smiled. It was far more complicated than that, and as intelligent as Ferrero was, he suspected that the young man only needed for him to confirm it.

"The fact is Galileo is an easy man to prosecute."

"He's arrogant."

"Oh...very," chuckled Bellarmine. "Even many of those that might defend him won't, because they loathe his manner."

"Yet you are, Eminence," countered Ferrero.

"Yes."

With that one word, Ferrero noted a slightly tender, if affectionate expression around the Cardinal's eyes. A moment of silence followed. For Bellarmine it was due to the very private recollection. For Ferrero it was out of respect for his mentor. Finally, the young Jesuit looked over the many documents on the table and frowning at the great question that had plagued him since the beginning of his involvement in the case, said, "I'll confess; I still wonder. Is brilliance enough?"

•

Maria Celeste was half-way down the hill with her empty basket when she looked up and saw the anxious, hurriedly approaching faces of her father's students, Vincenzo Viviani and Evangelista Torricelli. As they got closer, she could see that their rapid pace and the steep climb had taken a physical toll. Their cheeks were red and sweaty, and they panted as they slowed to a walk and then stopped in front of her. Both men leaned forward with their hands on their knees and sucked wind, trying to overcome the oxygen debt that their unconditioned bodies had incurred. They weren't athletic by constitution, and a life spent in sedentary study hadn't helped.

Viviani held up a pudgy hand for a moment's indulgence as he panted away. Of the two he was the shorter, and plumper, but Torricelli, while tall and angular, was apparently no better equipped for the exertion. Finally, their breathing caught up with their physiological deficit and they straightened up.

"The *Doctore*, we heard he had been taken," said Viviani.

Maria Celeste couldn't help but feel a grateful surge of affection at the look of genuine alarm on their faces. They loved her father as intensely as she.

"Yes," she said soberly. "The Inquisition."

That one word was enough, and with it the color drained from their faces. They both knew the stories. Everyone did. To be charged was to be guilty already. If the victim, the accused couldn't overcome the bias of the charge, which was virtually impossible, then a confession would have to be offered, and if that weren't given voluntarily, then extraction would be in order. All of them had seen the results of a "purification by pain" in the crippled and deformed bodies of so-called heretics who had been retrieved from Satan's grasp by way of the rack, the whip, and literal tongues of fire applied to their flesh.

The thought that such could be the fate of their beloved mentor and intellectual leader was almost too much to bear. Tears formed in Viviani's eyes.

"Is anyone speaking for the *Professore*?" asked Torricelli.

"I am told that Cardinal Bellarmine has agreed to be his counsel," said Maria Celeste.

That was at least some reassurance. Both students nodded.

"He has known him a long time and loves him," said Viviani.

"How is *Doctore* Galilei?" asked Torricelli.

Maria Celeste allowed a dry smile.

"He is, as he always is," she said. "Undaunted, defiant...old."

They all chuckled at that.

"I took him food," she continued.

"And wine, I hope," interrupted a smiling Viviani.

"And wine. Of course. I wouldn't dare go without it."

They chuckled again. Just the familiarities conveyed by the thought was restorative.

"They wouldn't allow him anything with which to write," she went on.

"He won't like that," said Torricelli.

"I suspect not," she said. "They only allowed him a spoon."

"A spoon?" frowned Viviani.

"He was using it to carve something in the wall. Letters."

Viviani and Torricelli smiled.

"What was he writing?" asked Torricelli.

"I don't know," she said. "But from what I could see, he was very committed."

•

The sudden knock at the door of the interrogation room was a formality, a warning. It swung open before either Ferrero or the Cardinal Bellarmine could acknowledge it, revealing the cretinous guard with one beefy hand encompassing Galileo's thin bicep. It was an overt gesture of control and completely unnecessary. The old scholar gave no indication of resisting or non-compliance. In fact, the ever-present twinkle of mischief on Galileo's face, indicated that rarest form of rebellion, a sharp wit, was engaged as he looked at the two priests. Then he glanced back at the guard and assumed a look of mock outrage.

"I have guests, and this is how you apportion them?"

He sounded more like a wealthy proprietor than a prisoner. Turning back to Bellarmine and Ferrero, he bowed slightly. "My friends, a thousand apologies, but the help here is simply not up to civilized standards." He gestured at the strewn papers covering the table. "Normally when I entertain, I set a much nicer table."

He looked back at the guard and clucked his tongue disapprovingly.

"I will note this in my next report to the management," he said admonishingly.

"The fare is more than adequate, honored *Doctore*" smiled Bellarmine, getting up and coming toward him.

Almost like a reflex, the guard relinquished his hold on the prisoner in deference to the Church officer. It wasn't lost on Galileo.

"Very good," he said as if the guard were suddenly some lower-level servant. "That will be all."

Probably from the sheer audacity and self-assurance of his prisoner, the cretinous guard looked alternately confused and offended. He even went so far as to take a hesitant step backward. Then he caught himself and in a reaction to his own embarrassment and anger, blustered and reddened. Not knowing what else to do, he cleared his throat. It sounded like a primitive attempt at reasserting his authority. The others in the room looked at him.

"Uh, if, uh, it would make... I mean if you would be more comfortable, I could always chain the prisoner to the table," he offered hopefully.

Galileo looked at Bellarmine with a mocking expectant grin and raised eyebrows as if he were perfectly all right with the idea.

"Thank you, but I don't think that will be necessary," said Bellarmine diplomatically. "In fact, you may go."

The cretinous guard glared at Galileo, then squared his shoulders. With a half-disappointed look, he nodded to the Cardinal, and exited closing the door behind him.

Bellarmine smiled and reached out, clasping Galileo's with both hands.

"My old friend," he said. "Please, sit down."

As they took their seats, Galileo looked over, taking stock of Father Ferrero for the first time. The Jesuit didn't look as pleased to see him as his mentor. To Galileo's quick assessment, Ferrero had already made his mind up about the case, and the verdict wasn't good.

"And who are you?" he asked.

"This is my secretary, Father Leonardo Ferrero," introduced Bellarmine.

Galileo nodded, but just enough that his eyes never left the young Jesuit.

"*Professore*," said Ferrero respectfully. The tone was neutral, not entirely approving.

"A fellow of the cloth," said Galileo.

"Father Ferrero has just been named a Monsignor," said Bellarmine.

"Congratulations," said Galileo. "And a Jesuit, I see?"

"Yes," said Ferrero easing up a bit. He considered that perhaps he had been a little judgmental about the old man.

"So almost an intellectual?" teased Galileo.

Instantly, the look of disapproval was back on Ferrero's face.

"*Doctore* Galilei has always been something of a flatterer," chuckled Bellarmine sarcastically.

Turning his wit on Bellarmine, he responded, "And you have always been something of a scholar, as I recall. He seems an appropriate associate."

It was one thing for Galileo to spar with him, but something about his tone in speaking with the Cardinal caused Ferrero's temper to flare. For a brief moment he forgot himself.

"On the subject of scholarship, I'm suddenly reminded of a passage from the Bible. Acts 1:11." Ferrero began reciting "'Ye men of Galilee, why stand ye gazing up into heaven?"

It was a reference to a sermon famously given by the conservative Dominican Father, Tommaso Caccini. The last name of Galilei was just too close to the pronunciation Galilee, and the reference to idle stargazing seemed a scriptural gift from God himself. The first time he had said it from the pulpit, the resulting laughter that flooded back at him sounded like a resounding endorsement. From then on, it became a stock item in every one of his sermons. The other orators in the audience took note and soon a recitation of the verse was accepted as a universal joke with the irritating heretical upstart as the butt.

At that moment in the interrogation room though, Bellarmine looked as if an act of protocol or decorum had been breached. He was apparently on the verge of apologizing when, Galileo's appreciative chuckle at the comeback, stopped him.

"Yes, I've heard that one a few times," he said, then looking at Bellarmine and nodding at Ferrero added genuinely, "He suits you."

CHAPTER THREE

With the new age of reason, or enlightenment as they were calling it, the novel enterprise of secular publishing was quickly taking its place along with the more established arts of painting, musical composition, theater and sculpture. Unlike the rest, the written word was a unique combination of both information and art, and no longer the sole domain of the intelligentsia and clergy. Now, a machine could democratically place any idea before the greater masses, provided of course, that there was someone who could read it. In Florence, where literacy had been a calculated push, reading was all the rage. The printing press might have been invented in the German states, but the only content worth putting to type, as the Florentines liked to brag, came from Tuscany. Among the burgeoning middle class, this broader accessibility to books led to a universal surge in education, especially when it came to their children. Latin might still be a challenge, reserved almost entirely for the aristocracy, most notably those select offspring that had been placed in the Church, but literacy in the common tongue of Italian was changing things...for everyone. The

Holy Roman Church's greatest fear – that a humble member of the congregation might ask a question or might challenge an interpretation of God's work – was perilously close to being realized. It was widely whispered among their leadership that something would have to be done.

While it was ultimately true that an informed populace might be good for the health of society overall, this social shift was a very real threat to those in power. The ruling class depended on a docile and controllable proletariat, and the changes brought about by this spread of intellectual freedom had terrifying potential. For others like the printer, Enrico Parma, who was also Galileo's publisher, it was a bonanza. Not a half-mile from Galileo's own home, Parma was thriving. In just the last year he had become a member of the upwardly mobile merchant strata. Of course, expanding his business, buying the heavy press and having it shipped had been expensive and a risk, but that wasn't all. There was the skill of typesetting. He had to hire costly artisanal workers who knew the right way to ink the plate and apply the subtly perfect pressure for a sharp, clear text on the sheets of paper. In the end though, it had been more than worth it. Within a few of months of the printing press's acquisition, he had acquired yet another skill. He had become a master of marketing. At first primers were a big seller, but as the pool of readership spread, so then followed an appetite for more sophisticated fare. That quickly divided into two classes of work; books that informed and books that entertained.

Very special work, did both, which is how and why he had made the acquaintance of *Doctore* Galilei. He remembered that first encounter, as if it were yesterday.

He had just hired several new employees specifically to bind the works of a popular poet. The demand for the music of language was a capricious thing, and he knew that he needed to sell as many copies as he could before the ardor cooled, or God forbid, people started to share their used books. He was overseeing the new binders who were rapidly stringing the edged sides together when the door to his shop opened, and two odd-looking men, one tall and one short and round, entered carrying a manuscript. From their protective nature, one might have assumed that they were delivering sheets of gold. Soon enough, Parma would learn that the manuscript was far more valuable than that.

Both Viviani and Torricelli had insisted that he secure the text before they would leave the shop. It wasn't that unreasonable a request. In those days, a paginated volume was an easily imperiled and delicate thing. Paper was vulnerable to everything from a mouse's mastication to fire to even the slightest water damage from a small leak in the roof. Thomas Jefferson's polygraph was still two-hundred years away, so an original copy of a book had to be protected in the utmost. The process of copywriting, duplicating a volume by hand, was an excruciating, labor-intensive enterprise, and Parma recognized the inherent writer's paranoia as the two men walked up. The difference with these two, Parma observed, was their quiet, anxious zeal as they insisted that they witness how and where the manuscript would be secured. Fortunately, Parma was ahead of his publishing peers and had installed a small iron vault, a buried box in the floor of his shop, where single copies could be assured of complete protection. These two were more on edge than most, so he even went so far as to let them watch him place the document inside. They literally sighed with relief as the door clanked shut. Watching them turn to go, Parma chuckled to himself at the near absurdity of their obsession.

It wasn't until later when he read it that he understood why they had been so anxious. The *Sidereus Nuncius* was unlike any book he had ever seen. In truth, he doubted that it was like any book ever written. As he sat poring over it, by candlelight, he felt a growing sense of excitement. Not only was it spectacularly groundbreaking, a proof of celestial interplay, but it was written so convincingly and so clearly that any literate person would be able to understand it. More importantly, the businessman in him realized with glee that it was also in Italian. Galileo had written for all the people, and in the process had committed a very subtle, revolutionary act. By the time he had finished the book, Parma knew that he had to meet Galileo.

He got up, walked into his daughters' bedroom and sat down on the edge of their bed. The soft rhythmic breathing was like sweet music, and he smiled. It was a regular ritual for him, these nightly visits. They were his pride and, since their mother's death, his heart. Normally, he would just sit and watch them, listening to the reassurance of their gentle slumber, but tonight he was going to give them a gift.

He gently nudged them both.

"Francesca, Veronica, wake up."

They grumped and half-responded, so he jostled them again with slightly more insistence until they yawned and opened their sleepy eyes.

"What is it?" asked Francesca.

"Papa has something you must see," he answered.

They yawned again and stretched and sat up. Francesca rubbed her eyes.

"What is it?" parroted Veronica, his youngest and a namesake for the famous poet and courtesan, Veronica Franco.

"A book," he said reverently.

"Is it a special book?" asked Francesca.

"A very special book."

"Can we read it?" asked Veronica.

"I don't know," he teased gently, "can you?"

It was much too early for a lesson in grammar, but Veronica knew the exercise and gave in quickly.

"May we?" she corrected.

"You may," he said with pride. He had educated his daughters. Some had warned him of the dangers in that. They criticized him for violating the social compact, but he was determined that they would not be put at risk in a world of incurable male obstinacy. Making sure they could read was their best chance at freedom.

"Do you see the name?" he said.

"*Sidereus Nuncius*," read Francesca slowly.

"Someday," he said with pride, "When you are very old, you will be able to tell people that you were among the first to see this."

"Is it a holy book?" asked Veronica.

He thought about that for a moment before answering. He suddenly remembered the fresco on the ceiling of the Sistine Chapel, the yearning he had felt when he saw the proximity of God and Adam, their fingers mere inches apart and yet still failing to touch.

"No, my darling, but I think it has been touched by the hand of God," he said.

He didn't sleep that night, and it was all he could do to wait until a decent hour to hurry over to the Galilei home. He actually ran the distance, he was that anxious to meet the genius, the mind that had discovered this and that had put it down so that the rest of the world could know. He was still breathing hard when the door opened, and the nun inside peered out with a look of concern.

"Are you all right?" asked Maria Celeste. "Can I help you?"

"I must see *Doctore* Galileo Galilei," he said.

"What is this about?" she asked cautiously, not opening the door any wider.

"I am Enrico Parma." He paused as if what he was about to say next was both important and life altering. "His publisher."

Maria Celeste smiled and opened the door.

"He is in his study. He has just finished his night's work."

She turned and led him through the front of the house to the door of the study. She paused and knocked gently.

"Papa, you have a visitor," she said.

Soft, muddled grumping came from inside.

"It's...your publisher," she said, and glanced back smiling at the equally pleased Parma.

Inside the room, Galileo shuffled and moved about.

"Well, bring him in then," he said.

•

That was years ago, and Parma smiled at the memory as he walked along overseeing the work of the book binders. Galileo had not been what he expected. Too many sermons had him ready for the glowing face of a beatific spiritual pilgrim, staring upward into the blissful favor of God. Instead, what he found was a grumpy hedgehog, whose hair and beard needed trimming and who stared at him with a penetrating and mockingly judgmental eye. The word, beatific, didn't enter into the description at all. Yet, there was *something*.

The first edition of the *Sidereus Nuncius* was a smash, and Parma soon found that he had underestimated it in terms of its ultimate market. When word spread that there was a description of the true nature of the moon and the voyage of the heavens, the book disappeared from the shelves faster than it could be printed. Requests for copies were so immense that Parma pulled every other book scheduled for printing and focused solely on cranking out as many copies of Galileo's book as he could. He took on extra workers so that the press could continue running day and night. As soon as a copy had dried, the surplus binders hurriedly stitched them together. Even then Parma couldn't keep up. He had never been happier or richer.

Everything was going perfectly, that is until the Church showed up.

Parma knew Cremonini and Colombe from an earlier petition to have their own works published. As members of the Holy Academy, they were well-subsidized, and in what would someday be counted as a vanity publication, Parma set their work to paper for an upfront fee. To be fair, it wasn't bad writing, but it didn't sell. When a copy of Galileo's work came to their attention and they learned how popular it was, they came to Parma for a reckoning. Thinking back on it, he wished he had been more astute. At first, he assumed it was simply a matter of jealousy that brought the inquiry. In retrospect, it was the beginning of something much darker and more terrible, a perilous descent into the most picayune and trivial aspects of human nature.

Ironically, they, the pseudo-intelligentsia, the canon-scholarly, took their arguments with Galileo to the least educated in the Church. It was a clever strategy meant to find a proxy to carry their message and generate controversy. This treatise by Galileo, they said, was nothing short of heresy, a direct rebuttal of the book of Genesis and an affront to the word of God. They stirred the village priests to lament from the pulpit and to present Galileo's work as a mockery and a product of the devil. In no time, the highly popular scientific text had become incredibly polarizing. Politics had reared its ugly head.

With the population divided into two very emotional camps, the discord and furor were soon an issue for His Holiness, Paul V, and while the head of the church, he was also a king with the same concerns for popular favor as any other. Not a particularly gifted scholar and in poor health, he was a perfect target for the soft, sinister whisperings of the two vocal church scholars. By the time Cremonini and Colombe had finished with him, the Pope was all but ready to have Galileo imprisoned and would likely have signed the writ, but for the fateful intervention of one, Cardinal Maffeo Barberini, a very special friend of the *Doctore*.

•

Like Bellarmine, Barberini met Galileo when all three were students in school. He had been dazzled by young genius' irreverent brilliance, and while accomplished in his own scholarship, he was admittedly like a donkey racing a stallion when it came to competing with Galileo. Given his ego, that was not easy. He hated having to admit such subordination, but Galileo had always been kind to him, and so quickly Barberini became an adoring fan. It was also why he made sure that Paul V assigned him to preside over Galileo's first heretical inquiry inspired by the *Sidereus*. With his keen political sensibility, he fashioned it, not so much as a trial, but as an examination by the College of Cardinals of how the data would be considered. It was elegant, face-saving, and potentially an allowance for Galileo to continue his work. It would have worked were it not for the general clerical paranoia generated by the agitators, Cremonini and Colombe. In the end, a compromise was reached, and Galileo was called to an audience with Cardinal Bellarmine to be informed of the judgment.

Almost from the second he entered the palatial hall, an air of oppression encompassed Galileo. If there was any doubt about the serious nature of the charges or the political intrigue surrounding it, the looks he received upon his entrance made it clear. Every head turned to follow him, and if he hadn't known better, he would have looked down to make certain he was fully dressed.

When he crossed to the far end and arrived at the table in front of his old friend Bellarmine, he paused and bowed formally. The serious expression on his friend's face forewarned him that the news wasn't good.

"Galileo Galilei," Bellarmine started officially, "I have been directed by His Holiness, Pope Paul V, to read to you the findings of the College of Cardinals in the matter of the examination of potential heretical acts."

Galileo straightened and stood waiting for the determination. With a cold sense of apprehension, he considered he might also be about to receive a sentence of punishment.

"In their wisdom, the College has determined that the concepts behind your discoveries and publications are deemed heresy."

Galileo looked for a moment as though he were legitimately afraid. He well knew the terrible fate of many who had been turned over to the Inquisition and the horrifying physical methods for the purification of their souls.

"However," said Bellarmine, "As you are not the originator of the Copernican theory, you have not technically, in the eyes of the judges, committed heresy. Therefore, you will not officially be labeled one, nor tried."

Galileo suddenly let out a tense breath that he hadn't realized he'd been holding.

You must not, however"—Bellarmine emphasized with a grave expression— "proceed with any further prosecution of the work in any fashion. You must not publish, orate, or teach about your observations through the telescope. You are not to publicly offer any opinion about the movement of the earth"—Bellarmine held up the scrolled document that spelled out the findings of the examination of theoretical heresy and fully formalized the constraints against Galileo— "from this point forward. If you do, you will be disobeying a papal directive. That," he offered with an admonishing raise of one hand, "will be punishable by a tribunal of the Inquisition, and no one will be able to save you."

Galileo did not say a word. He simply gave a curt nod followed by a tense bow. He turned and walked hurriedly across the hall. Not slowing a step, he opened the heavy wooden doors and continued out. To the casual observer it looked like a tacit acceptance of the terms. To Bellarmine's practiced eye, it was much less certain.

•

The prohibition of the *Sidereus Nuncius* was admittedly an initial financial blow to Enrico Parma, but soon enough, the enterprising publisher discovered another opportunity. While sales dwindled within Italy, save for the newly emerging black market, the appetite for the work was only just heating up in the principalities of France, Germany and the Netherlands. Even orders from as far away as England began to pour in, and the sales didn't stop there. Parma soon learned about a strange proportionality in publishing controversial work that comes with predictable certainties. The smarter the written word, the greater the number of idiots there are to rebut it. In the end, that was sure to add up to serious money.

The argumentative clergy, the lesser scholars and intellectual pretenders came in droves to the shop carrying their treatises and tomes, many with repetitive, drawn-out, inefficient texts that attempted by volume, to overcome Galileo's lean arguments and proofs. The resulting business model that came with it was staggering. They offered sacks of coins to see their work produced and eagerly handed over more and more money to move up in the queue at the backlogged press Soon, he was pricing their efforts of vanity by the pound and the estimated volume of ink. Ironically, he was making more as a publisher from bad writing than from the genius work, but the cash box couldn't tell the difference.

When Cremonini and Colombe laid their pamphlets

before him, he knew better than to gouge. Those two were the sort that could make serious trouble, so he smiled, thanked them, and agreed to prioritize their printing. He even demurred tactfully when they disingenuously offered to subsidize. They weren't officers of the Church, but they had access to the ears of those that were, and it was better to have them beholden than aggrieved. Not that their work sold. It never did, but that didn't matter. In a pseudo-biblical analogy Parma was laying up treasure in a very different way. One that amounted to a tenuous form of protection.

That was why, on the fateful day of Galileo's arrest for the *Dialogue*, Parma looked up from where Francesca and Veronica were watching old Marco the master binder and felt a sudden sense of alarm. Coming through the door were Father Inquisitor Maculani followed closely by Cremonini and Colombe. He had never met the Inquisitor, but there was no mistaking who he was. Of course, he bore the papal seal of the Inquisition on his robes, but even without that, his identity was unmistakable. Half zealot, half legal prosecutor, his dark penetrating eyes blazed like some retrieved coals from the hell to which he could send an accused. With his black hair close-cropped widow's peak in perfect alignment with the sharp point of his beard, he looked to Parma like a perfect imitation of a hungry bird of prey.

"Go, behind the screen. Now!" said Parma urgently to his daughters.

Without turning, he reached back and gave them a quick push. Francesca looked up as if to argue, but something about her father's tense posture stopped her. Without a word, she and her sister ran to the back of the shop and stepped behind the tall, wooden-slatted frame where the freshly printed pages were hung to dry. It was a good privacy barrier if one didn't look too closely, and the girls watched through the lattice as the serious-looking men approached their uncharacteristically nervous father. Old Marco had gone back to his needle and twine binding as if he were wearing blinders, but they could tell that his ears were pricked acutely.

"Father Maculani," Parma nodded respectfully, and turning to the scholars, acknowledged, "*Professore*s Colombe and Cremonini. Welcome."

Maculani tilted his head curiously.

"You know me?" he said, suspended between being flattered and suspicious.

"I don't think there is anyone who doesn't know the papal Inquisitor."

He nodded at the seal. Maculani looked down at it and back to Parma. The simple explanation was sufficient. He smiled, sizing the publisher up. It was clear from his expression that he wasn't quite convinced that the man was an ally. Adroitly, the publisher was already addressing his two colleagues.

"Gentlemen, I regret that we have not yet sold any copies of your work."

Parma sounded genuinely sympathetic, and Maculani smiled as much at the scholars' embarrassment as at the way Parma had innocently managed to call out their failure.

"That is not why we are here!" reacted Colombe.

Maculani looked at the table where old Marco was working quietly. He reached over and picked up a copy from the stacks of books. Parma studied the Inquisitor as he looked at the cover of the *Dialogue*. The man showed nothing, but Parma had a sense of being enclosed in a shroud of danger.

The feeling only worsened when he looked up from the page and said neutrally, "You published this."

It wasn't entirely clear if it was a comment, an assertion or a question. While Parma tried to decide, the Inquisitor looked over at the subtle movement of the girls behind the screen. He tilted his head slightly and stared at them with a sudden reptilian detachment. The girls' eyes widened, and they took an involuntary step backward. Behind him, Cremonini and Colombe read what was coming. They smirked as he turned back toward Parma who appeared to wilt slightly.

"Did not Our Lord say, 'Suffer the little children to come unto me?'" he asked. He extended his hand and beckoned gently to the girls.

All eyes went to his hands.

The nails on each finger were as long as a woman's and shaped to a point like a talon. At the sight of them, the girls recoiled even further and turned fearfully toward their father. Knowing better than to disobey an Inquisitor, Parma forced a reassuring smile and motioned to them that it was all right. They stepped out and walked forward timidly until they were positioned with their father between Maculani and themselves. The Inquisitor smiled coldly, appraising them both. Again, the reptilian quality of it was chilling.

"Such beautiful daughters," he said, letting the words, and their implication, just hang there.

The girls looked frightened, and Parma fought an impulse to physically move over and block Maculani's line of sight. The smile on Cremonini's and Colombe's faces broadened in genuine enjoyment at the printer's discomfort.

"*Such* beautiful daughters," continued Maculani with an unhealthy tone Then looking at Parma, he added. "We see so many who have not the protection of their fathers." He stared at Parma evenly. "The world can be so dangerous and cruel."

The threat was deliberate and apparent. Parma understood. Italy was enjoying a reconsideration of many social norms, but it hadn't yet extended to women. Two parentless girls were still the most helpless members in a society.

With no legal or social standing or rights to inheritance of any sort, their options were limited and terrible, even to the point of sexual slavery and subjugation to the lowest most abused strata. Terrified, the girls looked up at their father as an intimidated, emotional flush spread across the back of his neck.

"And a good father would never do anything to affect his ability to protect them," pressed Maculani.

The two observing scholars grinned smugly. It was almost enough to obliterate their embarrassing comment about the failed sales of their book. Almost. Parma took a breath and sighed in surrender.

"What do you want?" he asked.

CHAPTER FOUR

Galileo looked across the interrogation room table and smiled tightly at Bellarmine and Ferrero. They had indulged in pleasantries long enough. Now it was time to get on to the matter at hand.

"Not that I'd question any excuse to be out of my cell, but why have you come?"

"I've been chosen by His Holiness to represent you at your trial," said Bellarmine.

Galileo's eyebrows went up. "Chosen?" he said.

A scoffing sound, half-cough, half-dissention escaped Ferraro as he turned away. It was pretty clear. He wasn't happy about the assignment.

"You sound parched, Brother Ferrero," said Bellarmine diplomatically. "Perhaps you could get us all some water."

"Eminence," he said crisply and stood up to leave the room. He was angry, but his respect and deference for his mentor kept it in check. When he had gone, Bellarmine looked at Galileo. His posture changed suddenly and when he spoke, his tone was different. It carried the gentle familiarity of one talking with an old, valued friend. Underlying it was also a tone of pragmatism, as if he were about to share a difficult concept.

"It was the Pope's writ that authorized the Inquisition. This is a very complicated matter now."

"How is Maffeo?" asked Galileo.

It sounded a little too familiar, even flippant, and Bellarmine flushed slightly.

"His Holiness Urban VIII is not called by that name anymore," he corrected.

"He is still my friend," said Galileo.

Bellarmine hesitated.

"Perhaps not so much now," he said grimly.

Galileo went silent.

"You once said that nothing inspires greater opposition than a revolutionary truth," said Bellarmine.

"And yet nothing is more stubborn and contagious," countered Galileo.

Ferrero detected something in the exchange and looked at his mentor.

"I asked the Pope—" Bellarmine started in, then paused, struggling with the best way to continue. "You know, when it first came out, he loved the *Dialogue*. I never saw him laugh like that."

He paused, pleased by the memory.

Galileo watched him a moment, allowing the indulgence before making his next point. "He said I could not advocate my celestial theories. No one said the characters in my satire couldn't."

Bellarmine's attention snapped to that. A flash of temper showed and then dissipated almost instantly. This was dangerous business, and he wasn't up for any verbal banter.

"He is convinced that the idiot in your satire was meant to portray him."

Galileo looked incredulous.

"How is that possible?" His eyes darted. "What could possibly have made him think that?"

•

The publication of Galileo's *Dialogue Concerning the Two Chief World Systems* was a bomb with a slow burning fuse. The initial demand for it had been so immense that the publisher couldn't keep up, so its spread was sporadic and intermittent. That only served to heighten its impact. Like interrupted courses at a banquet, the starting and stopping only seemed to stoke the popular appetite all the more and also explained why it had been out almost six months before it was seen at the *Accadémie* where Cremonini and Colombe held sway.

It was an otherwise beautiful day. The citrus tang of the distant orange groves wafted in through open windows throughout the university. Both professors had concluded their lectures and were walking down the long hall when they saw a cluster of laughing students gathered around something with intense interest. With unsuspecting smiles, they approached and leaned in. What they saw melted their pleasant expressions immediately.

They recognized the work, especially the captivating phrasing and tone. What bothered them the most, however, was the spell it cast on the students. They pored over the document, and with each chorus of laughter and exclamation at the humor, the two scholars became ever more offended and angry. Noticing them, the students looked up and made their subdued obedience in the form of verbal "*Professore*s" and respectful nods.

The effect of the work on all those impressionable faces was a call to intellectual arms and they arranged to have a copy brought to them immediately. From the first page, they both experienced a sense of despair, not just in its content, but in the accomplishment of the writing. To their consternation, both Cremonini and Colombe had to admit, it was that good.

"The bastard has made a farce of the sacred argument," griped Colombe.

"Even worse, he made it funny," lamented Cremonini.

"I don't see the humor," said Colombe.

"I do," sighed Cremonini without so much as a trace of a smile. "He has constructed it as a dialogue. A sage, a scholar and a fool having a conversation. Too clever. I recognize Galileo's rhetoric, and even"—he scanned the document— "some of his own phrasing coming from the mouth of the sage. The scholar is clearly all the Archimedeans that support Copernicus. But the fool..." He let the word hang in the perfumed air.

"Yes?" said Colombe, not following at all. "What are we going to do?"

Cremonini didn't answer. His eyes were locked on a sentence. He looked up at Colombe, and the corner of his mouth lifted in a crooked smile.

"I think we should share this with a certain audience."

•

Long before he was ordained Pope Urban VIII, or had even attained the rank of Cardinal, Maffeo Barberini had known and been enchanted by the genius of Galileo. He first met him at the University not long after the miracle of the pendulum experiments. Galileo was, in fact, the person young Maffeo wanted to be, and while he might not be a genius and a prodigy, his status as the child of a politically prominent family necessitated that Barberini achieve the next best thing. He would claim Galileo as a friend.

He was present that day, inconspicuously in the audience of luminaries, as Galileo debuted the artillery compass in the lecture hall. It was Bellarmine who saw in Barberini an inevitable star in the canonical hierarchy and introduced them. Everyone wanted to be next to the intellectual phenom, but young Barberini had acted on it and elbowed his way through the crowd. Even the few heads that turned in offense at his pushiness quickly muted their outrage when they saw the expensive nature of his scholastic robes and entitled demeanor. Unlike the object of celebration, here was someone of elite means, connected, and though they had no idea who he was, they weren't risking the potential enmity of an obviously powerful scion.

As Barberini broke through the mob and presented himself, Galileo had looked at him with a kind of intrigued amusement. What was missing in his expression was even more telling. Galileo didn't look intimidated or even impressed by Barberini's superficial finery. He looked right through Maffeo. It was a startlingly different experience for the young social climber and took him aback in a completely disarming manner. As a result, he felt something akin to immediate infatuation.

From that very moment, their friendship and continued acquaintance was fated, and in a short time, Barberini's inclination soon turned toward adoration. Every new discovery, every publication, every gasp of amazement by society at Galileo's achievement was an opportunity for Barberini to revel in it as a reflection on himself. Just being able to say to others, "Yes, he told me when he first thought of it," gave Barberini a sense of inflated esteem.

It was almost as good as having the talent himself, and years later when the debate within the Church about whether Copernicus' theory of heliocentrism re-arose, he sought out Galileo privately to understand why he was in support. The university system in Italy was an extension of the Church, so it was appropriate that the matter be considered in a forum there. Barberini was no intellectual donkey, and he, like many, agreed that the evidence was plain. He had always prided himself on being on the right side of any argument, and he immediately joined the ranks of the Archimedean thinkers, disciples of the philosopher and scientist who, in a lesser manner, applied a primitive form of the "scientific theory." At least that was what Galileo called his new process for testing a hypothesis or belief. Experimentation, validation, proof. At the time their opponents, the Aristotelians, were supporting a position that the heavens were perfect and moved in synchrony around the earth. While no definitive evidence was permitted to be presented, the mathematically inclined, those rarified few of the *Lincean* academic society with Galileo at their head, had the better argument. Even so, Barberini was on a fast track to the position of Cardinal himself, and in case the debate went wrong in any way, he wanted to make sure that his ascendancy would not be impacted.

So, he arranged to preside as moderator, a neutral and apparent judge. That way, regardless of the outcome, he could still claim triumphant insight and most importantly, the privilege of pontificating authoritatively at dinner parties in its aftermath. He chose Venice for the venue, arguably the most elegant and exciting of Italian cities, in no small part so that the after-hours enjoyments of drink and carousal could be indulged with prejudice.

But that had been so long ago.

Now it seemed to the Pope that the memory belonged to an entirely different person. The lively idealistic Maffeo Barberini was a distant dream of someone he only yearningly recalled. The trappings of his office, of the old man that looked back from the mirror each day, and the inherent loneliness that came with the office of the Holy See had rendered him exhaustively changed. In his most secret heart, he still loved Galileo. His attendance at his coronation as the head of the church had been a particularly special pleasure, but as Urban VIII he was obligated to give up the freedoms that the younger Maffeo had so enjoyed.

Still, an intellectual fan of the *Sidereus*, it was he that had allowed Galileo to resume his work. With one condition. He had to include a consideration of the opposing view.

He looked up from his reading as his attendant, Father Antonio Barbarossi, approached.

"Antonio?" he frowned with mild irritation. "I thought this time was reserved for my personal study."

"Apologies, Holiness. There are two *Professore*s that say they must speak with you urgently. They insist it is of the greatest importance."

He looked past Barbarossi where Cremonini and Colombe were standing anxiously in the doorway holding the document. He sighed wearily and nodded. Antonio beckoned, and the two scurried forward to bow excessively.

"What is it?" asked Urban VIII.

"An abomination. An affront against you, Your Holiness," said Cremonini offering up the text.

He took it and read the cover.

"You are aware that I have given Galileo permission to write about his theories?"

"Holiness that is not the offense of which I speak," said Cremonini. "He has ridiculed your person in this document."

He looked up. As Pope he should have known better. As much as Colombe was a clumsy fool, his counterpart was cunning.

"What do you mean?" he asked.

Cremonini stood.

"He has presented the arguments you allowed through a conversation among three personas; one is reason, one academic, and the third a fool," he said thumbing through the document until he came to the most indicting passage. "I would have you note the line quoted by the fool."

Urban VIII looked at the referenced text. A second later, his face went as scarlet as a Cardinal's robe.

"Prepare a writ," he said angrily.

•

"I've never understood why you did that?" said Bellarmine shaking his head. "You used his favorite line. I can't even begin to calculate how many times we both heard him say, 'God could have made the universe any way he wanted to and still made it appear to us the way it does.'"

"Yes," affirmed Galileo.

"Then why did you have to attribute it to a character you so obviously named Simplicio?"

Before he could answer, the door to the interrogation room opened and Ferrero returned with a jug and glasses. He set them on the table and shot a look at the two old men. Something important and private had been discussed in his absence, that much was evident. He trusted Bellarmine, but he also knew that the old Cardinal's judgment was clouded when it came to Galileo. Even all these years later, he was still a little star struck and ran the risk of making a mistake. Partially out of a sense of protection, Ferrero wanted to make sure that Bellarmine didn't indulge the arrogant genius too much and put himself at risk.

"Thank you, Father Ferrero," said Bellarmine.

He gave Galileo an insistent look, encouraging him to say something polite.

Galileo smiled softly. "You know, you may find this hard to believe, but as a young man I almost entered the clergy myself."

Ferrero looked piqued by the confession. Then he frowned curiously, as if reconsidering some minor judgment about the man.

"And the reason you did not?"

"I thought studying the works of God was as important as studying His word," said Galileo.

It was a good answer, simple, profound and not what Ferrero was expecting. Bellarmine smiled and glanced at the young Jesuit for his reaction.

"You believe in God?" asked Ferrero with a note of surprise.

Galileo looked stunned at the question.

"Of course," he said.

Ferrero's eyes darted again, processing a thought.

"Yet, you violated a directive by his Holiness, God's earthly manifestation and head of the Church."

"What a depressing comment from one assisting in my defense," said Galileo with a slightly mocking tone.

The words landed hard with Ferrero, who was at heart a fair man. Even more so, he was diligent, and the insinuation that he would underserve was strong and worrisome.

"Brother Ferrero is young and devout. He is also dedicated and competent," said Bellarmine defensively. "He has my trust, so perhaps you could go a little easy with him."

Galileo nodded. His old friend was right.

"I'm delighted to have your assistance," he said to Ferrero and then added, "they say age is supposed to temper impetuousness, and dull the edge of a sharp tongue, but I don't find that to be the case." He settled before taking a more conventional tone. "You were asking me about my faith in God."

"Yes," said Ferrero. "I was simply noting your point about choosing to study the heavens."

Galileo smiled. "Well...certainly a heavenly body." His face softened with a complex distant recollection.

Ferrero looked at him keenly like he had seized upon an insight. "Ah, so you were in love."

It could have been an assertion or a question. It didn't matter. Galileo had all but left them and was staring off into an overpowering memory.

"You're an educated man, Ferrero," he said almost abstractly. "You must know that with respect to the Greek classics, *love* is a varied and complex word."

•

The banner at the front of the cathedral hall in Venice announced much more than a simple debate. Young Bellarmine, who had taken his vows, was still years from attaining his Cardinal's robes, but he was already a confirmed and respected member of the Académie. Right now, however, none of that mattered. Right now, he was nervous. Being selected to head the Archimedean side of the argument was a great honor, and he knew he was more than capable of it, but without any physical evidence of the earth's movement, he needed his best mathematical ally and Galileo was nowhere to be found.

Seated at the front of the hall, ready to preside was Barberini. He might be a philosophical advocate, but despite his leanings, he wouldn't, and in fact couldn't, slant the outcome. Barberini was already learning the politics of power and more importantly, the appearance of it. He looked across the room at the Aristotelian cohort. In particular, he took note of the presence of Cremonini and Colombe. He knew that while they were wrong-headed on the issue at hand, they had proven quite skilled at generating popular support. He also noted the nervous look on his colleague Bellarmine's face.

It was well past the starting time for the discussion, and Barberini knew if he wanted to appear impartial, he couldn't wait anymore. He cleared his throat, and the room went quiet. That was quite a feeling; that a simple gesture from him could silence them all. It fed something not entirely healthy in his head. Across the room, Bellarmine looked up with even greater alarm at the subtle notice that the proceedings were about to begin.

"The College of Rome and His Holiness have allowed this discussion of the state of God's firmament so as to illustrate"—Barberini lifted both hands toward the heavens— "his...greater glory."

In the opposing gallery, Cremonini and Colombe were smiling. Bellarmine knew this was about to get tricky, and worse, Galileo still hadn't shown. A slow creep of panic began to ride up his spine.

"I know many of us have been intrigued and some even seduced by the writings of *Professore* Copernicus," continued Barberini.

Just then, the side door of the cathedral opened, and an out-of-breath Galileo entered and rushed over to sit down next to Bellarmine, who glared back with a mix of relief and exasperation. From his presiding position, Barberini forced a disapproving look at the new arrival even as he stifled a grin. Galileo looked at him innocently.

"You are late," Bellarmine whispered harshly.

"What? I had something to do," said Galileo.

Bellarmine's eyes widened in agitation. "You are the one that wanted this debate. Now you almost miss it and leave me to risk a charge of heresy!?"

Galileo looked at him like he had lost his mind. "Heresy? It's an academic discussion, and a good one to have, I might add."

Barberini cleared his throat. Again, the room resumed a rigid silence. The resulting smile on his face showed he was really warming to the power.

"In regard to Copernicus, I will remind everyone that his works have been declared heretical," Barberini continued emphatically, "and an offense to God. So today, be mindful. Only a purely philosophical discussion of heliocentrism is permitted."

Cremonini and Colombe smiled again. Galileo frowned. Bellarmine looked at his friend.

"Take care," he whispered. "This just became very tricky."

"How tricky could a philosophical discussion about a fact be?" said Galileo with slightly sarcastic bitterness.

"There can be no advocacy for any physical proof," said Barberini.

Cremonini and Colombe looked at each other with smug satisfaction.

"I think our Barberini just performed an academic castration," whispered Galileo.

"Better academic than literal," responded Bellarmine.

"We will begin," continued Barberini, "with the proponents of the Aristotelian theory."

Colombe stood up to offer his argument.

"The philosopher Aristotle has proposed that the universe is perfect, and this perfection coincides with what the Holy Bible teaches us about the Creator. For how could it be that an all knowing, all seeing, all loving, perfect God"—he paused and looked around for emphasis— "how could He create anything less than perfect?"

The Aristotelians applauded emphatically at what they considered irrefutable logic.

"Thank you *Professore* Colombe. An excellent opening statement with much to consider." Barberini turned toward the Archimedean side. "Who will provide a response?"

For a moment, silence followed. Bellarmine looked at Galileo who had expected that he would only be called on to address the mathematical argument.

"Or do you concede to the points just made?"

"No," chorused the Archimedeans. Bellarmine put a firm hand on Galileo's shoulder and gave him a shove to stand up.

"Perfection," said Galileo, letting the word suspend for a moment.

The power of silence on an audience being an awesome thing, Barberini took note. He would certainly want to employ it in the future.

"God...is perfect." Galileo looked around at all the attentive faces. "On that we can all agree."

The crowd muttered its affirmation to the simple point.

"But," he tilted his head to the side and squinted quizzically. "In a universe where some calves drop three-legged, odd goats have wayward horns, and babies can come with crooked backs, then how can everything be created perfectly?"

Both Barberini and Bellarmine smiled.

"Why, even I myself was late this morning," punctuated Galileo.

A smattering of chuckles answered from both sides. Galileo didn't let up.

"And Paradise itself was lost by God's first favored two, so imperfection must have been in play?"

Cremonini couldn't stand it.

"Blasphemy," he shouted. "God is infallible."

"Not blasphemy at all," countered Galileo. "I agree with you completely. God is infallible." His eyes narrowed cunningly. "But perhaps he knew that offering us anything of obvious perfection was beyond our capacity. Don't believe it? Look then to our Savior's example. He was given to mankind in His perfection, and mankind tortured and murdered him."

Once again silence filled the great chamber. Galileo looked around waiting for any kind of rebuttal. When nothing came, he glanced at Barberini and gave a quick wink. Then he turned back and sat down next to Bellarmine.

"What do you think?" he asked.

"I think," responded Bellarmine, "that if this were swords, they'd be cleaning up the blood for weeks."

"And I haven't even started in with the mathematics," said Galileo.

•

"That was a very good day," said Bellarmine, and his wrinkled face contorted in a smile punctuated by a sparkle of youthful light in his eyes.

"You won the debate," said a captivated Ferrero.

"No," said Galileo. "The Pope, Paul V, at the last minute before we began, instructed Barberini to keep the discussion as a philosophical exercise. There would be no mathematics, nothing undeniable nor objective. Since most of them couldn't understand the physics anyway, and without an instrument to measure the heavens, it was all comfortably theoretical." He stared off again like he was looking back into the past, and with a disgusted tone added, "They fell back on the last refuge of the mentally lazy and impoverished. They called it a matter of faith."

The silence that followed was the same as it had been there that day so many years ago.

Finally, Ferrero asked, "So what was the decision then?"

Bellarmine looked embarrassed. "They called it a tie."

Ferrero looked back at Galileo, who wasn't showing anything like a man saddled with a distasteful memory. More, the look on his face was one of an insight into bliss.

"It was a triumph," he said with a slightly abstract tone. "The day was a triumph."

Bellarmine knew, he wasn't talking about the debate.

•

Every day at midday in front of the cathedral, the Venetian market became much more than just an exercise in capitalism. It was a social phenomenon like farmer's markets would be in a few centuries, or town squares after that, or even eventually what would become the shopping mall experience. Certainly, coins passed hands and fortunes were made and lost, but for the hours that the wares were spread, the market became the neural and social center of the city. All elements and enterprises were in play. Overlying the soft brine scent from the archipelago were the comingled bouquets of the aromatic herbs for sale, the organic dye of cloth, the human and animal sweat, the amine tinge of the fresh bounty of the sea, and the liberated aroma from the various spice bins that met the nose with the same gratifying, exotic complexity that their colors did the human eye. The young lords of the great families lounged with a casual ease, as they gathered and looked with laconic eyes over the milling crowd until something so exceptional came into view that even they could not pretend boredom.

"Look, there she is," said a young man in an expensive robe and cap.

The others sat up and leaned forward.

She. They all knew exactly who he meant, and like most days, her arrival was a noteworthy and lustful indulgence. But there was so much more than just lust.

Her name was Marina Gamba, and in a world where a single germ or unlucky injury could ruin beauty, and the odds against arriving at womanhood without some discounting scar or flaw were astronomical, her perfection was phenomenal. It also made looking away, for the voyeuristic gang of young men, quite impossible.

"I must have her." The words broke from an emotional young aristocrat. The resulting laughter of his friends made him recoil sheepishly for a second.

"You would, but she doesn't belong to your house," laughed a dark-eyed scion whose carriage and attitude indicated his noble rank. "Alas, she doesn't belong to mine either."

As she moved between the fishmonger's bins, Marina seemed happily unaware of her effect on the group. Not that she didn't know how her external beauty was received. The various, gap-toothed smiles that responded automatically as she looked pleased at each merchant's clear-eyed, finned or healthy, seaweed-wrapped shellfish offerings was reinforcement. A simple smile from her landed like a magic spell and left each man and woman with a pleasant afterglow. Great beauty, whether in the form of a poem, a painting, a scientific calculation, or a friendly face was a small miracle and universally irresistible.

Far off beyond her attention, the doors to the cathedral flew open and an agitated, red-faced Galileo stormed out with Bellarmine hot on his heels.

"I don't know why you are so angry. Did you really think they would let you champion that idea and prevail?" asked Bellarmine.

"They are idiots," spat Galileo.

Bellarmine was moderately corpulent even as a young man, and he hustled to grab Galileo by the arm.

"Yes! But they are idiots with power, and they can be dangerous, Galileo."

The genuine concern on Bellarmine's face impacted his friend much more than his words. In a second, Galileo's frustration defused, and he smiled good-naturedly.

"You worry too much. Remember, because of my compass, His Holiness' army spends half what it used to on gunpowder."

Bellarmine looked neither reassured nor convinced.

"So, what were you doing that was compelling enough to make you late?" he asked, redirecting.

Galileo raised a superior eyebrow.

"I was at the Arsenal, by the harbor."

Bellarmine looked intrigued. "Again? What now?"

"The Harbor Master has hired me to design a more efficient oarlock in the galley ships."

"For how much?" asked Bellarmine.

"A lot," said Galileo happily. He reached into his robe and produced a bulging leather bag, heavy with coins.

Bellarmine's eyes bugged, and thunderstruck, he crossed himself. Galileo took note.

"I know," he affirmed to the non-verbal reaction, "and the best part?" His excitement could barely be contained now. "I didn't have the heart to tell him that Archimedes already gave me the solution."

Bellarmine thoughtfully worked the concept. Then arriving at it, he spoke. "Give me a lever long enough and a place to stand, and I will move the world."

"Exactly. You always had a better memory than I," said Galileo. He touched his friend on the shoulder. "You know what's even better?"

"Hmm?" muttered Bellarmine.

"This is only half the money!" He held up the bag again. "I already spent the rest at the optician."

Bellarmine groaned. "Not more lenses?"

"Of course." Galileo said enthusiastically. "Don't you see?"

They had arrived at the steps to a canal bridge, and Galileo took a few steps upward so that he was looking out over the market. Bellarmine followed him up with obvious consternation. All this physical activity was almost too much to endure.

"Must we do this?" he asked.

Galileo ignored the statement. He gestured skyward. "When I can measure the movement of the heavens, I can show that the earth itself moves!" He was getting worked up too emotionally. "I can prove Copernicus was right, and"—his face screwed up with disdain— "there will be no more of these...debates." When he said the last word, it came out with unmistakable bile.

Bellarmine looked out across at the broad array of tents and canopies where prospective buyers wove and plucked, sampled, and smiled. It was a pleasant enough sight, but the pleasure was no match for the pessimistic cloud that had swept in with Galileo's declared intent.

"You really think they will acknowledge that?"

"They will have to acknowledge the facts," countered Galileo in a manner that Bellarmine saw as defiant and naïve.

"My friend," agonized Bellarmine, trailing off and shaking his head.

"Here," he said. "I'll show you," insisted Galileo.

He reached into his robe and pulled out a thick piece of parchment and two heavy, glass lenses. He rolled one end of the paper into a tube around the first lens. Then he inserted the second lens and peered through it at the distant market.

Given the fixed focal length, only some of what he was looking at was in sharp focus. As he scanned the enlarged subjects at greater distances, they went from clearly detailed to slightly blurry to large fuzzy masses.

Bellarmine looked up at his friend with no idea what he was doing. He had only an abstract knowledge of a telescope and had never actually seen one, not even a toy. He certainly didn't know what Galileo meant to prove with it.

He was about to find out.

"Ah," clucked Galileo happily.

In the distance a filthy old garbage collector walked along pulling a cart loaded with rotting vegetables and fish guts. Already some of the merchants had set out the unmarketable items from their bins on the distant stones for collection. The old man stopped at one and began loading a pile of old wilted cabbage leaves. What made it interesting enough to elicit the exclamation from Galileo was the relationship in terms of distance to a stone manse several meters beyond.

Galileo nodded for Bellarmine to look through the telescope, holding it in a perfect alignment so that the subject would be easy for his friend to see.

"Now, look there at the man with the cart."

Bellarmine leaned in and peered through the scope.

"Notice his position in relationship to the fixed stone," he said.

"Yes," answered the squinting Bellarmine. "I see. The lenses make it clear."

"Now," said Galileo taking the scope back and looking through it again.

The man had finished with his pickup and was on the move until he came to another pile farther away from the first stone.

"There," said Galileo excitedly preparing to offer Bellarmine a look. "While he seems not to have moved, in reference to the stones you'll see that his position is different."

He was just about to hand it over when Marina walked into his line of sight. She was at just the right distance to be in perfect focus, and as a result Galileo could make out every aspect of her beautiful face. It was one feature, however, that made the greatest impression. The light was slanting in at just the perfect angle to bring out the spectacular fire of her eyes. They glowed with a golden amber hue, and while she couldn't see him, the direction she was gazing made it seem as if she were making eye contact with him through the instrument.

Galileo gasped.

"What is it?" asked Bellarmine.

Scientists are notoriously unsentimental as a group, but Galileo was also an inventor, and that aesthetic vein of imagination and creativity carried with it all the makings of an artist. In that moment his artist's soul was touched by something like a lightning strike.

"What is it?" asked Bellarmine again.

"My God, she is perfect," said Galileo emotionally.

Bellarmine leaned in to take a quick look and saw Marina, who glanced down at another seller's goods with a quick penetrating expression of intelligent amusement. Even as a man who had promised his chastity to God, he was affected.

Recovering only partially he said, "Uh huh. But don't you remember what you said about the impossibility of perfection in the debate?"

"I take it all back," said Galileo quickly.

"I would love to see the look on the Aristotelians' faces if they heard that."

Galileo didn't answer. He just handed the makeshift telescope to Bellarmine before running off down the steps. Bellarmine looked through the scope again. After a second, his face broke into a smile. Galileo was sprinting across the square in pursuit of the beautiful young woman.

"Of course," he said and was just about to lower the telescope when he noticed something beyond. Relative to the large stone manse, the filthy man and his cart had moved. He lowered the scope, blinked at the concept his brilliant friend had proven and what it could mean in relation to measuring the heavens. A moment later, a sense of slight uncertainty began to build at the implications of what Galileo had done and what he knew the Aristotelians might do in response.

For the first time in his life, young Galileo understood the phenomenon of a stag in the rut. Granted what he was experiencing was more elevated than that. He was a man, after all, not a base animal, but for the ardor he was experiencing as he ran across the marketplace, he might as well have been some antlered thing racing through the woods.

Marina had moved on from the spot where he had first seen her, and as he arrived there, a momentary panic overtook him. He looked around in desperation. He suddenly imagined himself decades later, telling some bored young listener about the great beauty he had seen at a distance and lost to the supreme regret of his life. He was on the verge of apoplexy when somewhere in the near distance, a glimmer caught his eye. It was the sun shimmering off her hair. He darted off through the crowd, getting closer, then he stopped just before his pursuit became obvious. As she casually moved from bin to bin, he found himself immediately enamored with the elemental mundanities of her perusals. In anyone else they would have been nothing, ordinary actions, not worthy of the slightest notice, but performed by her, they were enchantments. Galileo was enthralled.

She picked up a bunch of grapes and closed her eyes as she inhaled and savored the aroma. The simple epicurean nature of it was overwhelming for him. It was, in a word, sensuous, and it took all his control to keep him from rushing up and making a fool of himself. She opened her eyes just then, looked at the merchant, an old man with a kind face, and smiled. Then she reached into her purse and paid him. He nodded and smiled, spellbound like everyone else, as she moved off toward another row of fishmongers.

Without stopping, she leaned forward and sniffed at a rack of fresh oysters. Her blouse slipped down on one shoulder, providing the oysterman with just a hint of the swell of her bosom. He smiled at the happy accident but said nothing. The light aroma of the mollusks met with her approval, and she looked up at the monger and smiled. His grin widened. She reached into another bin and lifted a healthy-looking snapper. Closer inspection, however, showed that the eyes were already taking on a slightly milky quality. That was not unusual; under the Venetian sun, dead fish deteriorated quickly. The finned, scaled, and gilled life forms might have it all over the lower, stationary bivalves in their natural habitat, but in the austere non-marine environment, the biologically slower creatures had better stamina.

Marina wrinkled up her nose and set the deteriorating fish back down with the rest of the catch. She straightened up and held her palm to smell it. Not liking the result, she grasped a sprig of basil from among her purchases in her basket and rubbed it between her hands. She tested her hands again under her nose. It was better. With a purposeful look, she moved on.

Galileo continued, following along, held at a distance by propriety and her arresting beauty, but like any conflicted connoisseur, struggling with the compulsion to get closer. It was tricky. To enter into an engagement too quickly with anything rare, be it wine, a fine meal, the estimation of a work of art, or an encounter with a potentially great love, was to cheat the overall. To do it properly, one first looked. They studied the details and invested them in memory. In later years, those memories would be a sustaining and important component. It was why the most common question a child would inevitably ask a parent was, "Do you remember the first time you saw mother or father?" So, it was no cheap voyeuristic motivation that kept him following along at a distance, entranced by the subtle changes to her face as she considered the market's wares. No, it was because he knew that this was a moment he would remember forever, and he wasn't about to shortchange the experience.

It was the right decision. She was back among the spice merchants now with the warm sunlight continuing to catch and bathe her. Only now it was in a glow of liberated ocher, umber, and crimson powders that rose and suspended to give the scene a magically spectral effect. It took his breath away.

She had stopped in front of a bin where a merchant was watching her intently. Unlike the fishmonger, the spice seller's look carried with it a cunning capitalistic assessment. Marina looked from his wares to his son playing with a small circle of marbles behind him and smiled at the boy. The boy smiled back, subject to the same magical effect as the rest of them. Like the one flawless pearl dredged up from a million oysters in the sea, she was a startlingly beautiful accident of nature for her era, and more importantly to the merchant's thinking, for her social station. He knew quite well that no lady of a noble family in Venice entered the marketplace, except on rare occasion and then only with a bodyguard. Marina had come alone. The world was dangerous enough for any woman, but for one as pretty as she, it was even more so. No, she might be well-dressed and with an adequate purse from her mistress, but *she* was common. That much he knew. It was why he decided that what he would attempt next was worth the chance.

As Marina looked compassionately at his son, the merchant reached under the bin to a wooden shelf where he kept a number of small, almost perfectly round stones. He plucked one and with the deftness of a magician, slipped it into a waiting bag on his scale. It was an incredibly subtle move and one that escaped the kind and unsuspecting Marina. It did *not* escape the sharp eye of Galileo.

"Shopping for the kitchen, *Signorina*? For your mistress?" the crafty merchant asked pleasantly.

She smiled. "Yes."

"Very good," he said. "What would you like?"

"This one." She pointed at a small mound of ground clove. "Only an ounce, though," she added.

The merchant reached down with a scoop and carefully began to measure the amount into the loaded bag.

"Just a moment!" Galileo called as he approached and nodded to the startled Marina.

His abrupt intrusion at first triggered a surprised and defensive look on her face, but his assured nature as he returned the withering glance of the spice merchant told her that he might not be the true threat after all.

"Pardon me," said Galileo to the merchant.

He reached over, hooked his finger in the edge of the bag and tipped it over on the scale. The spice-dusty marble rolled out of the bag onto the metal pan. Marina looked from the stone ball to the merchant with an incensed expression. For a second, no one said anything.

"My apologies, *Signorina*," sputtered the merchant. "I...I do not understand."

He was good. Like all confidence men, the merchant was a fine actor when caught in the act of cheating a customer. It was all there in his impromptu performance. He took on an innocent countenance, and his words spilled forth genuinely. He looked around as if the circumstances were beyond his comprehension until he spotted his son, obliviously playing with his marbles. Offering an "aha" look he viciously smacked the boy on the ear. It was a completely unexpected attack, and the child howled with shock and pain.

"How dare you cheat the beautiful *Signorina*? Wicked, wicked child. I shall beat the devil out of you!"

It was obvious the boy had no idea what had prompted the derision and abuse, but he was covering up against the punishment all the same.

"Wait! No! Stop!" said a genuinely alarmed Marina. "Don't hit the boy. No harm was done."

Galileo liked that. As he kept a suspicious eye on the lying merchant, he was moved by her compassion. Instead of focusing on the outrage of being deceived and robbed, her attention and energy was on protecting the child. The beauty of this woman, he realized, went way beyond the happy accident of her face and form.

The merchant turned back to Marina and with the sincerest look said, "The boy, he is always doing these mischiefs. Please, I will give you a little extra."

Marina didn't react at first. She was mostly relieved that she had ended the attack on the boy and was not quite prepared for the quick readjustment to material negotiations. The merchant gave the watchful Galileo a resentful glower as he scooped a large portion of the spice and dumped it into the bag.

"No charge, of course," he added.

Marina looked over at Galileo and smiled appreciatively. He grinned back. The merchant closed the bag and handed it to her, ready to be done with the whole matter.

"Thank you," she said and started to move along. After a step she looked back and seemed not too displeased to find that Galileo was still walking along with her.

"I suppose thanks are in order to you as well," she said.

"I'll leave that to your discretion, *Signorina*," he said respectfully avoiding any presumption of familiarity.

She seemed to like that and chuckled musically.

Given her looks and social station, she had not always enjoyed the decorum of gentlemanly behavior. The same lecherous motivations that had made the market place a danger to the fairer sex had already been visited upon her a few times in her life. First with an uncle, then with certain gentlemen whose position in the aristocracy gave him a sense of entitlement to the daughters of the proletariat. She had seen the uglier, lustful side of men. In an even more outrageous unfairness, on those occasions when the unwanted attention had been forced upon her, despite there being no acquiescence or compliance on her part, her reputation had been the one damaged. The Renaissance was changing things for some people, but when it came to sexual violation, the privileges and power of noble station still provided an undeniable and abusive social inequity, and the blame unfairly remained with the victim.

She took a quick assessment of Galileo's fine clothing. He didn't act like a young count, but he was clearly of an elevated level in society. He was not an officer of the Church, she thought. Maybe an academic, but usually they weren't as well-apportioned. What she liked most was how suddenly ill at ease he was, almost shy now. The slight shift in their interpersonal power let her know she was safe, if only because he seemed so disarmed by her presence.

"What I mean," he stammered, "Uh...well...I mean...I did do you a...service."

She chuckled again. Like magic, it seemed to momentarily overwhelm him. He almost stopped in his tracks and a few seconds passed before he could recover himself. Once something of the usual Galileo had been restored though, he pointed at the small bag of spice, and quipped, "I also added a little spice to your life, did I not?"

Marina glanced at the bag and laughed outright.

"I don't even know your name, *Signore*," she said with just the slightest hint of coquettishness.

It was the opening he had prayed for. With a flourish worthy of the royal court, he bowed and said, "I am Galileo Galilei dei Linceo."

She stopped. Now her face had a look of surprise and appreciative familiarity. She recognized the name, but more importantly, she knew about the Academy of the Lynx, or the Lynceans as they were becoming known, a nickname for the best and brightest. She was also aware that the scholar-star in front of her served as its intellectual epicenter.

"I have heard that name," she said.

"Oh," he said, straightening up with a validated look. "You have heard of *me*?"

She was interested in him, but propriety would not allow her to reveal it so quickly. She simply responded in a teasing note, "It wasn't entirely good."

He seemed suddenly crestfallen, and she regretted it immediately.

"What did they say?" he asked defensively.

Hoping to restore his good humor she added with a slight hint of flirtation, "That you are a genius. Impetuous, but a genius."

He smiled. In her eyes he thought he saw something that was a perfect match to what he was feeling.

"And you are?" he asked.

"Marina Gamba."

It had the sound of an agreement to much more than the simple exchange of nomenclature. He stepped closer and offered his arm for an escort. She blinked and then gently looped her arm in his. It was a simple act, but one that joined them in more than just the physical as they started to walk on together.

CHAPTER FIVE

Love, for anyone, is a bewilderment. The inaccessible nature of its process, what might be called the phenomenon of love was, for a mind like Galileo's, a tantalizing thing, and as compelling as the amorous state itself. Had he any hope of breaking it down and discovering how it worked, he would have thrown himself into the creation of an instrument to calculate or map it, but somehow, as he stared at the object of his affection in the dim light of his room, he knew this was better left a mystery.

It was not the first time that he had been with a woman, but it was the first time that in the aftermath of the act of love, he had felt such a sense of peace. It was incredible, and he knew undeniably, in that moment, that she was the love of his life.

"I'm hungry," she said.

He lifted his head from the pillow as she rose from the rumpled bed without bothering to dress.

"Me too. And yet, I am oddly satisfied," he replied humorously.

She glanced back at him with a wry smile.

"It's about time."

She crossed the small apartment to the kitchen next to the open hearth and began taking fruit from a small bag. Then she leaned forward and picked up a bottle of red wine.

"Wine?" she asked.

"Always," he answered.

She chuckled, and once again the music of her laughter warmed him. He sighed and looked over at the tiny table next his bed. The two lenses and the sheets of parchment that he had used to fashion a makeshift telescope for Bellarmine earlier that day were lying there. The paper was still partially curled, almost begging to be employed again. He reached over and set the lenses again then pointed it at Marina. Without the ability to finely adjust it, her body was mostly a mass of flesh-colored blurs. Only every now and then as she moved did some part of her anatomy come into startlingly graphic detail. Overall, it was worth the effort, he thought. He also realized that for the purposes he had in mind, some innovation would be needed. The telescope was still a primitive tool – two lenses and fixed focal length that could not be adjusted, but already he had some thoughts on how that could be addressed.

The consideration of that came to a sudden halt as Marina's breasts moved into focus.

"You and your little toy," she said moving toward him with the fruit and wine.

"It's a scientific tool," he countered with mock offense.

"Oh?" she smiled, handing him his glass of wine.

"It makes things appear larger so that their...*properties* can be studied and truly appreciated."

She laughed again.

"Give it to me."

He sat up and, being very careful to prevent the expensive lenses from falling out, handed it to her.

"Hold it like so," he said and positioned her hands, so she had proper control of it. "Now," he touched the near end, lowering it so that it pointed toward his lower region. "Keep that other end to your eye and look through."

She laughed at first with a slightly shrill outrage, then continued with a salacious smile.

"Now, that *is* useful," she chuckled.

•

Galileo stared ahead, warmed by the recollection. For just a moment, he was not old and not in the interrogation room. He was back in Venice with a horizon of happiness before him. For a moment, Bellarmine and Ferrero didn't say anything out of respect. Then he roused.

"So, you see," he said looking at Ferrero. "It was love...of many kinds."

Ferrero's look of disapproval had tempered.

"What happened with the Arsenal?" he asked.

The question jarred Galileo a bit, and he looked first at Ferrero and then to Bellarmine who was looking at him as if indulging his own pleasant recollection.

"What happened at the Arsenal was Archimedes," he teased.

"Archimedes," echoed Bellarmine.

•

Galileo stood at the lagoon side of the great Arsenal of Venice and looked out at a damaged, burned barge.

"Barbary pirates," said Duca Delarosa, the Harbor Master. "It was found floating just short of the archipelago. None of the crew were aboard."

"What happened to them?" asked Galileo.

"Slavery? Death? The only two fates possible," he said grimly.

It was true. Piracy was an economic and humanitarian problem in the Mediterranean. There were horror stories of noblemen taken captive and enslaved or held for huge ransoms. The treatment of noble women was far worse. Something had to be done. The leaders of the Venetian high counsel had called on Galileo to design some kind of countermeasure, to come up with an answer to the superior speed of the pirate ships. In short, a faster Venetian fleet was required in order to survive, and they sensed the answer would be in the engineering. The near legendary tales of his artillery compass and his presence in Venice for the debate made for a perfect opportunity and they weren't about to waste it. As for Galileo, he knew that if he could arrive at a solution not only would his reputation be made, but so also a small fortune. Now, despite the vision of tragic violence that floated before him, Galileo considered the damaged merchant vessel with a rising sense of optimism.

"Can you help us?" asked Master Delarosa.

"Of course, I can," said Galileo confidently.

The solution was simple enough and extremely effective. A narrowed galley aperture and an elongated oar stock would provide three times the thrust and generate what they needed. Galileo looked over at a docked ship.

"That one," he said, moving to a table where a pen, ink and paper awaited.

He quickly sketched the ship with remarkable accuracy and then drew a longitudinal opening above the waterline. Then he sketched a row of long oars extending in a perfect close alignment.

"That," he said straightening up, "will do it."

Delarosa nodded. He understood the alterations though he wasn't as certain of the effect to come. What he was sure of was the confident manner of the genius who was now giving the orders. He nodded again, turned and gestured to his shipwrights to get started.

A week later when the maiden voyage of the Doge's flagship was put to a race and defeated the next closest finisher by sixteen boat lengths, Galileo was awarded with a golden commission. The benefits of his new responsibilities weren't simply in the form of professional respect. It meant that he could now afford a great house and the supporting staff necessary to maintain it.

He went to the home where Marina was working in the kitchen. She had a knife in her hand and was just about to slice a chicken when he walked in and without a word, took it from her and set it on the table.

"Go and tell your mistress that you'll be leaving now," he said.

Officially, Marina Gamba was to be his housekeeper. In reality, she was everything and more to him. She was the one that selected the prime house overlooking the Bridge of Sighs with its grand salon and luxurious apartments, and from that moment on, her position was never again like that of a servant. While formally undeclared, she was in all ways the lady of the manor. Galileo saw to it that she wore only elegant dresses of the finest material, befitting one of the burgeoning merchant class, and his treatment of her was consistent with the role of wife and mistress of a grand house. On the day of the provincial regatta, a celebration of the official fleet, she sat in the box with him just a few feet from the Doge, the King of Venice, himself. If any of the same entitled party who might have commented on her shopping in the market were inclined to remark now, they held their tongues out of respect and deference to the celebrated guest of honor with whom she clearly belonged.

"They move so quickly now," she said, watching the long oars pulling the ships efficiently through the waves.

At the waterline, the oars completed their submerged circuit. Then they rose and swung forward, in a spray of silver drops, before repeating the action again. With every stroke they seemed to pick up even more speed. Gasps and exclamations of surprise and delight escaped the members of the gallery, verifying her love's magnificent achievement.

The Doge turned and looked at Galileo.

"*Magnifico,*" he exclaimed happily.

That emotional remark was worth almost as much as a formal knighting.

As the great ships raced along in review, Marina smiled and leaned in toward Galileo intimately. He rested a hand on hers and smiled as blissfully as a newlywed, for marriage was his ultimate intent. She already shared his bed, and he felt she was as much a spouse as any who had knelt in ceremony before a priest.

A month later, when she told him that their child was on the way, he was already crafting a letter to the Duke of Tuscany to introduce her and obtain permission to formalize their wedded state.

But no reply came.

Not that it mattered. They were happy. Soon enough, he would be back at the university in Florence and he could make his request in person. The world was changing, but not quickly enough and as a commoner, despite his favored standing, he dared not attempt a wedding without the endorsement of the church and his civil lord. He was in the final stages of preparation to leave when a summons came that would change his life forever.

Marina was tending the small herb garden in the courtyard of the house when the heavy knock of a wood striking wood sounded at the door. She opened it to find a messenger bearing a staff with the winged lion's crest of the Doge. For most in Venice, the appearance of such a person was usually a serious matter and a reason to worry, but the pleasant look on his face at that moment said that this mission was different. Even so, Marina was cautious.

"Yes?" she said.

"*Signora,*" he said with a respectful nod, holding up a sealed document.

She relaxed. It was only the delivery of a message.

"This is the house of Galileo Galilei?" he asked.

"It is."

"A message for the *Doctore.*" He handed her the document, which bore both the seal of the Doge and the mayoral crest.

Whatever was within, she knew, represented the determination of the city's entire power structure.

"*Grazie,*" she said taking it.

The messenger nodded curtly again as she closed the gate. Then she turned and carried the letter across the courtyard and up the stairs to the studio where Galileo was at work on a new form of telescope. He looked up at her entrance and smiled. Then he noticed the sealed paperwork in her hand. She handed it over, and as he quickly inspected the stamp and seal his eyebrows raised.

"Very official, apparently," he said with amusement.

He broke the seal and began to read. Marina watched his face for any sign as to the nature of the contents. Showing nothing, he set it down and stared ahead.

"What is it? What does it mean?" she asked, unable to restrain herself.

He smiled at her with just a tinge of sadness.

"It means that no good deed goes unpunished."

Unique among Italy's cities, Venice was a series of contradictions somehow existing in harmony. Strictly ruled, it was also the most libertine place in Europe. Staunchly Catholic, its masked balls and celebrations were exhibitions of some of the greatest acts of debauchery since the Roman Empire. A city-state composed by an archipelago of separate and distinct islands; it was connected by arching bridges that made it somehow seem intact. Finally, while it was solid *terra firma* upon which the houses, buildings, galleries, and cathedrals stood, it was also comprehensively sinking.

Some of the older structures had descended enough that their lower floors had been closed off like perpetually flooded basements, and while that strategy had served for a while, those in charge knew that something more substantial had to be done. For Galileo, the timing wasn't good.

He had intentionally avoided communicating with his parents while he sought the approvals of the Church and the Grand Duke Medici to wed Marina. His mother, Giulia had always been a class-conscious woman, and he knew that it had been her wish that he marry advantageously, so that the family might elevate their status to nobility. To alert her that he intended to marry a maid, a woman of even lower social standing than themselves without a fortune to recommend her, would have been pure folly. His plan was to arrive in Florence with Marina, obtain both civil and clerical permission, marry and be done with it before he announced anything to his parents. By then there would be nothing his mother could do, and she would have to accept the situation.

The new summons in the document, however, put an end to any hope of leaving Venice any time soon.

The audience for the discussion was held in the fabulous *Palazzo Ducale*. As Galileo entered the hall and looked up at the ornate golden molding and crafted wooden adornments, it occurred to him that the setting had been chosen for its effect. No one passing through could avoid feeling the sheer power that lived and breathed within the building. When he entered the salon for the interview, the constitution of the audience was just as overwhelming.

The Doge of Venice sat next to the Harbor Master, who was seated next to the newly ordained Cardinal Maffeo Barberini. Galileo's first impulse was to acknowledge them as the holy trinity of governmental power, but his sense of self-preservation stilled his irreverent tongue from saying so. He paused at the door and bowed, making his initial obedience. Then he walked halfway across the room and repeated the process.

"Oh, come now, we don't need all that do we?" asked Barberini of the other two.

They looked back at him with slightly offended expressions. It was clear they were enjoying the genuflection entirely. Barberini stood up and walked over to Galileo.

"Maestro, we should be the ones bowing," he said with the unabashed adoration of a fan. Then with a twinkle added, "Alas, genius is not a recognized municipal rank."

"Eminence," said Galileo.

"Oh please," waved Barberini. "I was Maffeo before, I am Maffeo now, and for you, I am always Maffeo."

Galileo respectfully nodded his compliance.

"Do you know," said Barberini enthusiastically turning to the others, "when we were in school, all anyone ever spoke of was Galileo, Galileo, Galileo. At first, I wondered who is this Galileo? He cannot possibly be so great that no one can challenge him." He paused and smiled at Galileo. "I was very foolish as I soon learned. Of course, God was generous enough to replace my arrogance and resentment with adoration for my very great friend."

Barberini turned to Galileo. His eyes darted greedily trying to take in all aspects of his friend's face. The look betrayed something too intimate of Barberini's affection, and both the Doge and Harbor Master shifted uncomfortably in their seats.

Barberini must have sensed it. He quickly suppressed his exuberance to resume the reserved nature of his station and said almost ceremonially, "The city of Venice requires your service, Maestro."

Galileo placed his hand gently over his heart and bowed.

"Whatever I may do," he affirmed.

They were fateful words. As the three began laying out the task, Galileo realized he was literally being asked to save the city. With a sinking heart, he also realized that his plan to hastily return to Florence and marry quickly had just been thwarted.

•

"You did it, though," said Ferrero. A hint of genuine respect was coloring his tone now, and Bellarmine looked pleased at the transformation.

The old scholar sighed and nodded. "Yes, the mathematics alone took six months. Once again, I looked to Archimedes."

"The screw," said Bellarmine. He couldn't help himself. He was enough of an academic at heart that an appreciation for the mechanics overcame his silence.

Ferrero looked confused.

Galileo explained, "The Archimedean screw was the simplest way to lift water. The threads of a giant screw inside a barrel with its end below the surface displaces the water up the screw until it spills out the top. The only limitation is the length of the screw and the power to turn it."

Ferrero considered that.

Then Galileo added, "It was both a blessing and a curse. My first child was born, and as happy as that made me, I knew that time for securing my family was slipping away."

•

Every parent believes their child is the most beautiful in the world, but as Galileo looked at the writhing newborn bundle in Marina's arms, he was certain that in his case it was the truth.

"What shall we call her?" asked Galileo.

Marina looked up at him. Somehow despite the ravaging pain and depletion of labor, she had never seemed more beautiful to him. He leaned down and kissed her.

"Virginia," said Marina as their kiss ended.

"Virginia," he repeated.

The baby clucked and sputtered gently like she approved of her name and a small pearly bubble formed at her lip.

"She's hungry," said the old midwife that had attended Marina.

Marina bared her breast and held the child up so she could latch. Regardless of what he might eventually witness through his instruments or find among the stars, he knew this was the most marvelous and beautiful thing he would ever see.

Marina looked up from the baby with a smile on her face. Galileo looked tired. Her brow knitted with concern.

"What is it?" she asked.

He shrugged.

"An unprecedented project in terms of its foundational mathematics, engineering, with instruments that must be invented to complete each critical task...all to push back an inevitable force of nature?" He grinned. "Not a problem at all."

She reached up and caressed the side of his haggard face.

"My poor man," she said lovingly before smiling, "and soon you will have to change diapers."

"Another instrument I'll have to invent," he chuckled.

It was one thing to joke, but his estimations of the requirement of the project were dead-on. Two forges worked around-the-clock to make the giant metal screws that would run in series to displace the waters of the archipelago and lighten the structural burden on the land mass. The carpenters at Galileo's command constructed huge wooden platforms and trusses to suspend the pumping chambers. For powering the massive device, Galileo designed special horse tracks affixed by long lever arms that attached to the top of each giant screw. Nearby, the stable of draft animals was stocked and maintained so that the horses could be run in teams, night and day, if necessary.

In the end, it would take four years to complete. Not that it was all bad. Galileo's value was recognized and rewarded. The numerous inventions he came up with yielded patents that enhanced his fame and reputation throughout all Europe. He was named professor at the illustrious University of Padua. By the time the project was finished, he and Marina had added two more to their family, a second daughter Livia and a son, Vincenzio. Unfortunately, in the critical matters of society, he could not acknowledge them, and during the census accounting, they were all listed with the surname of Gamba instead of Galilei. In the eyes of the church and state, they were not yet his. It was a fact that ate at him constantly.

Without the benefit of marriage, if anything were to happen, none of his possessions could pass on to Marina nor would his name to his children. It would be as if she had simply been a promiscuous woman, and the paternity of her children would forever be a source of conjecture and shame. They would be, in a word, damned.

That was why so many nights of late he had awakened and stared into the darkness as he listened to Marina breathe. Sometimes he would get up and go to the other bedroom to look at his children. It was surely impossible, he knew, that word of his growing family and domestic situation had not gotten back to Florence. Only the fact that he had not received an angry, objecting letter from his mother kept hope alive that he might yet make it back and arrange a marriage before cruel fate interfered.

CHAPTER SIX

"It wasn't cruel fate," said Bellarmine sadly. "It was your mother."

Ferrero looked from the Cardinal to a nodding Galileo.

"She objected that you lived in sin," said Ferrero.

It was such an abrupt statement, not intended as a condemnation but merely an observation in the context of church position on the matter. Even so, Bellarmine winced and looked uncomfortable. Galileo didn't react at first, no flash of temper. The memory was like a scar, deadened and impervious, rind thick, but even so, it had been pressed and reawakened. Galileo shrugged slightly.

"It didn't feel like it to me," he said. "I was in love. Despite of the rules of the world." He looked thoughtful, like a man mentally reviewing the details of a critical mistake. "I just didn't move quickly enough."

•

The ride back to Tuscany was certainly different than his trip to Venice had been years earlier. This time everything from the mode of transportation in a luxurious carriage to the company of a wife and three children seemed as though it was happening to a completely different person. In some ways Galileo was. As he watched the golden city on the Adriatic disappear through the window of his carriage, a sense of unease occupied him. Ironically, it made him think that while they were moving inland away from the ocean, they were in fact heading into stormy seas of a different variety.

By the time they arrived in his hometown, he had made up his mind to address the issue head on, and he directed the driver to take them to his parents' home straightaway. Almost before he was ready, the carriage pulled up in the small cobblestone drive that formed a semicircle in front of the house and stopped.

They knew he was coming. At the stop the night before, he had sent word ahead with a rider. As the door of the carriage opened, Giulia and Vincenzo, the namesake for the infant boy, rushed out of the house with broad smiles to embrace their son. Vincenzo was still smiling when Marina climbed down, but the look on Giulia's face was anything but welcoming. She looked from Marina to the children and back at their mother. Only Galileo noticed as her expression went from surprised, to offended, to something far more alarming.

He had expected his mother to be displeased, but her opposition to every aspect of his new family was beyond anything he could have anticipated, and it wasn't just in matters of disposition. Giulia stared at the children like they were a personal insult, like living, breathing assaults on her aspirations for her son's social ascendance. It was also clear to him that the one she blamed was not him. It was Marina.

There would be no winning over his mother, and he knew he could never depend on her support. As with all other problems, this social dynamic seemed to Galileo to need only logic to solve it. He couldn't have been more wrong. Perhaps he had indulged the supposition because of the wonderful news that had come to him and fueled his hope. Bellarmine had been named Cardinal and had taken over the academic responsibilities of the church in Florence. As the presiding clerical officer, he could give Galileo and Marina the blessing to proceed with an ordained marriage. Galileo knew the way to his friend's favor was through his appreciation for genius and so without further confrontation or discussion with his parents, he disappeared into the back room of the new house he bought for his family and set to work. In what would soon be his lifelong, permanent study, he took up his tools and with remarkable concentration, began construction on a new device, a metronomic clock of unparalleled precision, powered by a perfectly balanced, swinging pendulum.

Through a bolted magnifying glass, he worked the tiny gears and attachments within a stylish housing. This much he had learned from the Venetians. A functional apparatus was not enough. To truly dazzle, one had to present the brilliance with commensurate style. It was not quick work, but Galileo had his family around him, and the time passed quickly. Granted, there were occasional setbacks. One day as baby Vincenzio began to crawl, he crossed the threshold to his father's study and looked up to find a single terrifyingly giant eye staring back at him from the opposite side of the magnifying glass. It took over an hour before the child could be consoled.

For the most part, though the work went smoothly, and by the time Vincenzio was tottering on two legs, Galileo was ready to make his presentation. He wrote a letter and requested a meeting with the presiding clerical officer in Florence. Just addressing the familiar name gave him a charge of optimism.

When newly installed Cardinal Bellarmine received the formal request for an audience with his old debate partner and friend, he knew what was going to be asked of him. He also knew it would be odd. This wasn't just a reunion of friends. This was a dialogue, tinged, perhaps even compromised, by his new office in the Church. Still, he missed Galileo and wanted to see him, so he granted the request.

Professore Galilei, despite his brilliance in so many things, still lacked an awareness of these types of tricky negotiations. A day later when he optimistically exited the carriage at the University, dressed to the nines in his finest cloak and cap with the tapestry covered gift in his hands he wore an expression of pure certainty. He was just sure that if his friend had any reservation at all in giving his blessing, the scholar in him would be won over by the novel device. He walked through the great hall to the private reception area with a broad smile on his face. The second he saw Bellarmine in his scarlet vestments seated on the throne-like seat of religious power though, a sense of doubt overtook him. This was still his friend, of course, but also something more now. Seeing the many attendant Monsignors and Fathers comprising his staff, Galileo paused and nodded respectfully.

"Galileo!" shouted Bellarmine encouragingly. "All hail the savior of Venice."

Galileo smiled and laughed. "Your Eminence," he said bowing again.

"Please," he said dismissively but spying the gift added eagerly," is that for me?"

He sounded almost like a child. Galileo handed it over.

Bellarmine, as if dragging out the anticipatory pleasure asked, "What is it? Something new?"

Galileo nodded coyly at Bellarmine who slipped the cover off to reveal the time piece. The beautiful housing of the clockworks was composed entirely of molded brass, but underneath the steel arm of the pendulum swung the rounded bell, like an inverted lollipop, back and forth within a cylinder of glass. It was a perfect combination of style and functionality, and as he expected, met entirely with Bellarmine's appreciation of their shared history and the science on display.

"You did it. The pendulum," exulted Bellarmine.

"A perfect arc, keeping perfect time," said Galileo.

For a moment, neither of them said a word. They just watched the beautiful mechanics at work. Bellarmine looked truly moved and amazed by the brilliance of the gift.

"It is an honor to the Church, His Holiness, and to me," he said.

Galileo's smile faltered. The encounter had suddenly become so oddly formal. He was now talking to Bellarmine in his official capacity, and once again his earlier confidence began to wane.

"Your Eminence," started Galileo.

The Cardinal's upheld hand stopped his carefully prepared speech.

"I have spoken with the Duke, and I am pleased that he has wholeheartedly approved your appointment as the Chief Mathematician at the University of Pisa. The appointment is for life"

Galileo frowned. "Pisa?"

As if he hadn't heard, Bellarmine continued with his official announcement.

"And he has authorized your continued work in the *Disegno* philosophy." Bellarmine looked at the clock again, dazzled still. "Science elevated to art."

The way he said it sounded almost like a beloved incantation. Galileo, however, was not distracted from the reason for the visit. He gave the Cardinal a considered look.

"And what of my request to marry?"

Bellarmine sighed and sat back in his elaborate chair. When he finally spoke, his tone was flat, reserved.

"The marriage of an appointed scholar is a state matter and at the discretion of the Duke of Tuscany."

"You know that Medici has said no," said Galileo.

Bellarmine looked down. "Your mother made an appeal to him...against it."

Galileo didn't say a word. The air was poison now and even drawing breath to reply seemed like a fated action. He nodded, turned and left as Bellarmine watched with agonized eyes.

•

The last thing Duke Frederico Medici wanted to get involved in was a Galilei family squabble, but the matriarch of the highly regarded clan was not the type to be put off. Plus, the musical work of the father and the remarkable genius of the son made ignoring her a peril. In the old days even a talented family of their station could have been ignored. They would have known their place, and feared becoming a bother, but times were changing. The name Galilei was famous enough that others among Medici's subjects might take umbrage if word got out that he had brushed off the mother's appeal. He was, after all, the civil authority on such matters.

It was simple really. He could easily grant a dispensation for Galileo to marry his housemaid if he wanted.

But the mother... he didn't finish the thought, because she was entering the salon with a member of his house staff.

"*Signora* Galilei," he said magnanimously.

She bowed.

"Don Frederico," she said humbly.

He smiled warmly, disguising his apprehension.

Her argument was emotional and outrageous, but also effective. Her son had been bewitched by a prostitute in Venice. To allow the witch, as she called her, formal membership, approved by himself, into Tuscan society would reflect badly on both the Galilei family and Medici. He didn't believe it, of course. It was ludicrous, but it also wasn't worth the time and energy for an obviously futile argument with an emotional mother. Besides, young Galileo had not come to him first.

He would not approve the marriage.

Signora Galilei was in the kitchen, happily preparing the evening meal when her son arrived at the house fresh from his appellate audience with Medici. At first, he just sat in his carriage outside, staring at the home that once sheltered, supported and nurtured him. Now it was an empty husk. As Galileo looked on, he realized that he was about to lose not one, but the two most important women in his life.

Giulia was still focused on her task when he appeared quietly in the doorway behind her. She didn't hear him at first, and he did nothing to give away his presence, but somehow, a few seconds later, she felt him there and turned around. Whatever justification she'd conjured to support her matrimonial obstruction, one look at his face and she knew that this was the last time she would see him. Even so, tragically, her obstinacy wouldn't yield.

"It is every mother's duty to protect her son," she asserted before he even said a word. "Even from his own tendencies."

The righteous tone of it was infuriating. He glowered back, his rage and misery growing.

"Maybe even more so then," she pressed.

Still, he said nothing. His silence was a stony impact. She stopped talking and stood there, staring back at him. Not that she was moved to reconsider her words. If anything, in silence she became even more resolute.

When he did speak, Galileo's voice was changed. It barely even sounded like him. His throat was raw and creaked with the words that rushed out in an even more devastating condemnation than if he had shouted them.

"You have damned your own grandchildren."

Now it was her turn to say nothing. For a moment, it seemed that maybe his words had gotten through, that she would acknowledge the terrible part her intrusion had played on his happiness. How she had destroyed of all their family. But no. She simply set her jaw and glared back defiantly. He knew. She was beyond hope, and so then was he.

It didn't stop his heart from crying out though.

"You would doom your own blood," he spat.

She scoffed.

"They are not mine," she countered.

"How can you?" he started to say more before giving up and shaking his head.

She had one last, venomous barb.

"A woman like that? How can you know that they are yours?"

They were the last words she would ever speak to her son.

•

The sun in Tuscany is not like the sun anywhere else on earth. Galileo had heard people say that since he was a boy. It wasn't very scientific, he knew, but as he looked down the terraced hill at the vineyard workers clipping back the tendrils and shoots along the fruiting arms of the vines, he felt there was also no scientific evidence against that assertion. The vineyard below where he and his family had stopped to picnic occupied a rich terroir. The rootstocks and scions were easily the size of his ankle, and the heavy, groomed fruit suspended in perfect lines with just enough leaf cover to protect the ripe berries from too much direct light. Venice had been great for him. It gave him love, fame and a small fortune for a man his age, but it lacked the warmth of home.

Yet now as he looked at the laborers, it did not feel so warm.

"What is wrong?" said Marina, looking up from Vincenzio who was sucking on a plucked grape.

She had been surprised when he told her to pack up the children and prepare for a picnic above the vineyards, and now it was apparent that his motivation came from some deep disturbance.

"I was just thinking about the fortunes of a grape," he said.

She leaned over and kissed him. It was warm and delicious, almost enough to distract him from his worries.

"I didn't know grapes had fortunes," she said. "Fates perhaps." She chuckled. "I knew they had fates."

"Do they, now?"

"Oh yes," she replied. "It is quite the drama."

The girls, especially Virginia, were looking at her with interest. Their mother was a good storyteller, and the fairytale of the grape had the potential to be quite entertaining. Galileo leaned back on one elbow, momentarily alleviated of his concerns.

"At first, it begins humbly, small, green and hard"—she wrinkled her nose at Virginia who laughed— "then, the sun"—she pointed upward— "whispers to them...little indelicacies until they become embarrassed and blush. The better the secret shared by the sun, the more they blush until they grow fat and plump and as happy as a grape may be."

Her audience was hooked. Galileo's eyes glowed with admiration. If possible, he thought, I love her more right now than ever.

"And then what happens?" asked Virginia.

"Well, then comes the time to harvest. They are cut from the vine and taken away and crushed."

The children looked horrified. Livia's lip trembled and a fat tear rolled down her cheek. Vincenzio was too young to follow the story or even know what was happening, but he took his emotional cue from Livia and began to cry as well. Galileo looked at his children with complete surprise.

"No, no," protested Virginia emotionally.

Marina had the opposite response to the emotional reaction of the children. While poignant and endearingly sweet, she also found it quite funny. The whole brood had taken up the empathetic cause of an acre of grapes.

"My, what a bunch of little sentimentalists I've borne. It is all right," she said throatily overriding the impulse to laugh. "Because while it is the fate of almost all grapes that they are crushed in this world, it leads to something wonderful happening."

It was perfect, and as it happens with affection, Marina's spontaneous crafting of the tale of the grape was so sweet, poetic and tragic that it set the wheel of love spinning anew for him.

The children were not that easily appeased. They continued their snuffling, but the promise of a happy ending made Virginia cough and sniff and ask, "What?"

"They become wine," said Galileo interrupting, "and nothing"—he looked at Vincenzio happily sucking on his grape— "well, almost nothing, is a better way for a grape to end up than that."

It was a complex consideration for children of their age, and while they thought about that, Galileo stood up and walked over to a vine. A thickly clustered bunch of grapes hung ripe and ready. Looking around surreptitiously, he reached and pulled it free. Then he turned and handed it to Marina.

"The luckiest ones end up as a treat for Vincenzio," said Marina, plucking another one and handing it to the boy.

"One lucky bunch, saved from a crushing fate by the Galilei family," he said.

"I am glad you saved them, Papa," said Virginia sympathetically.

The sunlight was beginning its sideward slant, which brought out the amber muted tones of the vineyard. The picnic was over, and they gathered their belongings to head home. Marina's hair was lighter now, a product of exposure to the sun, and her skin glowed with a slightly darker warmth. The resulting pang for Galileo was a delicious agony of overwhelming emotion that reinforced his marvel at the mystery of love.

It was still there that night as he sat by the hearth and watched the rest of them interact. He had a home. He had a family. He looked at his wife, completely oblivious of him and moving around with the children performing the most mundane of tasks. It was intoxicating, natural, magical. Yes, Galileo was certain, he had a wife. He was suddenly overcome by an adoration for her that instantly gave way to a sadness and most profound pain.

The next morning, he went to see Bellarmine again. This time as a friend. There was no pageantry, no pomp. He did not have a gift. He was simply Galileo, a man trying to protect the thing he loved most.

One look at him and Bellarmine knew. He waved to the others in attendance to go. Whatever was coming was going to be deeply personal, and he wanted to protect his most admired friend.

"Please sit," he said, and then thinking better added, "would you like some wine?"

Thinking of that picnic in the vineyard, the resulting smile on Galileo's face was bittersweet.

"Perpetually," he said.

Bellarmine poured two glasses and handed one to the *Doctore*. Galileo held it up and stared at it against the light.

"What better fate for a grape," he said.

"I heard you went to see Medici," said Bellarmine.

"Yes." He took a sip.

Bellarmine had never seen his old confidante and colleague more wretched. As a friend he would have done anything to help, but as an officer of the Church, he knew he had to hold his tongue.

"What are you going to do?" he asked finally.

Galileo took another sip and set down the glass. When he spoke his voice was controlled, his comments thoughtful as if he were describing a detached phenomenon.

"It is a crushing world," he started. "Daughters born out of wedlock, without a father's surname have no future except for the mercy of a husband who is willing to forgo a dowry. To assure the proper type of man and oblige him to decency, it would require more money than I have."

He paused and thought before continuing.

"And I have two daughters."

Bellarmine understood. There were only three other options outside of marriage. A woman if she were lucky, might become an elevated courtesan, or she could take a nun's vows and seek the sanctuary of the cloth, or she would be left to the savagery of the world.

"What can I do?" asked Bellarmine gently.

"Virginia and Livia," said Galileo.

Bellarmine nodded and leaned forward to place a promissory, assuring hand on his beleaguered friend's shoulder.

"They will have a place in the Church," he said. "You have my word."

Galileo sighed. It sounded like both a resignation and relief.

"*Grazie*," he said.

•

That night Galileo watched his family again, as if imbedding each image, each detail as a memory that would have to sustain him for the rest of his life. In a way it was like that first day he had seen her at the Venetian market. He knew he needed to capture every aspect of the moment. When the children were asleep, he and Marina made love, but something in the intimate physical act seemed different. Again, he was indulging in a sensual cataloguing. There was a gentility and something else that in the end left Marina disquieted as she lay with her head on his chest. He closed his eyes and inhaled the warm aroma of her hair. It was like the liberation of the sunlight that had been captured during the day, like the respiration and little enzymatic processes and interactions that occurred in the vines in the cool of the evening. These were the special indulgences. As he felt the weight of her head lift, he worried that in the years to come, without the refreshment of the sensation, the memory might fade. It was that potential that was the most disturbing to him.

"What is it?" she said.

The moonlight was slanting now and bringing out the luminous quality of her eyes, just as the sun had that first time, he saw her through the telescope. While the muted lunar light didn't show the flash of her soul's fire, it displayed something cooler, more intellectual perhaps that made him love her all the more.

"I saw Bellarmine today," he said.

This was bad news. She knew her husband too well and his flat tone now explained why he had been so different that evening. It also meant that what was yet to come was going to be even worse.

"He will make sure that the girls have a place at convent."

She stared off as she absently ran her hand across his skin.

"I see," she said sadly, "and Vincenzio?"

"We have time," said Galileo. "A man does not require a dowry to wed, and while it will be slow, I can eventually get permission to give him my namesake."

It was unfair and true. A boy was easier, or at the very least, it was easier for a boy in that regard.

For a moment they just stayed still, saying nothing, focused on the simple physical contact of their bodies against each other.

"What else?" she finally said with a tone that indicated she already knew.

They would never be allowed to marry and if anything happened to him, or when eventually something did, she would cease to exist in society's eye as having any application to her life with him, no status save that as a household servant.

"You are sending me away."

It sounded horrible, empty, heart-breaking.

"We are being punished for indulging our love, for daring to be happy without asking first," he said bitterly.

"I don't care," she said. "I won't leave you."

He sighed. It was all too hard.

"If you don't, in the end, after a lifetime together, they will obliterate me from you. You will be excluded from your home and have no claim to any aspect of our life. They will prevent you even from occupying a proper place when I am buried. I cannot bear the thought of that. I cannot allow myself such selfishness...just because I love you."

"I don't care," she said again defiantly.

"And the boy," said Galileo, playing his last card. "If you remain, they will punish him. They will deny him the claim of paternity. Whatever chance he has at a place in this world will be gone...all to punish us."

It was terrible and completely true.

She kissed his chest.

"If I am a million miles from you, if I am to never see you again...I will always be...yours," she said haltingly.

The word "tears" was not adequate for what came next.

•

There was really only one option, but it was too terrible for them to consider, at least aloud. To a nobleman, Marina would have been a trifle, a dalliance, and now with children, she might even be seconded into a household and her children subordinated to the labor force or worse. It was a common enough story, for common people. Despite the changes in the world, the world was not yet kind enough to the common person.

That left Reynoldo Bertoluzzi. In Venice, long before Galileo came along, he had asked her to marry him. He was a commoner, but an accomplished craftsman, and he loved Marina and was actively wooing her with marginal success until the day that Galileo appeared. More importantly, he was a good man, kind and had never hidden his continued affection for her, even as he stepped aside. Nor had he shown any animosity toward Galileo. He saw how she felt and had docilely relinquished the field in favor of her true happiness. If Galileo were going to indulge the unthinkable and look to someone for her domestic security and protection, he couldn't find a better candidate than that very decent man.

The next day he told Marina.

She refused.

The day after, he mentioned it again.

Again, she refused.

Finally, he reminded her of the impact it could have on their son. She said nothing. She just sat staring off as if her heart had stopped and she was awaiting her inevitable death. Of course, she didn't die, but when finally, she moved again, her life as she had known and loved it was at an end.

•

Father Ferrero was no sentimentalist, and his austere nature was a perfect fit for a Jesuit. His tendency in anything had always been to go first with the intellectual and then only reluctantly to the matters of the heart afterward. Now though, as he listened to the story of Galileo's family, he felt an emotional ripping that defied cold thought. Now, he simply listened and stared with a distraught look on his face.

Bellarmine too, looked morose, remembering his part in the matter. While Galileo had arguably been the most affected by those past events, he was somehow the least incapacitated as they sat in the interrogation room. As he looked at the other two, it seemed to him that the power of absolution and catharsis was in his hands, not theirs.

"It must have been hard for you to perform the ceremony," he said gently to Bellarmine.

The Cardinal roused and looked at him with anguished eyes.

"Thank you for doing it, though."

Bellarmine's face contorted a little. He seemed unable to accept the gratitude and comment.

"You saved her," said Galileo definitively.

•

For Bellarmine the memory of that ceremony was torture. He was just finishing the matrimonial liturgy in the small chapel when he looked up and saw Galileo, standing in the doorway, watching from the back of the church. No one else saw. They were all facing the other way, paying attention to the bride and groom. Reynoldo smiled happily, affirming the vows he had just taken. Marina looked beautiful, but her eyes expressed an undeniable sadness.

Even years later, Bellarmine was sure he was the only one that noticed. In the span of a second, she dismissed it and looked back with a smile at Reynoldo as she prepared for the final kiss. It took everything he had not to look away and as he tried to take a breath, Bellarmine found it didn't come so easily. When the couple finished the ceremonial act of affection and turned to face the crowd, Bellarmine looked over and found that his friend, Galileo, had gone.

•

"My life was altered. My happiness in the manner of love was at an end," said Galileo to Ferrero. The weight of his words felt as though the stones in the roof had collapsed upon them all until Galileo sat back and added, "And from that point I pursued happiness purely in manners of the mind."

It was the reprieve the two clergymen needed, and they both released a breath of air that neither was aware he had been holding.

"You did that with a vengeance," said Bellarmine appreciatively.

"Perhaps. I do know I pursued it in two directions. First, from the heavens to earth," he said trailing off to settle into another memory.

•

Of all the universities under the Catholic administration in Italy, the college at Pisa, was one of the most secular. By modern standards it might have been considered progressive in both its philosophy and intellectual daring.

Subjects that would have been difficult on a Roman campus or anywhere really, were far more easily engaged there. In fact, it was as close to free thought exchange as could be found anywhere in the empire. Experimentation, the testing of scientific theory, a new approach that had been championed by *Professore* Galilei was almost exclusively practiced there. It was daring, brilliant and the most important step in understanding the world without superstition. Even so, there were those that thought him a little reckless and even more that were envious and felt threatened by him. This was especially evident when he began his work with falling bodies.

He had made it plainly known that the Aristotelian concept of *mass* determining a body's properties in the physical world was wrong.

"I will prove that it isn't mass, but *density* that matters when it comes to displacement and gravity," he said that fateful day in the lecture hall.

He looked around at the young scholarly faces. The fact that the students were even present was a testament to their promise. Only the very best, the most talented minds were chosen for the *Lincean* and *Disegno* programs.

"I will be taking on two assistants for the study" he added, looking around the room. "I am looking for brilliance, of course, but also"—his eyes came to rest on the broad shouldered and portly Viviani and the tall, lanky Torricelli sitting next to him— "and perhaps as importantly, strong backs."

At first, they looked delighted that the great Galileo had taken notice of them, but a week later as they made their fourth trip up the winding staircase inside the tower of Pisa with an iron cannonball in each hand, they were having second thoughts.

The iron spheres were of slightly different diameters and circumferences. They had been carefully designed by Galileo and his meticulous and nattering oversight of the poor blacksmith that crafted them had been almost too much for the poor man to take.

"Different masses, identical densities."

It was like a mantra, he kept repeating. It was also why he wanted to use the tower. The drop would provide enough distance that the similarity in the rate of fall could not be denied. To Viviani and Torricelli, who were incidentally enough, the two top *Physik* students in university, this methodology was exciting and made perfect sense. Proof, it was a new concept in science. Driven almost primarily by Galileo, it employed techniques drawn from another genius, the great Leonardo Da Vinci. It also stole from a host of others, a fact that the good *Professore*, readily and happily admitted; such names as Archimedes, Welser, and, yes, even Aristotle were credited. Galileo, however, was the first to apply rules, structure and instrumentation to an experimental model, which was why the two sweating, panting scholars were lugging the iron balls up the stairs.

"Do you think... this time...will be...enough?" said Viviani gasping for breath between the words.

He paused and leaned against the wall of the tower.

"I...certainly...hope so," gasped Torricelli, contorting his neck to try and wipe the sweat from his forehead on his shoulder.

"I...don't think...I can...do this again," said Viviani.

"Perhaps... this time... he'll be satisfied," opined Torricelli.

Just then the impatient voice of Galileo rose from below.

"I am waiting!"

The two students looked at each other and with resigned expressions began their slow upward climb. Eventually, they reached the loggia, the open upper deck at the top floor of the tower. For Viviani this was the most nerve-racking part. He was uncomfortable with heights in general and the slightly tilted, smooth stoned, unrailed platform that offered no protection from a terminal drop with a single misstep had him basically horrified.

They slowed and carefully, cautiously waddled to the edge. Looking down they saw Galileo standing right in the middle of a pockmarked landing site.

"I wish the *Professore* would stand a little farther back," said Viviani with genuine concern.

"You could run down and tell him. Then run back up," teased Torricelli.

Viviani said nothing at first as he processed the exertional requirement of that.

"I am sure he knows what he is doing," he said finally.

Torricelli chuckled. He had to admit that he wasn't sure which would be worse, falling to his own death or accidentally crushing one of the greatest minds of the age. Down below, Galileo was waiving his arm impatiently for them to get on with it.

"Ready?" asked Viviani.

They took a tiny step forward to suspend the cannon balls over the edge.

"*Un...due...*" started Torricelli.

"*Tre*!" said Viviani, and they both released.

The balls dropped in the atmospheric lean of the tower where no breeze or other impedance could interfere. Outside of an eight-story vacuum chamber it was the best setting to prove Galileo's hypothesis, and while he might have been brilliant at devising an experiment, he was already showing a certain disregard for his own safety that would come back to haunt in the future. This time it was just his physical safety that was in doubt.

From the vantage point of the two volunteer scholars above, it had to be luck or God's own providence that was in play when the two cannonballs struck at exactly the same moment, only a few feet from the exuberant Galileo. The heavy iron spheres hit and imbedded slightly in the earth with a thud like a geological expression of discomfort. They rebounded and rolled past him, but the happy scientist wasn't even aware. He was too busy scribbling the results of the simultaneous strike – a perfect replication of the previous drops – into his notebook.

•

The loss of her love and giving herself over to another man, while excruciating for Marina, was only a small part of the true diminishment she would experience. Perhaps even harder was the fracturing of her maternal claim. Vincenzio was still a baby and would go with his mother and Reynoldo to Venice. The girls, though, were old enough that they could begin their instruction in the Church, so from that moment, they were lost to her forever. It was for the best. She knew that, but it did little to mitigate the pain. Still, she was grateful for the help of Cardinal Bellarmine as the girls were entered into the convent of *Santa Caterina de Siena*. It was the best place they could be, the place where the daughters of Tuscany's most illustrious families were placed. It also enjoyed a singular reputation for providing a liberal education and was the only institution that allowed the expression of women, rivaling what their male counterparts enjoyed at the *Disegno*.

It was the home to the celebrated Sister Plautilla Nelli who had painted the rival canvas to Da Vinci's *Last Supper*. An unprecedented and unique female artist, she had even been permitted to autograph her work with the phrase, "Pray for the Paintress." Granted her own painting had the beloved John, next to Christ with a certain feminine countenance, and she had substituted the fare depicted on the table with the same enjoyed by the nuns: a whole roasted lamb, bread, and fresh fava beans – an obvious wink of tribute to the Florentine cuisine.

So, it was the perfect place for a child of Galileo's, that is if she couldn't be with him. Since the permission for travel or visitation by any occupant of the convent was at the discretion of the officiating Cardinal, Bellarmine saw to it that Virginia, who upon her vows was thereafter known as Sister Maria Celeste, spent almost as much time with her talented father as behind the monastic stone walls. Soon enough, her quick and nimble mind had accumulated enough knowledge that it made her a perfect match and assistant to Galileo. Within a few years, at about the same time that Enrico Parma was publishing her father's seminal proof of the effects of density, not mass on falling bodies, she was allowed to move in and attend to his work.

On Motion was the first breakthrough work describing Galileo's scientific method. The audacity of the principle and the use of an experiment to prove a concept that had been argued for ages, told everyone who heard of it that intellect now had a means for overcoming conjecture. Soon requests for copies were flooding in from all parts of Europe, and for the first time, Parma experienced the fiscal and reputational rewards of publishing a hit.

It hadn't been a year since he had handed the first edition of the limited run to Viviani and Torricelli. He had no way of knowing its potential as they left his shop, and had someone suggested it, he would have laughed them out of the place. For the two scholars, seeing the work they had supported in print was an intoxicating experience. They hustled up the street alternating who got to carry the text every few blocks. It was a magical thing, that manuscript, and because of their part in helping create it, they too felt empowered.

"Here's to immortality," said Viviani exuberantly holding it up.

"And our part in it," affirmed Torricelli.

They entered Galileo's house with the familiarity that comes from working intimately with someone and carried their precious cargo into the study. Maria Celeste heard the door and came out of the kitchen just as Galileo took the manuscript and started to look it over. He waved to her, and she approached and draped herself against his neck to read over his shoulder.

Meanwhile Torricelli was looking at the latest iteration of Galileo's thermometer, one that had involved a few of his own suggestions. It sat just inside the open window that had such a perfect view of the sky at night. Inside, the large glass cylinder was filled with distilled alcohol, a micro-atmosphere in which different colored glass balls, each with a measured weight, rose and fell. Between the improved properties of the balls in the liquid and the change in temperature, the pewter number on the weight displayed a perfect measurement of heat or cold.

"A hot summer day," said Torricelli consulting the device.

"Yes," said Galileo abstractly, his attention far more dedicated to proofing the text, "and now you know exactly how hot."

Torricelli looked like he wished he had said a little more.

Viviani pointed at the document.

"*Signor* Parma sends his apologies, but just as we arrived, he received a request for 50 copies of the book. From Germany." He paused, then added. "He thought it was a prank at first."

Galileo and Maria Celeste looked at him with mild indignation. In that moment, two thoughts crowded for priority in Viviani's head. One was that they both had the same look, an intimidating similarity especially around the eyes, and the other was that he had placed his foot squarely in his mouth.

"No, I...uh, what I meant to say was," he stammered, clumsily trying to clarify.

Torricelli saw that his friend was about to drown in his own apoplexy and inserted to rescue him, "What he meant was that *Signor* Parma, has never had that large an order and so was not prepared. He thought you would want the public to benefit before you had a copy of the work, since you already know what it says."

Galileo smiled. "*Signor* Parma was correct...and is forgiven."

•

"So, I had studied the properties of the world from the heavens to the earth," repeated Galileo to Ferrero and Bellarmine, and for emphasis, he held up a finger and brought it down against the table mimicking the *thud* of the falling cannon balls. "Now, though, I had something else in mind." He looked at them for effect before continuing. "I would study the heavens from the earth."

"The *Sidereus Nuncius*," said Ferrero looking disquieted.

It was, after all, part of the reason they were in the interrogation room.

Before another word could pass, Bellarmine cleared his throat.

"It was not the subject, it was the way you dealt with it that caused the furor," he said firmly.

"He is right," said Galileo turning back to Ferrero. "He is absolutely right. If one kept their argument purely philosophical, they could advocate for the earth's moving around the sun." A mischievous twinkle followed, and he added, "At the top of their lungs."

"But you set out to prove it," countered Ferrero.

Galileo looked at him, and for the first time Ferrero understood the hushed, intimidated tone that those who had worked with Galileo resorted to when they shared some anecdote about his formidable nature, particularly when he was displeased. Just in that one look, he saw the full weight of someone who irrefutably knew more, could reason more, and whose intellect would always dwarf his own. It was impressive and, in that moment, without saying a word, he experienced the sense of a wrongheaded schoolboy being admonished by his teacher.

"Actually, I did prove it," said Galileo devastatingly.

It took a lot for Ferrero to muster a retort, but to his credit he did manage to finally say, "You could have remained silent."

Galileo sat back with his expression changed. There was no mocking affect now. Instead, it something more like professorial compassion, as if about to impart a truth that a slow student hadn't considered.

"A man who is unaware of the truth is a fool, but a man who knows the truth and doesn't say it, is a criminal," he said.

Bellarmine smiled.

Ferrero mulled the comment. It was profound, quick, and indicated a logical finality, but this was not an issue of logic. If it were, Galileo would not be in prison, and his soul and future freedom would not be in jeopardy.

"And yet, Sir, you are the one on trial for contradicting the word of God."

Suddenly his tone was back to prosecutorial.

Galileo smiled and turning to Bellarmine said genuinely, "I'm liking him more and more." He looked back at Ferrero, took a small breath and delivered his coup de grace. "The Bible shows us the way to heaven, young Jesuit, not the way the heavens go."

Ferrero had to admit. It was an excellent line. One for which he had no response.

"You see," continued Galileo, "all I did was discover the means to map them."

•

The breakthrough that made it all possible occurred in the Netherlands, as far a place in terms of climate and temperament as one could get from Italy. To the minds of a century's worth of Popes, the farther North one went from Rome, the more dangerously free-thinking was the inclination of the people. There had even been a theoretical discussion on the nature of winter and its negative spiritual effect on the faithful. How else, they wondered could the actions of Martin Luther be explained, not to mention the incomprehensibly heretical actions of Henry VIII of England. No, they surmised, the farther one got from the perpetual nature of the sun and summer, the further they risked being away from God's Son.

Even Dante Alighieri had agreed, or so they assumed. In his deepest circle of hell, the ninth, it wasn't a blazing cauldron of molten rock and fire. It wasn't heat that characterized the punishment. It was ice. In the absence of physical proof, as the upstart Galileo was always employing, this divine inspiration of Dante was considered an irrefutable argument by the Church scholars. No, it was certain. If they came from the North, the more people needed to beware of new ideas. Now, it was a transformed element that was going to risk the souls of men and with the same subtle cunning the Devil often used, its introduction seemed completely innocent.

For the longest time, an ocular lens had to be ground down from a single crystal or manufactured block. It was painstaking, inexact and the quality of an individual lens was subject to the carver's ability. The application of the large convex lens had been the master stroke of an eyeglass maker, Hans Lippershey, but it was the work of a German mathematician and astronomer, Johannes Kepler, that would dazzle Galileo and bring his attention to the miraculous potential that the telescope could provide. Even so, the quality of the lenses themselves were still a problem until a miraculous breakthrough occurred in the creation of glass molding. By creating a hellishly hot kiln and working the clear, liquefied sand into a perfect shape, a lens of near perfect acuity was possible, and even more importantly, different diameters could be specified.

According to the reports sent back by the German, Danish and Dutch Catholic clerics, the factories themselves were like an insight into the afterworld of the damned. Whole floors of large warehouses had been converted to blistering smelting works. Giant, open-ended furnaces blazed with higher temperatures than had ever been achieved by man, while broad-backed craftsmen, stripped to their waists, stoked the coals to even greater intensity.

On the opposite side, artisans, held long armed blowing tubes into cauldrons of molten glass. In some cases, as they withdrew the long tubes, they would begin blowing and shaping. In others they simply ladled the heated material into a shaped mold. Thus, the famed "Dutch perspective glass" came to the attention of one, Galileo Galilei. He placed an order the same day.

The two lenses, one twice the diameter and size of its mate arrived at his study six months later encased in a heavy wooden box, packed carefully in a nest of excelsior shavings. To Maria Celeste's recollection, Galileo's expression was as if he had looked into the manger at the infant Lord for the first time. He gently lifted the shaped glass and placed it in the brass conical cylinder that he had completed months earlier. It had stood teasingly empty for so long that the arrival of these two pieces was more than just a relief. It was a triumph. From what he knew of the limitations of focal length, with his usual anticipatory brilliance, he had crafted the body of the telescope so that the length of the tube itself could be adjusted between the lenses without letting in any additional light. This, he was sure, would revolutionize its clarity. Now he was dying to see if he had been right.

The only problem was that it was still noon. Sundown was hours away.

"I suppose there is only one thing to do now," he said.

"I'll get the wine," she answered.

Finally, the evening arrived. The sky shifted from the yellow of day to gold, and from gold to the light blue of dusk, then the light blue, deprived of its sustaining sunlight, deepened to a spectral array of pink and red and then a final lavender. When the stars presented themselves, he called Maria Celeste into the room. It was going to be a magnificent moment, a moment that would change the world, and he wanted her to see it, to experience it with him. This, more than paternity or protection or anything else. This was the greatest gift he could give her, to be there at the moment of scientific discovery.

They sat down at his desk where the three-foot-long telescope was angled up at the moon.

"Go ahead," he said stepping back.

Maria Celeste leaned in and squinted into the eyepiece. A second passed and she blinked and looked. Then she stepped back. It was not the look of wonder and awe Galileo was expecting.

"What is it?" he asked.

She simply shook her head.

He leaned down to look. The magnified moon was there, but the sharpness of detail that he was anticipating was not. He grasped the middle of the cylinder and extended it. Then he gestured for her to take another look. When she did the size of the moon had not changed, but the detail improved. It was sharp, as bright and crisp and accessible to her eye as if it had been stationed right outside his window. She gasped with surprise and smiled happily, but when her father looked, he didn't share the same exuberance. She could tell, something was still wrong.

There are those problems that vex the mind, and almost without exception, there is a direct proportion between their difficulty and the satisfaction and grandeur of the solution. This problem was not an easy one, and Maria Celeste watched over the coming weeks as her father studied and read and stared out the window. He was looking not at the Tuscan countryside, but into some vast consideration of the universe that only he saw. He scribbled formulas relentlessly and took out the lenses to peer through them one at a time.

And yet, it, the answer, eluded him.

Her mother had often teasingly complained that by being with him, she had chosen to give up any hope of a satisfying night's sleep. Too many times, he had abruptly risen in the middle of the night, in a frantic, pressured search for his pen and paper. Driven by some only partially awakened consciousness, he would stumble around until he could write down the idea, calculation, solution or fragment of inspiration that seemed peculiarly loosed at the threshold of sleep.

That was how it ultimately happened with the scope. When Viviani and Torricelli followed Maria Celeste into the maestro's study that fateful morning, he was asleep on his couch, one leg hanging off, his head at an odd angle, snoring away as the ink-stained fingers of a dangling hand bore testament to his late-night seizure of creativity. It was all on the desk for them to see, the mass of calculations and optical angles, drawn from the larger convex lens to a focal point at, not another convex lens, but a concave one.

"Oh," gasped Maria Celeste.

Her educated mind comprehended something extraordinary in her father's work, and as she had listened to him postulate and agonize over the last weeks, she understood the issues of the adjustment and focus that plagued the primitive instrument. It could be enlarged and still the clarity remained fine, but what he required was greater magnification and acuity without having to enlarge the tube. This though, along with the refined adjustment at the eye piece had solved it. Just as her father had wanted to give her the gift of seeing a change in the world through the eyepiece, she was seeing it now, in a far better way, via the magic of mathematics. This was inspiration and the moment of breakthrough. This was special and reserved for the select few that could see it. She, because of him, because of how much she was like him, could do so completely.

"He's done it," whispered Torricelli.

"Yes," affirmed Viviani a little too enthusiastically and a little too loudly.

On the couch, Galileo's eyelids fluttered, and he sat up. He gave a slight cough and then let out a groan. As he straightened, he grabbed at his neck and rubbed it, trying to alleviate the obvious stiffness in the muscle.

"I slept wrong," he yawned.

"*Doctore*, is this what it seems?" asked Viviani, pointing at the drawings.

He grinned and started to get up only to find that his leg had fallen asleep from its odd alignment. He stamped his foot several times, to circulate the blood until it could support his weight and then stood and took a cautious step like a giant toddler.

"Are you all right, Papa? Can I get you anything?" asked Maria Celeste.

He nodded.

"Wine, please."

She darted from the room and by the time he had made it to the drafting table, she was back with bottle and cups. Galileo took a respectfully savoring sip and followed it with a greedy swallow of the rest. He smacked his lips and scratched his head.

"Yes," he said to his audience. "This will enhance the view and enlarge the image another threefold."

They all looked pleased at first. Then Viviani pointed at a small diagram of a pencil- shaped device with a small, geared gage attached.

"And this, *Professore*? Is this something new?"

Galileo smiled and looked at Maria Celeste. She could tell from his one, raised, bushy eyebrow that he was testing to see if she recognized the product of his labor. She looked at the drawing and the straightened up and smiled.

"It's a micrometer," she said.

His smile widened, but instead of offering any congratulation, he just held out his wine cup and waggled it to be filled. Viviani and Torricelli leaned in closer, studying the calculations and the clean smooth lines of focus between the lenses as Galileo drank. When he had finished, he looked over the night's work and, satisfied, rolled the paperwork and placed it in a leather bag.

"Have a copy of this made and send it to Kepler at once," he said.

The round trip for the drawings and the return of the concave lens took just long enough for Galileo to construct his own version of the micrometer. Between the extension of the tube itself, the high quality and clarity of the superior glassworks and the adjustment to the eye piece, Galileo was certain that by the time he had finished, he would be truly in a position to, at long last, move forward the understanding of the universe.

The day it was completed, almost as if with divine endorsement of his work, God provided a night sky that was completely cloudless. Even as it took on its last lavender hue before night, the stars were already showing through. Like greedy actors on an opening night, they seemed to be peering out from behind the curtain as if to review the house. Maria Celeste had made sure that they opened a particularly good bottle of wine, and just as Viviani and Torricelli hurried up the street, the edge of the horizon succumbed to darkness.

"I told you we should have left earlier," said an irritated Torricelli.

"I'm sorry, the tailor is to blame. I wanted the new robe for the occasion," said Viviani.

"The *Doctore* was very clear. We must be there by dark. He said if we missed it, we would regret it the rest of our lives."

The words served as a spur and Viviani hustled, increasing almost to a run. Almost.

"Well," he panted, "at least we know he has not lost his gift for understatement." He gasped facetiously, but the exertion mitigated the desired effect.

They charged around the corner and up the street, straight to his house. Defying all propriety, they opened the door and barged in. A few steps later and they entered the study panting and gasping before leaning over with their hands on their knees to gulp for, air.

Seated at the table was Galileo staring up at the sky with the look of an eager child. The telescope was pointed at the full moon. All around, books surrounded him.

"Ah, perfectly on time," he said turning and smiling at the two oxygen-depleted men.

He nodded to Maria Celeste. She picked up two of the large books and handed one to each of them.

"What are these, Master?" asked Viviani.

"*De revolutionibus orbium coelestium.* On the Revolutions of the Heavenly Spheres," read Torricelli aloud.

"Copernicus," said Maria Celeste thoughtfully.

"*Harmonices Mundi*. The Harmony of the World," read Viviani.

This was an advance copy of the brilliant German's summation of his theories about celestial correspondences, and it tied together the ratios of the planetary orbits, musical theory, and the Platonic solids. He and Galileo had been corresponding for some time and their mutual respect had fostered a lively, if intermittent conversation that was instrumental to the moment, they were all about to experience.

"Kepler," muttered Maria Celeste.

Galileo smiled. She had read them all, including the one in her hand.

"*The Astronomia Nova.* The New Astronomy," read Torricelli.

"Kepler again," she said and looked over at her father.

He was beaming.

Lying open at the base of the scope was a copy of *The Epitomes of Copernican Astronomy.* It seemed perfectly fitting. He picked up the bottle of wine and filled several cups. Then he handed them out to the others in the room and took one himself.

"To my good friend, Kepler, whom I have never met," he said raising his cup. "If his works weren't so good, I might envy that I hadn't written them myself."

The others laughed.

"And to the foundation of what is about to come, to Copernicus," he said.

"Copernicus," echoed the others before they drank.

The view through the new telescope was a revelation. With the micrometer's adjustment and the adapted lens' increased magnification, the clarity was ten times what anyone else in the world had been able to accomplish. It was as equal in its importance to mankind as the discovery of fire and, beyond what any of them could possibly know, was the first step toward someday planting a foot on that distant glowing body.

Galileo stood back and let them all take a look.

Viviani gasped, dumbfounded.

Torricelli reacted the same way when it was his turn except that afterward he crossed himself.

Then it was Maria Celeste's turn. Galileo wanted her to go last. He wanted her to be able to stare for as long as she liked. As she leaned in to look, her reaction was perfect.

Her eyes widened and her pupils contracted then enlarged as the reaction to the increased luminance gave way to an attempt to take in everything about the image. With the increased magnification, details of the surface were revealed as never before. She saw mountains and scarred craters like a great artillery battle had been waged. There was the upheaval of ridges that framed vast irregular plains. Her lower lip dropped as she suddenly realized something important, and she drew a quick breath. She stepped back staring downward at the floor for a few seconds as she processed her thoughts and the significance of what she had concluded.

"The moon is not smooth," she said, looking at her father. "The heavens...are *not* perfect."

Galileo smiled.

It was no small declaration and certainly not a benign one. The Church scholars' philosophical argument of Aristotle's postulate, that the reproducible array of stars each night meant that the heavens were perfectly created and that the moon itself seen from a distance without instrumentation was a perfect orb, as smooth as glass. The Church scholars had taken this assumption of the perfect heavens as an extension of the perfection of God himself, and any attempt to dispute it was an affront to God and the very tenets of the Church.

To prove it, was considerably dangerous, and everyone in the room that night seemed to realize it. All, that is except for Galileo. To him the proof was no affront. For as he had said, the church scholars themselves with their individual flaws were not an affront to God, why then should be a phenomenon. Unfortunately for Galileo, those men were flawed in other ways, with arrogance, paranoia, inflexibility, laziness in understanding a new concept and petty in the fear of some diminution of their authority.

"No, they are not," said Galileo happily.

"Aristotle was wrong," said Viviani.

"Yes, in this matter," affirmed Galileo.

CHAPTER SEVEN

Bellarmine looked across the interrogation table at Galileo.

"You finally won our debate in Venice," he said with a mixed tone of appreciation and sadness.

"Yes," said Galileo.

"And you did not see the danger in that?" asked Ferrero.

Galileo smiled at the young Jesuit. "The truth is patient," he said. "I finally had the instrument to reveal it. Why should we fear that?"

It sounded so simple, almost childlike in its innocence, that fact and truth could overcome the ridiculous, small natures of men. In a completely separate way, it warmed both of them to the purity of his motives. It also spoke to an additional challenge in his defense.

"It was invigorating," he said to Ferrero. "I was suddenly seized with a certainty that I had to share it. The first person I wrote to was Kepler. I mean, when I had first read him, it was like discovering I had a twin, if only in matters of the mind."

"A German twin," said Bellarmine with a slightly mocking, sour note.

As if responding to a joke, Galileo smiled and said, "I was a little puzzled by that myself."

"He influenced you," said Ferrero, thinking of a tack he could take in arguing for Galileo at the trial.

If Kepler had seduced Galileo, perhaps they could offset the rage of the Church by exploiting its generally xenophobic considerations toward the Germanic states. They were, after all, so much farther north.

"Ah," said Galileo, getting it.

His expression said he didn't completely agree with that direction, though.

"You are referring to the map."

"Yes," said Ferrero.

•

It was one thing to postulate, another to show and prove his concepts, and quite another again to document and share them. Galileo knew that for the breakthrough discovery provided by the scope to truly impact the world, he would have to publish. He also knew that words would not be enough. So, he moved his grand experiment out into the walled garden beyond his study. It was the dry season in Florence and the coming months of a sky absent clouds and crisply low humidity made for the perfect opportunity to combine science with art. For Torricelli and Viviani, it meant more labor, but they didn't care. This was exactly the type of breakthrough for which they had hoped when they agreed to serve the *Professore*.

They lugged two heavy tables out of the study and set them up so that one could support the telescope, while the other could serve as a workstation for its documentation. They sharpened black charcoal into pencils for sketching and set out pots of ink and pens to fulfill the drawings. Everything had to be right. This work was going to alter history.

The sheet of parchment upon which he was going to draw was so large that it took all of them to carry it out and spread it on the table. Galileo looked through the scope and let out an awed breath. Then he chuckled and turned to make a first sketch. A true practitioner of the *Disegno*, his artwork was every bit as good as his science. His first sketch was a perfect reproduction of the jagged mountains on the surface.

The map of the moon took an entire month to draw. When it was finished a young painter, Lodovico Cardi, was invited over to view it. A bit of a rebel himself, he had studied under the fervid mannerist, Allesandro Allori, but of late had taken to a new art form known as the *Counter Maniera*. It was a throwing off of the conventional and a bold new take on the artistic interpretation of the world. In Galileo's mind, the Tuscan maverick was a perfect *collaborateur* when it came to reproducing his work in smaller forms for the publication he had in mind. He also knew that like himself, like any great spirit, Cardi, who was already signing his work with the invented persona "Cigoli" carried with him a unique desire and ability to advance the world view.

When he first entered Galileo's study and saw the huge drawing of the moon, he stopped stone still. Rendered speechless by it, he stared for a full minute, barely breathing, as if he were having an epiphany.

"It is fantastic, Maestro," he said abstractly.

It wasn't the first time that term had been used in reference to him, but just then, coming from Cigoli, Galileo felt a true validation by the word.

To the wise eye of Maria Celeste there was something else to the choice of Cigoli as an associate in spreading her father's discovery. Cigoli was popular. Already he had been recognized for his Biblical scenes, but it was really his clever inclusion of the likeness of the patron commissioning the work as the face of Abraham or Saint Peter or

Saint Paul in the scene that made him a favored artist. It was politically brilliant, and given the earthshattering nature of her father's work, she suspected that having that sort of astute ally might be critical. Regardless, word soon spread, and their small home began receiving a constant parade of enlightened scholars and artists. Galileo seemed to feed on it. Enrico Parma visited, and seeing the celestial mural, pleaded with him to hurry the accompanying text. He had already gotten a taste of the enthusiasm that the world had for Galileo's work, and almost salivated at the potential of the coming windfall that would result from it.

As for Cigoli, while the map of the moon was fascinating, what really drew his interest was something that at first glance wasn't nearly as impressive. Being just a series of celestial bodies in alignment, it seemed rather crude. It didn't have any of the artistic detail of the map, but on the scientific front, it was far more significant.

"What is this?" he asked.

"Oh, just a little representation of the heavens," responded Galileo.

It didn't sound like much, but something about the way he smiled, some aspect of his eye said differently. Cigoli could tell there was more, but instead of pushing, he just let the absence of words do the work.

Galileo looked out the window and smiled.

"You know with the improvements"—he gestured at the telescope as he took on a musing reverent quality— "I can see ten times the stars than are visible with the naked eye."

"Remarkable," said Cigoli.

"Yes," he nodded. "And yet, I am left to wonder how many more are out there."

He glanced over to see if Cigoli understood how magnificent that was. The artist's smile said that he did.

Galileo pointed at another drawing. The alignment of figures drawn in the shape of stars formed a swooping line.

Like the belt around a fat man's waist, thought Cigoli.

"Orion's belt." It was Maria Celeste.

"Yes," said Galileo, "and that is not all."

He pulled another sheet from the table. A different array had been drawn with all of the six-pointed stars, shaped like snowflakes spread out in a straight line from a large circle in the center. A few inches lower the same linear drawing showed a different position of the snowflake-stars, and an additional, smaller eight-point variety had been added next to the circle. A few inches below that, the spacing changed again. And so, it went.

Cigoli frowned with confusion. "I don't understand."

"Those are the bodies of Jupiter." It was Viviani. "That is Jupiter." He plopped a fat finger down on the circle. "And those"—he dragged his finger along the line of stars— "are the revolving stars of Jupiter."

"You see how they appear to change? It is how they move," said Torricelli, weighing in.

Galileo didn't mind their interruption. In fact, he loved that they also felt ownership of the discovery. He studied Cigoli's face. The artist was impressed, but he obviously didn't understand the full implication of the sketch. Maria Celeste knew, and though she didn't say a word, she looked at her father with concern. He ignored her and carried on.

"Those bodies move, yet Jupiter remains the same. They are in different positions depending on the time of year. That tells us that the heavens are in flux, while the sun remains the same."

He looked particularly excited now.

"What does it mean?" asked Cigoli.

"It means that the earth moves."

Cigoli's eyes widened. It was more than just revolutionary. Proof like that could be dangerous. He looked at the stars stretching out from Jupiter. An idea was forming. Something he had experienced might just be of benefit.

"Have you shared this with your peers in the Church?"

"No," said Galileo. "Not yet."

Cigoli nodded. "Maybe you shouldn't yet."

Now it was Galileo's turn to look confused.

"And these stars of Jupiter..."

"Yes?" said Galileo.

"Jupiter was the king of the gods, yes?'

"To the best of my recollection," answered Galileo tentatively.

"But I don't believe he had a treasury," said Cigoli.

Galileo's head tilted. He thought he might have an idea where Cigoli was headed, and it made sense.

"And maybe, in this case, a Duke would be better than a king" he chuckled.

•

In the aftermath of its publication, the effect of the *Sidereus* was like nothing the world had ever seen. Not even *The Copernican Treatise* had set off such a response. It was like a literary earthquake and its force was felt in all directions. In a prescient nod to Newton, however, the reaction to the work was equal and opposite in magnitude, though the nature varied, ranging from hostility to outright adoration and love.

From as far away as England, those that recognized the truth in it and loved it, responded with adulation and with works of art of their own in tribute. Poems were composed and daily letters fed into the Galileo home. The great Johannes Kepler published an open letter throughout Europe, enthusiastically endorsing Galileo's credibility. Artists included the findings of the book as components of their work. The German painter Elsheimer's mural of the flight into Egypt contained a sky in conformation with it. The Italian Sacchi did likewise, and of course, Cigoli incorporated the constellation into the night sky of his work, *The Assumption of the Virgin*.

Those that hated it claimed that the work was uninformed and flawed. They assumed and spread the rumor that the Medicean stars as he had called the Jupiterean bodies, were defects in the lens of his instrument, although not a one of them had actually seen the telescope. Others especially those in the Church, saw it as the end of their domination of common thought, and a terrifying threat to their control.

In the end they would prevail, but only in a muted, incomplete fashion.

Galileo had taken Cigoli's advice and lead. Instead of painting the faces of the Medici brothers, who luckily numbered exactly the same as the stars, he had named them for the family. Spurred by the flattery, the younger brothers championed him with the eldest, Cossimo, the Grand Duke, who when he saw the twinkling lights through the scope, took on the defense of Galileo's work as a matter of State.

It struck Galileo as sadly ironic that where the Medici's had failed him in the matter of supporting his matrimonial ambitions, they had come to the aide of his other love. To that end, their treasury had underwritten the creation of more Galilean telescopes, one for each of their embassies in every court in Europe. This, he realized, would ultimately bolster the greatest contribution that the *Sidereus* made to the world.

Galileo had proven his theories and had, in the process, established a modern scientific method. Soon others were reproducing his findings in a similar fashion. Verification versus pontification was a radical concept and was about to constitute a quantum leap in all areas of science.

•

"That book was a huge success," said Father Ferrero neutrally.

It wasn't that he expressed any negativity. It was the complete reservation of even the slightest positive tone that impressed Galileo as a declaration of his sentiment.

"Yes," said Galileo.

"And even now you speak of it with a kind of wonder I cannot fathom," inserted Bellarmine, hinting at a curious insinuation of envy.

Galileo looked at him with unuttered encouragement.

"I mean to say," he went on, "The look, your aspect as you talked about it, it is like you were seeing it all again for the first time."

Ferrero watched Galileo closely. Something important was happening, just then. It was a challenge but the likes of which he had not seen, and he was fascinated to hear his answer.

"I suppose," he began, "it is because, just now, in a very real way, I was."

Ferrero looked surprised by the answer.

"You see, there is something monumental about discovery. To be the first to see or discover something, marks you, and that moment, is like being touched by God. It never fades."

For the first time Ferrero looked like he might understand Galileo, and Bellarmine smiled as his protégé's expression softened.

"I saw comets, in all their blazing, icy glory revealed in such detail," said Galileo professorially. "The twinkling of the stars of Jupiter, and Venus like the goddess herself, revealed in all her naked form. It all showed undeniably that the earth was moving."

A respectful silence passed as he indulged the memory.

"But in answer to your question, Ferrero, yes, his book was much more than just a huge success. It was a phenomenon read by almost everyone. In every country," said Bellarmine. With a slightly melancholy note he continued, "Loved by many, even His Holiness, though he had more latitude to love it as he was just 'Cardinal Barberini' in those days."

"It was also hated by a few," added Ferrero pragmatically.

Galileo smiled.

"What more could any author want?" he joked.

"That *was* brilliant, dedicating the satellites of Jupiter to the Medicis," conceded Bellarmine.

Galileo shrugged deprecatingly.

"A rare moment of political insight on my part." He paused, his eyes twinkling a bit. "I recovered quickly from it."

"But then came the opposition," intruded Ferrero, back on task.

"Yes, well. That was to be expected."

•

If it hadn't been for Cardinal Barberini, the discussion about the *Sidereus* might have had a completely different outcome. Cremonini and Colombe had barely finished reading the text when they rushed to arrange their audience with Paul V. As a Pope he was old, tired, and more an administrator than an intellectual or academic. Mostly, he didn't like dealing with all the new abstract concepts and theoretical considerations spawned by the Renaissance and preferred his gospels literal and easy. Fortunately, he relied heavily on the judgment of Barberini, and made sure to have him close by when the two scholars rushed in with the book.

He listened to their arguments only comprehending about half of what they said, but that wasn't important. He assumed an expression of understanding and nodded as they took on their emotional pleas with an apparent amenable consideration. Cardinal Barberini had prepared him well, and when they finally ended their appeal, he cleared his throat and said, "*Professore*s, the College of Rome has established that *theories* referencing Copernicus are not heresy, have they not? Debates were held in Venice on this very matter."

Cremonini hadn't expected that, and he now knew that this was not going to be as easy as he hoped. Then something important occurred to him. This was all Barberini. He glanced past the pontiff to the Cardinal with narrowed eyes. In that moment, and forever after, the battle was on.

Meanwhile, Colombe was still inanely pleading the fundamentals to a man who could barely hear or comprehend him.

"But Holy Father," he sputtered, "that was simply a theoretical discussion. Galileo now maintains to have proven it."

The old pope was starting to look uncomfortable. Barberini noted his exasperation and jumped in.

"But Galileo's work just states that Venus and other planets go around the Sun, in conformance with the Copernican System."

Colombe reached into his robe and began hauling out a document. Barberini could see it was a publication of his own very simple treatise. Cremonini saw it too and Barberini thought he almost saw a look of irritation on Cremonini's face.

"Holiness, if I might offer, my own work, *Against the Earth's Motion* which avoids the sin of proof," Colombe whined.

Barberini smirked at the absurdity. It also avoids the skill of writing, he thought.

Cremonini picked up on that and while he didn't know exactly what the Cardinal was thinking, he knew it was time to try a different approach.

"Your Holiness, men of God are speaking out from the pulpit against Galileo's subversive work," and with emotional emphasis he added, "the faithful are confused."

His tone was perfect; cautionary, concerned and measured. From the alarm on Pope Paul V's face, it was also apparently having the desired effect. He looked at Barberini for help, as if to say, "Is this true? Are my children at risk?"

For a moment Barberini considered that he might have underestimated the two scholars, or at least Cremonini. Certainly, Cremonini was more formidable than he'd guessed and would have to be handled carefully in the future. His intellect, though motivationally flawed, was not to be discounted.

"Not scholars though, Holy Father," he countered.

"No," said Cremonini raising a triumphant eyebrow. "*Only*...men of faith."

It was well played. He had turned the argument from one of scholarly insight to politics. The Pope, like any ruler, wanted all good quiet. He knew that anything that stirred up the parishioners could have dire consequences.

Colombe had finally caught on to the direction Cremonini had taken them and seeing an opportunity, piled on adding, "Francesco Sizzi, Brother Tommaso Caccini, Brother Nicolo Lorini...they all are preaching that this is blasphemy."

"Brother Caccini was censured by his superiors though, was he not," interjected Barberini.

It was true that the inflammatory rhetoric of the loose cannon, Caccini, had touched on a number of sore points for the Church, and while he had been disciplined and admonished by the senior clergy including the archbishop, it was not entirely because of his opinion about Galileo or Copernicus. Barberini also knew that this attack was not entirely directed at Galileo. Caccini had spent the greater part of a year as the prior of the Dominican monastery in Cartona as he lobbied Barberini incessantly for a promotion and patronage. The downside of family wealth, as Barberini had learned painfully, was that parasites and morons like Caccini were always trying to attach themselves to it. In Caccini's case, he had left a wake of intellectual carnage wherever he went. The fool had even presented himself before the Inquisition to rail against Galileo. Fortunately, the Inquisitors at the time were more confused by his oratory than moved to outrage. Undaunted, he sent a redacted version of Galileo's work to other church scholars who, in the same way that they learned of the omission, were forced to back off from their own emotional statements. Like a phenomenal precursor that would someday characterize McCarthyism or other ablating secular persecution, Caccini had wrangled paranoia, confusion and hyperbole to attain a position of Master and Bachelor of the Santa Maria in Rome. It was said he had higher ambitions and, while an idiot, he had certainly enjoyed the advocacy of Cremonini and Colombe.

Colombe looked personally offended by the comment. He drew himself up to a righteously indignant posture.

"These are men who have dedicated their lives to God. Are they to be ignored by the Holy See?" he asked emotionally.

Barberini glanced over. It was having a concerning effect on the Pope. Cremonini noticed it as well and with the same demeanor of a proficient player throwing down a trump card, he produced a letter.

"Brother Lorini has authorized us to file a formal complaint with the Inquisition," he said handing it over.

Now, he really had the Pope's attention. It was true. As Preacher General of the Dominican Order, Lorini carried considerable political weight within the Church. While a Pope might outrank a Preacher General in terms of ecclesiastical potential, the advantage with the faithful resided with Lorini. He had taken up the argument that the scriptures described the sun rising and the earth as fixed to condemn Copernicanism and Galileo in particular. Additionally, he had roused his congregations to fury at the attempt to disprove the word of God.

"May I read his justification, Your Holiness?" asked Cremonini.

To Barberini's helpless concern, Paul V nodded. Cremonini smiled, opened the letter and started to read.

"To the Holy Father Paul V, all our Fathers of the devout Convent of St. Mark feel that the writing included in the *Sidereus Nuncius* by *Signor* Galilei contains many statements, which seem presumptuous or suspect, as when he states that the words of Holy Scripture do not mean what they say; that in discussions about natural phenomena the authority of Scripture should rank last, he is taking it upon himself to expound the Holy Scripture according to his private lights and in a manner different from the common interpretation of the Fathers of the Church."

He looked up, satisfied with the power of the implied threat. Unfortunately, the solemnity he was trying to impart at that moment took counteractive hit when Colombe chose to interject.

"And do you know, Holiness, he has also called my own scholarly collaborative the Pigeon League?"

If the momentum of Cremonini's argument wasn't still a concern, Barberini might have laughed. It was true the nattering, cooing, erratic group of emotionally worked up imbeciles had been called that by many. Even Barberini himself had spread its use among his trusted colleagues within the intelligentsia. It hadn't originated with Galileo. He knew that for a fact. The artist Cigoli had been the first one to use the name. He had even drawn a caricature of them as frantic anthropomorphic "squabs" with identifiable but beaked human heads and feathered bodies, pecking indiscriminately and erroneously away in a large nest, feathered by the most superstitious members of the cloth. Cigoli was highly regarded and a favorite of the most powerful members of secular society, and while insulting to the pigeons, there was little to be gained and much to risk by attacking him. Regardless of the truth, they attributed the characterization to Galileo, and the reaction among those who had not committed to his condemnation, was an instant inspiration to join.

Pope Paul V looked at the emotional little man with weary eyes.

"I am not sure how that affects the charge of heretical discussion," he said flatly.

Cremonini saw his advantage slipping and was just reaching out to touch his colleague admonishingly on the arm when Colombe blurted out, "Holiness, even the painter, Cigoli, is creating portraits in homage to his lunar observations."

"What does that have to do with anything?" reacted Barberini, capitalizing on the foolishness of the comment.

"The people are in danger!"

This time it was Cremonini responding emphatically. He knew he had made progress with the Pope, and he wasn't giving in on his fundamental point.

For a moment it looked like the two men were on the verge of physicality, but before either could do anything, Pope Paul V threw his hands in the air in irritable exasperation.

"Enough!" he said.

Silence filled the room as the old man rose to go.

"We will convene a panel of qualifiers to examine the subject," he said. "Cardinal Barberini, you will make the arrangements."

It was done. Pope Paul V made the sign of the cross.

"Holiness," said Barberini meekly lowering his eyes and nodding.

From the opposing side of the room, Cremonini looked at Colombe and smiled.

CHAPTER EIGHT

The Order of the "Poor Clares" to which Sister Maria Celeste belonged was unique in many ways. A resource for spiritual ministry, it also served as the closest thing to a hospital for the poor. That day as she walked through its gates after spending the morning helping her father, she could detect the odor of the electuaries that were cooking. There was the slightly acrid smell of rue, the yellow flowered herb that relaxed muscle and formed the basis for a number of treatments from plague to arthritis. With it, was a sweeter odor of reduced, dried fruit extracts. Just by the strength of the aroma, she could tell that the cooking brew was just about right. The Convent of San Matteo had become the leading pharmacological resource in the region, in large part because of Maria Celeste and her skills. A gifted apothecary, she had taught the rest of her order her recipes and preparations, so that with them at work, she was freed to support her father as well as the Church.

Now she took another appraising sniff of the liberated vapor on the air and nodded to herself. The current batch was going to be a good one.

The Order itself fit her. Established by the brilliant Chiara Offreducio, a student and colleague of Saint

Francis of Assisi, "Sister Clare" as she was invested, was the first woman to achieve an approved Rule or spiritual discipline by the Church. She advocated that worldly possessions got in the way of spirituality. More incredibly, she was the first to establish an unprecedented order that administered itself with almost no masculine oversight. For a forward-thinking nun, it was an attractive concept and as soon as she heard of the "Poor Clares", Maria Celeste knew she wanted to be one them.

That was not to say that life there was easy. The Order was known for its poverty and the hard labor it necessitated upon the members. Their victuals were meager and their accommodations spare, but the contributions provided by the earnings from her father's inventions had become a silent sustainment. As she looked up at the tired clay tiles of the roof, she noticed an old bird's nest extending from under the eaves that gave it a shaggy, ragged look. Nearby, the clay had cracked, and pieces marked the ground below. She reached into her robe and closed her hand around the small pouch of coins from her father.

She smiled. Done right, she knew that the simple act of fixing that roof, just like all of their ongoing work, would only bring them closer to God. The money would make that possible. She walked through the door to the common room where her small bed was situated. As usual, she did note the stark chromatic differences between her father's house and the convent. In the company of Galileo, in his study overlooking his garden and the distant vineyard terraced hills beyond, the world was all light and color. It's vibrancy alone was an exciting stimulation that matched the ingenious energy that crackled within him. The convent, by distinction, was a wash of all that, well-lit of course, but much duller.

Today she wasn't thinking about any of that. Today she was concerned. Her father's work was having an impact, but she also had heard rumblings that there were forces within the Church that wanted him silenced. As in any controversy, she knew that the issue at the heart of their consternation was being amplified by their own egos and opportunism. She also knew that despite her father's genius, there were situations in which he could be his own worst enemy. In fairness, he liked the energy and action of thumbing his nose at the pompous and powerful. At times, it almost seemed he received an odd gratification in tempting fate with them, like he believed his brilliance was a force that could ultimately prevail regardless of the opponent. What he didn't consider – that she did – was that in this contest, it was not simply a battle of wits. It was something far murkier and more dangerous. This was a political campaign.

She set her bags down on the bed and walked into the large open kitchen area which had been converted for the day to a pharmaceutical manufacturing enterprise. Stoves blazed under each cauldron. The slow bubbling solutions of the rue, fig and nut extracts were boiling down to syrupy consistency. At prep areas at the open end of the room, chlorophyll-green-stained cutting boards evidenced the volume of plant material that had been chopped, ground and rendered for maximum yield in the pots. Next to one, an older plump woman with a red face mopped her brow as she stirred.

"Welcome back, Sister Maria Celeste," said the sweating Mother Superior.

"Mother," said Maria Celeste nodding respectfully.

The older woman's metabolic stress was not entirely due to the heat in the kitchen. Menopause was a reality in the Renaissance even if the concept was not.

"Here," said Maria Celeste, "let me take over."

The Mother Superior sat down and fanned herself as Maria Celeste manned the spoon at the large pot. After a couple of vigorous turns with it, she turned and handed the sack of coins to the old Mother who looked at it with a certain relief and then crossed herself.

"How is the *Professore*?" she asked.

Maria Celeste just turned and gave her a non-committal look. The Mother Superior chuckled.

"I wonder," she said, "if the Holy Father knows what he does for the Order."

"My father is a curious man. I sometimes think nothing would scare him more than to be appreciated for anything other than his genius."

The Mother Superior crossed herself again. "I will pray that God helps him with a new perspective."

"He probably would be the One to do it."

The old Mother chuckled again. Then her face grew serious.

"He has enemies, you know?"

"Yes."

"Vocal ones."

"Yes," said Maria Celeste, stirring methodically.

The old Mother looked like she was hesitant to say what else was on her mind.

"They are preaching for his excommunication from certain pulpits," she said at last.

Maria Celeste nodded. The look on her face said much more, but before she could speak, a disturbance at the door caused her to turn.

Her sister, Livia, now known as Sister Arcangela was standing at the entrance to the kitchen as if paralyzed. Her hands were shaking, and her mouth hung open as tears streamed down her cheeks.

"What is it?" asked Maria Celeste.

Sister Arcangela couldn't answer at first. Then she choked out the one chilling word that would change everything.

"Plague," she said.

•

The hearing brought on by the *Sidereus* was going to be a panel, not a trial. Cremonini and Colombe were in the courtyard of the *Collegio Romano* eating their lunch when the messenger arrived with the papal writ. It was not what they wanted. As he read the news, Cremonini's face turned scarlet.

Colombe noticed the change and realizing that something terrible was happening, set down his food and asked, "What is wrong?"

Cremonini gritted his teeth. Then he lowered the paper and spat the reviled name.

"Barberini."

Cremonini and Colombe might have won the battle during their interview with Pope Paul V, but Barberini had flanked them behind closed doors. This was not going to be a real charge of heresy as they had hoped, as they had felt sure was coming when they left His Holiness that day. This was going to be a gentle discourse, a conversation of the concept of the heliocentrism, and even if Galileo were found "guilty" the repercussions would be an admonition at the most.

"What are we going to do now?" asked Colombe.

That question would have to wait.

A new player had been introduced in their little drama and was about to take center stage. *Yersinia pestis*, the plague – though it would be centuries before a scientists would understand and name it – was sweeping the continent. At the time, the understanding of how it spread was lacking. There were two schools of thought to its origin, aligning almost in perfect proportion to the two schools considering Copernican theory. On the one hand, were the traditionalists, which included Colombe, Cremonini and most of the Galilean detractors. They believed that disease was a result of a humoral imbalance brought about primarily by godlessness and they hinted that it could be specifically attributed to interaction with Jews. The more progressive were only marginally better and supported the supposition that a pathological miasma floated in the fog and early morning mists. Regardless, they all acknowledged that there was no cure, and within a month, physicians were conducting their daily rounds, dressed in the monstrous ensemble of waxed, hooded robes, bird-beak masks, black broad brimmed hats, and long leather gloves. They walked the streets like terrifying emissaries of death, reminding anyone who saw them of the peril that could strike at any moment. In their hands they carried, the most terrifying instrument of all, a long narrow staff that was used alternately as a walking stick, a surgical instrument and a weapon to hold off desperate victims. In the latter enterprise they were particularly effective, not so much because they were injurious in and of themselves, nor because physicians were particularly skilled at self-defense, but because everyone knew the true purpose and use of those staffs. Those that hadn't seen them in play had heard the stories of the sharp end being used to puncture and drain the swollen, weeping, black lesions in the armpits and groins of infected patients. Those large, painful pustules called buboes, stained the staff tips and when they were brandished as the physician walked down the street, most people acquiesced and yielded the thoroughfare.

Just the sight of surreal epidemic garb struck terror in the heart and as they drew near, doors closed, and windows locked tight. It didn't matter though. Soon enough the bodies stacked, and the night skies were lit up with the hellish auroras from the pyres that burned constantly. The days were not much better. Dark offending smoke hung in the air and gave each affected town, a halo of damnation, as if to warn all approaching travelers that here was no place to enter.

That was how that the word reached Rome that Galileo, the subject of the panel review had been exposed, and as a result, his spiritual examination was put on hold, much to the pleasure of Cardinal Barberini.

Galileo's part time housekeeper, *Signora* Sarti, a kind woman, who had served him quietly, almost invisibly for several years, was already ill that fateful day when she left his house never to return. It was no surprise when the heavy knock on the door by the sinisterly outfitted doctor and his attendant, carrying a bucket of blue paint sounded a few days later.

Galileo looked at the curved beak of the mask. He knew was stuffed with theriac; a compounded garni of herbs, cinnamon, myrrh, and other filtering materials. He looked into the man's eyes behind the glasses in the mask that were clouded with a condensate of sweat and gave a clear indication of the stifling nature of the protective gear.

"Are you all right?" asked Galileo.

The physician's eyes widened a little in surprise. No one ever expressed any consideration for *his* condition. Usually, they were too busy reacting emotionally out of denial, self-interest, and fear.

"*Grazie*," he said genuinely touched. "I am well, *Professore*."

His voice was muffled and sounded quite distant through the thick mask, but it was clear enough for Galileo to understand. He looked past him and noticed that the attendant stood with a slight postural defect as if perpetually stooped. It could have just been the heavy bucket and brush he was forced to lug around that caused it, but Galileo's keen eye for engineering noted that one leg seemed slightly bowed. The poor soul looked up curiously at the doctor who seemed to him to be engaged in a polite conversation with the newly quarantined patient. Having little patience for it and feeling the burden of the bucket, he stamped his flawed foot like a nervous pony.

"I suppose, you come bearing unpleasant tidings," Galileo said mildly as he looked at the blue paint in the bucket.

"Yes, I am afraid you are under quarantine, *Professore*. *Signora* Sarti has the plague."

Galileo didn't look particularly concerned although he knew how serious this could be. It was a purely outward act. Inside a chill went through him. No one was anymore immune to the fear than they were to the disease.

"I understand a nun visits you regularly," the doctor continued.

"Yes, Sister Maria Celeste, of the Convent of San Matteo. She assists me in my work, but she has not been here since *Signora* Sarti visited last."

The doctor seemed to consider that. Then arriving at a clinical conclusion, he nodded his beaked head. "You may appeal to her to support your quarantine, but you may not leave your home until we are sure that you are safe."

Galileo considered that line and the recent summons he had received from Barberini on behalf of the College in Rome.

"That...may be a very long time, *Doctore*," he said with just a touch of irony.

It was done. He closed the door and looked out the window. The attendant stepped forward, dipped his brush and then applied it, painting a big blue cross on the wood. When he'd finished, he turned and followed the doctor as they resumed their unenviable duty of delivering bad news and punching holes in large black boils. Galileo was considering that when he noticed something. All along the length of his street and well beyond the corner where he could see other distant homes, almost all of them were designated by similar blue crosses.

In the end, Galileo did not die. He also did not get the plague despite his exposure and the prevalence of the disease in Florence. Maria Celeste credited it to the rue and medicinals she and the other sisters prepared at the convent and delivered in little packages to his doorstep each day.

In Rome, Cardinal Barberini made an irritating point of Galileo's good health. Around the members of the Pigeon League, he wondered aloud if this might be a sign of God's Holy protection in keeping Galileo safe. He also wondered aloud if perhaps this was a sign that he also favored the provocative genius. The commentary only inflamed the opposition. Upon receiving word that he had been alleviated from quarantine, they insisted that, plague risk or no, Galileo had to be brought before the panel.

Barberini begrudgingly agreed, but he had already put the delay to good use in preparing his panel of qualifiers. Mostly they were Jesuits and reasonable Church scholars. They were not completely supportive, but they were impressed enough with Galileo's intellect historically and would not be swayed by simple religious fervor. That, apparently, was going to be the strategy employed by the accusers.

The trip to Rome would prove uneventful. Barberini had generously provided a carriage bearing the seal of the Church, which received a priority of transit. In reality, the insignia simply designated an urgency and implied a request for expedition by any secular official in charge of the roadway. Of benefit to Galileo, it also meant that Maria Celeste could accompany him, and while they could not sit in the same sections in a Cathedral or in the large hall where he was to be judged, they could at least spend some pleasant, if only transitory time together. The request had gone up from the priory of San Matteo, which she served, and needed only the Cardinal's authorization to travel, not as the accused's daughter, but as a representative of the

Church as well. It had been quickly granted by one, Cardinal Bellarmine.

Now they rode, looking out at the countryside. On the outskirts of Florence, they passed an olive grove. Galileo noted that the trees were heavy with ripe fruit. Too heavy, he realized. Missing were the white canvas ground cloths to catch the shaken fruit as well the necessary workers to make it happen. Their absence was as telling as the fires that lit up the city at night, another result of the plague. Unlike others who might have lapsed into melancholy at the thought, Galileo studied the trees, calculating the force necessary to loosen the ripest olives, and the potential of a machine that might be able to do it. It would not be simple nor easy, he thought and filed away the idea for future consideration. In the meantime, even the loss of the crop would not amount to the tragedy it seemed upon initial consideration. These olives would be a bounty for some lucky birds and creatures, and those that weren't consumed would renew the soil and be drawn back into the source trees for investment in future generations of fruit.

In a way, he knew, scientific discovery and knowledge were like that. An olive tree like himself, could bear its discovery, but the nature of the harvest was beyond his control. There were some that chose not to acknowledge the harvest and some who had no idea how to use the fruit of his treatises. Others could turn it into something delightful and valuable.

"We will want to make sure to stock up on olive oil," he said.

Maria Celeste looked out at the grove. She thought she knew exactly what he meant, and that he wasn't just talking about the product of the trees. She knew that this phenomenon of the plague would have a long-term effect on the world. Then again, as she took in the sunny vista of olive, grape and wheat in the distance, the *world* seemed just fine. *People* were dying. Mankind was at risk and in the ultimate consideration of hubris, extended his definition of personal crisis to the rest of the world. A miasma, a sin, a plague, whatever was the cause, these were threats to only one of God's creatures, but in a most forbidding sense then amplified in the individual to a point that it seemed to threaten all of creation.

Almost as much as a new idea, she thought, looking at her father.

He stared a little out at the world a little longer and then suddenly said, "Is your mother well?"

It was so simple, and so sweet and, thus, so painful; it took all her control not to throw herself to embrace him. As for Galileo, he kept his face away looking out.

"Yes," she said. "She's well."

He nodded that it was good. Then went silent. There was nothing left to say.

Of all the indications of the prevailing danger in the world, none was more telling than the fact that their coach driver was afraid. There was no denying that. They could tell, just from the pace of the team of four he was driving. Normally the horses would never be pushed to a run and only sporadically were encouraged to a canter. Any faster and a highly trained, extremely valuable team of horses would be at risk for injury. The roads were uneven, and the slightest off angle of a horse's gait could lead to a break that required the animal to be put down. If one calculated the amount invested in the rearing, training and feeding of just one of the team, then one hoof of one horse was worth more that the driver's annual pay. That was why the crack of the whip and verbal charges to maintain the galloping pace was so telling to the passengers inside.

Finally, at long last, they heard him call out that they were entering Rome. Both of them realized that while one threat had been passed uneventfully, another potentially greater one, awaited.

The large hall in the College of Rome was an impressive venue. Meticulously crafted, its majestic stone walls were apportioned with stained glass representations of great Biblical events. As soon as anyone entered, they were met by the angelic sound of a boys' choir that was a perfect accompaniment to the beautiful chromatically illuminated scenes of the sermon on the mount, the miracle of loaves and fishes, the miracle of the vacant tomb and the Ascension of Christ. Together, they made for a backdrop of sanctified endorsement of any proceedings within.

Such was the case when Galileo walked through the doors on the day of his examination. The audience galleries were already packed, an indication of the controversy and success of the *Sidereus*. The hearing itself had intumesced to something far more than a philosophical or religious discussion. This was entertainment, a sporting contest of the soul and even the potential threat of plague did little to discourage the numbers that crowded into the observing sections. Ironically, Galileo's own daughter an authorized attendant of the Church was segregated from the prime area exclusively because of her gender. Corralled in a much smaller area off to the side, she took her place among the other representative nuns.

At a small table, almost like the desk in Galileo's study, was a single empty chair. This was where he would sit. Opposite was another table with Cremonini and Colombe already waiting. Behind them, a row of seats for invited guests and speakers was occupied by the rest of the dreaded Pigeon League, including Lorini, Caccini and Sizzi.

In between, on a riser at the head of the hall, sat the presidential throne occupied by Cardinal Barberini, and next to it, the panel of qualifiers, almost every one a Jesuit. Right in the middle and possibly most importantly was Cardinal Bellarmine.

The gentle murmur of the crowd in the hall came to an abrupt stop as the accused walked its length to take his seat. Barberini placed a gloved hand to his lips to hide a smile at the incredibly bored expression on Galileo's face. For the Cardinal it was absolutely glamorous of him.

Galileo dragged the chair out and looking around neutrally, sat down. It was obvious that if Cremonini and Colombe had meant to intimidate him by assembling the overwhelming number of decriers, they had failed miserably.

"We will begin this examination of the philosophies and theory presented in the work in question, the *Sidereus Nuncius*," said Barberini turning toward Cremonini and Colombe. "We shall first hear the articles of concern as drafted by *Professore*s Cremonini and Colombe of the papal Collegio.

"*Grazie*, Your Eminence," said Cremonini. "I would defer to our most Holy Brother, Tommaso Caccini, Master and Bachelor of the convent of *Santa Maria sopra Minerva* in Rome."

At the mention of his name, Caccini all but leapt from his seat. A tall, thin man in a starched cassock, he smoothed his garments with his hands as he took a breath. He was nothing, if not a consummate showman in the pulpit, and his reputation for fiery rhetoric promised to make this quite the show. Manifesting a look of fierce indictment at Galileo, he walked forward and picked up a copy of the Bible as he faced the panel.

"I submit for your consideration"—he bowed slightly and extended the Bible with both hands, as if offering up a sacrifice upon an Old Testament altar— "the only book that matters, the most Holy Bible."

Galileo had to admit that it was a fantastic opening, if possibly a little too heavily influenced by the *Comedia*.

"We are acquainted with the book," said Cardinal Barberini with understatement. Then he diplomatically added, "And there is no need for you to part with it. It is accepted in principle and guides us all in this examination."

Caccini straightened up and kissed the book before returning it to the table.

"The sun rises!" he shouted as he turned back to the panel. "And the sun sets. Ecclesiastes, Chapter one, Verse five. The Bible tells us so. Yet, *Signor* Galileo—"

"*Professore*," corrected Barberini gently.

Caccini nodded politely, though his face acquiesced to nothing.

"*Professore*"—from his lips, the words sounded like an expletive— "Galileo has offended that passage by his obscene observations through his little glass. Are we to believe that the Holy Bible is to be abandoned for the rantings of some voyeur?"

A chuckle swept through the crowd. The titillating terminology was a bonus in terms of the contest, and the salacious reference was a thrill they weren't anticipating.

"Silence!" commanded Barberini.

Galileo looked completely disengaged, beyond bored now. His lids almost drooped and he seemed on the verge of a yawn.

"Continue please," said Barberini to Caccini, though in his heart he hoped he was done.

"First Chronicles, Chapter sixteen, Verse thirty, 'He has fixed the earth firm...*immovable*.'"

Again, a murmur passed through the onlookers. Father Caccini was in full sermon mode now and enjoying the sound of his own voice. This was turning out to be a better show than the onlookers had hoped, and Galileo hadn't yet begun to respond.

Caccini paused, letting the impact of the Biblical citation sink in.

"Psalms, Chapter ninety-three, Verse one, 'Thou has fixed the earth immovable and firm.'"

More murmuring responded, a little louder this time. Maria Celeste looked around with alarm. The crowd was fickle, and thus, dangerous, she knew. She looked back over at her father.

Galileo was not even listening to Caccini's performance. He was looking down at a piece of paper and was scribbling away at something. Among the Pigeon League, Colombe was smiling. This was going even better than he had hoped, or so he thought until he looked away from Caccini and saw Galileo, completely unaffected. His eyes narrowed and he looked back at Caccini with renewed intensity.

"Again, in Psalms," called out Caccini boldly. "Chapter ninety-six, Verse ten, 'He has fixed the earth firm, immovable." He worked the last word hard for emphasis. "The hundred and fourth chapter, fifth verse, 'Thou didst fix the earth on its foundation, so that it can never be shaken."

The crowd was with him even more now, and some were calling out encouragement. The members of the panel of Cardinals, frowned uncomfortably. Barberini looked concerned. Still, Galileo obliviously scribbled away.

Barberini held up his hand for quiet and waited for the audience to settle down. Among the panel, Father Paolo Foscarini leaned toward Bellarmine and whispered, "That Caccini is as ambitious as Lucifer himself."

"Hmm," murmured Bellarmine.

"I have it on good authority that he said that he was far less concerned about prevailing in his objections toward Galileo than he was about the opportunity to advance his own reputation as an orator here."

Bellarmine glanced over at Barberini who wore an expression of controlled irritation.

"You know he appealed to Cardinal Barberini for patronage?"

"Yes," said Bellarmine.

"So, he has taken his case to the masses now it seems," said Foscarini.

"Nothing unites, like a common threat," said Bellarmine pessimistically. "Especially when it appeals to a confederacy of dunces."

"Do you have anything to add?" asked Cardinal Barberini.

Caccini looked around the hall. It had been one of his best performances. He could tell from the look on those faces. It was the same as he had come to expect from his most successful sermons. He also knew that the most powerful thing a speaker could do when he had the crowd behind him was to leave them wanting more. He turned toward Barberini and bowed humbly.

"No, Eminence. Unlike *Professore* Galilei, I find the word of God complete, requiring no further comment."

Barberini nodded, and Caccini turned giving Galileo one last withering look before walking back to resume his seat. Galileo, just as before, didn't appear to have heard a thing.

Barberini looked at him, then cleared his throat. As if responding to his name, Galileo looked up from his writing.

"*Doctore* Galilei, do you have any response to Father Caccini's"—he looked like he was searching for the most appropriate, but diplomatic word— "recitations?"

The room went quiet, waiting for something equally emotional and fiery. Even Maria Celeste found herself leaning forward a little. Galileo looked thoughtful, like he was considering the question. Then he answered pleasantly, "No, he recited the passages accurately."

He smiled and went back to his writing.

Bellarmine couldn't contain himself, and like several others in the panel, smiled as well. Barberini maintained his neutral visage and looked over at Cremonini and Colombe.

They looked not only cheated that Galileo hadn't responded with vigor, but also that he was completely impervious to their strategy.

"Your Eminence," said Colombe standing. "I would like to pose a question to the accused."

Barberini looked mildly off-put.

"*Doctore* Galilei is not accused, *Professore*," he corrected and speaking more broadly to the audience added, "this is not a trial. It is an examination of the spiritual merits of the *Sidereus Nuncius* and respectful discussion to determine a proper consideration and place for the work alongside the Holy Scriptures."

"Of course. Apologies, Eminence," nodded Colombe.

"You may ask your question," said Barberini.

Despite the admonition for civility, it was evident that Colombe was still on the attack.

"*Professore* Galilei," he said.

Galileo looked up.

"Yes?"

"You have heard the viewpoint offered by Brother Cassini."

"I did."

"What is your response?"

Galileo frowned curiously, as though he thought he had already answered the question.

He set his pen down, considered Colombe, and said, "I would offer that by denying scientific principles, one may maintain any paradox."

Faces in the panel smiled. Sister Maria Celeste shot a quick look at the common gallery. It hadn't had the same effect there even though a few chuckles could be heard.

Colombe heard them too and not happy about losing ground, he added emotionally, "Your Eminence I would like to have *Contro il Moto della Terra*. Against the Motion of the Earth, circulated among the panel for review."

Barberini nodded wearily. Colombe eagerly grabbed copies of his leaflet and handed them out as Galileo looked on with amusement. Almost none of them looked at it. They already knew what it said. A clumsy attempt, it offered no proof, only a lengthy, emotional, and poorly written diatribe against Galileo's study of the heavens.

"Are you acquainted with my own humble work on the subject?"

"I am," answered Galileo.

Taking a page from Caccini's performance he turned and faced the common audience and said, "And are you aware of the numbers who subscribe to its merit?"

The sentence had the sound of a triumphant note.

Galileo looked amused.

"Well, I suppose there is a literary appetite for anything," he said flatly.

This time more chuckles resonated in the audience. Sister Maria Celeste placed a hand against her mouth as she gently joined them. Even Barberini couldn't contain a smile. Cremonini took note, and his brow furrowed with frustration.

"How then do you reconcile the differences in our work as not heresy," Colombe fired back.

It was a big gamble. Galileo was not on trial for anything, least of all heresy, and in truth only the Pope or a Grand Inquisitor could determine if someone were to be charged. Just the use of the word was a huge step beyond propriety, but before anyone could react, Galileo sat back and smiled.

"I read God's transcripts in the heavens, while you just read the scribblings of others on a page."

It was a devastating retort. Colombe simply blinked, blasted beyond words. Cremonini turned scarlet. Behind him, Father Ignoli's jaw dropped.

Now even a few members of the panel chuckled.

"You have been refuted by Church scholars, *Signore*, including the beloved Father Ignoli. Would you insult his work so casually, as well?"

This was tricky. Ignoli was well-regarded, and Barberini looked at Galileo, wishing he could counsel him to be less himself and more the diplomat in that moment. When Galileo did speak, it was almost like he had heard what Barberini was thinking.

"God," he said clearly, "is known to us by nature in His works...and by doctrine in His revealed word."

It was brilliant. The elegance and simplicity of the response worked on the crowd instantaneously. In the panel, Bellarmine smiled. He knew, he should have expected no less, but still, even when he expected brilliance, Galileo had a way of dazzling.

Maria Celeste's disquietude dissipated as well. Sometimes, she thought, it is easy to forget what he is capable of summoning in the moment. He could be irritating, demanding and ever trying, and just when it didn't seem worth tolerating, he would write, or say or hypothesize something so extraordinary that the world was reminded that here was a god and all of them were simply intellectual mortals.

Colombe was beaten. It was evident to everyone watching. He started to speak, then hesitated, then finally came out with the best he could muster.

"You, Sir, would do better to seek refuge in the word of Our Lord than in the observations of your little toys."

It sounded pathetic, and only made Galileo's simple, elevated earlier utterance seem even more impressive. Cremonini reached out and touched his floundering colleague on the arm. He stood as Colombe, with an angry vanquished expression, retook his seat. Much more controlled and calculating, Cremonini looked at Barberini and awaited permission to speak.

"The chair recognizes *Professore* Cremonini."

Cremonini turned and when he spoke his voice was polite, innocently curious.

"*Doctore* Galilei you know of the precedence that has determined Copernicus' assertions are heresy?" It sounded coolly careful.

In the panel, Bellarmine leaned forward with concern. He knew Cremonini, and there was real dangerous potential in the coming exchange. Galileo, however, didn't seem fazed.

"Surely, it is harmful to souls to make it a heresy to believe what is proved," said Galileo evenly.

Cremonini smiled. It seemed a fabricated substitution for a preferred sneer. He nodded and stroked his chin like he was thinking about the answer. He even paced a little for effect.

"How then do you answer Brother Caccini's argument that your assertions are an affront to the books of Ecclesiastes, Psalms, Chronicles...to the very acts of God?" he asked, pointing at Caccini.

The room went quiet.

"*Professore* Cremonini," started Galileo calmly, "the prohibition of science is contrary to the Bible, which in hundreds of places teaches us that the greatness and the glory of God shines forth marvelously in all His works."

He pointed upward. Unlike when the others did it, his action appeared natural and genuine.

Maria Celeste looked around quickly. Faces everywhere were engaged and affected. She knew why. He was saying what he really thought and felt. The truth was the most compelling of arguments.

He continued. "And it has to be read, above all, in the open book of the heavens."

Barberini smiled proudly.

•

"I have read the transcripts of that examination," said Ferrero searching for them among the clutter on the interrogation room table. Finding the document, he held it up for emphasis. "I would suggest that your tone and approach be different this time."

"You will not have the same level of advocacy, and the stakes are greater," Bellarmine nodded.

"You were clever," conceded Ferrero, "but this time, clever will not be enough."

Galileo knew they were right. At the mention of the stakes involved, he remembered the days after the examination.

•

For reasons that were not shared initially, the deliberations of the panel of Jesuits took longer than either Galileo or Sister Maria Celeste expected. Everyone that had been present agreed, the Pigeons had been plucked, rightly. Galileo had won the argument, so something greater had to be in play. Why else would the decision take so long?

In the marbled side corridors of the Vatican, despite their vicious defeat during the deposition, the Pigeon League had not given up its fight. As a matter of fact, the murky backrooms where unanswerable, political intrigue ruled was much better suited to their kind of arguments anyway. As they gathered in the anteroom to the papal chambers, they knew that while the verdict of the Jesuit scholars would go against them, the resulting actions were still in play and at the discretion of His Holiness.

Paul V was not well and had sat out even a casual attendance of the meeting, relying entirely on Barberini to address the matter. What Barberini thought was widely known. The Pope, however, was concerned with a legacy as he prepared to meet his Lord and he didn't want to risk doing something wrong as a last official act. It was just the opportunity that the Pigeons were seeking.

The interval in the waiting area dragged on, and as the time passed, Cremonini sensed that perhaps the Pope's audience with his God was closer than had been initially stated. Finally, the inner door opened, and the Holy Father emerged. It seemed impossible, but since the last time they had seen him, the man had withered. His vestments hung on his skeletal frame and his eyes, once falcon-sharp were sunken and looked around with a diminished acuity.

For a moment, no one spoke. They were just too stunned. If they had not seen him there, among the symbols, and in the robes of his office, they might not have recognized him as the man who carried the charge of St. Peter. He walked stiffly toward his throne and when he reached out to steady himself on the arm of the chair as he prepared to sit, his hand shook like a reed in the wind. Flanking him was Cardinal Barberini, and seeing the immobility of the audience, he cleared his throat loudly to rouse them. Reflexively they crossed themselves and bowed.

Paul V sat down gently and responded by making a wavering sign of the cross.

"Holy Father," said Cremonini hesitantly. "Thank you for meeting with us on this important matter."

"I have read the disposition of the panel, provided by Cardinal Barberini," he said hoarsely. "Do you dispute their interpretation or judgment?"

Barberini was focused entirely on Cremonini. He knew that they knew, they had lost in the formal discussions in the great hall, but in the analog of a trial where the verdict and the judgment are separate, so was the potential with the Pope right then. Unlike the others, Cremonini was a clever politician and had clearly only conceded the one aspect of the argument. Influencing the pontiff's judgment was where he was headed now.

"No, Holy Father, not at all. We"—he gestured at the other members of the Pigeon League— "concede the intellectual argument." Feigning humility, he added, "We are, after all simple scholars and men of the cloth."

Barberini's eyes narrowed suspiciously. This had the all the ear markings of an ingenious bait-and-switch.

"No, Your Holiness, our concern is that like us, the common members of the church, your people, are also not intellectually inclined."

Barberini looked at Pope Paul V. The old man was listening. Of all the arguments that Cremonini might try, he had landed on the one that might pluck at the fears of a dying man the most. Paul V blinked, and his eyes, almost childlike now, showed a hint of vulnerability. Barberini knew he needed to speak, to break the spell that Cremonini was weaving, before it went too far.

"Holy Father," he started, but before he could utter another word, the pontiff held up a bony finger for silence so that Cremonini could continue.

Cremonini smiled.

"Our concern is that these good and simple people will be at risk for losing their souls if the panel determines that the contradictory evidence should be placed alongside scriptural statement. It's that elemental. We may argue and discuss and even understand the concepts but," his voice grew ominous, "those that would employ doubt to further Satan's purposes, will see this as an opportunity and point to the apparent differences and the disposition of the panel on this matter, and so, your people, will be lost for eternity."

Barberini listened with a sinking feeling. Paul V was obviously affected. His old eyes watered with a combination of alarm and agitation. The last thing he wanted to do now, at this point in his life and papacy, was to yield a single soul to doubt and rob them of God's grace. Cremonini saw it too. Studying the dying man's face, he bowed humbly.

•

Brother Giordano Bruno was a heterodoxical thinker, which was the Pigeon League's way of saying he was dangerous. Initially named Fillipo by his famous soldier father, he seemed naturally predisposed to a bellicose style in making a point, and as a result, he could turn a neutral discussion with only a slight philosophical difference into an excoriating attack on and opponent. A Dominican scholar, he had studied at the illustrious monastery in Naples, where Thomas Aquinas had taught, and upon taking his vows chose the name Giordano as a tribute. Initially schooled in the Aristotelian philosophy, he was soon attracted to new streams of thought, among which were the works of Plato and Hermes Trismegistus, the gentle prophet who some said may have been a gentile contemporary of Moses. Seeing himself as an intellectual champion in the face of traditional thinkers, he soon accumulated several professionally bruised enemies. It was, however, his extraordinary memory that alternatively provided him allowances of forgiveness and bouts of extreme envy and, for the most part, kept his detractors at bay. His capacity to recall whole passages of a text from a single reading, or to recall long and complicated lists of items made him something of a celebrity, and soon he was being called to the courts of nobility and even the Vatican to put on entertaining displays of his divine gift.

For several years this aspect of celebrity was protective, and had he confined his arguments to mere oratory, he might have been all right, but where his tongue was a sharp and lancinating instrument, his touch with a pen was even more so. His first book, *Cena de le Ceneri,* The Ash Wednesday Supper, argued blatantly in favor of the Copernican model and heliocentrism. When a raw version of the text was discovered by the head of his order, his name was referred for review by the Inquisition. Hearing of the potential for trial and being "Put to the Question" a hushed euphemism for examination by physical pain and torture, he abandoned the Dominican habit and fled to France. Incredibly, while on the run he published another book, *De l'Infinito, Universo e Mondi*, On the Infinite Universe and Worlds, in which he argued that the limitlessness of the universe, and that it contained an infinite number of worlds, and that these were all inhabited by intelligent beings. The Inquisition was not as strong an influence in France, and as he was no longer an agent of the Faith and still quite entertaining, the French were more than happy to offer him refuge. The love affair lasted seven years. Unfortunately, it was to remain an affair, not a marriage.

He had accompanied the French ambassador on a trip to England and hearing of his magnificent memory, he was invited to discuss the ideas behind his books as well. English universities then, as they would ever be, were given to no-holds-barred, rowdy verbal exchanges, and while the deans and faculty at Oxford could dish out their challenges, they were not prepared for the response from the fiery Giordano.

Once back in Paris he was no more amenable to being disciplined by the ambassador and so had fled to Germany, where he lived first in Wittenberg, then Prague, Helmstedt, and finally Frankfurt. As before, each time he seemed to have found a favorable patron, some word or assertion, some reaction to what he perceived as ignorance would set off his ungovernable tongue, and a new situation would be necessary.

Finally, just as he seemed to have exhausted his options, a letter arrived from Venice. The Doge was still enamored with his intellect and offered his munificence. Within a few months he was back in his native land. The deal was simple enough. All he had to do was offer an apology and recant, not for ideology, but for the offense of his manner and abandonment of his status as a Dominican brother. Whether the Doge knew what they really had in mind is doubtful, but a few months after Giordano arrived in Venice, despite the conditions he had met, Father Maculani and the Inquisition came to call.

There was going to be another trial. This time Giordano would have to recant all his theories and works. Copernicanism, heliocentrism, the infinity of the universe, all would have to be renounced. Before he could even answer, he was arrested and transferred to Rome. To Giordano it was as if by recanting anew, and including his entire life's work, his own existence, his soul would cease to be.

Now, the thing about persecution and torture, the thing he didn't know, was that the goal varied depending on what the persecutors truly wanted from the accused. In some cases, the goal was only to eliminate the source of consternation. In such situations, a confession and attrition were not the outcomes the Inquisition wanted at all. In fact, it was the opposite. In fact, mathematically speaking, it was often inversely proportional. The guiltier the individual, the less useful the confession when the elimination of an idea or its expression was the real goal. Extracting an admission of guilt from the innocent was far easier. The less an accused knew and the more innocent they were, the more likely that their honest response would quickly turn to a willingness to say anything to make the pain stop. In many cases a strange dynamic emerged. The persecuted seemed equally as eager to restore the good graces and forgiveness of their torturers as to achieve relief from the torture.

With that in mind, Maculani made it clear to the Examiners, not to push Giordano past his limits of resistance. He wanted his refusal. As long as he did not recant, they could keep him in prison. They could silence his voice.

Having him in a dungeon would make it even easier. Eventually, then, if they determined that it was in the interest of the Church, they could still his tongue permanently in any horrible way they chose.

That was why as Galileo and Maria Celeste climbed back into the carriage to return to Florence that the one of the two documents he carried had such meaning. Although neither of them had seen it, the disposition of the gallery had been filed. The decision of what would be required of the *Doctore* because of it was still a mystery. He was just picking up his bag to go when the door to his room opened, and Cardinal Barberini walked in.

"Eminence," said a surprised Galileo. Then he frowned. "Do you have word?"

Realizing the ominous potential of his presence, Barberini reacted. "Oh no, no! Calm yourself, Maestro."

Galileo nodded, then looked puzzled.

"I wanted you to have this," said Barberini reaching into his scarlet robe to withdraw a single folded piece of paper.

"What is it?" asked Galileo.

Barberini looked embarrassed. "I, it's just something." He was fumbling like a love-struck schoolboy. Then he looked at Galileo with adoration. "Your words. With the whole world against you and only your words to arm you"—he looked down thoughtfully— "the others never stood a chance."

Galileo wasn't sure how to respond, but before he could, Barberini continued.

"I wrote a poem," he said. "Just, just a poem. I do not have your gift, but I wanted you to know that you have a brother who loves you."

Galileo looked particularly moved.

"I will treasure it."

Barberini nodded awkwardly then stepped forward and embraced Galileo. When he was done, he sighed and smiled. He was just about to go when the sound of hurried, approaching footsteps stopped at the edge of the room. In the doorway was a Jesuit messenger, and from the look on his face, the reason for his errand was not good.

"Speak," said a suddenly concerned Barberini.

"Eminence, I have this for you," he said handing over a document with a wax seal that Barberini recognized as signifying the Inquisition. Galileo watched as he broke it open and read. His eyes darted over the page, and as he comprehended the message, his face changed to a severe politically concerned expression, that Galileo had recently seen perfected.

Barberini paused and looked at the messenger.

"When?"

"This noon, Eminence. Brother Maculani had the decree read publicly," the messenger elaborated.

Barberini sighed and after a thoughtful moment, looked up at Galileo. "I fear we are entering a treacherous time, my friend. My dear friend—" He sounded profoundly saddened. Then with a note of genuine concern, he added, "You should take care. Return to Florence and quietly pursue your work."

There was something ominous in that gentle, genuine guidance. There was threat, not conveyed as coming from Barberini or even his office within the church, but from something greater, and much vaguer and more dangerous.

"What has happened?" asked Galileo.

"Giordano Bruno has refused to recant, and is to be burned today," he answered soberly.

For a moment the words just hung in the room as Barberini appeared to struggle with something more.

"You know, when he was arrested in Venice, among his correspondence were letters from you," said Barberini.

Galileo tilted his head slightly, estimating the connotation of that.

"Half of Europe has a letter from me on its desk, I'd guess," he countered.

Barberini smiled thinly. "You don't have to convince me, nor anyone who reasons, but it seems there are more dragons than reasoning people on the earth these days."

He stepped forward and embraced Galileo tightly again. His hand touched Galileo's. A moment later, he broke with him and left the room.

Galileo looked down. It was a charge of expedition, a safe passage document bearing, not a Cardinal's crest, but the Pope's. Barberini was that concerned about him making it home.

Outside, the carriage was waiting. All around, though, an energetic flood of people was rushing up the street in a hurry. Like fording a stream, he worked his way through them to enter the carriage where Maria Celeste reached out with a worried look on her face. He grasped her hand and stepped up and in just as the crush of humanity surging around them increased. Galileo thumped the carriage roof and felt it lurch forward slowly. The horses didn't like the thick traffic any more than the occupants, and they nickered and whinnied, nervously as they stamped and pulled through the mass of bodies.

The fearful look on his daughter's face told Galileo that she knew what was happening, and the energy of the mob only made her concern more valid. There was a vicious, furious, happiness about them. Their wide eyes were seeing without insight. Mouths were open in full-throated cries that didn't articulate. A common thread of something electric and overwhelming had them in its horrifyingly energized grip. Galileo saw it too, but rather than being frightened he was fascinated. It was like a metamorphosis was taking place. The faces were not those of unique men and women, capable of love and rage anymore. Now, there was something that had been sacrificed to a consensus brain. They were no longer individuals, but individual cells of a greater, more terrifying beast and subject to its motivation and inertia.

Barberini's comment came back to him.

"There are more dragons than reasoning people on the earth these days."

It was the right word. Dragon. The dragon had assimilated and was sweeping past the carriage now. This was the beast that haunted the edge of the maps. He thought of the mariner's recitation at the margins of the oceanic guides. Beyond its known limits, there were supposed to be monsters. Now, he clearly saw, some of them were here.

The carriage continued forward steadily but slowly. Occasionally the driver called out alternating between reassurance to the nervous team and in warning to the people getting too close. The progress was excruciating. After an hour, as the sun was approaching midday, they were only just approaching the main square. Outside, the constant rhythmic murmur of a thousand voices had grown like the throaty growl of a huge beast. The crush of the throng was increasing by the second, and in no time was so thick that the carriage had ceased to move. Moments later a huge roar went up that made the horses whinny and stomp in place.

Galileo and Maria Celeste looked out. Across the plaza a line of banners from the various offices of the Inquisition moved above the crowd toward the center of the square. Following behind, seated on an elevated litter so that all could see, was Giordano. He was being subjected to an *auto-de-fe*, the ritual of penance and public humiliation. It was clear, the intent was not a reclamation of a lost soul by the Church, but a vile entertainment for the raging mob and a display of the power of the Inquisition. Giordano was bent forward on the sedan chair. A *coroza*, the degrading, conical, three-foot-tall dunce cap signifying his extraordinary shame and sin, sat on his head.

Shortened chains around his wrists held him to the base of the chair and forced him into a slumped position, further enhancing the appearance that he had been cowed by the power of the examiners and minimizing his posture for the crowd's amusement. His arms were bared, and he was clothed in just a swaddling cloth around his hips, so that he was nearly naked except for the black *sambenito*, the small placard style vest that bore his sentence in pictogram form. This too was intended to stoke the illiterate mob. The sins and sentence were not written in words, but represented by a simple drawing of red flames, signaling to everyone that Giordano was about to be burned.

Even from that distance, the terror on Giordano's face was evident, and when they arrived at the stake set high on a stack of kindling and thorny wood, he struggled pitifully and cried out for a last reprieve of mercy as the executioners grabbed him. Prison and unrelenting torture had weakened him, and he could barely stand. In the hands of the muscular, hooded men, he appeared even more wretched and pathetic, but instead of inspiring even a shred of compassion or merciful tendency, the crowd responded with renewed vicious passion as though being fed by his fear and agony as he was dragged. Maria Celeste and Galileo could do nothing but watch with gaunt depleted expressions as he was roughly tied to the stake and bombarded with a fusillade of rotten vegetables, excrement, and offal as soon as the officials were clear.

When the supply was depleted, crosses atop long staffs rose and surrounded him, just far enough away that he could not reach them with his lips. Maculani had made it clear, he was not to be allowed an opportunity for last-second mercy. A moment later, a waft of smoke rose up, thin at first, like almost nothing; it was soon followed by more, thick roiling clouds. The pyre had been ignited.

Unlike most in attendance, Galileo knew what was going to happen. From his time studying medicine, he was acquainted with the physiological changes and manner of death caused by burning. The best Giordano could hope for would be a would be an excruciating immolation of his skin and nerves, followed by inhalation of flaming gas, liberated coals and smoke. That was the best.

At worst, depending on the way the pyre burned, the wind and any actions taken by those attending the flames, he might literally be roasted over time with his internal musculature and organs destroyed by a slowly rising blaze. The skin would shrink as the fat and water reduced until it split and ripped free. Until the nerves were consumed, the agony would be intolerable. Then the musculature and tendons would shorten until they tore away from the bone, or if the bone were simultaneously weakened, they would snap and twist changing the body into unnatural positions that the mob would interpret as the evil spirit contorting and being driven from the body. In that way, it was a horrible and self-fulfilling fantasy. Inside, the organs would expand with vaporized gas and rupture if hollow or rip free as they desiccated and pulled free from their vasculature to begin hemorrhaging. Finally, in the very worst of cases, the brain would boil as the lining of the lungs sloughed away.

That was the theoretical.

In reality, the flames had risen and were in full force now and Giordano shrieked animalistically behind the wall of fire. Maria Celeste crossed herself and clasped her hands in a white knuckled prayerful pose. Her lips moved silently, rapidly beseeching God for mercy. Galileo, continued to watch, with mournful eyes, forcing himself not to look away from either the braying celebrating crowd or the burning atrocity that inspired them. When finally, the screams ended and there was no more horror to sustain them, the mob relaxed, and the dynamic, like a sexual aftermath, ground down, alternating until they were again a population of people, no longer consolidated by a mad emotion.

In a way their return to everyday people was even more disturbing to him.

•

After that the trip home was muted for a number of reasons. The country was still in the grip of plague, and as they approached each town, the rising cloud of crematory smoke reminded them of the terrible display in Rome. With a thump and a call to cover from the driver, leather flaps were drawn over the windows of the coach so that as they went through each municipality, no deathly miasma could get in. It was always the same. The horses' pace would pick up to a fast gallop, and the coach would jostle roughly depending on the quality of the road. Inside, Galileo and Maria Celeste were tossed about until the agitation slowed and the curtain lifted to show once again a sun-drenched countryside devoid of the concentrated horrors of man.

Galileo was noticing something, and a thought was just starting to form when Maria Celeste spoke.

"You should take care, Papa."

He looked at her. Her expression was darkly worried. He knew what she was thinking, and while his hearing had not been a trial of heresy by the Inquisition, his enemies had shown themselves to be vocal and highly motivated. They both knew of the deception that had led to Giordano's capture and execution, and so the assurances of the clement nature of his own examination were not completely calming to her.

He sighed and looked at her warmly.

"Giordano was a proponent of the earth moving, yes. But he could offer no proof for his position. I have shown proof."

He said it like the matter was just that simple. Maria Celeste looked back at him as if she knew something he did not.

"I'm not entirely sure that proof is protection, Papa," she said.

Deep down, he wondered if she might be right, though he said nothing. He just patted her hand and looked back out at the sunlight. Just that quickly, his mind was on to other matters. He was seeing something right then, a pattern in the way the light shined on a small river near the road. Along the shoreline, the texture of moss showed well above the old watermark of the limestone bank. This was a tidal river, linked to the influences of the sea. He looked up. It was one of those days when the position of the moon made it show even in the daylight.

A wave rolled and for a moment showed the reflection of the moon. Then just as quickly, it disappeared. He blinked.

Then he scratched his head. There was something there. By the time they arrived in Florence, he knew what it was. Another new concept concerning the great silver moon was beginning to form.

•

The decision of the Panel of Qualifiers, and the resulting papal determination regarding same, took three months to finalize. It took another three months to write. Barberini had chosen Cardinal Bellarmine to oversee the transition from discussion to copy, a task he accepted grudgingly. Even so, it might have been simple enough had it not been for the Pigeon League's constant efforts to circumvent him with the scribes in order to alter their own representation in the document, and worse, to place in it that which might later be used to prosecute Galileo again. Finally, after so many months of institutional subterfuge, paranoia and an exhausting amount of scrutiny, Bellarmine had a document that was true to the findings of the panel.

As Barberini read it, he smiled with something like relief, then looked up with appreciation. The strain on his face told Bellarmine that he wasn't the only one who was feeling the effects of life in the twisted unstable court of a Vatican on the verge of papal change. It had been some time since the Holy Father had been a mentally cogent vessel for God's philosophy. Those closest to the pontiff knew it best. In the recent weeks, he was more like a newborn babe, only without the charms, or promise. Even feeding him took the services of another as a spoon defied his unsteady hand.

I wonder, Bellarmine thought, if Galileo would have been so sure in his bold words, if he knew the rising danger in the world to one challenging the status quo. Then he thought again. For Galileo there was no other way. He remembered how he had given up his family to save them all, despite his obvious pain. It was just another act in the continuum of his character. To consider that he might discover a truth of the universe and withhold it was inconceivable. Fact, science, the absolutes of God's creation, these were his loves now, and to deny any of them, to underserve them, was as he had said not just a sin but a crime against the Lord. In that he was a dedicated servant without compare.

Barberini handed the finding and the directive to Bellarmine.

"Uncompromising men must be protected," he said. Then looking especially weary he added, "If only from themselves."

"I only hope it will be enough," said Bellarmine.

The thought still plagued him, days later as he climbed into a carriage to bear the message to Florence.

The scribbling that had occupied Galileo during his argument in Rome were a precursor to the inspiration of the moon's image on the water that day when he and Maria Celeste were riding home. It seemed to him, a divine reminder, a celestial nudge that despite the recent horrors, he should be back about his work. The waters of the earth were like the breath of man. Something drove the tides just as surely as the body inhaled and exhaled. Staring out the window of his study at dusk, he knew. It was the moon herself.

All along the wall stretched a mural he had drawn, cataloguing the phases of the moon and the corresponding measurements of high and low tide for the past six months. Once again, his method was proving beyond doubt that a correlation existed. He set down his pen and looked at the letter that had come that afternoon. His son Vincenzio was a man now, and Marina had written asking a favor.

Galileo looked at the handwriting. He ran his finger along smooth curves of her distinctive script and a flood of emotion possessed him. For a brief moment, he allowed himself to consider what might have been even though he knew that avenue would lead nowhere but to pain. Eventually, he gently folded the letter and set it aside. Unfair though it was, daughters were one thing, a son another. A petition of paternity would require no dowry and, though meager, his fortune would be more than enough to warrant a designated heir. A name cost even less, and he knew that unless that name bore dishonor, it might still be worth something.

The sky was dark now, and he looked through the eye piece at the splendid moon. She was just coming full, and if his hypothesis were true, the reports from the tidal basin would show that the waterline had topped out again. He smiled and made a notation. It was going to be hard to sleep that night in anticipation of the measurement. He picked up a bottle of wine and smiling, poured himself a glass.

"In the meantime," he said to the moon, "there is always wine."

He lifted the glass in tribute to her and took a sip.

CHAPTER NINE

The next morning when the coach with the Church seal on its door pulled up in front of his house, Galileo was asleep on the small couch that more than once doubled as a bed in his study. Maria Celeste had arrived earlier and found him in the all too familiar position with his head, crooked on the cushion at one end and his foot dangling off just above the floor at the other. She gently lifted his foot and placed it on the couch, then picked up the empty bottle and glass on the floor next to his ink-stained hand. His eyes opened and he smiled.

"Help me up, dear girl," he said.

She grasped his arm and pulled him to a seated position. He yawned.

"Perhaps just a few more minutes," he said and stretched back out.

She was in the kitchen when she saw the coach come to a stop. The driver jumped down and opened the door then set a small stool on the pavement. A second later, the scarlet-slippered foot of Cardinal Bellarmine stepped out. Travel by coach might be one of the more civilized modes in its time, but the distance between Rome and Florence was tiring. Bellarmine was road weary, and not just because of the demands of the trip, but also because of the news he carried in the cloth valise at his side. He stretched and straightened, betraying a certain stiffness. Then with a serious expression he started for the door.

He had just reached it and was about to knock when it opened suddenly. Standing back, in a deferential bow was Maria Celeste.

"Sister," he said by way of greeting.

"Your Eminence," she answered. "*Professore* Galilei is in his office. If you would like, I will announce you."

She knew Bellarmine was a fan and a friend of her father, but the image of him sprawled on the couch was not the sort of presentation that would do either of them any good. Besides, she could tell there was something weighing heavily on the Cardinal's state of mind and if bad news were coming, for dignities sake, she wanted to make sure Galileo was at least awake.

"Of course," he said and stepped inside just across the threshold with his hands folded to wait.

She hustled to the study door and knocked. From inside a grumpy voice muttered, "Enter."

She opened it and stepped in. Fighting the impulse to cross herself in gratitude, she sighed at the sight of him seated at his table, pen in hand. If a more professorial posture were possible, she couldn't imagine it. Nodding to Bellarmine, she cleared her throat.

Galileo did not look up or acknowledge her cue.

Bellarmine entered and paused with a look of amusement at Maria Celeste's discomfort. She cleared her throat again, this time much louder and with greater emphasis.

"Are you feeling ill?" Galileo asked, still not looking up from his work.

She'd had enough.

"Cardinal Bellarmine," she announced insistently.

That roused Galileo. He set down his pen and turned. He smiled at first, then recognizing the emotional state of his friend, his eyes narrowed.

"Come to deliver good news?" he asked with a trace of sarcasm.

Bellarmine looked uncomfortably away.

"That bad, is it?" said Galileo.

Maria Celeste gestured that the Cardinal sit. He crossed the room to a chair and placed the valise on the floor next to it. Then he sat down with a slightly exhausted sigh. He was having a tough time.

Galileo looked past him to Maria Celeste and nodded. She turned and left the room, then a moment later, returned carrying a bottle of wine and glassware. She set the items down and waited in silence.

Bellarmine knew there was no point in putting off the unpleasantness at hand, so he reached into the valise and withdrew the verdict and disposition. He opened the document and began to read aloud.

"The unanimous decision of the Panel of Qualifiers delivered this day," he began.

"Unanimous?"

The word came sharply, cutting off Bellarmine. Suddenly all the keen sharpness of Galileo's attention had zeroed in on that one word.

For a moment, Bellarmine, almost faltered. Then recovering himself, he answered, "You know that regardless of any dissention in the panel's vote, a decision is always issued by the Church as unanimous."

"Mm," muttered Galileo. "God's perfection in all things."

It sounded like a derision, not of God, but of all those that were only too ready to speak for Him. Despite his tone, Maria Celeste recognized that he could sense what was coming, and he was compensating for the imminent injury of it.

"What was the vote?" he asked.

"It doesn't matter really, does it?" asked Bellarmine.

"It does to me," he answered earnestly.

Bellarmine lowered the document to speak unofficially.

"The majority found for your argument."

Galileo nodded. There was at least some gratification in that. Bellarmine looked like he found no pleasure in continuing, almost vexed at what he had to say next, as if it was some admission of a shameful fact. His eyes darted as he searched for a way to express it best.

"But it was His Holiness's opinion that the minority vote would prove problematic if it were not supported."

"Ah," said Galileo and he looked out the window.

Bellarmine resumed reading.

"The proposition that the sun is stationary and that it is at the center of the universe is both foolish and absurd in philosophy."

Maria Celeste was listening and watching her father. He didn't seem to be listening at all. His attention was apparently occupied by the sun-drenched laborers that were hard at work in the fields far away. It was a ruse though. She knew him too well. Not a single word was escaping him.

Bellarmine, on the other hand, looked like the emotional effort of reading the decision was equivalent to climbing a mountain, and he struggled as he pushed through the rest of the text.

"Such assertions are to be," he continued, "and are formally considered as heretical, since in many places, they explicitly contradict the sense of Holy Scripture."

Maria Celeste looked frightened now, and a soft involuntary sob escaped her. The recent memory of what had happened to Giordano Bruno was still fresh in her mind, and the fact that the word heresy had been included sent a chill, bone deep.

"As a result, the Pope has ordered that you be censured and that you abandon the Copernican opinions," said Bellarmine.

Galileo's eyes closed as if enduring a physical pain. He sighed.

"You must abstain completely from teaching or defending this opinion."

"Opinion?" said Galileo bitterly. Coming from his lips it sounded like an abomination.

Bellarmine pressed on, trying to finish the horrible task as quickly as possible.

"And from discussing it. To abandon completely, the opinion that the sun stands still at the center of the world and the earth moves, and henceforth not to hold, teach, nor defend it in any way whatever, either orally..." He hesitated, almost verbally staggering as he assailed the next few words. It was almost like they were wounding him as well. "...Or in writing."

He dropped the paper to the floor and slumped back in the chair, completely exhausted and depleted. He was sweating, far too heavily for the temperature in the room, and his breath was labored, catching up to some great incurred oxygen debt. With his last reserve, he spoke the final line of the directive.

"If you resist this decree, stronger actions will be taken."

Galileo was angry and frustrated. The moratorium decreed by the papal verdict was an assault, not just on him, but on all freethinkers. Its application was greater than just to the parties in the room. As he took stock of Bellarmine, he knew that a few perfectly applied words by himself would annihilate the man. Then again, he thought, poor Bellarmine looked like a worse punishment was already underway.

Galileo let a few more seconds of silence pass as he looked at his distraught friend and said, "I can think of no better rebuttal for information like that than wine." He smiled ruefully. "Maria Celeste, would you be so good?"

She picked up the bottle and started to pour.

"And be sure and pour a glass for yourself," he said.

Her brows knitted, and she almost shook her head in protest before shooting a quick look at the Cardinal. He was her superior in the Church, and to take the liberty of serving herself without his permission was a significant violation of protocol. Father or no, well-intended or not, Galileo had put her in a very difficult position. Fortunately, Bellarmine took note.

"Please," he said answering the unspoken question.

"Thank you," she nodded and filled a third.

They each picked up their glass.

"To my infamy," toasted Galileo with wry bitterness. Then he went on, "And perpetual improvement."

Unlike the usual pre-drink tribute, none of the three looked at the others as they sampled their cup. Each seemed to be considering a future bound by the parameters set forth in the document. What they did all have in common was a subtle temperance of sadness.

Then they noted the taste of the wine. It was that good. Slow smiles spread, and they looked impressed as they experienced the small but simple truth that even in the face of something ominously daunting, a simple pleasure was salvation. In that moment, like with most of his determinations, it was obvious that Galileo had called it right. Good wine was the perfect response.

By the time the bottle was finished and the warm glow in Bellarmine and Galileo was rivaling that of the sun on the distant vineyard's leaves, a resolved equilibrium had set in. Some might have called it anesthesia. That was certainly how Maria Celeste saw it as the two lubricated colleagues chatted in the study. The contention generated by Bellarmine's official duty had dissolved in the libation consumed, and the talk turned to more comfortable subjects. The plump Cardinal was back to his devotee status with her father. He held up his glass and sipped it down to one remaining swallow.

"Is it true what I heard?" he asked happily.

Galileo considered how best to answer a question that was clearly assuming a context that hadn't been established yet.

"Hmm?" he finally muttered.

"That you mathematically calculated the geometric area of each level of hell from the description in Dante's work?"

Galileo smiled at the memory. Of all the things he had invented, discovered, accomplished and written, that one indulgent act of amusement always seemed to come up.

"*The Divine Comedy*," he said chuckling. "Yes, I liked it. Smart. I also agreed with Alighieri as to the hierarchy of sin and his particular scale." He grinned again. "So, I thought, there is achievement of sin, just like in all things, and while he qualitatively determined the escalating punishments, well, mathematically, I wanted to make my own contribution."

Bellarmine was enjoying this.

"How did you estimate the area?" he asked. He was enough of a mathematician in his own right to be interested.

"Well," mused Galileo leaning forward intimately. "If you promise to never tell a soul?"

"Of course," answered Bellarmine with an earnestness that only comes from being fairly inebriated.

"As I didn't have an instrument to measure, I was forced to...*guess*," said Galileo with an impish gleam.

It took a second for the joke to land, but then Bellarmine laughed out loud. His face turned a deeper red and he slapped his thigh.

"Oh *Doctore*," he said breathily. "You are a genius."

"Well, I'll confess, given certain parties' estimation of my eternal destination, I thought it might be good to know what to expect."

Bellarmine laughed again and waved his plump palm dismissively.

"You do know," he said seriously. "You've a friend in Cardinal Barberini. When he heard that you had done that, he was tremendously amused. In private of course. You are something of a secret guilty pleasure at least among the Vatican court"

"He has always been a good friend," said Galileo ignoring the rest of the statement.

Bellarmine held up his glass. There was only one decent swallow's volume left in it. After a proper consideration of its garnet color, he tilted the glass, drained it and smacked his lips. Then he frowned quizzically.

"What was it you called wine? It was clever. I remember that, but you said—"

Without any prompt, Galileo cut him off.

"Wine is sunlight, held together by water."

It was simple enough, and he recited the words with a kind of mellow comfort, but Maria Celeste saw something more in his expression. It was like he was looking into the magic behind the phrase.

•

"I could do with a glass right now," said Galileo looking at Ferrero and Bellarmine.

Both old men were smiling at the memory of that long-emptied bottle. Fererro, however, had no such connection, and his face wrinkled a bit with renewed impatience.

"As you brought up the verdict and directive of the Pope, I must point out that you did not desist, did you, *Doctore*? You just couldn't still your pen."

The pleasant memory dissipated like mist subjected to a punishing sun. Galileo was back to business. He looked back at Ferrero evenly.

"No," he said flatly.

It was the tone more than anything that irritated Ferrero. He was wholly unapologetic, not conceding a thing in terms of his willful disregard of the Pope's instruction. It was a reminder that hit hard with Ferrero and made him question himself for his varying feelings about the accused. It was frustrating. Most wrongdoers were monochromatic in terms of their offense and their natures generally reinforced their crimes. Galileo was something else entirely, and despite his personal feeling, already Ferrero had to admit to himself that in just the course of the interview he had swayed between sympathy, admiration and offense. Frustrated, he grabbed a document and held it up.

"*Disputation on the place and stability of the Earth, against the system of Copernicus*," he recited.

It was the name of the pamphlet. Ignoli's rebuttal of Galileo's assessment of the heavenly dynamic.

"Mm," muttered Galileo dismissively. "Ignoli's book. A terrible title, by the way."

Bellarmine held up a hand to hide his resulting smile. A moment later, he had regained control.

"You should take this seriously," he admonished.

Galileo looked nonplussed.

"Ignoli was an idiot. Kept arguing against Copernicus.

"One might argue that you were one as well for replying," parried Bellarmine.

"His pamphlet was simply a manuscript, not published. No one worth his ink and type would put it out. Therefore, I simply indulged in a semi-private correspondence."

The way Galileo said it sounded so innocent, so benign, but they all knew that nothing he wrote in any form was benign, not after the *Sidereus Nuncius*.

Ferrero ignored it. In his opinion this was pointless sparing. They needed to prepare for a real examination. He held up another document. This one was different, not only in style and type, but the quality of the lettering and accoutrements. This had been produced by a skilled publisher.

"And this? *The Discourse on the Comets*?" Ferrero pointed at the authorship. "Mario Guiducci?"

Galileo smiled. The effect on Ferrero was like a flaming accelerant.

"There is not one person in Italy that doesn't know you authored this yourself," he said emotionally.

Galileo gave a conciliatory shrug. "Good name though, don't you think?" he said wryly. Then with complete joy he indulged himself in repeating the name. "Mario Guiducciiiiiii," he said drawing it out like a celebratory cry.

Ferrero was not amused in the least.

"I would point out, that it hasn't been condemned," said Galileo.

"A rare distinction," countered Ferrero with just a hint of snide.

Suddenly Bellarmine leaned forward and picked up another document, a deadly serious look on his face. It was *The Dialogue Concerning the Two Chief World Systems.*

"This one has been, though," said Bellarmine emotionally. "And all because you made an enemy of one who loved you."

Ferrero looked at him. The reaction was uncharacteristically emotional for his mentor, but what he noticed most was the sweat that was just as suddenly pouring from under his pileolus. The small skullcap was actually quite soaked, and the escaping perspiration cascaded down his ruddy face to darken the collar of his robe. This was no ordinary strain impacting the man, and both Ferrero and Galileo looked concerned.

Bellarmine didn't seem to realize the effect he was having and ran a fat hand across his face as he took a ragged breath. The room suddenly seemed extremely warm and for some reason even the very air had become heavy and hard to take in.

Ferrero's frown deepened. "Eminence?" he said anxiously.

•

The death of Pope Paul V, two years before the arrest of Galileo by the Inquisition, was a significant moment for the Catholic world. Certainly, anytime a pope died, there were a hundred intrigues. A certain apprehensive energy consumed the faithful as well as the College of Cardinals, but with the world in such a state of peril, the absence of a pontiff made the current situation particularly delicate. The immediate convention of cardinals and bishops agreed that summoning the leadership for Conclave would have to be expedited. The plague was still raging, and the Inquisition was running without the Holy See's check. To have a strong and established head of the church determined as quickly as possible was critical. Without it, the balance of power and direction of the Church was in jeopardy, so even before the customary waiting period of the funeral and burial had been completed, one hundred and twenty summoners on horseback were dispatched at a run throughout Christendom.

One such recipient of the charge was Cardinal Bellarmine in Florence.

The road leading up to the Cardinal's residence was easy to see from his office, and as he looked out at the shiny bay horse approaching at a gallop, he reactively crossed himself and appealed to God for strength. As it got closer, he could make out the froth of lather along its bridle line. It was obvious, this news had traveled a good distance in a hurry. He also knew that no good news came with such urgency and he would want the Lord's strength to meet whatever challenge was carried in the saddle bag.

The rider reined in his mount at the last minute, and the animal's hindquarters dropped so that its hooves skidded across the gravel. Even before it had come to a stop, the man was out of the saddle and running into the chapel with the bag. Bellarmine descended the stairs and arrived just as he was handing off the message to a member of the Order. The Brother turned with a wide-eyed look on his face that said instantly that the seal on the parchment was that of the Vatican.

Having finished the first leg of his task, the rider bent forward. He placed his hands on his knees and gasped for breath. Bellarmine walked over to the thunderstruck brother and removed the document from his hands. He opened it and read.

"What does it say, Eminence?" he asked.

The panting rider looked up. He was curious as well.

"Expedite with all prejudice, all responsibilities in subordination, to this summons to Conclave of Cardinal," he hesitated before saying the last word, then with effect added, "Electors."

The Brother gasped and crossed himself. At a distance, the rider did the same without straightening up. Nothing more needed to be said. The Pope was dead, and the Church needed Bellarmine's service.

Normally, the call to this kind of service, though predicated upon tragedy, was an honor. For most like Bellarmine, it represented one of the greatest privileges and responsibilities imaginable. It also meant that as a member of the Conclave, he was automatically a candidate to be the new pope. No humble member of the clergy would suppose himself likely, but in too many cases, the elevation to the position of cardinal made humility a casualty of rank. Even the trip to Rome was often a splendid affair. It became a minor pilgrimage made special by the task waiting upon arrival. Most never experienced it in a lifetime. Those that did, took steps to savor every aspect. They were going to have a hand in Church history. It was immortality in a way, and they planned each aspect down to the most minute detail. Even the very robes and cassocks would forever carry special meaning. This time, though, none of that could be indulged.

Bellarmine turned to the Brother and said, "We leave at first light."

While a team and carriage could never match the speed of a single horse, Bellarmine's driver did his best to minimize the difference. The Cardinal smacked his hand several times against the top of the carriage to tell him to slow down out of fear for the health of the animals. Even though he had been muted in his reaction to the summons, the word had gotten out about the imperative. From the monks assigned to his packing, to the driver who seemed intent on running the horses into the ground, they all felt the pressure.

Somehow, because of a miracle perhaps, they arrived in Rome intact, both man and beast. As soon as they had stopped, Bellarmine disembarked the carriage and entered the Apostolic Palace. It wasn't the first time he had been in the Sistine Chapel, but on that day, as he entered, the song of the choir seemed more angelic, the frescos above more illuminated and brilliant. God was granting him a new insight, a perspective that he hoped to carry into the closed session. That night he and the others would gather in St Peter's Basilica for a mass to invoke the blessings of the Holy Spirit, and then they would seal the doors, which would not open again until white smoke billowed from the chimney.

The process was set in the oldest tradition and was elaborate in its ceremony. The first order of business was an indoctrination with an oath of secrecy taken by each cardinal. There was to be no discussion nor anything resembling a political process. The secrecy was to isolate each heart to preserve its motivation and protect its spiritual influence. Among the one-hundred-twenty, there was immediate discussion as to who should be considered. No names were used. Only descriptions of character and personal skill were designated in code, but just the same, there was very little doubt as to who the prime candidates were.

Bellarmine looked around at his peers. In his own mind there was only one option. Barberini had the scholarship and an understanding of the office. His family wealth provided immunity to bribes and financial influences and with his intellect and academic prowess, he would be very difficult to flank. Plus, he was well-liked. That was not to be overlooked.

Oddly, as Barberini considered the room, his eye was on Bellarmine. There was only one problem there, Bellarmine's health. It was a concern shared by other members of the Conclave. While there were other members of the clergy with even more girth and body mass, Bellarmine was known to suffer from bouts of humoral apoplexy, or shortness of breath and he experienced pains in his chest from even limited exertions. They had just buried a pope and replacing him with another of even greater fragility was in no one's interest.

Just the same, he wrote the name on his ballot and folded it over twice.

The first ballot was almost always ceremonial. In many instances, members who would have no chance of carrying any type of majority would write their own names. Once each member had folded his ballot accordingly, they formed a line and began a silent walk up the long staircase that ended at Michelangelo's fresco where a silver chalice, the progenitor and symbol of the legend of the grail was placed. Each then kneeled to pray, crossed himself and dropped his ballot in the cup, before heading back down.

As expected, the reading of the first ballot was little more than a roll call, a recitation of the membership. That was customary. Most everyone had voted for themselves, not so much because they thought they should be pope, but just so they could hear their own name echo under the rarified ceiling of the chapel. So, the secretary of the proceedings read each name, allowing for enough time for those that would never be mentioned again to look around at the others for approbation. Despite the need to expedite, vanity still had to have its moment.

From there they settled into business.

The ballots were gathered by the three cardinals chosen as "recorders" who governed the voting and then stacked in the chapel stove, the source to the chimney that would signal to the common throng each day's progress. In one pail next to it was a mixture of coal, anthracene and sulphur. This would produce the black smoke that would billow as they set a torch to the vanity electoral cards.

Next to the black pail was another, the famous white pail containing Greek pitch; a mixture of crudely refined lactose, potassium extract and clear pine resin. As the black smoke swept upward into the chimney, the cardinals wondered how long it would be before they could they could dip into the other bucket.

According to tradition, votes would be taken four times each day until a majority of two thirds was established for one individual. No candidate could advocate or speak on his own behalf in any deliberation, which meant that alliances and parties of support were pursued with all the maneuvering of a partisan political campaign. It lent itself to a certain hypocrisy, as the four prime candidates addressed questions carefully behind the scenes and always in the abstract.

For example, when queried by a cardinal from Germany about his vulnerability to tribute, Barberini for example, didn't answer directly, but chose to say, "I would offer only this; surely we would all want a pope whose own means made the temptation of outside appeal, irrelevant."

The meaning was clever and obvious, as he came from the most affluent family and at least two of his rivals were from more provincial and less wealthy backgrounds. He hadn't advocated for himself at all, and yet still had managed to instill doubt about the others.

There was still even more afoot in those privately chambered moments. As the number of potential candidates decreased, the emphasis of discussion shifted from exclusion to favoritism. To have an obligated or favorable history with a newly elected pope was a generational investment, and they all knew it. For some it was a promise of church office, for others patronage of pet universities or some family member. As the days passed, it seemed everyone had their hand out.

And then, when enough deals had been struck, the slow trudge up the stairs to the ceiling of the chapel rendered a decisive chalice. When the recorder read the vote count, the faces remained stoic with a practiced neutrality. As Bellarmine watched he could see, with the mounting votes in favor of his friend Barberini, a soft slackening of disappointment manifested in the faces of the losers.

Barberini was the right choice and even his political opponents grudgingly admitted he would do well. As for Barberini, when he heard the news, he lowered his face into his hands and prayed openly. To Bellarmine's observation, it was a genuine response, truly possessed of pure emotion and the spirit. The other members of the College of Cardinals looked on impressed at the reaction and almost contagiously crossed themselves as well.

The ancient white-headed Dean of the College stood and said in a clear, resonating voice, "Cardinal Barberini, do you accept the verdict of the College?"

Barberini looked up tearfully.

"I do," he said humbly.

An affirmative murmur spread through the group.

"And by what name will you be known to all of Christianity?" asked the Dean.

"I shall take the name, Urban," he said.

Another affirmative murmur followed.

"Rise," said the Dean.

Barberini stood and followed the attendants to the Holy apartments. The others stood and bowed, all that is except for the recorders, who were busily gathering the ballots and carrying them to the chapel stove. With a smile, they dug into the white pail and sprinkled the savory material onto the paper as they struck a flame. The cloud of swirling white smoke rose into the chimney stack. A few minutes later, the distant roar of the gratified crowd outside shook the stone walls.

•

Galileo's decision to travel to Rome for the inauguration of Urban VIII, as his good friend would now be known, was driven by more than one factor. First and foremost, he was genuinely happy for his friend and wanted to do him honor. Another was in the lesser consideration that it would not hurt to be viewed favorably by the head of a church that had previously, effectively gagged him. Finally, and most importantly, he wanted to make the case for science. The past months had been insufferable. Not that he had not worked. His writing and studies in matters of the tidal connection to the moon, the shape and mapping of the heavens and his studies of mathematical forces had been the same as before the censure. Even so, the inability to broadly express himself to the rest of the world had rankled him.

The new pope would be a landmark for the office. He was intellectually sharp and able to read with an understanding of nuance. For the first time in Galileo's memory, the discoveries of science would be reasonably discussed alongside the writings of faith. Upon word of Barberini's selection, he had written a letter to his friend and sent it off in advance of making the travel arrangements for Rome. Just days before he was about to depart, a response came back.

"You have a letter," said Maria Celeste from the doorway.

He was busy deciding which books to take with him as he stuffed them into a bag.

"Read it," he said.

"It is from His Holiness," she said. As a nun she was far from immune to casually handling a papal letter, even if she had known the Pope from his less elevated days.

"Who?" asked Galileo, still sorting through his library.

"The Pope," she said with a little more emphasis.

Galileo looked up.

"Oh"—he seemed to consider that before deciding—"well, unless the letters are blazing through in tongues of fire, you will still have to open it and read."

She gave him a dismissive smirk and opened it.

"My dear friend, Galileo," she began, "only a letter from you could make this wondrous event in my life even greater. I am honored to learn that my beloved should want to attend and welcome your presence as always. Please make haste. The requirements of the Holy Institution are such that no delay in the ceremonies may be taken. It would be to my immense joy and delight, to have you, one who is so dear, present for my coronation. I will direct that you be placed in an honored, and beloved position so that you may share in this with me and that we may speak at length."

She paused and looked at her father. The letter read more like some affectionate suitor's invitation than from a spiritual king about to take the throne. As for Galileo, he didn't seem to be listening fully. All he heard was that they would soon speak and obviously assumed it meant he could anticipate future intellectual freedom. She knew that her father was certainly a genius, but she was reminded that he also had his blind spots. She only hoped he was right.

The place of prominence described by Cardinal Barberini was not only located within the Sistine Chapel, but it was in the row of eminence generally reserved for ranking members of the clergy and special servants of the Church. Galileo's seating status was meant simply as an honorarium, purely intended to include a valued friend, but in his moment of magnanimity, the new pope forgot that where there is piety and godliness, the devil is never far removed. Without the intrigue of the papal selection to occupy them, the ubiquitous network of Vatican gossips and spies had turned their attention to the arrangements of the coronation ceremony.

There were many who would be interested in the hierarchy of proximity and access to Urban VIII during the ceremony, not the least of which were the senior scholars Cremonini and Colombe. While initially gratified with the previous pope's decision to censure and still Galileo's comments about the movement of the earth, they had been suspicious when the works of Mario Guiducci circulated. It didn't take a genius to guess at the true name of its authorship. Their inability to prove it only made them angrier.

"His Holiness is placing a heretic in a place of privilege?" said Colombe as he stared resentfully at the list of honored guests.

"Not a heretic," said Cremonini flatly. "A proponent and circulator of heretical concept. And, as far as can be proven, he has adhered to the directive since the determination of the true nature of his writing."

Colombe looked vexed.

"That"—he pointed emphatically at the gallery so

intimately close to where the coronation would take place— "that place, that man, there." He seemed on the verge of sputtering. "All of Christendom will see him raised up."

"Yes," said Cremonini coolly. "An elevated perch for so careless a flier."

Colombe understood. He turned and looked at his colleague, with a smile on his face.

The objection had to be handled carefully. No one wanted to establish a relationship with a new and powerful pope by throwing a wrench in his plans. Instead, Cremonini and Colombe turned to a trusted friend, one they knew Galileo hated even more than them. Father Caccini had just been approved for a permanent place in Rome and his appointment was due, in no small part, to certain conservative factions of the church supporting his apparent defense of faith against science. As such, he had been selected for one of the many committees involved in support of the ceremony. His having to share a place assigned to the despised Galileo was like throwing turpentine on an open flame and exactly what they had hoped.

In the end, Galileo was reassigned despite Barberini's irritation, and while he was still in the chapel, he was unnoticeably out of the way. It mattered little to Galileo though.

On the day of the ceremony, as he sat in the lesser box, and listened to the arias rising and swirling beneath the vibrant scenes on the brilliant fresco, he was happy. Perfect young boys in spotless robes, walked before the members of the College of Cardinals They carried the long chains of the swinging, smoking, golden thuribles that left in their wake, an incense-sweetened invitation to the faithful. They made certain to pause with each step toward the altar and execute three full swings in remembrance of the trinity. In a tribute to the gifts of the nativity, smoldering sources of frankincense and myrrh wafted through the vents of the swinging instruments. When they had taken their places, the choir-song changed, indicating the arrival of the holy processional.

"*Pater Sancte, sic transit gloria mundi* . Holy Father, thus passes the glory of the world," called out the loud voice of the Senior Cardinal Deacon as a symbolic reminder to set aside materialism and vanity.

For the last time as Maffeo Barberini, the future pope walked down the aisle, his head lowered in a humble posture, praying with each step. All around, the full cathedral grew quiet. Faces of all colors and hues, representing the global range of the Church, watched in silent awe as the Senior Cardinal Deacon in a ceremonial robe stepped forward. Barberini kneeled at the altar as the Confiteor, or seminal prayer, was offered. The audience bowed and when it was finished, watched as he sat for the coronation. Then three Senior Cardinal Bishops stood and approached the incipient pontiff.

First the Cardinal Bishop of Albano said, "God, who are present without distinction whenever the devout mind invokes you, be present, we ask you, we and this your servant, Maffeo Barberini, who to the summit of the apostolic community has been chosen as the judge of your people, infuse with the highest blessings that he experience your gift who has reached this point."

He affixed the *immantatio mantum*, the long circumferential gown, and enclosed Barberini in the raiment symbolic of the divine hand around him.

Then Cardinal Bishop of Ostia said, "God, who willed your Apostle Peter to hold first place in the inner fellowship of the apostles, that universal Christianity overcome evil, look propitiously we ask on this your servant, Maffeo Barberini, who from a humble position is enthroned with the apostles, on this same principal sublimity, that just as he has been raised to this exalted dignity, so may he likewise merit to accumulate virtue; in bearing the burden of the universal church, help him, make him worthy and for thee who are blessed may merits replace vices."

Finally, the Senior Cardinal Deacon placed the ecclesiastical vestments of the pallium on Barberini's shoulders saying, "Accept the pallium, the plenitude of the Pontifical office, to the honor of Almighty God, and the most glorious Virgin Mary, his Mother, and the Blessed Apostles Peter and Paul, and the Holy Roman Church."

He turned, lifted the bullet-shaped, bejeweled tiara, and held it suspended a few inches above the new pope's head. In a loud clear voice, he announced, "Receive the tiara adorned with three crowns, and know that you are the father of princes and kings..."

In the crowd Bellarmine looked on emotionally. No Catholic, and surely no one that had dedicated their life to the cause of Christ could witness this and not feel an overwhelming sense of piety. While pettiness and human nature would reassert soon enough, right then he felt at one with the world through God's grace. He crossed himself humbly.

The Senior Cardinal Deacon went on with the litany, "The ruler of the world, the vicar of our Savior Jesus Christ on earth..."

Sister Maria Celeste knew that her father was inside the chapel, but once again, as a woman and secondary in status among the clergy, she had made her pilgrimage with the other members of her order and now remained just outside the doors of the church. Even so, the voice of the Senior Cardinal Deacon was loud and clear enough that she too was impacted by the moment. Clutching the crucifix that hung on the chain around her neck, she closed her eyes and tenderly pressed her lips to the figure of her suffering Lord.

"To whom be all honor and glory, a world without end." With that, the cardinal released his hold on the three-tiered crown and withdrew his hands so that it crowned the brow of the new pope.

The choir exploded in a resumption of the *Gloria*. Maffeo Barberini no longer existed. Now in his place and forever more would be the person of Pope Urban VIII.

Galileo smiled and crossed himself, genuinely happy for his friend. Cremonini and Colombe did likewise, but their indulgence of the moment was of a greater, almost painful fervor. It was telling, a hint at the sort of force of purpose that their faith manifested. Bellarmine saw it, and it occurred to him that herein was not a consideration of love, but of power, control and judgment.

On the holy throne, Pope Urban VIII looked above all worldly concerns. A beatific smile covered his face as he stared upward to heaven. He was energized, illuminated, changed by God's holy light.

In his first act as pontiff, he looked out at the massive crowd, made the sign of the cross and spoke the words, "*Urbi et Orbi*. To the city and to the world."

The choirs exploded in joyous expression once again as the new pope rose and made his exit from the chapel.

Now he would enter the chamber of tears, the sepulcher where a pope appealed directly to God for guidance, chose his colors and style of vestments, everything that would symbolically define his papacy. Even the most minute of items; cassocks, head gear, and the signature pileolus would be distinct and selected here. As he looked at it, Urban VIII smiled. The "zucchetto" was how he had known it as an Italian and a boy, but never would again. A bittersweet sense of some human things that were as gone as if he had physically died overtook him at that moment, but just as immediately this sense was replaced by an overwhelming expansion of spirit.

God was possessing him, raising him to a higher purpose and consideration. He could no longer think just of himself or even as himself. Now he must always remember that any decision, any word stood not for a man such as Maffeo Barberini, but for the whole of Christianity. He could not indulge his personal wishes or views any longer, no matter how dear they were. Like St. Paul's illumination on the road to Damascus, he realized that he was not even himself anymore, but something greater, embodied of God, a condition which would take priority in all things he would do.

•

The cable that carried Galileo's invitation to the coronation mass also included a further invitation for a private conversation with his old friend. He was standing out in St. Peter's Square when the reedy young papal attendant, Father Antonio Barbarossi approached to lead him to the papal apartments. Galileo was still feeling the magnitude of the first public appearance of Urban VIII on the balcony above and while of an irreverent nature normally, even he felt a certain humility as he followed the slender Jesuit up the stairs.

Barbarossi led him through the outer offices, where senior deacons, archbishops and cardinals were waiting for their own private audience. They looked up, as if trying to determine whether this new entry would mean a delay for them. It had not been a full day since the ceremony, and already the politics were back. It reminded Galileo of the ever-returning tides.

The question now, he thought, was how high is this one going to get?

Brother Barbarossi walked to a panel in the wall, pressed it and magically transformed its alignment from an apparent barrier to the portal for entry. The symbolism of that was overwhelming, but Galileo didn't have time to consider that long. They were moving too fast, and he was too occupied by the details of the apartment.

"You may sit here, *Doctore* Galilei," he said.

His manner was polite, but Galileo detected that the decorum, while courtly left no doubt that it was a distant, temporary tone of courtesy, without any assumption of real familiarity. He was in a word, "formal" to a fault.

Galileo sat down in the beautifully upholstered chair, feeling very much the visitor, but not quite a guest.

Barbarossi nodded and with that same unfathomable, unreadable expression, exited the room through another door to the next level of Vatican privacy. A few minutes later, it opened again, and he returned, this time followed by Pope Urban VIII.

Galileo stood up quickly.

"Your Holiness!" he said bowing.

Urban VIII had his arms already spreading to embrace when he saw his friend's formal gesture. Sighing with the slightest note of acquiescence, he lowered his hands. Galileo leaned forward taking one and without looking up kissed his ring. There was still enough of Barberini left, that the gesture was painful.

"Please, my friend, sit," he said.

They each took a seat, and unable to contain himself, the Pope leaned across and embraced his friend. Although not completely comfortable, Galileo returned the intimacy. Mercifully, the new pontiff sat back after just a second.

"Would you care for some wine?" he asked brightly.

"Constantly," he said. The impish twinkle was back in Galileo's eye.

Urban VIII chuckled and gestured for Barbarossi to pour.

"It has been a difficult time for you, hasn't it my friend," asked Urban VII as he picked up his glass.

"It has been nothing, Your Holiness," said Galileo, brushing it off.

The Pope did not look completely convinced. With an expression of mock admonition, he smiled and said, "You know, you should not lie to a pope."

Galileo smiled back.

Urban VIII took a sip of wine and with a note of warm familiarity added, "I have known you a long time and loved you as well."

Galileo nodded deferentially.

"You also know, I have read everything you've ever written and worshiped every word."

Galileo glanced up at Urban VIII. He knew him, or used to, and he felt sure the choice of words was not something incidental.

"I am honored, Holiness," said Galileo carefully, though he was obviously, genuinely moved.

Urban VIII was looking at him intently and leaned in close so that what he said next could be whispered and understood clearly.

"I have missed those words to which I am now pleased to offer a reprieve." He leaned back smiling as happily as if he had endowed a gift.

Galileo wasn't sure exactly what that meant.

"Holiness?" he said with a curious note.

Urban VIII just continued to smile. "You know I am a scholar at heart too." He let the silence fill in tantalizingly before continuing. "I want you to continue with your work."

Now it was Galileo's turn to smile. He couldn't believe it at first. It was like he had just been released from prison, or at the very least, his pen had been. Then his face relaxed with a kind of invigorated happiness. He leaned forward and clasped the Pope's hand, kissing the ring again. This time it was with an unabashed enthusiasm.

Urban VIII looked down at Galileo's bowed head and smiled, then glancing up at Barbarossi who had remained a discreet distance away, tilted his head as if reminded of something else. The attendant betrayed nothing, staring ahead as if no one was in the room, but him.

"Of course," said Urban VIII, his tone changing to broader consideration. "In order to allow that as pope, I am obliged to consider all of Christendom and not just my own inclinations."

He was speaking to Galileo, but glanced at Barbarossi, who despite his apparent inattention, was memorizing every word. In that skill, he was renowned as the late Giordano Bruno.

"I want you to continue your work and your writing," said Urban VIII. "You may write whatever you choose, but you must also be fair."

"What?" asked Galileo.

"You must be fair," said Urban VIII.

"I don't understand, Your Holiness."

Something more was afoot here, and Galileo waited for the explanation as Urban VIII poured another glass of wine. When he had taken a sip, he gave his old friend a calculating look that made him immediately uncomfortable. Suddenly the warm chamber of the apartment was more like the court of inquiry he had endured not so long ago. He glanced at the attendant. It all suddenly made sense. He was present as a witness.

The disappointment was almost immeasurable. That his friend, even as pope would manipulate him or require a qualification after initially dangling complete freedom of his work, stung like a slap. Galileo sat back and for the first time since the coronation, looked at him with his characteristic daunting scrutiny.

"What exactly do you mean by fair?" he asked with just the hint of an edge.

Urban VIII frowned slightly like he was struggling with exactly how to put his next point.

"God is all powerful," he said. "We can agree on that?"

It was a test or perhaps, even a trap. Galileo was certain, but to what purpose was not quite yet clear.

"Of course, Holiness," he answered evenly.

"God could have made the universe any way He wanted, and still make it appear to us another."

Galileo couldn't believe what he was hearing.

"Could make it appear the way it does when it was not that way. Could He not?"

Barbarossi was still standing in the same spot, wearing that same neutral disengaged expression, but his eyes had shifted slightly. He was watching the *Professore* intensely.

"Could he have not?" repeated Urban VIII, this time with an insistent edge to his voice.

Galileo looked at his old friend.

"Is that what you believe, Your Holiness, that God is playing a trick on us with the stars? That my observations were in error? A heavenly joke?"

He looked wounded by the very possibility that Urban VIII could even entertain such a preposterous thought and stared at his once great colleague and friend like he had never seen him before.

"I believe what you believe, Galileo," he said, raising an admonitory eyebrow, "but you must think of others. You must be patient that they take longer to be taught."

Galileo just frowned. His old defiance was rising despite the setting and the audience.

"That has always been a problem for you," said Urban VIII authoritatively.

Galileo tilted his head studiously, as he glanced up at the attendant who was barely pretending not to eavesdrop. He looked back at Urban VIII, this time with an expression of certitude and profound thought.

"You cannot teach a person something he does not already know," he said clearly. "You can only bring what he does know to his awareness."

It wasn't what either of the other two were expecting.

For a second, Barbarossi's eyes darted between the new pope and his academic sparring partner. Urban VIII took a moment to gather himself as well. When he spoke again, it sounded like he was trying to guide Galileo.

"To be fair, though, wouldn't it be unwise and harmful to assert that so many are wrong?"

Galileo didn't answer that immediately. He stared ahead, then drew a breath for control before giving his response. Barbarossi was watching keenly now.

"In questions of science, the authority of a thousand is not worth the humble reasoning of a single individual."

The attendant's eyes widened. Mild as the statement might be to anyone else, to say such a thing to the Pope was egregiously impolite. Urban VIII didn't say anything in protest, but he did seem mildly rebuffed, and something new, offended. His hand bearing the ruby ring moved gently back and forth on the arm of his chair.

Galileo noticed and nodding his deference, he added, "You have always been a reasoning individual, Holiness."

It was enough. Urban VIII smiled his acceptance of the embedded apology.

"Nevertheless, I will allow you to resume your writing. You may write in support of heliocentrism, but you must also fairly represent the alternative view."

Galileo looked like he was about to speak, but before he could utter a word, Urban VIII held up his hand commandingly.

"You do not have to advocate for it," he said firmly.

Galileo knew this had stopped being a discussion some time ago. Perhaps it had never been nor intended to be. He bowed his head politely. His eyes narrowed thoughtfully, and an idea forced its way to the forefront of his thinking.

"I will represent it...fairly," he said.

•

Someone had gotten to his friend, and while Galileo could still recognize certain aspects of him, he could also tell that a metamorphosis had occurred. The candidates of change were numerous. There were enemies in those cold stone halls, and while Urban VIII was a spiritual king over all the world as they had declared in the chapel, he was not immune to the princely influences around him. The most telling, of course, was the resurrection of advocacy for a fixed earth. He knew the Pope didn't believe in that. Something or someone had gotten to him.

He was just exiting the crowded waiting area where a clutch of Cardinals was standing up to follow the attendant, when his eye caught two familiar figures moving down the stairs. Cremonini and Colombe were walking with a retinue of Vatican scholars, including the newly elevated Tomasso Caccini. Just the looks on their faces told him that once again logic and science were being trumped by the forces of politics and ego.

Turning away, he hurried down the stairs, all too eager to be away from the place. The beautiful effects of the chapel which had dazzled him before, were now just reminders that the works of genius were too often only backdrops to the petty machinations of lesser men. He crossed through the chapel as an aria swirled about and exited the doors to the warm sunbathing St. Peter's. Like a man bursting through the ocean's surface from a great depth, he took a breath.

Waiting for him was Maria Celeste.

Her father's demeanor was not what she was expecting after an audience with the Pope.

"What did His Holiness say?" she asked tentatively.

Galileo looked at her. She hadn't seen him look that unsettled for a very long time.

"He wants me to be fair," he said crisply.

She frowned.

•

The sweating Bellarmine waved a flat hand.

"I am fine. Continue," he said.

"And do you think you were fair?" Ferrero reluctantly resumed his inquiry.

The memory had rekindled something in Galileo and Bellarmine noticed. The *Doctore* was angry, just as he had been that day when he was directed to treat a lie with respect.

Galileo looked at Ferrero as he had at Maria Celeste. Immense control was in play. With a stony tone of defiance, he said, "Entirely. I included both viewpoints fairly."

"You did not write a scientific treatise. You wrote a satire," corrected Bellarmine.

Galileo gave him a hard smile. It was just as defiant as the words.

"A debate between a wise man, representing you, and a fool you insultingly named Simplicio? The simpleton?" elaborated Ferrero incredulously.

It was obvious. Galileo wasn't budging on this point.

"I was writing from experience," he said neutrally.

Bellarmine looked physically uncomfortable again. He was really sweating now. With a finger tucked into the collar of his scarlet cape, he took a sip of water. Then panting slightly, he wiped his face.

"You mocked anyone who refuted heliocentrism," he said shaking his head.

Galileo started to speak, then noticing the cardinal's distress, held his tongue and looked concerned.

"And in so doing handed your enemies the one advantage they could never achieve on their own," said Ferrero irritably. Galileo's unwillingness to admit he had written the piece purely to provoke had him completely distracted.

Bellarmine looked like he might be recovering his breath now. Galileo looked from him to Ferrero.

He had to admit, the young man was right.

CHAPTER TEN

There are times when anger is the greatest propellant of the written word. All the impurities, the chattel and drag are excoriated in the heat of emotion and the words arrive clean, winnowed and sharp like tempered steel. Usually, it only lasts a short while before burning out, but there are times when the blast furnace continues to stoke. Such was the way *The Dialogue of Two Chief World Systems* was created. Originally, perhaps to avoid a red flag of suspicion, he had simply titled it, *A Dialogue on the Nature of Tides.* Despite the likelihood that ruse would not work, but it didn't matter. In his state of mind, there was no stopping his pen.

Each time he thought of the conversation with the Pope, an up-swell of anger, disgust and even betrayal would consume him and no matter what he was doing, he would feel the compulsion to return to the pen and strike back. The page was the only venue in which he was allowed to fight and fight he would in the most savage manner he knew.

It didn't hurt that he had his fans. Mostly they were members of an enlightened nobility who maintained a subservient, but resentful power dynamic with the Church. For them, it was difficult to hold sway over land, people, and treasure, to be endowed by birth and still have to lower one's head to the likes of a Maculani or Caccini. So, when word came that they could remain completely distant from the fray and yet see their pompous rivals lampooned, they were only too happy to quietly subsidize the angry genius. It provided great joy and amusement to see Galileo turn his high wattage intellect into a vicious pursuit, and the outcome promised to be highly entertaining and gratifying.

Of course, there were also those like Federico Cesi, who had founded the Lyncean Academy, named for Lynceus, the lynx, the mythological character renowned for his unusual sharpness of sight. It was the kind of Utopian academic collective that only someone with the absolute protection of noble birth and a vast fortune would have the nerve to take on. For Cesi it was a natural progression of his own life. A descendant of the powerful Orsini family, he had been drawn to the principles of Copernicus and had balked at the desire of his father that he take on more statesmanlike endeavors. More importantly, he was also his mother's son and enjoyed both her emotional and financial encouragement and so, was free to go his own way.

For Cesi, Galileo was a god.

He also knew Maffeo Barberini from his days as an intellectual confederate. Given his connections, he had gotten word that as Urban VIII he had given Galileo permission to write again, and he had also heard the rumor that he had hobbled the *Professore* with a ridiculous condition.

When Galileo confirmed that, Cesi had made him an offer, an alliance that seemed both perfect and intellectually protective. The Academy, which had long adored and fostered Galileo, would subsidize the work and they would silently underwrite the cost of printing. It would also serve as a venue for its cataloguing and dissemination throughout all of European scholarship. All Galileo had to do was write.

The instructions by the Pope had been simple. Be fair.

Maria Celeste knew there was something different about her father after the meeting in the Vatican. The tidal change in his mood from the optimism when he entered to the suppressed determination in his face when he walked out were indicators of that. Now, she saw something else that worried her even more. She had seen some of what he was writing. He had asked her to look, and to give her opinion. At first, she didn't know what to make of it. It seemed like a scientific argument, but the context was a completely different and the combination of styles and possibly even intent were novel and difficult to immediately grasp. This was no scientific paper in the purest sense. This was a drama purporting the scientific principles of its main characters.

"What is this?" she asked.

"My new work."

She furrowed her brow at the curious nature of his answer.

"Who do you intend to read this?" she asked as he gave her a dry little smile.

"Why, the world, my dear. The world."

He was playing some sort of game, and she didn't like it. She also didn't like the potential risk of this new effort.

"I notice you chose not to write in Latin." She looked over the top of the paper at him. "It's in Italian."

"You see a problem with that?" he asked.

She concentrated for a moment as she formulated her answer. "There is a certain sophistication to the message that seems contradictory to the choice of language. You really think a hod carrier or swineherd is going to understand this?

He shrugged. "I don't know, but he should have the opportunity to try."

Her eyes shot off the page again. "Or perhaps she?"

He smiled appreciatively at her point.

"I was intelligent before I was educated, and so were you. Others likely are as well. Why should I deny them such an insight by writing in Latin?"

He had a point. She nodded, moving on. Once again, a certain democratic quality, defiant of the exclusion of class structure was creeping into his work. It wasn't the first time he had attempted such a thing, and Maria Celeste felt certain that understanding what he was really up to was even more important now.

"It has the style of a drama," she said. "Almost a production, and these three characters..."

"Yes," he chuckled.

"This hero of your story is obviously Salviati?"

"Yes," said Galileo.

"Named after one of your old teachers?"

"Yes. Fillipo Salviati was a great man."

"But the words he is using in his argument with the bystander Sagredo and the idiot Simplicio, those words are yours."

His smile widened. "Yes. What do you think?"

"I think it is brilliant. I think it is dangerous."

"Those often go together," said Galileo.

She looked a little weary at that. She was trying to be honest with him. She cared for and loved him. He was trying to be clever and yet was potentially doing so at his peril.

"I think," she said and paused before pushing ahead. "I think, where you have no rival in the work of science, you may not be as sure-footed in the subjective realm of art."

He instantly flashed, but before he could speak, she went on. "The physical laws are absolute, metrics that can be reliably measured and objectively discussed. Drama is a shifting sand, unpredictably variable even with the same audience. It depends on factors that have no logic."

He nodded. Sometimes she seemed to be more his daughter than at others. Now was definitely one of those times.

"I do have a question," she said.

"Yes?"

"Perhaps the most critical one," she continued.

"Go on," he said.

"Who is Simplicio?"

Before he could answer, they were interrupted by the sound of a horse stopping in front of the house. Both of their faces showed concern. They knew, an unexpected visitor at the home of Galileo Galilei was more often than not, a harbinger of bad news.

When the door opened of its own accord without a polite knock, they stiffened, but the tread was light, not a heavy menacing approach. A second later, a young man appeared in the door. He was dressed well and bore a striking resemblance to a younger version of the old man seated at the desk. He did not look at all comfortable.

"Vincenzio!" said Maria Celeste, her facing breaking open in a huge happy smile.

She rushed over and hugged him. Galileo rose from his chair and walked over with his arms wide. He closed them around both of his children and for a moment indulged in the sense of what he might have had if life were a little less unforgiving all those years ago.

The hug finally separated and before he could say a word, Maria Celeste was already walking to the kitchen.

"I know," she said," this calls for a really good wine."

"She is my daughter," said Galileo chuckling.

The choice of words appeared to hit Vincenzio poignantly. His daughter. Intellectually, he understood that his father had been forced to give them up, but in this matter, there was far more than just the intellectual at play.

Galileo turned and gestured toward a chair, indicating that Vincenzio sit.

"Are you well, my son?" he said.

"I am," answered Vincenzio.

"And your studies?"

Maria Celeste walked back in with the wine and cups. Vincenzio didn't answer at first, but instead looked down reluctantly. Maria Celeste and Galileo looked at each other in silent conference. They both knew that this was not simply a cordiality. Vincenzio had something significant to tell them.

"I want you to know, I have appreciated your continued support. You did not have to pay my tuitions. I know that," he began.

"I wish"—Galileo looked aggrieved— "I could have done more."

"I am leaving the study of laws," said Vincenzio.

Galileo and Maria Celeste stopped short and looked at him.

"What?"

"I am going to do something else. I want to study music."

"The law is a profession that champions the truth," said Galileo emotionally. "And you...would have protections in this world." With an incredibly painful expression he added, "Without those protections, the very things you love can be taken from you."

Maria Celeste looked at her father. There was so much more in that statement.

"I am going to study music."

The irony was completely lost on Galileo. He didn't think about a similar conversation he had so many years ago with his own father when he told him that he was forgoing medicine for the less compensated field of mathematics. He also didn't remember the identical emotions in play that day.

He drained his cup of wine and poured another.

"My teachers say I have a gift. I am going to be a lutenist."

"Oh, well, so you have made up your mind. Do you expect me to support you in this?" said Galileo, emptying the cup again.

"It would help," said Vincenzio. "I plan to marry, you see."

At that both Maria Celeste and Galileo looked shocked, almost like they hadn't considered him as a man, of an age that such things were done. For her it was excusable. With the dowry requirements the lack of legitimacy would necessitate, she had put the possibility of love, marriage and family out of her mind. Even if she were legitimized, to make her attractive to a decent husband would have required more money in dowry than he had. No dowry would be necessary for Vincenzio, though Galileo's support while he was establishing himself would help.

For once Galileo was at a loss for words. He went to reach for the bottle. It was empty.

"I'll get that," said Vincenzio as Maria Celeste started to rise. It was almost like an opportunity for relief had presented itself, and he wasn't about to neglect it.

He grabbed the empty bottle and walked from the study. With the same look that every father since Adam has given his son, Galileo said, "He is nothing like me."

"And yet, exactly the same," said an amused Maria Celeste.

Galileo looked at her with mild shock and offense. Then seeing the near mocking nature of her expression, his own face relaxed, and he smiled.

"Well, his grandfather was the most celebrated lutenist in Italy, so I suppose he comes by it honestly."

"And the obstinance?" she chided.

"Perhaps his mother's side of the family," he said dryly.

Maria Celeste chuckled.

"Beyond that, it's a mystery." He could barely contain his smile.

•

"You did not approve of the marriage?" asked Ferrero.

Galileo roused from the recollection and looked at the young Jesuit.

"It was not the marriage, nor his choice. It is an inconvenient absolute; an old man's and a young man's estimation of connubial readiness are never aligned."

Bellarmine looked amused. He understood what Galileo was saying completely.

"So, it is like high and low tide, then? Always in opposition," said Ferrero.

Galileo looked at him and smiled with surprised delight. It surprised Ferrero how good the genuine appreciation of the old genius suddenly made him feel.

"That's very good, Ferrero," he said, and continuing his original line of thought, "The girl he loved...Sestilia Bocchinieri, was a fine a girl. Beautiful, in the way all the great paintings of women are beautiful, and in life, she had a certain"—he searched for the right word before smiling slightly— "music about her."

Galileo's smile faded and he looked thoughtful and a little sad.

"I didn't begrudge him the love I was forced to relinquish." He shot a look at Bellarmine, who glanced away. "And while I was not without some means, there were so many mouths to feed. The baby birds, especially in the Catholic nest had bottomless beaks."

At that Ferrero looked a little off put. "I don't understand," he said.

"I was supporting two of the Poor Clares. I had been prohibited from publishing for several years. My funds were not unlimited." He smiled as a thought came to him.

"Even the ocean has a bottom, my dear man. Besides, the boy was right. His teachers were right. He was a born lutenist. Though for a while, my refusal kept him away."

•

Just about the time that Galileo was putting the final touches to his new work, in far off Rome a new enterprise was getting started that would eventually be the rock against which all the work of his life would collide. It was called the Congregation of the Inquisition, and it was described to the new Pope as something that would provide a means of tempering the outrageous behaviors that were being reported in heretical Spain by forming a bridge between the prosecutorial inquiries and the statutes of Holy Rome. In short, it was billed to Urban VIII as a way to reestablish the Church's control of the rogue enterprise. Soon though, even as politically connected and adroit a mind as Urban VIII's would discover, harnessing that beast was almost impossible.

He had allowed them to convene with the qualification that papal officers be included in the proceedings, but it was as much to have a spy embedded as to drive any objectives. As he might have predicted, the more conservative players in the Collegio began lobbying immediately. The Pigeon League and Father Caccini were proving indefatigable in trying the turn the world to their own devices, and where unctuous flattery could serve better than intelligence, they flourished. In particular, they identified a champion in the severe and menacing Father Maculani.

Their first order of business was to draw up a list of books that would be forbidden. Copies would be kept, but only in the custody of the Vatican archives and only under seal of the Inquisition. It was a calculated power grab. Once designated, not even the Pope could unilaterally release a book for broader consumption.

Now, despite his pragmatic and disappointing audience with Galileo in the aftermath of his coronation, Urban VIII was still a champion of scholarship, and when the proposal of a ban on books was disclosed to him by the Deacon Cardinal, he flew into a rage.

"These men of faith," he growled through his teeth, "who do they think they are that they could presume to fetter a mind given to a man by his God?"

The attendants in the papal apartment said nothing. This was the one place a pope was permitted to indulge his impulses as a man. The Deacon Cardinal waited until he had finished his rant and then softly spoke.

"Holiness, the Inquisition represents a powerful element and has enriched the Holy Mother Church in places such as Spain, where Christianity had been polluted and eroded by those very minds given to men. Perhaps when minds are in the grasp of the unholy one, they need fettering."

He knew the Deacon Cardinal was right, Spain had been overrun by infidels and Jews. In the minds of most of the church hierarchy, the reclamation of holy icons to increase the Vatican treasury's wealth and the expungement of those opposing influences could only be accomplished by the force and fear of the Inquisition.

There was little he could say, but in that moment, his mind went immediately to concern for his beloved Galileo.

"These will be a judgment on all works published to date?" asked Urban VIII.

"And going forward, Holiness," said the Deacon Cardinal. "An exception would require a papal bull."

That, Urban VIII knew, would be a declaration of civil war within the Church. It was done. He smiled and reached out his hand to the deacon cardinal, who took it obediently and leaned forward to kiss the ring.

•

It is no small thing to ban books. For one thing the logistics alone make it an arduous undertaking. On the plus side, human laziness on the part of the burners could be counted on to mitigate. Those that would have zealously read every line of every text were in short supply, and so the initial screening of flagged books was assigned to junior scholars pressed into service by the Congregation. While there might be little the more progressive minds in the Church could do to stop the process, they weren't obliged to simply sit by and allow it to have widespread effect. That was why the very private letter from Cardinal Bellarmine arrived at the Galileo home with the admonition to take care with the new work allowed by His Holiness.

When the first draft of the *Dialogue* arrived for review at the Congregation, the clerk who'd been assigned, didn't see much to worry about. Even the title, *A Dialogue on the Nature of Tides*, seemed mild enough, but when he saw the name of the author, he knew to ask for a senior scholar. As luck would have it, that was Lodovico Delle Colombe. To say that the text itself was not what he was expecting was a colossal understatement. He was still struggling with it days later as he sat in the portico of the *Collegio*.

"What is it?" asked Cremonini when he saw his colleague's baffled expression.

"Galileo's book," he said, not quite sure how to continue.

Just those two words were enough, however. The mention of the dreaded name seemed to have stimulated some innate alarm, and Cremonini rushed over to lean in and read. After a few moments he frowned too.

"What is this?" he asked.

"I don't know," said Colombe. "It seems that *Doctore* Galilei has abandoned science for the *Comedia delle Arte*."

Cremonini didn't look convinced.

It took them a week to figure out what he was up to. When they brought the text and the disposition on its acceptability back to the clerk, their notes made the volume almost half again as long.

"Send this to the *Professore*," said Colombe snidely.

When Galileo read their response, a wide smile spread across his face. It was almost too good to be true. They seemed to have overlooked the substance of his argument. They objected to the title and the veracity of the discussion of tidal movement, as they said it could be interpreted by some to describe a moving earth. Picking up his pen, Galileo struck through the title. Now, it was simply "*A Dialogue*." Remarkably, they had not objected to the conversations of the characters. He'd been smart to characterize his own voice as that of Salviati, the academician in the fiction, so they had raised no objection. As there was no such real character, and no one would want to claim the mantle of the satirically ridiculous Simplicio, he felt sure he had managed to indirectly make his case, but he had made one critical error.

The science behind his points was flawless and elegantly put. As a satirist though, he had included a line, a line that when the revised copy returned to the Congregation, Cremonini was only too happy to see remaining.

"Has he published this yet?" he asked Colombe.

"Enrico Parma has already disseminated a hundred copies in Florence," he answered with a nasty smile.

From there they wasted no time in arranging a meeting with Urban VIII.

•

It had already been enough of a trying day for His Holiness when Father Barbarossi leaned in to remind him that the two eager scholars were waiting. His face showed it. Nothing other than a trying encounter came with those two. The only question was, "How big a problem would result?"

"Bring them in," he said wearily.

They almost ran into the room, before genuflecting dramatically to kiss his ring. Even before they straightened up, Colombe was offering up the *Dialogue* like a sacrifice. Urban VIII took it from him and seeing the authorship, smiled with a keen, pleased look. To Cremonini, this was perfect. When he showed Galileo's great offense to the Pope, the reversal of joy would make his anger even hotter. Like with any *Comedia* it was all about timing.

"Oh? Galileo has written a *Comedia*?" Urban VIII said with interest.

"Indeed, Your Holiness," said Cremonini calculatingly.

"How clever." Urban VIII" scanned it quickly. "A scientific discussion among colleagues." He looked impressed, even delighted at the literary innovation. "Oh, ho," he chuckled. "I would imagine, you two are not pleased as he has the fool, holding with principles much like your own."

The Pope was mocking the two of them, assuming that they were there to try and get his support in condemning his old friend. Surely though, he thought, they must know I agree with Galileo.

That's when Cremonini made his move.

"Oh Holiness, we would not intrude upon the Church's business and your attentions simply for our own offense."

He lowered his head and placed his hand over his heart. Both Urban VIII and Barbarossi looked piqued.

"Not at all, Holy Father," echoed Colombe.

"What is it then?" asked the pontiff.

Cremonini looked up innocently. He started to take a step toward the throne of St. Peter, then hesitated as if uncertain as to how to assist. It was all a performance. Urban VIII knew that. Nevertheless, he waved a hand for

Cremonini to approach. He stepped up next to the seat and reached across to turn the pages to the indicting passage. Lowering his head in an act of humble embarrassment for the Pope, Cremonini pointed at the offending line of dialogue.

At first Urban VIII said nothing. Without betraying his own effort, the adroit Barbarossi looked down at an angle and read as well. A second later, Urban VIII's face began to assume a slow spread of flushed rage.

Without looking up, Cremonini smiled.

•

"You had Simplicio, the idiot, say that God could have made the universe any way he wanted to and still make it appear to us the way it does," said Ferrero emotionally.

Both Bellarmine and he showed what they were thinking. For such a smart man, Galileo had allowed emotion to cloud his judgment, and gave his enemies the one opportunity they needed. In fact, if he had tried, he couldn't have designed a better downfall for himself.

"Yes," said Galileo with a tone of regret.

"You put the Pope's favorite argument of compromise in the mouth of the person who had been ridiculed throughout the dialogue," said Ferrero.

"And you removed the one ally who could save you," said Bellarmine.

Galileo looked like the gravity of that conclusion carried a physical toll as well.

"Simplicio was Cremonini and Colombe," said Galileo futilely.

Bellarmine sighed heavily, as if trying to get his breath.

"You know, as a satirist, you make an excellent scientist," he said haltingly.

Galileo smiled bitterly. He looked like he was just about to speak when the sound of Bellarmine's chair scraping harshly on the floor intruded. Both Ferrero and Galileo jerked to attention as the portly cardinal coughed weakly, then clutched his chest and fell forward.

"Eminence!" cried Ferrero leaping from his seat.

He grabbed Bellarmine by his shoulders and turned him onto his back. The old man's eyes were wide with unreasoning terror as his failing heart pumped an inadequate amount of blood to his brain. It occurred to the alarmed Ferrero that in that moment, his mentor looked like a giant infant; sprawled, helpless, unable to rise, eyes clearly unfocused and disoriented.

"Guard! Help!" he yelled as Bellarmine's breathing became precipitously less effective.

The door swung open and the heavyset, cretinous guard rushed in. He looked immediately at Galileo.

"What has he done?" he asked, looking at Galileo.

Ignoring the stupidity of the question, Ferrero looked up and yelled, "We must get him to the infirmary!"

•

Galileo never saw Bellarmine again. Given his corpulence, the dying cardinal was too much for the cretinous guard and the skinny young Jesuit to carry from the room. By the time others arrived to provide the additional help, Bellarmine was gasping, and his color had gone from an inflamed sanguine to an ashen demise.

Ferrero knew, but, as with any situation in which a beloved is dying, he denied the inevitable, and insisted that they carry his mentor to the surgeon. They lifted him and shuffling their feet, lumbered down the stone corridor as Galileo was hauled away in the opposite direction to the prison cells below. It was no minor trip for any of them. The heavy cardinal went from a kind of wriggling agitated mass to literally dead weight by the time they left the stairwell and started across the courtyard. Even the most optimistic had to acknowledge that the fixed stare and absence of movement of his chest and belly meant only one thing. It was confirmed when the physician dragged the cover over Bellarmine's inanimate face and crossed himself with finality. Instantly, the rest in attendance did likewise.

Now the advocacy for Galileo fell squarely to Ferrero. It wasn't a duty he would have taken on under any other circumstances. While he had come to respect him and appreciated his brilliance, he still didn't particularly like Galileo even though the man was smarter than anyone he had encountered. Ferrero guessed that must carry with it a certain irritation and impatience, and over time, a certain irascibility, but still, there was something about the way he just couldn't avoid conveying it that was always a little infuriating. In contrast, Bellarmine was also a brilliant man, but he didn't convey it in a heavy handed or punitive manner. Of course, he was not a genius, and Ferrero considered that maybe that accounted for some of the difference. That difference was what led to the distinction for Galileo that amounted to hate in so many.

No, this was not a duty that Ferrero would have chosen, but as he looked at his fallen mentor and friend, he knew that he could not abandon it now. He sighed. He would make it work. He convinced himself that he was not just defending Galileo, but he was defending the cause of intelligence, of real scholarship in the face of ridiculous suppression. In that, Ferrero could find a meaning he could hold onto. The cause was suddenly bigger than the man.

That night Galileo resumed his etching work in the cell wall with the handle of his spoon. The words were already finished, but he decided that he should take the opportunity to furrow them deeper. The recent reminder of why he was really on trial made him a little less certain that his brash cerebral argument would prevail, and it somehow made the idea behind his defiant declaration in the stone even more important.

He was still at it when he heard the heavy metallic tread of the guard approaching his cell. Brushing off his robes, he walked back to his cot and sat down, pulling the table with its single candle closer to him to shroud the graffitied wall in darkness.

The letters disappeared from view, just as the cretinous guard leaned his broad face against the bars and simply said, "Cardinal Bellarmine is dead."

With no more ceremony, he turned and walked off as Galileo stared into the darkness.

CHAPTER ELEVEN

If Urban VIII ever wondered if his reaction to Galileo had been engineered by Cremonini and Colombe, it might have been when he was so quickly presented with the *Formal Authorization for Heretical Examination by the Inquisition*. Even in his raw emotional state, the speed with which the papal writ was placed beneath his pen for authorization was suspicious. Of course, by then it was too late to reconsider. He had already given the scholars permission to prepare the text.

Now it seemed likely that it had already been prepared well before he was given Galileo's book. As he looked at the parchment, a significant pang of loss and sadness arose, but feeling the scrutiny of the scholars' eyes on him, he lowered the tip of his pen and slashed his signature.

I'm not the one casting the first stone, he thought, but he also had to admit that he wasn't the one turning the other cheek either. The pretense was heresy. The reality was affection spurned.

Now with the Pope's approval, Cremonini and Colombe gathered the document and almost ran from the room with glee.

Not since Torquemada had the name of an Inquisitor inspired such apprehension as Maculani's. Unlike where his predecessor had been a hammer of prosecutorial power, Maculani was more like a scalpel. Possessed of a special wit and intelligence, he was incredibly effective when examining a heretical candidate. Almost like a forerunner of a devastating criminal prosecutor, he could weave a line of questions that would tighten with each answer until the noose was close around the defendant's neck. Originally trained as a military man, he approached his Inquisitorial duties with the same order, strategy, and discipline of a field marshal. In short, he was a very dangerous man.

Yet, just then, when Cremonini and Colombe hurried toward him with the document in hand, he didn't appear immediately eager to begin his examination.

Perhaps it was because he had just sat down to his lunch and knew he would not be able to eat in peace. Perhaps it was because the unabashed petty joy they displayed was so irritating to him. Even so, his eyes cut to the unmistakable scroll.

"His Holiness has finally agreed to refer the matter to the Inquisition?" he asked.

"Yes," said Colombe.

"We felt certain when His Holiness saw the blasphemous writing and how Galileo mocked his generosity, he would have no alternative," said Cremonini.

Maculani dipped a small piece of bread in a bowl of soup with his long sharp fingernails and chewed thoughtfully.

"Yes," he said. "Galileo should have been charged with heresy the last time. That mistake has allowed evil to flourish."

His dark eyes shined at the prospect of an opportunity to address an offense to Christianity via the Inquisition's powers, when the Church proper had been too liberal.

"His Holiness," he said crossing himself, "was distracted by his love for the genius of a man and he allowed an affront to God."

Cremonini and Colombe crossed themselves and smiled.

They had found exactly the right man for the job.

•

The heretical trial of Galileo was not like most trials for heresy. In the vast majority of cases, the accused was some poor ignorant peasant or member of a disenfranchised group such as a Muslim convert or a compelled Jew. The evidence against them was usually hearsay or circumstantial at best. In the case of the former, it was often the mere utterance of an accusation by a jealous neighbor or vengeful landlord that set the wheels of persecution in motion. In the latter, it was the prejudicial accident of birth to some hated demographic. In either case, the compulsion for the accused was always to avoid being "Put to the Question," the chilling euphemism for torture.

In rare cases, an actual trial was conducted, and real evidence considered. Then, if judged by some composition of a jury, usually clergy, to be guilty, the condemned heretic would be put to a purification of the flesh, also a euphemism for torture. This would go on until the subject agreed to publicly recant or until he or she died in agony.

Since Galileo had not only written the offending words for which he would be tried but had also enlisted a publisher to spread his harmful ideas, his trial and purification would have to be every bit as public a spectacle to send a warning to others. From Maculani's perspective, it was fantastic. The presence of real evidence created a unique opportunity with a subject of Galileo's stature and favor. The world would be watching. From the most common to His Holiness, the cause and power of the Inquisition would be on full display.

In the future, there would be many so called "trials of the century," legal proceedings that gripped the attention of the world or a nation, but the examination of Galileo, was the first, and it would prove every bit as sordid and public as the ones to follow. With his compulsion and intimidation of the publisher Enrico Parma, Maculani now had the means to make sure that every detail of the hearing, and how he conducted it, would be shared everywhere. As pamphlets describing the coming charges of heresy were read, an excitement among the public heightened with the very human desire to see the high and mighty brought to heel. Soon, word swept across all of Europe. And since Galileo had chosen to prosecute his blasphemous theories in Italian, the language of the common man, so would the details of his own prosecution be shared for their entertainment and gratification. In that way Maculani was as farsighted as Galileo. He and the Pope understood that in the new social awareness of the Renaissance, the average person could not be taken for granted. This trial provided an opportunity for something new, a populist political form of power.

Parma had not been happy about his conscription by the Inquisition, but any time he reconsidered his involvement, he would look at his daughters and remember the gentle caress and veiled threat of Maculani's claws against their cheeks. Nevertheless, he made sure that each time a new edition for the press was dictated by the Pigeon League, that Viviani and Torricelli received an advance copy, which they took immediately to Sister Maria Celeste.

She brought these copies with each resupply of food and wine to Galileo, tucked carefully within the weave of the basket to avoid detection by the guards. At first, her father chuckled at the poor copy, the weak language skill and the absurdity.

"This must be killing Parma to have to print such, excrement. If only because of the style," he said picking through the delicacies in the basket.

Silence followed, and he looked up at the somber faces of Ferrero, Viviani, Torricelli and Maria Celeste.

"What is wrong?" he asked.

"For a brilliant man, sometimes you don't seem to understand the dangers around you," said Ferrero.

"Papa, everyone is reading this. Many have already been convinced that the *Dialogue* is a work inspired by Satan," implored Maria Celeste.

Viviani and Torricelli nodded their agreement of the assessment.

"Satan?" said Galileo incredulously. "I have simply documented the work of God!"

Ferrero hesitated to speak at first, but a look from Maria Celeste was clearly a charge to explain.

"You are not seeing it, *Professore*. Perhaps because you know what you intended, perhaps because you are in here and cannot observe the changes in the world right now. When the *Sidereus* was being considered by the College of Cardinals, it was not with the weight of heresy. It was an assessment of the compatibility of the work with scripture."

"Yes," said Galileo.

"Now though, you have been charged with heresy, not just for the content of the work, but for your intentions, for disobedience to a directive by His Holiness, for an offense against the authority of the Church."

Galileo looked ahead thoughtfully. This had nothing to do with heresy, he knew. This was about vendetta and politics and committing a far greater offense than of one to God. He had bruised the feelings of men in power, and if history had proven one thing, there was no surer path to the gallows or pyre than that.

Arrogant though he was, Galileo was still almost purely an intellectual creature, and as such he had been blind to a fundamental mistake.

"An offense against the authority of the Church." Galileo repeated Ferrero's words.

"Yes, that is the charge they will formally bring," said Ferrero.

"So, the merits of the work, its validity, its truth and support of God—"

"Irrelevant, I am afraid," said Ferrero.

"Well, if this is simply a matter of embarrassment as to my method, perhaps I might consider a limited acknowledgment of that, while maintaining that the science is still legitimate?" he offered.

Ferrero looked like he didn't know how to answer the question, but his expression showed that there was no such simple answer.

"What?" asked Galileo.

"It seems that your sin, my brilliant father, is not in the Holy Word nor even in your beloved *Divine Comedy*. The truth is that you have committed the only really unforgivable sin, and that is the embarrassment of power," said Maria Celeste.

While it wouldn't have seemed possible mere hours before, Galileo considered that the mood in the dank cell had just gotten darker. He looked at Ferrero.

"There is more, isn't there?"

Ferrero looked at him. His eyes carried an awful awareness. For the first time, Galileo looked like he was having a moment of doubt.

"Yes," said Ferrero.

•

As he dressed that morning Urban VIII found himself in an unsettling, unprecedented position. He rose and bathed as he always did, then stood for his attendants to dress him in his *mantum* and pileolus. All of that was normal and a ritual he had come to like. Today, however, a strange sense of conflict that possessed him. Today, he would be facing something no other pope ever had.

As the signatory of the authorization for the coming Inquisitional hearing, he was obliged to preside over the same trial where he was also the aggrieved party. That would have been enough to challenge most pontiffs but adding on the deep-seated personal emotions he felt toward the accused made it almost feel like the word "trial" applied to him as well.

It was a test of his objectivity, certainly, and in any other mortal would have cast doubt on the legitimacy of the dual function. In fact, only God could assume to do such a thing, but as God's instrument on earth he was expected to possess the capacity. Besides, he knew that the sharp-fanged officers of the Inquisition and their slathering chorus among the Pigeon League would see his refusal of the duty as betrayal of his position.

And so, as he sat in the great seat and looked out at the capacity crowd in the galleries and the formal Jury of Cardinals, who would decide on the guilt or innocence of his former beloved friend, he couldn't help but feel a diminution of his own soul. The joy and spirit of God that had possessed him the day of his coronation was a scant flicker in comparison. He was questioning himself. He had let a very human emotion drive him to sign the order for the trial, and his solicitation of Bellarmine to aid their mutual friend was his attempt to make it right. When word came that Bellarmine had died, it seemed to him a sure sign that God had turned his face away from what was about to happen.

Maculani sat at the prosecution table waiting, a calm, deadly look on his face. Stacks of papers and copies of Galileo's publications were neatly arranged at his elbows like stacked arms awaiting a battalion. To his right, a council of Vatican scholars including Cremonini and Colombe loomed like eager vultures at a distance. Next to them, Tomasso Caccini sat at the recorder's table ready to capture every detail.

The far door opened, and Galileo entered flanked by prison guards. Even though he was old and small, the number of armed men surrounding him gave a casual impression of extreme danger. Following behind were the similarly benign figures of Ferrero, Viviani and Torricelli carrying their documents from the interrogation room. Ferrero, in particular, didn't look good. The loss of his mentor and the burden of defending Galileo alone against the Inquisitor was apparent to anyone who bothered to look. He glanced over as he passed at the women's section and made eye contact with Maria Celeste. She smiled, but it was a poor attempt at encouragement. Both knew what she really thought. In a telling move, Ferrero looked away and hurried on toward the empty table where Galileo was just sitting down.

At the opposing table, Maculani noticed and smiled.

Ferrero was taking his place when he looked over and saw Maculani's amused expression. It was offensive and intimidating at once, and everything in him said, "Don't look away," but he just couldn't stop himself.

Leaning over, the rattled young Jesuit whispered to Galileo, "I beg you, do not give Maculani anything with which to work."

Galileo looked back at him and said nothing.

"Remember, your intellect is not on trial," said Ferrero.

"Good," said Galileo dryly. "In my experience the greater the intellect, the greater the penalty."

That wasn't the answer he was hoping for, but before Ferrero could say another word, Urban VIII raised his hand. The room went quiet in anticipation. Maculani looked up. Caccini dipped his pen and prepared to write.

Unlike the last time Galileo had answered a charge in the chapel, the sense in the room was much graver. This time there were wolves.

"Inquisitor," said the Pope. "You may begin."

Maculani stood and turned toward Urban VIII. He bowed reverentially. It was almost too much. Cremonini and Colombe, stifled smiles.

"Your Holiness," said Maculani.

Urban VIII made the sign of the cross.

Turning toward the Jury of Cardinals, Maculani made a similar obeisance. "Your Eminences," he said.

The Cardinals nodded their acknowledgement. Finally, Maculani turned toward Galileo.

"*Signore*," he said, with a similar nod.

Cremonini and Colombe smiled. Caccini grinned as he scribbled the introduction into the record. It was a calculated insult, foregoing his earned titles. Galileo didn't bite. He just stared at Maculani. Next to him, however, Viviani, Torricelli and Ferrero flushed with anger. In the women's section and in the papal seat, two other faces showed slightly more restrained but similarly offended reactions.

"*Professore*," corrected Ferrero vigorously.

Cremonini saw an opportunity and stepped up next to Urban VIII and whispered something.

The Pope sighed softly. Betraying nothing, he just nodded and said, "Monsignor Ferrero, this is not a trial, but a tribunal of faith. We will be guided by the Lord and need not act like lawyers."

Ferrero looked confused and quelled. It was true. The rules of an Inquisition tribunal were often constructed as it went along. That made the defense even more difficult. In the most extreme cases, if the accused were suspected of intermittent possession by witchery or the devil, he or she could be gagged and prohibited from offering any counterargument. Ferrero had half-risen. Now, with the abrupt rebuke from the Pope, he shrank back into his seat. Galileo watched his former friend and, seeing the desolate misery on his face, suddenly realized the gravity of his own disadvantage.

Maculani smiled tightly. The restraints were off, and he was free to attack. He looked Galileo in the eye as he announced loudly, "Galileo Galilei, you are accused of heresy and disobedience to the instruction of Rome. Do you deny it?"

Galileo stood slowly. The room went silent again, and everyone leaned forward ever so slightly, so as not to miss a word.

He cleared his throat and in an even, strong voice answered, "As I have said before, I believe that it is harmful to souls to make a heresy of that which is already proven."

The members of the Pigeon League, groused at the response, and the Cardinals in the jury didn't look impressed with his cleverness. Ferrero could tell that unless something miraculous occurred, the best they could hope for would be a merciful judgment. That, he knew, would depend on him and how vigorously and effectively Galileo responded to their questions.

In the scholarly cohort, Colombe leaned over to Cremonini and whispered worriedly, "We should have pushed for censure. He is too clever to be allowed to speak."

Cremonini was watching the Pope. What exactly His Holiness was feeling each time the accused *Professore* opened his mouth wasn't completely clear, but it seemed from his misery that each word struck like a tiny painful dart.

"No," said Cremonini calculatingly. "The *Doctore* flies on the wax wings of Icarus." He grinned. "So much greater then his fall."

Colombe didn't understand him completely, but he had learned to trust Cremonini's judgment and sat back with a comfortable smile.

Unlike during the academic hearing years before, Maculani was not affected by Galileo's wit.

"Then you do not deny it," he said.

Galileo didn't flinch or hesitate. "I do not think it is necessary to believe that the same God who has given us our senses, reason, and intelligence wishes us to abandon their use."

A slight murmur rumbled through the audience, an a few faces in the jury of Cardinals even looked impressed. Despite the severity of the situation, Galileo's coolly profound answer had made an impression. Urban VIII's eyes welled up slightly, though only the attendant standing closest to him noticed.

Despite the momentary win, Viviani and Torricelli still looked worried. Ferrero, who was watching Maculani, saw something that made him even more concerned. Maculani was enjoying the buildup and resistance by Galileo, as if it would make was coming have even more of an impact.

For a moment, Maculani just stood there staring at Galileo, then he turned and picked up a document. It was not a pamphlet, nor a book. It wasn't even a scientific paper. From where she was sitting Maria Celeste recognized what the Inquisitor was holding and felt a sense of the world dropping away beneath her.

It was a letter.

Holding it up between the tips of his sharpened nails, Maculani, didn't even bother to look at it. His attention was focused entirely on the accused.

"*Doctore* Galilei," he said, emphasizing the title with an edge of disrespect. It was a clever method for communicating how little he thought of the intellectual process of an academic when applied to matters of faithful obedience. "Have you ever referred to the Holy Academy and its officers of the Church as an *ass*?" he asked.

A gasp ripped through the chapel. The mere accusation was beyond outrageous. It was heresy in and of itself.

Ferrero looked desperately worried, and not just for Galileo. Depending upon how he was perceived in this line of questioning, and especially if Galileo were judged guilty, he could also be punished. Even if he weren't, his ambitions within the brotherhood might never recover. Suddenly, everyone had something at stake. By far the greatest impact was registering in the one spot Galileo couldn't afford, the charge of giving offense. The cardinals were sitting bolt upright, posturally on the warpath. Even if Galileo could somehow convince them that whatever Maculani held in his hand were not a direct insult to them, their mood had changed. The current of a corresponding wave of agitation rippled through them.

Finally, Urban VIII held up his hand and the room quieted again.

"If I have, the incident escapes me," said Galileo genuinely.

Maculani was good. He paused a little too long allowing the power of silent tension to build. Then he lowered the document in his hand, preparing to read. When he spoke, the menace was rapier sharp.

"Then I shall now read from your letter to Johannes Kepler," he said lethally and looked at the indicting text. "My dear Kepler, I wish that we might laugh at the remarkable stupidity of the common herd—"

Ferrero looked over at the jury. The effect on the members was devastating. Their ego was taking a direct hit, and Maculani was not letting up at all.

"—what can one say about the principal philosophers of this academy who are filled with the stubbornness of an ass—"

Ferrero didn't bother to look. The resulting cascade of audible gasps, outraged billowing, and indistinct angry shouting buffeted around him. He suddenly recalled the story of the Red Sea collapsing on Pharaoh's army. He could understand the sense of doom the Egyptians must have felt completely.

"—and they do not want to look at either the planets, the moon or the telescope, though I have freely and deliberately offered them the opportunity a thousand times?" read Maculani.

Now even Urban VIII looked angry.

Galileo, however, didn't show the slightest sign of emotion. He simply stared ahead as if completely immune to his own destruction. Maculani continued the assault. He was just getting to the best part.

"Truly, just as the ass stops its ears, so do these philosophers shut their eyes to the light of truth—"

Maria Celeste looked on in terror as most of the jurors were on their feet in protest. Cremonini and Colombe were openly smiling now. It was perfect. Even better than if he had been tried for the heresy of heliocentrism, Galileo was going to be judged on the charge of arrogance, and in that, they knew, not only was he universally guilty, but his punishment would be intolerable.

Even then, Maculani was not done.

"—and who can doubt," he started again only to almost be drowned out by the chorus of angry reaction. "And who can doubt," he repeated, "that when those devoid of any competence are made judges over experts and are granted authority to treat them as they please, it will bring about the ruin of the state."

He finished and looked up, smiling like a victor already. He crossed to the jury and handed the letter so that it could be shared and confirmed among the cardinals. As they saw it with their own eyes, the discharge of outrage boiled up anew.

After giving them just enough time to come to another crescendo of wounded pride, he turned to Galileo.

"How do you answer?" he asked.

All eyes turned. Galileo just looked calm, even, as if he had not expected the outcome to be any different. If anything, he seemed even more defiant in that moment of sure defeat than he had when he was making the case for the movement of the earth. He looked around, briefly making eye contact with his students, with Ferrero, and ever so briefly with Maria Celeste like he was saying goodbye to something.

"Long experience has taught me this about mankind. In matters of thought: the less people know and understand, the more positively they attempt to argue."

Defiant to the very end, thought Ferrero, as all around the room devolved into chaos. The jury was beyond control. Caccini scribbled frantically attempting to capture every letter of his heresy. In the galleries, a very small minority, including Maria Celeste tried to remain calm as the mob began braying its encouragement of a finding of guilt.

In the ranks of the scholars, Cremonini smiled and said to Colombe, "There are times I find it very hard to dislike *Professore* Galilei"—his smile broadened— "but then he opens his mouth and speaks."

Ferrero was watching the jury. As the cardinals reviewed the letter, their rancor continued to build to a consensus rage of indistinct expressions of vitriol and gestures of condemnation. It reminded him of a volcanic eruption he had seen as a boy, the *uber* explosion punctuated by extreme vapor and heat. What he witnessed now seemed just as deadly.

Looking concerned, the prison guards gathered up the one calm person in the room and nearly shoved him out the same door he had entered. Whatever was coming, it would have to be prescriptive and official for the satisfaction of the Church, but until that time they had to make sure he was protected. Otherwise, the cretinous guard knew, he would be the one paying with his flesh.

•

The deliberations were short. Not that anyone expected anything different. They could have given their verdict without even removing Galileo, but appearances and proprieties had to be met. Plus, there was the nature of the sentence. He had been proven a heretic, not for substance, but for disrespect and disobedience of a papal directive. At its worst, this could warrant excommunication if Urban VIII so desired, but in his heart, away from the baying pack, he knew he could never consign Galileo's soul to hell.

Not that there weren't those who tried to convince him. Cremonini and Colombe, made their appearance to congratulate him on upholding the dignity of his Holy Office and in a roundabout way tried to nudge him toward the ultimate punishment. To their disappointment, he declined to commit, but they departed happily to celebrate that at the very least, neither Galileo nor his irritating undeniable principles would be a bother to them again.

He was just about to shed his vestments when Barbarossi appeared with one more request for an audience. It was Maculani. Nodding wearily, the Pope signaled to let him in.

When the doors swung open, the Inquisitor was already wearing the same anticipatory smile he had shown when he realized his moment of victory at the trial. In an instant, Urban VIII felt both anger and worry. Sensing that, Maculani suppressed his smile and genuflected with humble extravagance.

•

Galileo sat in his cell and looked at the last of the wine waiting in the bottom half of his glass. It wasn't a sense of economy that kept him from finishing it off. It was the thought that therein was the last remnant of sunlight he might ever see. Even cast in the poor light of the candle, the garnet liquid still gave off more color and spectral texture than simple reflection should warrant. He was still considering allowing it to remain when the distant sound of approaching footsteps and the growing glow of an accompanying torch made him down it in a single swallow. His justification? That with the uncertainty of his fate, leaving wine in the glass would be a greater sin than anything the Inquisition could manufacture.

He was prepared for the large rough hands to close on him at any minute and drag him away to whatever doom awaited, when to his relief, the face of Ferrero and Maria Celeste suddenly appeared outside the bars of his cell.

"You're not here to celebrate, are you?" he asked wryly.

It was almost enough to bring a smile to their faces. Almost.

Getting into the prison had been tougher this time. The guards seemed to have already anticipated the verdict, and the moderate courtesies they had extended while there was still some doubt had all but evaporated with the day's resolution. If Maria Celeste hadn't been a nun, they wouldn't have let her through, but the power of the habit and the displayed crucifix won the moment.

The cretinous guard gave Galileo a menacing look as he unlocked the door.

"I don't mind staying," he said ominously to the guests.

Maria Celeste set the basket next to her father and smiling pleasantly answered, "Thank you. It won't be necessary."

Grudgingly, the guard stepped out and locked the cell door.

"Bang on the bars when you are ready to go," he said before moving away.

Galileo was already pawing through the basket. Finding what he was after, he lifted a bottle of wine and looked at it.

"Here's something worth celebrating," he said.

Ferrero and Maria Celeste looked immune to his levity. Galileo looked at Ferrero with a wise conciliatory expression.

"You think you failed," he said gently, and with a whimsical look that defied the peril he was facing added, "I think you have accomplished something in failing, that no one else could by any successful venture."

"What is that?" said a confused Ferrero.

"Our failure has managed to unite the Inquisition and the Holy See as never before."

His ironic perspective didn't seem to help their mood.

"You are worried what will happen," he added softly.

"I am worried that I know what will happen," replied Ferrero.

"I am guilty of being an intransigent. I am guilty of telling the truth. I am even guilty of almost holding good wine in worshipful consideration," he said pouring a glass.

"No other gods before me," said Ferrero absently quoting the prohibition from the commandments.

"Exactly!" said Galileo. "But I am not guilty of disobeying His Holiness, nor of offending God by sharing his accomplishment in the heavens. And if I am not mistaken, that was what I was being tried for."

Maria Celeste looked worried. Ferrero shook his head in frustration.

"They are not constrained by logic, *Professore*. The Inquisition may discover and condemn on other matters as they find them." He seemed hesitant to continue, but a grim encouraging nod from Maria Celeste and he took a breath and went on, "I am afraid they will push for more.

If the Pigeon League and Maculani can use the landslide of sentiment against you, they will do it.

Galileo held up his hand.

"I will not allow them to destroy a hundred years of scientific truth. No matter what they threaten to do to me."

Silence followed. There was not much either his daughter or his counsel could say. They both looked devastated. It touched Galileo's heart, and to encourage them he offered, "I cannot rely on his friendship, but once our pope was a true scholar. If within him, some remnant of that remains, then there is hope."

•

Unlike the day of the trial, the verdict morning saw the chapel almost completely empty. Despite Maculani's objection that the Pope's subjects needed to see the righteous judgment of God in action, Urban VIII had said no. He had already made enough concessions. A public spectacle would be playing to the Inquisition's one strength, intimidation, and he was inherently opposed to that. Now, only certain church officers and others wearing the designation of the Inquisition sat in the public galleries. Even Galileo's daughter, a nun, was banned from the hall.

The order of introduction was different as well. This time, the guards brought Galileo and Ferrero in ahead of everyone. Trailing behind were Viviani and Torricelli who looked bad enough that one might think they were they accused. The fact that even now they wanted to be associated with Galileo was not only touching but warranted his respect too. Opposing them, Maculani was already seated behind the prosecutor's table. Today he did not have an arsenal of documents. It was only him, waiting and watching with the appraising stare of a serpent evaluating a wounded bird.

The guards stepped back as Galileo and Ferrero sat. They waited a few minutes. Then a few more. Between Maculani's expression and the delay, it seemed clear. Something terrible was manifesting outside the hall. Finally, a door opened, and the Vatican scholars filed in. Among them Cremonini and Colombe wore smug anticipatory smiles. For the first time, Maculani looked away from the defendant's table to make eye contact with his two confederates. Both Galileo and Ferrero took note, though Ferrero showed more concern as the rest of the scholars filled in their section and sat. A moment later the sober jury of Cardinals entered and were seated in their box. Ever hopeful, Ferrero scanned their faces. In contrast, Galileo didn't even glance their way. It was like he already knew. Finally, Urban VIII walked in, flanked by his attendants. He sat and made the sign of the cross, and all heads in the chapel bowed.

When the moment of invocation had passed, he announced, "The body has reached a conclusion."

The others in the room crossed themselves in affirmation. Urban VIII looked at Galileo.

"Galileo Galilei you have been found vehemently suspect of heresy for the opinions that the sun lies motionless at the center of the universe, that the earth is not at its center."

It was the announcement Ferrero had feared. Not an indictment of his disobedience. They had without even addressing it, gone after the Copernican principle that Galileo had proven objectively. Not one word had been directed to the underlying theory or the discussion. He had been judged on his manner of derision for the sheep-like mentality of the church scholars and convicted of something entirely different. Justice, it seemed, was also a victim in God's court.

Even so, Galileo didn't flinch, as within him, an indignant outrage rose. Urban VIII was betraying everything he knew to be true. Ferrero glanced over at Galileo and saw a slight tension increase around his jaw. In the stacked galleries, faces alternatively broke into triumphant smiles or vicious sneers and shouts of condemnation.

"Heretic!"

"Blasphemer!"

"Infidel!"

Urban VIII raised his hand for quiet and waited until he had it, before continuing.

"Galileo, do you denounce your statements for the salvation of your soul?" he asked.

Now the room was completely silent. For the first time, Galileo turned and looked at his former friend. What he saw was almost completely unrecognizable. Urban VIII looked like something vital had died. He had become entirely the Pope. There appeared nothing left of the man Galileo knew, the one who had once viewed the world in humble wonder.

Even so, it had no impact on his answer.

"I do not, Your Holiness," he said simply staring back.

It was a profound moment, and Galileo's lack of alarm only stoked the building rage in the room. In contrast, Urban VIII's eyes had gone empty, as if the sentence he was about to levy was as much applied to himself as his brilliant former friend.

"Then you shall be put to the Question, and your soul purified by a trial of the flesh until you are ready to acknowledge your sin and beg God's forgiveness."

Viviani and Torricelli looked stricken. They crossed themselves and clasped their hands in fervent prayer. Maculani looked satisfied as Cremonini and Colombe clapped each other on the back. Even the Cardinals nodded with righteous justification. Only Galileo and Urban VIII registered no emotion at all.

The guards were just stepping forward to convey the condemned from the room, when Ferrero, his hands shaking, leaped to his feet.

"Holiness, I humbly beg that I might offer counsel, during his purification," he said.

It was a bold thing to say. A young Jesuit, barely a Monsignor, was addressing God's instrument on earth, the highest-ranking member of the Church with an audacious request. Maculani shot a look at Cremonini. He jumped to his feet and started over to whisper to Urban VIII, who waved him away. He was looking at Ferrero and clearly had no capacity for more input.

"You have permission to try," he said.

Ferrero turned to follow him from the chapel.

CHAPTER TWELVE

Galileo did not remain in his cell for long that night. The cohort assembled by Maculani for the Question was not by chance. Among those in attendance were specialists, members of the Inquisition whose natures, they believed, God had made to intuit how pain might be best applied to maximum effect. In another time they would be called sadists for their insight, and enjoyment of another's suffering. In the service of the Church, however, they were called inspired.

Now they waited.

In another part of the prison, Galileo listened as the approaching footsteps arrived to take him for his purification. He knew too well what that really meant. He would be tortured, until either by reason or in spite of it, he chose to confess. It mattered little that his words would be driven by the very natural desire to see pain end. All that really mattered in this political pursuit would be that Galileo had said what they wanted to hear.

The soft glow of the torch changed from a vague insinuation of light to amber and then brightened to illumination proper as it got closer to his cell door. Finally, the details of the cretinous guard and Ferrero appeared.

Galileo took note. Ferrero's expression was even more morose than it had been the night before.

The cretinous guard withdrew a scroll from his robe and read.

"Galileo Galilei, you have been found guilty of heresy and showing no remorse for your offense. By order of His Holiness, Pope Urban VIII, the Inquisition and Almighty God, you will now be put to a test of the flesh in order to cleanse your soul."

Galileo just stared ahead, as if not listening at all.

"If at any time your heart opens to God's truth and mercy, you will be afforded the opportunity to admit your crime and receive His grace in the Holy Court."

Having finished, he rolled the scroll back up and stuffed it into his robe before sliding the key into the lock to open the cell. It turned with a rough metallic grating sound and then *clanked* as the mechanism tripped. Galileo stood up.

The guard was both hoping and expecting for some overt demonstration of fear. That was at least what he was used to. Though his experience with prisoners tortured by the Inquisition was admittedly limited, he had seen a few. Granted they were mostly the uneducated, some gypsies and Jews and even one witch, but all, when they realized what was in store for them, had dropped their pretense of defiance and begged for mercy. He had really hoped that Galileo would do the same, but even as they exited the cell, the little academician maintained his calm self-control.

So much the better, he tried to justify to himself. It will just make his screaming surrender that much more enjoyable.

They walked up the corridor, past the other cells, where men cowered in privation and terror, until they arrived at a barred door. Turning the key again, the guard opened it and they continued on, descending a different flight of stairs to another lower wing.

Even as they approached, it occurred to Galileo that this must be exactly what Alighieri had in mind when he described the levels in the Divine Comedy. The damp cold intensified as they approached a flickering light, and then as they got closer, he could make out the details of the flames.

All along the walls were unfettered torches. Farther ahead, the mouth of the tunnel opened onto a large room, and as they arrived, the temperature changed from the penetrating cold to a fetid sweltering heat. The light cast a hellish hue on the details of the room, but it was the combination of the altering illumination of the flickering flames, the smells and sound that brought the terrible nature of the place and what went on there to their full awareness.

At the far end of the room a huge rack with its dangling cuffs and the leveraging wheel awaited some perverse application The leather wrist restraints were stretched and worn from the too frequent service of slowly pulling the joints out of socket until in the worst cases, they separated so that the subject bled to death. Hanging next to the rack, two barred face cages were already occupied with huge brown rats, that scurried back-and-forth in a hungry agitation, anxious for access to the defenseless head of some unfortunate. All along the wall, whips and scourges, each with their own unique alteration, dangled threateningly. Some were split reed, which when applied would cut in narrow stripes to ooze blood slowly. Others had been modified with long leather strips attached to metal barbs so that when they hit, they bit into and held the tissue of the victim. Extraction would require a forceful ripping by the flayer to free them before being applied again. While horrible, this type of scourge, nicknamed the "cat" because of its embedding claws, was the kind that supposedly had been used on Christ by the Romans before his agonizing trek to Golgotha. As such it was deemed a fitting and often used instrument to cleanse the sinful. It required a skilled practitioner, though, as repeated blows across an existing stripe could cause the flesh overlying the lungs to open and collapse them. This had the undesired effect of rendering the tortured incapable of generating the breath necessary to confess and led to a foreshortened trial of pain as it killed too quickly.

From somewhere down another corridor, the searing hiss of white-hot iron being pressed into flesh was followed by a soul-deep wail that carried over to a sobbing groan. A second later, the acrid stench of burned skin and muscle flooded their senses.

Even the air itself carried with it a strange form of biologically generated humidity, liberated by the sweat, tears, blood and excreta of human bodies in pain to create a uniquely damnable microclimate. They were experiencing the beginning of a season in hell, and even the cretinous guard seemed offended by it as his face contorted in revulsion at the sounds and smells.

Somehow, throughout it all, Galileo had remained stoic. Rather than focusing on the effects of the setting, he was looking at the arrangement of the room. Seated at a small stool was Caccini with a tablet and pen on his lap. Across the room, Maculani stood at the foot of a long wooden bench shaped like a homunculus. Affixed with leather straps at four points, its anatomically caricaturized design and purpose was unmistakable. It had apparently recently been in use, as the surface was still wet with the dark remnants of piss, stool and blood, but that wasn't what struck Ferrero as most alarming.

Along the edge facing them, was a congealed rind of material, that at first could have been mistaken for hardening paraffin. Closer inspection, however revealed it as something far more horrifying. It was tallow, human fat that had been liquefied by some unimaginable practice only to solidify as it cooled in the aftermath.

Whomever had been on the homunculus most recently had been rendered, like a hog, while still alive. The awful process of that and the incredible suffering it caused explained the loss of control and presence of the other bodily fluids that resulted. At the business end of the wooden torture-board, a large man wearing a leather hood emblazoned with the seal of Inquisition was unrolling a leather pouch with pockets containing the metal instruments of torture. These were the tools of trade for the sweating purveyor of suffering, and as he removed and placed them alongside the bench, the purpose of many were chillingly apparent, even to the uninitiated.

First was a pair of large shears, sturdy enough to cut through an oxen's hide. Then he withdrew a long blade with double serrated teeth.

Ferrero swallowed hard, but it wasn't until the final item that the real silent, visceral effect took hold on all of them.

At first it wasn't immediately evident what it was. There were two arms with a handle at one end and a demi cup with a sharpened interior edge at the other. They were connected in the center by a small gear and when opened the instrument looked like a metal X. As the torturer grasped the handles and squeezed them together, however, the sharp two dish-shaped edges closed in, slicing against each other to form a small cup. This was a castrating rongeur.

Every face in the room showed the effect including Galileo, but he wasn't giving the others the satisfaction of seeing his fear. He knew they could torture him, but he also knew, the only thing that could imperil his soul in that room was a lie. To deny God's work, because of the desires of men would be the real sin.

"Why is he here?"

Galileo was referring to Caccini at his writing stand.

"He is here to document what is done to you, in detail. What damage is done, and how you respond. When you confess and plead for absolution, he will note that too," said Maculani coldly.

"Why would men of God want that?" asked Galileo.

"Because," said Ferrero softly so that the others could not hear, "they want to mutilate you. To humiliate you. Castrate you, in all ways. And they want everyone to know, so they will fear them."

The full, awful intent of the Inquisition was apparent now. This had almost nothing to do with anything spiritual. They were hoping he would resist. The best outcome for Maculani would be for a trial of pain to render Galileo publicly butchered, emasculated and humiliated for all time.

A combination of fear, dread and sadness showed all at once, as much for the despair it registered for his fellow man as for the perverted purposes of the Church he had worshiped and loved his entire life.

Seeing that Maculani spoke.

"Do you...recant?" he asked pointedly.

Ferrero looked panicked. He grasped Galileo by the wrist and implored him. "Recant, *Professore*. I beg you. Confess. Recant."

Thinking of his soul, all Galileo could say was, "No."

Maculani smiled, and Caccini dipped his pen to wait. The torturer began tossing pine shavings onto the floor to prevent any loss of footing in the blood that was about to be spilled.

"Do you recall when people pointed to Copernicus and warned you?" said Ferrero desperately.

Galileo looked at him.

"If you let this happen, they will point to you, and it will be far worse. You will be more than a caution! You will be a tool of suppression for anyone else that dares to think!"

That made an impression. Galileo blinked. The issue at stake was far greater than even the integrity of his own soul. His obstinacy could do damage to future truth.

For a moment, he felt as he did when he looked at his family that last night that they were completely his. No matter the pain, no matter the cost, their well-being had been more important than his interests or desire.

"You will be the example they use to intimidate all who come behind you," pressed Ferrero.

"If I recant. If I deny the truth, then I will be damned." It didn't sound mournful. It didn't sound self-pitying when he said it. It was flat, unemotional, almost like the assessment of a hypothesis in his new scientific method.

Now it was Ferrero that sounded damned when he said, "Therein is the cleverness of their evil."

The homunculus was ready and Maculani was just about to give the order to begin.

"I beg you, recant while your mind and body are intact," pled Ferrero.

"The time has come, *Signore*," said Maculani menacingly.

"Recant," said Ferrero, his voice becoming more strident. "For God's sake, recant."

Galileo stared ahead and down slightly like he was wrestling with an awful decision.

"It would not be for God's sake," he corrected.

"Then for your beloved future science's sake," said Ferrero.

Galileo looked defeated at that. He nodded.

Across the room, Maculani was watching the intense conversation. Though he hadn't heard the words, he could tell a lot from the expressions and the recent change in Galileo's body language. Now, seeing the capitulating nod, Maculani smiled.

•

The word of Galileo's acquiescence spread quickly. The explosive and outrageous details of his trial, and his prior fame had served to make for a public fascination that had never quite occurred before. With Maculani's adroit manipulation of the media in the form of the intimidated publisher Enrico Parma, every literate person in Christendom had followed the proceedings and now was aware that Galileo had quailed and given in. The Church and conventional thinking had won.

When the members of the Pigeon League found out, they celebrated and prayed in a self-aggrandizing fashion thanking God for exalting them in contrast to the heretic. Cremonini, with Maculani's endorsement, leveraged Parma to produce an announcement of the recantation of Galileo so that advance notice would already be out among the faithful even before the full details of the ceremony were decided. The goal? To generate enough of an interest and outcry so that the Pope would have to accommodate as large a public event as possible. It was the fastest that written word, in any form, had spread throughout Italy, and as political theater, Galileo's humiliation was all but assured on an unprecedented scale.

Urban VIII was considering the problem of building an arsenal for the papal army when Father Barbarossi approached and leaned in to whisper, "*Doctore* Galilei has admitted his sin and agreed to recant."

Urban VIII looked almost startled and then a little sad at the news.

"How badly did they hurt him?" he asked as if the answer would wound him as well.

"Not at all, Holiness. He acquiesced when he saw the chamber."

Urban VIII frowned curiously.

That seemed odd. Galileo was, if nothing else, at least two things; he was no coward and incredibly obstinate when it came to an intellectual point. Something else had triggered this. Of that Urban VIII was sure.

"We shall consider how this will be handled," he said working the idea.

"Perhaps Your Holiness should see this," said Barbarossi. He held out a flyer from Parma's shop.

Even before he read the body of the text, Urban VIII could tell what it was. By that he didn't mean the information delivered in the headline, "Galileo to Recant" or in the propagandized details of the disclosure. What *it* was to Urban VIII was the political flanking maneuver that the Inquisition with the support of the Pigeon League had hoped to accomplish.

Galileo had committed only one offense. He had injured the pride of the establishment. Heresy in and of itself rarely garnered the sort of obliterating punishment that was coming. It was an absolute of the human condition that institutional embarrassment was the truly unforgivable sin. It was not suicide, not offense to God, not the taking of an innocent life, but the hubris to offer an offense to the powerful that would always draw the greatest and most horrible sentence. The forces surrounding Urban VIII were making sure that no matter what mercy he might resurrect for an old friend, the inertia of politics would make certain that Galileo and his voice were destroyed in a landmark fashion.

In the lesser minds that had just triumphed, faith had prevailed over intellect.

By the time he had finished reading the text, Urban VIII knew that he could not control the attendance or venue, even if he wanted. The royalty of the Roman states having read it had sent letters requesting space for themselves and their favored subjects. From as far away as England, Germany and France, others were asking to be admitted so that they could see the exaltation of God's word over the insidious notion of heliocentrism. That was the part that rankled Urban VIII the most. The charge against Galileo had been for disobedience of a papal directive, not an advancement of a heretical principle.

Somehow in the murky politics, the issue had been adulterated and conflated against something even Urban VIII had entertained as scientifically reasonable. Now there would be two casualties in Galileo's humiliation, fact and the sovereignty of the papal hearing.

Urban VIII looked up at Barbarossi. Like a chess master realizing he has lost before the final moves are executed, his face showed his concession.

"With the number of requests, the only option will be the chapel." Barbarossi looked away as he said it, almost like he was apologizing for bringing it up.

Urban VIII nodded.

"In this we are overmatched, I fear," he said. "Make the arrangements."

•

Viviani and Torricelli had only been waiting a few minutes in the alcove of the Convent of San Matteo when the clouds closed over and a roll of thunder signaled what was coming. That time of year in Tuscany, the buildup of heat in the afternoon often resulted in the violent clash of inbound ocean air and the perfectly energized atmosphere. The sharp distinct odor of cracking ozone said that the nearby vineyards were in for a good dousing.

"Galileo would like that," said Torricelli looking upward.

It also meant that if they wanted to stay dry, they needed to get under the protection of the newly repaired roof's overhang.

They moved right as the first cool drops began to fall. Viviani was careful to make certain that the publication he was carrying stayed between his body and the wall of the convent so by the time Sister Maria Celeste and Sister Arcangela arrived to receive them, it was still perfectly dry.

Maria Celeste seemed to read their concern quickly.

"What's wrong?" she asked.

The two scholars looked at each other as if each expected his colleague to answer. Finally, Torricelli took the flyer and handed it to Maria Celeste. She read it with her sister looking over her shoulder while the two despondent academicians stared out at the falling rain. When she had finished the look in her eyes was a combination of anger, and determination.

"If they cannot emasculate him one way, they will try another," she said.

Then with the decisiveness of her father she turned to the two men.

"We are going to the chapel," she said.

The scholars almost startled at the directive.

"To do what?" asked Viviani.

"To save what we can. You two make the arrangements," she said and turning to Sister Arcangela added. "Get paper and a pen. I need to write a letter."

•

There are times that life delivers what the greatest fiction would blush to propose. The legal writ requesting official acknowledgement of his paternity by Galileo Galilei had been submitted to the Grand Duke and while it wasn't assured, Vincenzio Gamba had been led to believe that the potential was promising. There were several factors that made him optimistic. The first was that his mother had never made any formal declaration of paternity at the time of his birth, even though she and his father were expecting to wed soon. In fact, his official birth registration had the words "paternity unknown," which while singularly rather awful, were proving beneficial now.

The second factor was that Reynoldo Bertoluzzi, who to his credit, had acted the loving father and protector all his life, had never taken any official steps to assign the boy as his own son. Now with the risk of daughters and dowries out of the way and Giulia Galilei long consigned to the grave, there was nothing that might create a social stir for Medici if he gave his approval.

Despite the charge of heresy against him, Galileo's favor amongst the Tuscan nobility and his formal request to the Grand Duke that Vincenzio be recognized almost guaranteed a successful outcome. In the meantime, he had gotten on with his life. Abandoning the study of law, he had taken up music, and much like both his father and grandfather, he had discovered something new. It really was no surprise. Vincenzo Galilei had been a musical prodigy and the leading lutenist of his time. His father's innovative talents in a number of fields were known throughout the world, if even now he was being persecuted for them. So, when Vincenzio began to really work with the instrument, something, a germinal idea that took root in a combined method of musical composition and mathematical timing occurred. He called it the polychordal style.

It took off. Everyone who heard it, loved it. For the first time a single instrument could sound like an ensemble. The strings could harmonize with themselves. Soon, the leading musical experts of the world began writing and composing derivative works with acknowledgments to the young Vincenzio's genius. In a short time, his purse was full enough that he was able to wed. So, it was with no surprise that the Church's request for an original piece arrived with a sizable commission. He, of course, had no idea to what use it would be put.

•

In the days before his recantation ceremony, Galileo received more visitors than at any time throughout his trial. It seemed that every person of station or means wanted to get a look at him before the grand and decisive moment. The guards at the prison, realizing the financial opportunity, enjoyed a booming cottage industry as they charged a small fortune to accompany the curious and well-heeled to his cell for a look. Most, remarkably enough, had nothing to say. They just appeared at the door of the cell to stare at him before walking out.

For the most part Galileo didn't acknowledge them, though it did occur to him that he now knew what the incarcerated lynx in a zoo felt like.

The one who seemed most offended by the insulting enterprise was Ferrero. There was little he could effectively do, even though he tried. His appeal to the prison officials went unanswered as did a letter for leniency to the Pope. This was entertainment masquerading as social activism and something as pitiful as legal process didn't stand a chance.

On the morning of the ceremony, Galileo was taken from his cell to a large stone room, much like where the interrogation had taken place. In the center was a large tub full of steaming, water on which floated a sheen of scented oil and several *bouquet garni's* of lavender, thyme and cedar. They had been in the water long enough that the room was filled with the heavy aroma. Even the clean linen robes hanging on a stand in the far corner seemed to have been permeated by their fragrance as well.

It was quickly apparent what they had planned. He would appear in the chapel, submissive, corrected and no longer dirty and soiled by the prison. He would appear to be washed clean by his confession and supplication to the Church and its power. The inference in every mind that saw him would not require a single word of confirmation.

"Whose idea was this?" asked Galileo.

"Father Maculani, and *Professore*s—"

"Cremonini and Colombe," Galileo finished the statement in chorus with the guard who looked confused. Then he looked at Ferrero, who seemed even more despondent than Galileo felt.

"It will be all right, Ferrero," said Galileo taking off his filthy garments. "You will be rewarded for your good counsel. I would not have confessed, and this pageantry would not be happening if not for you."

Ferrero looked like he had been stabbed in the heart while the cretinous guard looked at him with new respect. Nodding to Ferrero, he backed out of the room. When he had gone Galileo stepped into the water and sat down

"*Doctore*," Ferrero started emotionally.

But Galileo held up his hand.

"I said it for his benefit and yours. You should not be punished for the kindness you have done me. I worried that perhaps Maculani and Caccini would malign you, but he"—he nodded in the direction where the guard had departed— "could never keep his mouth shut. The whole world will credit you with convincing me. Don't worry. You saved me from terrible physical pain. No man can stand up to that. Eventually he will break. He will lie. He will dispirit and dispute those things he holds most dear. He will admit to anything when a question is put to searing steel and blood."

Ferrero didn't speak, but the words did not seem to help. Galileo took note.

"Listen to me."

Ferrero looked up at him.

"You delivered me from a longer road to the same end, and I am grateful to you, but even more, you have served all those that might have been discouraged by what could have been. For that, the world owes you thanks."

He slid under the water then and held beneath its surface, as long as a baptism, allowing the bath and oils to surround and insinuate his hair and beard thoroughly. When he surfaced again, he had to admit, he did feel some element of ablution.

He took a breath of the perfumed air and heard a sound, harmonics that seemed at once lovely and intriguing on a completely different level. Someone was playing a song, but the intricacy and orchestral nature of the chords from the same instrument was unique and compelling.

"What is that?" asked Galileo eagerly.

"I don't know," said Ferrero, "but it is all that one hears these days. I believe it was a special commission for the ceremony.

"I like it," said Galileo. "It isn't," he searched for just the right word, "it isn't, easy."

•

The trip to the chapel was not in a prison wagon as it had been during the trial. This time he boarded a carriage bearing both the symbols of the Inquisition and the Pope on its door. Galileo was to be delivered in a style that spoke simultaneously of label, credit and reclamation of a celebrated figure. In his robed finery, smelling of the sweet natural fragrances of this world, he was a soul anew, or so the message was meant to convey as he rode past the chattering celebratory throng.

"Is anyone anywhere else in Italy today?" asked Galileo as he took in the massive attendance.

Ferrero did not smile. Galileo looked at him curiously. "What?"

Ferrero reached into his robe and withdrew a parchment.

"They would like you to say this," he said.

Galileo took it and read. His face didn't change at all.

•

Unbeknownst to Galileo, the ceremony itself and its tone had been a point of contention behind closed doors. The Pigeon League members had lobbied hard for a more public and dramatic presentation, outdoors in St. Peter's Square where even more people might be permitted to witness Galileo's degradation. They also wanted a broader declaration of guilt that would include a personal censure. Maculani didn't seem to care. The Pigeon League had served its purpose in furthering the Inquisition's goals, and as far as he was concerned, their personal grievance with Galileo was a lesser consideration.

As for the Pope, beyond his sense of justice being insulted and his intellectual disdain for Cremonini and Colombe, he had the integrity of the Holy See to protect. He had already conceded enough and with the Inquisition satisfied, he decided to take a hard stand against the others. The already large attendance indoors would be enough. Galileo's denouement was for God, not the popular appetite.

As he sat at the head of the room, he clutched the letter from Sister Maria Celeste. He had shown it to no one, not even Barbarossi, but its simple clear and straightforward request for mercy had reminded him of her father's light and clever gift with words and it had touched what was left of his heart. Now, he listened to the light melody that intrigued him with its effortless complexity and involved, intertwined chords. It was an amazing piece, compelling to him both in terms of its beauty and structure.

"What is that?" he asked Barbarossi as they awaited the arrival of Galileo.

"A piece commissioned for the church, by a young genius named Vincenzio Gamba."

Urban VIII looked surprised then almost subdued by the profound irony of that.

"It's extremely popular," said Barbarossi.

Urban VIII gave a dry smile.

Before anything else could be said, the sound of a commotion from outside told them that the moment of judgment was at hand. A moment later, Galileo entered, followed by Ferrero. He seemed impervious, resigned, and despite the sounds of the crowd around him, his demeanor was like that of a man completely alone.

A sudden surge of the old tender affection rose in Urban VIII at the sight of his former friend. Only the presence of the scholars, the jury of Cardinals and the masses wedged into the galleries to observe kept it in check as Galileo walked up and kneeled in front of the dais.

Off to the side, Maculani wore the same smile that had been on his face in the dungeon. Noting it, Urban VIII cut his eyes toward the scholar's section where Cremonini and Colombe looked delighted, reveling in the pleasure of seeing their enemy's abject posture. It was, as much as the letter, his own sense of regret that made Urban VIII determine what he was going to do next.

Fixing an expression of neutrality, without a hint of sympathy, he took quick stock of young Ferrero. The Jesuit looked more aggrieved than the kneeling accused.

Urban VIII held up his hand and made the sign of the cross. The room went quiet. Then he nodded to Maculani, who stood and said loudly, "Do you Galileo Galilei, confess to the crime of heresy against the Holy Mother Church?"

Without the slightest hesitation, Galileo answered, "I do."

A murmur of response and enthusiasm rippled through the crowd. Maculani allowed it to die down then continued saying, "Then now confess your sins before God and beg His forgiveness so that you may receive the penance of His Holiness."

The eager anticipation had the crowd silent. Not a one of them wanted to miss a word of what he said.

"I, Galileo Galilei, recant my statements and assertions that the sun... lies motionless at the center of the universe—"

In the gallery, several of the Cardinals smiled viciously.

"—and that the earth is not at its center nor does it move, and that it is contrary to Holy Scripture," he continued reciting the dictated script verbatim. He paused like he was gathering himself for what he was about to say next, then he sighed and repeated, "I do abjure, curse and detest these opinions and beg the forgiveness of God and the Church."

Maculani turned and bowed to the Pope with a satisfied smile. Then he stepped back to await the sentence accompanied by the murmuring approval of the crowd. Galileo remained in his humbled posture, staring at the floor. Ferrero swallowed hard. It was worse than he had expected.

Urban VIII knew that every eye was on him now. For what he was going to do, he needed to assure that he was seen as resolute and strong. He stared unemotionally at the humbled, genuflecting Galileo.

"The Church accepts the confession and rejoices at the restoration of Grace to your reclaimed soul. From this day, all your heretical publications and works will be banned. Nor will any future publication of any kind be allowed."

Galileo did not look up, but from their perspectives both Ferrero and Maculani could tell, he looked as though he had been physically wounded.

Urban VIII was not done.

"Furthermore, you shall be sentenced to formal imprisonment for the remainder of your life."

The Cardinals smiled openly. Cremonini and Colombe, clasped each other with hateful glee and in among the audience, the happy faithful viciously crossed themselves and thanked God that evil's voice was being silenced for all time.

Then the Pope held up his hand. The exultant mob grew anticipatorily silent as if awaiting another helping of cruelty.

"But we are not without mercy," said Urban VIII loudly.

Faces in the audience ranged from bewildered to cheated. Maculani, who had been smugly sure of the outcome, now frowned at the uncertainty of what might be next. Ferrero, for the first time, looked like there might be hope.

"This sentence shall be commuted to your house in Florence where you will remain under the discretion of the Inquisition."

The crowd began its murmuring again. As social drama, this was turning out to be better than they could have hoped with all the sudden twists. In the scholar section, sensing that their triumph might be at risk of slipping away, Cremonini stood up and moved next to Urban VIII. Speaking so softly that not even the attendant could hear, he offered a silent conference.

"Your Holiness, *Signor* Galileo is old, but disposed to obstinacy. Perhaps if he were to spend his time in required reading, the scriptures for instance, it would address the needs of his spirituality and curtail his nature by exhausting his vision."

The Pope didn't react at first. As much as he didn't care for the manipulative Cremonini, he had to admit that he was right about Galileo. He could not be counted on to stop his own intellectual curiosities and process.

With a slight gesture he dismissed Cremonini.

"So that you may not be tempted by your instruments of observation, you will direct your attention to the reading of the 7 Penitential Psalms each day," he said.

Galileo seemed to startle at that and for the first time since he had assumed the submissive position, he looked up directly into Urban VIII's eyes. His own expression was one of outrage and disappointment at the cruel addition to the sentence. Yet there was nothing he could say.

"Go in peace," said Urban VIII.

It was done. The Pope rose from his seat and walked from the chapel, followed by the Cardinals, and scholars. The crowd, having been properly entertained, stood up and shuffled toward the doors, chattering indistinctly about what appetite they would satisfy next. Some were hungry. Some wanted wine. Others, eyeing the courtesans in attendance, had less tangible, but as poignant a need to fulfill.

Ferrero rushed over to help Galileo to his feet. Unlike just an hour before when he had been surrounded by guards and every attentive eye was on him, now he was extraneous, invisible, irrelevant, and with what the Pope had just decreed, so would be his life's work.

His age and the long period he had spent in the damp cold of the cell had weakened him, and he accepted Ferrero's assistance in standing. To Ferrero the difference between his perception of the *Professore* based on the formidable nature of his speech and what he felt now as his hands encircled the thin arms of the old man was startling. The phenomenon of Galileo and the physical nature of the man were two distinctly different things.

Suddenly the devastating nature of the sentence that had been laid down made sense, and a soft grief filled Ferrero. Galileo was old. A day spent reading a text up close would fatigue the tiny muscles that changed the shape of the eye to accommodate his observation of the distant details of the universe. The scholars, with the decision of the Pope, had finally achieved what they had been after for decades.

"Here," he said gently, "let me help you, *Doctore*."

Outside the chapel, Cremonini and Colombe were exultant.

"A day of holy scriptural reading," chuckled Colombe.

"That should keep his ancient eyes from being able to see a thing through that abominable device," agreed Cremonini smugly.

They knew they were right.

CHAPTER THIRTEEN

To endure exile is to experience a strange sort of death sentence. It is execution by absence and irrelevance. On the one hand, Galileo was still physically alive. He ate. He drank. He slept and rose. On another level, in a fundamental and critical way, he had ceased to exist. The door to his home remained closed to the world. He was, absent from it and so in the public mind, his presence faded. With each day and each new distraction, their recollection of him evaporated a little until, like a ghost, the details of his face and voice, his work, and ultimately the characteristics that made him unique disappeared. That's what happened when you died, and it was what the brilliantly cruel architects of his sentence intended as the months and years passed following the trial.

His home was supposed to be his cell and knowing his unique capability for visiting the world without ever setting foot outside, his enemies had made sure that they closed down that opportunity as well. Even the use of the telescope was compromised. The reading of scriptures, ironically a review of a pronouncement of love, were put into service as a punishing and painful enterprise. It was entirely the opposite of what the original author had experienced and intended. Therein was the perversity of the task. It had the desired result though. After hours of it, his vision remained blurry, and no amount of adjustment of the optics could bring the heavenly bodies into merciful focus.

His inability to work would have been the end of him completely had it not been for Maria Celeste.

Whether it was a mistake by an inattentive or lazy scribe, or some clever alternate strategy designed by a merciful friend in power, the escape clause she found was all they needed. The wording only called for "a reading of the seven Penitential Psalms" not for the accused to be the one to do it. A truly diligent daughter of the Church might have asked for clarification but being Galileo's daughter and as much an independent thinker as her father, Maria Celeste chose to see the obliquity as a gift from God and exercised her own power of interpretation.

He was struggling at the table when she walked in and lifted the Bible from under his nose. At first, he looked confused, but then she sat down at a chair near the door to his study and began reading aloud.

"Remember not, Oh Lord, our offenses, nor those of our parents; and take not revenge for our sins," she began.

"What are you doing?" her father asked.

She looked at him with a strange assurance and just went on reading.

"Let all my enemies be ashamed and be very much troubled: let them be turned back, and be ashamed very speedily—"

He watched her as she continued and when she spoke the next line of the litany, an understanding grin crept across his face. Without actually saying it, she was telling him by emphasizing loudly the very lines in the psalms intended to punish him.

"—Blessed is the man to whom the Lord hath not imputed sin, and in whose spirit there is no guile." She glanced up from the verse at him for emphasis. She might as well have called him out by name. "Do not become like the horse and the mule, who have no understanding. With bit and bridle bind fast their jaws, who come not near unto thee," she continued emphasizing the word "mule". It was an ironically close reference to his own attribution of the word "ass" when he had described the obstinate ignorance of the narrow minded and blind church officers in his letter to Johannes Kepler, the very one that Maculani had used to condemn him.

She was saving him. He knew, and with that, he smiled and turned back to his table to dip his pen. After looking out his window at the vineyard covered hill and seeing it clearly, he began to write.

Outside the house, a bored guard holding a lance, leaned against the frame as the muffled sound of the psalmist recitation eked through the wood of the front door. This post was easy duty, though he couldn't imagine how much of a risk it would really be if the ancient Galileo actually escaped.

"I have watched and am become as a sparrow all alone on the housetop. All the day long my enemies reproached me: and they that praised me did swear against me," said the distorted voice from inside.

The guard looked up as a sparrow flew over. Then he yawned and leaned back. It was going to be another dull day.

•

Viviani and Torricelli were struggling. They panted as they chugged up the street with an armload of correspondence and supplies. In the year since Sister Maria Celeste had taken over the readings, Galileo's work had flourished. Though they did not attribute it to his sentence, it did seem at times that his explosion of intellectual discovery was a furious equal and opposite reaction to the intended persecution of his imprisonment. That meant that they were busy too. With him unable to leave the house, they became his legs and hands in the world. They purchased and fetched ink. They mailed his correspondence and picked up mail, packages, scientific work sent in by colleagues and fans around the world at the direction of his daughter. In spite of the efforts of the Inquisition, the Church and its so-called scholars, the influence of Galileo on the world was about to be greater than ever.

Now the two men hurried around the corner and up the street toward the door with the almost napping guard in attendance. To their calculation, he had put on a few pounds since his assignment. Guarding Galileo was as acaloric a duty as one could find. On top of that, the rich food and wine that Sister Maria Celeste kept supplying had made him as docile as an old horse.

"You know," panted Viviani, "if the Maestro were ever to try and escape, I am not sure his pursuer could keep up for long."

Torricelli laughed. "You are right. Then again, whatever could prompt the *Doctore* to want to leave? He has the world's attention and," he looked down at the bottles in the heavy bag, "all the wine he can drink, with no impediment to the ventures of his mind."

They arrived at the door and the guard, who had become quite at ease with them, politely opened the door as if they were old friends.

"*Grazie*," said Viviani.

"*Signore*," followed Torricelli.

The guard nodded and smiled. He was part of the team.

The two scholars entered the house and set their parcels on a table. The postmarks ranged from England to the Netherlands.

Maria Celeste walked out of the kitchen and handed them both a cup of water, and as they sat and caught their breath, she began sorting through the correspondence and supplies. There were a number of letters with names she knew her father would want to see, most notably, a dated postmark from his good friend, Kepler, but somewhere toward the middle of the pile, a small envelope emblazoned with the seal of the Church caught her eye. She plucked it up and opened it. What she saw, made her brow knit.

"What is it?" asked an observant Torricelli.

"The *Dialogue*," she said.

"What about it?" asked Viviani.

She sighed before continuing, "The Church has consigned it to the Index of Forbidden Books."

The words landed hard, and none of them said a thing at first. It wasn't that they hadn't expected it, but the official notice meant that the Church had not forgotten about Galileo. Whatever he might do in the future, they would have an eye on it somewhere. Not that such a thing could stop him.

They all looked over toward the door to his study. There was no light showing under its edge, like they might have expected normally.

"The *Professore*?" said Torricelli.

"Yes." Maria Celeste smiled. "Asleep. He worked all night again."

"And as soon as the stars dimmed?" asked Viviani with a leading tone.

"Yes, as soon as they dimmed, he went to work on the sun," she said.

His indomitable intellect was a source of amusement, encouragement and hope for all of them.

"He does too much," said Torricelli.

"That is not an argument you will win," said Maria Celeste sounding a little too experienced.

"It's good that you can read the psalms for him," said Viviani.

She rubbed her eyes and suddenly looked very tired.

"Yes, he is only required to reflect on them as they are read."

They looked at her with mild amusement, as if they knew she had more to say.

"Of course," she added, "he did point out that they didn't specify the amount of time spent in reflection."

Their smiles broadened. She nodded at the door.

"Go ahead and knock," she said.

Viviani stood and walked up to the door. With a tentative look back at the others, he summoned himself and knocked gently on the door. A second later, Galileo's voice responded forcefully through the door.

"Go away!"

Viviani took a trepidatious step backward. Maria Celeste just sighed, handed Viviani the letter from Kepler and gestured that he stand steady as she leaned in against the door.

"It's Viviani and Torricelli," she said and then with a pragmatic shrug added, "they bring wine."

A sudden shuffling sounded inside and then steps approached the door. It opened, revealing the almost entirely blacked out interior of the study. Maria Celeste stepped back so that Viviani and Torricelli could enter and plucked a bottle from the table before heading into the kitchen.

"I'll bring it in," she said just before disappearing.

The room was dark for a reason. Heavy tapestries were hung covering every one of the windows completely except for the one above his desk. That one was split so that the investigatory end of his telescope was extended beyond. Clips held the material tightly both above and below the scope so that no other light could enter.

Across the room, a sheet of parchment was tacked onto a wooden surface, tilted at such an angle as to be perpendicular to the eye piece. Incredibly, a beam of light expressed from the ocular lens and shot across the room to illuminate a perfect oval on the paper. Next to it sat a small pot of ink and pens. Surrounded by darkness the projected image of the sun was remarkably distinct, detailed and clear.

It wasn't the first time they had seen the room like this, but no matter how often they witnessed the set up, it never failed to impress. Galileo was mapping sunspots. They moved closer to look at the paper.

"Don't stare at it too long," said Galileo. "In fact..."

He stepped over and opened the drape around the telescope. Instantly the beam disappeared and the circle on the parchment transformed to the drawing that was a spot-on match for the projection they had just seen. Along the wall other such helioscopia or sun maps were arranged with each showing different dark spots mapped out across the solar face. As Torricelli and Viviani marveled at it, however, Galileo's attention was drawn to something much more earthbound in the distance.

Among the terraced rows of grapevines, workers were hard at labor bringing in the harvest. Galileo smiled and realigned his telescope so that he could watch them in detail. If he couldn't leave his house and visit, this was the next best thing. He made an adjustment with his instrument and the smiling brown faces came into focus as their sun browned hands cut heavy lustrous clusters of fat purple grapes and placed them gently in the large baskets.

"I marvel every time I see it," said a humbly impressed Galileo.

Torricelli looked up.

"*Professore*?" he said.

Galileo lingered in consideration of the happy faces. There was real joy in the community of workers engaged in such simple and measured labors.

"The sun," he said and paused, as if he were savoring the thought like he would eventually savor the vintage of those same grapes. "With all those planets revolving around it, dependent on it, can still ripen a bunch of grapes as if it had nothing else to do."

It was a marvelous thought.

Sister Maria Celeste entered with the open bottle of wine.

"Always looking ahead," she said picking up on his fascination with the vineyard, "but there is"—she started pouring— "some joy in the present."

Galileo turned back toward the room. On the edge of the wine tray was a letter. He picked it up, shooting his daughter a quizzical look. As always, a lot passed between them without a single word. He read and a dry tight smile replaced the bounteous open one the vineyard workers had inspired.

"The *Dialogue* has been exiled...just like its author," he said.

She held up another letter.

"And just as effectively," she said.

He took it from her and read.

"The Welser Institute," he said.

"Yes."

"What is it?" asked Viviani.

"Something about an award," he said with a less than enthusiastic tone. He looked up at the unspoken question on Viviani and Torricelli's faces. "If recent history has taught me anything, it is to be as immune to the world's praise as to its condemnation."

The award was not just some sentiment. The Welsers had placed a large amount of money in an account for him.

"And they are coming for a visit," he said reading further.

"But you are under arrest," said a concerned Torricelli.

Galileo looked thoughtful.

"Yes, *I* am," he said. "Not the rest of the world." With slight amusement he added, "People visit the residents of a prison all the time. I should know."

That made sense.

Torricelli and Viviani frowned, considering that. They still didn't look convinced. Maria Celeste took a sip of wine and decided to help them out.

"According to the specifications of Papa's punishment, he may not receive a visitor simply for their society, for the pleasure of their company."

They nodded.

"A professional visit or one for the purposes of scholarship is another matter," said Galileo.

"And so, the money in the account?" asked Torricelli referring to the letter.

"I suppose there is some benefit to Welser being a scientist as well as a banker," conceded Galileo. He reached over and opened another letter and reading, smiled again.

"Something good?" asked Maria Celeste.

"They are commemorating Kepler's camera obscura. You remember when he first wrote me about it?"

"Yes," she said flatly. The memory of the incident was obviously slightly different for the two of them. It was, in no small part because she recalled that it was that correspondence that was used to condemn him.

Before Kepler the study of the sun was not something that could be done directly, and while a number of theories about its composition, movement or lack thereof and the nature of the curious dark flecks that appeared and disappeared across its surface were being debated by the best scientific minds, the investigation was thwarted by the harmful nature of direct visualization. More than one reckless astronomer had suffered irreversible blindness from staring too long at it through the telescopic magnification.

It was a problem. That long a look at something so intense and great was damaging.

And then Kepler solved it, and in a remarkably simple manner.

Galileo remembered the day that he had learned of it. He still had Kepler's enthusiastic letter describing, in great detail, how he had gone up on the roof, toolbox in hand, how he had cut out a section so that the sharp image beamed in and projected onto the floor of his home. While an inconvenience, it was not reckless. He had, in a manner to rival Galileo, calculated the angle perfectly and turned that inner room of his own study into the means for a leisurely and safe examination of the transmuted, neutered beam of sunlight, without losing a single precious detail.

Galileo had been impressed, but as he had read aloud, his enthusiasm was not shared by Maria Celeste, when he delightedly announced that Kepler had cut the hole in his home.

"We're not planning to do that, are we?" she asked nervously.

He grinned, back in the modern moment. Maria Celeste seemed to be sharing the same memory.

Torricelli had moved on. Spotting a booklet on Galileo's desk, he frowned, not believing what he was seeing at first, then picked it up. On closer inspection it was exactly what he had first thought.

"*Professore*, this is Colombe's latest treatise," he said.

"Yes," said Galileo.

"Why would you read it? The man is a fool."

"That is a measurable fact," said Galileo lightly, "but I have never met a man so ignorant I couldn't learn something from him."

Viviani chuckled. Torricelli disdainfully dropped the document and reached for another piece of mail.

"And what did you learn?" asked Maria Celeste.

Galileo's face crinkled into a sarcastic expression.

"Precious little," he said dryly.

Torricelli lowered the letter that he had been reading.

"What is it?" asked Galileo.

"Your friend, Castelli. He's been named science adviser to the Pope."

Galileo's eyebrows went up.

"The Vatican was due to make a right decision," he said.

Maria Celeste shot him a look of concern. Even now, even after the close call and risks posed, the old intellectual defiance could not be quelled.

"Be careful," she said, "our guard is fat, not deaf. Anything heretical, he is obliged to report."

"What else does Castelli say?" he asked.

"Maculani has withdrawn as an officer of the Inquisition."

Torricelli looked up in surprise. This was news that had an impact on the rest of them.

"He is to be the new general of the papal army."

All eyes turned to Galileo for his response.

"A good choice. He will do well," said Galileo.

It made sense. Maculani had been trained for war. His theological instruction was a secondary academic discipline. His father and grandfather had served the Church as leaders of her army, and his involvement as a prosecutor had been a near accident. He had taken to it with the belief that God had a hand in all things and so he discharged his duty as he would eventually on the field of battle.

"I only wish he had been a little less strategically gifted in the courtroom," said Galileo ironically.

"Castelli is planning to visit," said Torricelli changing the subject. "He says, he would like to consult you on the matters of water properties, fluids and hydraulics."

Galileo picked up the wine bottle and poured. "Fluids and hydraulics," he said noting the vintage as it spilled into his glass. "Sounds wonderful."

The visit by Castelli was nothing new. In the latest years of his exile, despite the suppression of his work by the Church, an underground network of dissemination had managed to reinvigorate both the *Sidereus Nuncius* and the *Dialogue.* Word of his brilliant satire and the foundational scientific publications generated a whole new fan base in the more progressive and less Catholically stringent kingdoms of the Netherlands and the notoriously heretical England. Even certain works that had been disregarded were suddenly resurrected for examination and study.

It wasn't just the scientific community either. Artists in all nations, perhaps because they could appreciate the ostracism of those comfortably in power and their unwillingness to tolerate something avant-garde, had seen his story and his work as a cause celebre. Soon, Galilean characters began appearing in the *Comedia* as proponents of reason to thwart and ridicule pedantic, conventional thinkers. In England, the writer William Shakespeare's work *Cymbeline* featured a scene in which the god Jupiter was surrounded by four ghosts in exactly the same configuration of the Medicean stars. Even the way artists represented the sun and moon in murals and paintings mimicked Galileo's scientific drawings of heavenly bodies via the telescope. A new style of art known as Neoplatonism had become popular, in part for representing the concept that the fundamental realities of the world they perceived were entirely mathematical. The celebrated Cigoli visited often to sketch his friend so that the rebel figure could be reproduced in his secular commissions as part of the heroic cast. As these works would reside in the private salons of the aristocracy and their favor was politically necessary for the many projects of the ambitious Urban VIII, no protest was made. For the Pigeon League it was infuriating. They had done their best to try and stop him. With the trial they thought they had succeeded, but now at every turn, it seemed they had accomplished nothing.

Even though Galileo could not leave his house, he was everywhere.

In a way, Galileo himself became a light attracting the moths of intellect from everywhere. He was not the only free thinker who had suffered, but prevailing as he had, or rather with his work prevailing despite the suppression, his home saw a constant stream of genius coming and going like the tide. He was just finishing up a weeklong visitation by the polymathic Dominican Brother, Tommaso Campanella, when Bernardo Castelli arrived for his symposia on fluid hydraulics. Not wishing to overstay his welcome, Campanella was about to leave out of a sense of decorum when the sight of the back of Castelli's carriage laden with crates of wine convinced him to remain. By the time the sun set that evening, with the additional presence of Viviani, Torricelli and Maria Celeste, Galileo's study had achieved the enviable claim of the single greatest concentration of intellectual horsepower in the Western World. Of course, as the evening progressed, a few I.Q. points were sacrificed in the consumption of a substantial amount of a good vintage, but the loosening of tongues made it a small consolation.

Together the three scholars represented the various levels of favor with the church. Galileo, while out of favor now, had enjoyed a combined papal friendship and professional respect before his fall. Castelli was still valued as a papal advisor because of recent flooding in Southern Italy and represented a potential solution to a critical need for irrigation. Campanella had also served as a papal advisor on astronomical matters, but because of his own persistent championing of the *Sidereus Nuncius* and the Copernican philosophy, had spent the greatest amount of time incarcerated by the Inquisition. In many ways he reminded Galileo of the late Giordano Bruno whose fiery torture would never be forgotten. Unlike Galileo and Castelli, however, Campanella had felt the physical toll of the Inquisition's cruelty.

Campanella had been tortured.

As he reached for his glass of wine, the last two fingers of his hand did not extend. Above them on his exposed wrist, the distinct circumferential scars from the leather cuffs of the rack were discernable. In a compensatory fashion he clamped his functional digits around the cup and lifted it to take a sip.

"Here's to our own fluid hydraulics and the science of intoxication," he said cheerily.

Laughter followed as the others drank.

"You know," he said to Galileo as he had savored his wine, "you and I are a paradox."

"I'll drink to that," said Castelli with an understated humor.

"How do you mean?" asked an intrigued Galileo.

"We are similar and yet so different," said Campanella. "We both enjoyed the hospitality of Inquisition's chambers."

"True," said Galileo.

"You were threatened with torture. I was put to it," he went on, his tone becoming less jovial. "When I confessed the only thing that saved me from execution was feigning madness."

"Really?" said Viviani.

"Oh yes," said Campanella. "I raved, flung excrement and set fire to my cell."

"I hadn't actually considered that," said Galileo in an attempt to lighten the mood.

Campanella laughed.

"Yes, well, I merely feigned madness, but I think you might actually have achieved it."

It was a good joke and despite the terrible nature of the conversation they all laughed again.

"Of course, you can only claim madness once," added Campanella ruefully.

"Much like virginity," said Castelli.

Torricelli chuckled.

"We are, of course, quite different in another respect. Mobility. If you try to leave, you will be killed. I will be if I stay," said Campanella.

He was serious now.

"You are leaving," said Galileo. It sounded like a query.

"Yes. Apparently, I am considered intellectually dangerous again"

"Where will you go?" asked Castelli.

"France, I think," said Campanella.

The seriousness of his exodus settled in, killing the lighter mood. This was the last time they would probably see their friend. Campanella was having none of that, however.

"When it comes to heresy, the French take a more liberal view," he said with a slight twinkle.

Galileo caught that and added, "Much like with the commandments then?"

It was just what they needed, and the darker effect of the recent subject dissolved in the resulting laughter.

"What can I do to help you on your journey?" asked Galileo.

"A good horse would go a long way," said Campanella, enjoying the play on words.

•

The messenger on horseback had been going at a hard pace for most of the morning and his mount's withers were lathered heavily by the pace. As the animal cleared a hilltop, the rider saw the very top of the distant spires of

Rome. It seemed to him, in that moment, that if one wanted to get a true estimate of the health of the city, one often would be best served by viewing it from a distance. Within its walls, the tight clutter and overwhelming scale made a real assessment impossible. Only distance allowed real objectivity and estimation. Now, he saw several new structures rising, funded by the Barberinis in support of Urban VIII. The world was less certain than it had been for hundreds of years. With Rome having been recently sacked, first by the League of Cognac, and then by German mercenaries, stability and defense was a priority. On top of that the sway held by the spiritual authority of "God's kingdom" over the other European states had been slipping. Protestantism threatened to weaken the protective superstitions that kept the Catholic principalities in obedient line. The answer to that was money. As such, a rash of nepotism resulted in papal dynasties, with the mighty families of Italy funding their own monuments as long as their relations occupied the ranking positions. For Urban VIII, three immediate issues had required his attention. At the top was protection of commerce. His own family's power hinged on keeping the harbors open, and to appease the popular mind investment in the Vatican City was necessary. The considerations went hand in hand. Of course, with such wealth came a preponderant greed, so the army and an arsenal to support them were also being enhanced. As such, the city's vitality improved. The downside was that in the process, the Pope was becoming just another political figure in Europe's unsteady landscape.

The rider resisted the urge to spur the horse harder and leaned into the saddle with his knees as the road began a merciful slope between the stone pines. He relaxed and let the animal have his head as he galloped along. Soon the farmland became more compact, and the houses closer together. The scope of Rome transitioned to more individual detail, and as he entered its thoroughfares, he felt the energy of the city overwhelm him.

His horse nickered and rolled its eyes nervously. He felt it too.

"There, there now," said the rider, "we're almost done."

He cantered through a market for a few blocks that then opened onto the wide expanse of St. Peter's Square. Seeing the seal of a papal messenger, a young Dominican took the reins as he rode up and came to a stop.

"I have news for His Holiness," said the rider.

"I'll see to your mount," said the Dominican and immediately began a slow walk to cool the animal down as the messenger entered the cathedral.

He knelt in the doorway, made his obedience and crossed himself before hurrying across the stone floor toward the dais where Urban VIII was engaging in a discussion with the city engineers. Next to his throne were the ubiquitous scholars including the newly promoted Cardinal Caccini and his advisors, Cremonini and Colombe. On the other side were the Pope's counsel of bishops and cardinals. Seated immediately next to Urban VIII was Barbarossi, functioning as an administrative secretary for the matters of the day.

He picked up a drawing bearing the signature of Benedetto Castelli and handed it to Urban VIII. The Pope looked at its impressive, artistic representation of a river and tributary channels designed to divert waters during the floods and to retain them during the dry season. He handed the document to the scholars who looked at it and then gave it to the counsel. This was how business was done. With each new agenda item, Barbarossi loudly announced the subject and the whole process of viewing, approval and execution started anew.

He had just picked up another portfolio.

"An affirmation regarding an arsenal in the Vatican and arms factories at Tivoli and the fortified harbor of Civitavecchia," he announced.

He turned and placed it before Urban VIII to scribble his signature. Making the sign of a blessing, he handed it off to the scholars.

Urban VIII sighed. His face showed the deadening toll that the status of state, the tasks of power, and the duty of kingship was slowly taking on him.

Barbarossi picked up another portfolio and announced, "An affirmation regarding repairs and restoration of the Churches of Santa Bibiana and San Sebastiano."

It was a lot of money, but Urban VIII knew this was necessary to maintain a placidity among the church officers. This was the price of leadership, courtesy of his family's underwriting. He signed and looked up as the messenger approached.

"And the commission of a painting to be named the *Allegory of Divine Providence and Barberini Power* by Pietro da Cortona," said Barbarossi presenting another portfolio for signature.

In the gallery, Colombe leaned over and whispered to Cremonini, "He's commissioning a painting? I hesitate to guess what the church treasurer will say when it ends up hanging in a Barberini family salon."

Cremonini smiled. "Probably that it's where the purchaser dictated. Besides, it's more a tribute for the preservation of peace. Cortona is a decent enough artist, but it's really his uncle the Prince of Naples that makes this transaction worthwhile."

The messenger stopped in front of Barbarossi. He crossed himself and bowed as he handed him the dispatch. Barbarossi read it, eyes widening, then he turned and presented it to Urban VIII. The Pope studied Barbarossi curiously for a second, before reading the document. The emotional impact of the content hit him profoundly, and an interested quiet settled on the galleries surrounding him. In the scholar section in particular, there seemed to be a heightened interest. Taking an extra moment, Urban VIII considered the message before handing it back to Barbarossi who waited until the Pope nodded for him to read it aloud.

"By notice of his magnificence, the Grand Duke of Tuscany," Barbarossi gave a dramatic pause. "The States General of the Netherlands has awarded a subject of His Holiness, Galileo Galilei—"

A chorus of gasps and outraged murmurs ran through ranks of the scholars.

In an effort to regain control of the proceedings, Barbarossi, continued the reading loudly, "— subject of His Holiness, Galileo Galilei, for his measurements of the longitudes of the world by his observations of the satellites of the planet Jupiter, a gold chain worth 500 florins in recognition of his effort and contribution to all mankind."

He set the document aside and nodded that the messenger had leave to go. Behind him, Urban VIII stared ahead, haunted by regret, and something that in that moment looked very like defeat.

•

Galileo was smart enough not to accept the golden tribute from the Dutch States General. He didn't need it. The financial support generated by the interest from the amount in Welser's account, and the earnings from his inventions and writing, while not on par with the great houses of the princely states, were enough to keep an old housebound scholar in good wine and food, while maintaining a constant, generous patronage of the Order of the "Poor Clares."

To have accepted the gold chain would have been an acknowledgement of the sovereignty and approval of a foreign body. As the fiscal value would amount to more than his academic compensation by the Medicis or the Church, it would have been seen as an indication that his allegiance to them was diminished.

That was the thing that those who didn't know him misunderstood. Despite his position on Copernicus, despite the assertions of his contradiction to the scholarly interpretation of scripture, Galileo was still a pious spirit and faithful to his God. He simply still did not accept, despite his forced statement after the trial that thinking, and spirituality were incompatible. As such, he would do nothing to offend his Duke or his Church.

On the practical front, he had been left alone for years now to study and theorize as he saw fit, and without any closer scrutiny than the ever-present somnolent guard, his writings had escaped to travel farther than he ever could. They ranged from private correspondence laced with wit and observation, to heavy scientific discourse with contemporaries in all the academic centers of Europe.

One such private letter, had found its way to very special recipient.

It began as always, with him alone, at his table, an estranged witness to the world. From his vantage point of the window, he could see a young father carrying his tiny son, in the distant, ancient, thick-stemmed, post-harvest vineyard. The vines might be old, but they were productive still, though that year's vitality was now in the barrel, and the ruddy-leaved vines were heading into their woody, seasonal recovery. At first look, they seemed permanently in decline, but at the heart in the very central vein, the germ of next year's growth remained to return in leaf and floret like a mathematical law, a universal truth, like a family bond. That wasn't what had Galileo's attention, though.

He was focused on the father and son, the gentle interaction, between them. The boy was the same age that

Vincenzio had been when he was forced to give up his family. Seeing the precious moment played out as they walked down the rows framed by the autumn-spent canes, he was able to appreciate it, even though he was as removed as if watching from the moon. A moment later, Galileo picked up his pen.

He had more in common with the transitioning vineyard in decline than with the man and child now. His own body was past its flowering leaf and bearing, and soon, like the metamorphosing vines, his own constitution would turn lifeless and dry.

He was just putting the inked tip to paper when, in a perfect moment of synchronicity, he heard Maria Celeste clearing her throat. He turned.

Standing in the doorway was his son, Vincenzio. He was different now. A much more substantial man had taken the place of the boy that visited years before to plead for support as he announced he was leaving the law for music. It seemed ages ago, and the difference in him brought home to Galileo a sudden awareness of how the years had passed as he remained in the house. He felt a sudden tightening in his chest, a restriction of breath. It was, he was sure, just the overwhelming emotion inspired by his presence, that and the sight of his sister standing next to him.

Almost his family. So many years gone.

"Father," said Vincenzio.

"Vincenzio," then he added querulously, "Galilei?"

"Yes. Thank you. I received word from Medici that the name was granted."

"I am not sure what good it will do you now?" said Galileo with just a tinge of regret.

"It does me good," said Vincenzio.

It was the perfect answer. Maria Celeste looked on the verge of tears. She touched her brother on the shoulder encouraging him to enter the study and sit down. When he did, she left to get the one thing the moment called for.

She was just returning with the wine when she saw the bag next to Vincenzio's chair. He had brought his instrument.

"Aren't you going to play something?" she asked.

He looked a little surprised, but seeing Galileo nod, he took out the lute.

"I hear you are quite celebrated. Your work has brought you great fame," he said.

"Some," said Vincenzio, turning a peg to bring the strings into tune.

He looked up hesitantly.

"Unfortunately, the popular pieces were published back when I was known as Vincenzio Gamba," he said apologetically. "I would have liked for them to bear the name Galilei."

"That fault is all mine," said Galileo.

The tuning was finished, and satisfied, Vincenzio strummed the strings of the lute. The resulting chord was rich and beautiful. Galileo smiled warmly.

"You know this instrument played the accompaniment to my youth. Your grandfather was a genius." He laughed ironically. "He wanted me to study medicine, and I did for a while, but I guess it's a family trait. Sons find their own way, in spite of their fathers."

A slightly wounded look showed on Maria Celeste's face, though she said nothing.

"My friends are envious. You may not know, but you're not just a scientist to them. Everyone reads your satire." He looked around conceding a comically exaggerated nervousness. "In secret of course."

"That's the best setting for it," said Galileo.

"Play him the piece everyone loves," said Maria Celeste.

Galileo looked happily expectant as his son began an intricate fingering. It was a luxurious, almost a soothing, elevated and complex melody, but as he listened, his smile started to fade. His son could not have known. It was the same music that had played as he was marched to his recantation.

With an overwhelming sense of irony, his son's greatest professional triumph was irreparably linked to Galileo's greatest defeat. He decided right then. While Vincenzio would claim rights to his name and estate from that moment on, he would not ask that the name Gamba be changed on any of his prior work.

CHAPTER FOURTEEN

For years thereafter, Maria Celeste was more than just an attentive daughter caring for her disgraced and aging father, she was his partner in the practical matter of smuggling his works beyond Italy. While she knew the risk, the reward of late had been quite high. As she now read the letter from the great publisher, Louis Elsevier in the Netherlands, she learned that an expanded registry of banned books, the *prohibitum librorum* had been instituted by the Inquisition. It warned that any of Galileo's heretical works should be included. Considering how the Inquisition felt about Galileo, Elsevier wrote, that meant all of them.

Even so, she read, the publisher was going forth with more printings of the Dialogue regardless of the threat, in part because of its popularity and the demand, but also as a matter of principle. He was also interested in another concept that her father was addressing in his less structured correspondence. For most of his life Galileo had been studying the properties of bodies in motion. He called it the *De Motu*, and while he had often come back to it, he had never published. Elsevier thought he should. In particular, there was one concept that he found intriguing and of great promise. It stated that unless impeded, a moving body would remain so. He sensed it could be something great. Elsevier agreed and rather than risk its capture in transit, he had come up with a different strategy.

"He is coming to see you?" she said looking up from the letter.

"Here?" said Galileo. "That is rather bold."

Then he coughed.

Ironically, the letter had reached the house in Florence only a little ahead of the traveling Elsevier. The mail in those days was only as fast as the horse that carried it, and as Elsevier and his daughter Famke did not want to risk word of his arrival preceding him by too much, they had departed Holland the same day it was sent.

Elsevier was brave, his continued publication of the prohibited book had proven that, but he was also not a fool. The Inquisition's reach extended to the Netherlands, certainly, but traveling to Italy put him much closer to the body of the beast. He didn't want to give them too much time to prepare, especially with his daughter in attendance. As for Famke, she was eager to meet the greatest mind of the age and as their carriage pulled up in front of the house, she carefully held a bouquet of flowers in her lap so as not to bruise a single petal.

Unfortunately, the cough that had recently begun to rack Galileo was not to be shaken and he was spending more time in bed than at the window in creative thought. It reminded him again of his beloved grape vines and their dormant interval through the colder months. He knew they were just gathering their strength to burst forth in pink bud and green leaf, just when they seemed at their most lifeless. In his case, however, he wondered if he really had another season left.

Maria Celeste, Viviani, Torricelli seemed to sense it too and they had moved his bed down to the study so that he had less distance to travel to get back to the work he loved. Vincenzio was visiting more frequently and had made certain to introduce his children to their grandfather, as if he wasn't sure how much longer the opportunity would be afforded. Ironically the requests to visit were increasing too.

"God has a sense of irony," he said upon hearing of the mounting number. Then he frowned at another thought. "Or perhaps, he is just wiser."

Maria Celeste looked like she didn't quite understand.

"I mean, He has allowed me to work for so long, uninterrupted by fame," he chuckled, before dissolving into a paroxysm of coughing.

"I'll call for the physician," said a worried Viviani.

Galileo waved a dismissive hand. "I doubt his opinion has changed in the last week. There is no need to bother the man simply so he can confirm that I remain quite old."

Torricelli and Maria Celeste smiled subtly.

It was much more than that. His heart, the great symbol of his perseverance, determination and accomplishment was failing as a mechanical device. Unlike his magnificent pendulum, its rhythm was irregular now, and even with their limited medical understanding of its function, this was recognized as a cause for alarm. Of course, his physician's answer to the diagnosis was a prescription for bleeding, followed by thermal cupping.

Afterward he lay back on his bed, recovering in the muted light of the open window. The Tuscan sun was not at its full strength, impeded by a gathering cloud cover. As a result, the breeze that entered, carried with it a thermal announcement of the coming autumn. Galileo looked over at the thermometer seated just inside the sill. The glass balls were realigned, confirming what the breeze insinuated across his brow.

At that moment, a knock sounded at the door.

"I could tell them that now is not a good time," volunteered Maria Celeste.

"But then they might ask when would be?" he said raising a clever eyebrow. Once again, his sense of bemusement was contagious. She smiled.

"Are you sure?"

"I haven't put my hypothesis to a test, but I believe so," he said.

She nodded and walked out of the study. A few moments later, a tall, elegantly dressed, white-haired man and a young blonde woman with kind, corn-flower blue eyes appeared in the doorway. Upon seeing the recumbent state of their host both looked immediately alarmed.

"Oh, forgive us, Maestro. If we had only known," started an apologetic Elsevier.

"Actually, I should apologize for not getting up," he said thinly.

There was a quality to Elsevier that Galileo had seen before and that he recognized immediately, an unhurried nature that allowed for indulgence of the amenities. It was the undeniable hallmark of a certain level of wealth and privilege. It insulated and alleviated the pressures of any objective. In certain circles it was called manners, but it was more than that, Galileo knew. It was a kind of invincibility available with privilege, an echelon of ease that was usually reserved for a precious Olympian few. And yet, it was Elsevier who had put himself out to travel, to pay homage to a man with precious few invincibilities.

"Ah," said Elsevier. "I am forgetting myself. I am Louis Elsevier." He turned to his daughter. "And this is my daughter, Famke. It is quite the honor to finally meet you, Doctor Galilei."

Famke hurried over and placed the flawless bouquet on Galileo's chest. Galileo held them up and squinted.

"They are lovely, as are you," he said.

"We only just received your letter," said Maria Celeste.

"Now I must apologize. Allow me," said Galileo. "This is my daughter, Sister Maria Celeste."

They nodded to her.

"And my colleagues, Vincenzo Viviani and Evangelista Torricelli."

Within the orbit of Galileo, the two scholars had long accepted their place as lesser satellites, but by the world's standards both were exceptional academicians and accomplished on their own. Elsevier's reaction upon hearing their names served as proof of that.

"Oh, yes, of course, *Professore* Viviani. Your book on calculations is a marvel indeed," he said, his face breaking out into an impressed incredulous smile. "And *Professore* Torricelli, have you completed your work on pressures..." He searched his memory. "The instrument you are constructing?"

"The barometer," said Torricelli.

"Yes," said Elsevier. "How is it coming along?'

"Quite well, thank you," he answered.

"We look forward to publishing your work," said Elsevier.

"I tell them often, they are wasting their time here," said Galileo. "The future belongs to young men. Old grape vines like myself are best considered by their past accomplishments... fermenting in the dark."

Famke laughed. Viviani and Torricelli objected, but Maria Celeste saw something just then in her father that separated her from the rest. He was growing old, and while his demeanor and fascination with the world was still that of a curious boy, there was no denying the practical effect of time and what was physically happening.

"Speaking of publishing," said Elsevier. "I have some items I thought you might find interesting."

Viviani and Torricelli were on it.

"In the back, the wooden crate," yelled Elsevier and then turning back to Galileo reached into his coat and produced a bottle. It had been kept cold, that much was obvious from the condensation forming on the outside of the glass. "I did not know of your misfortune of health, or I would not have presumed."

Galileo waved his hand dismissively.

"What is it?"

"White wine, from Germany," said Elsevier. It is best served while cold, so we made sure to load it in ice and shavings for the trip.

"German wine," said Galileo with just a hint of doubt.

"I assure you, it is quite good," said Elsevier. "Of course, given your health..."

"I have seen many doctors," said Galileo with a teasing edge. "They argue constantly about everything from diagnosis to how best to make me miserable while keeping me alive. However, they do agree on one thing. I am best sustained by an unlimited and constant ingestion of wine." He looked at Maria Celeste. "Would you?"

She took the bottle, opened it and began pouring. Then she handed a cup to her father just as Viviani and Torricelli walked back in with the cargo. He took a sip.

"Well?" asked Elsevier.

"The scientific method has proven your hypothesis," grinned Galileo. "My compliments to the Germans."

They laughed and drank and for a moment, the clock rolled back and once again Galileo held his intellectual court as he had years ago, but Sister Maria Celeste could tell that the interval of his humor and life spark was shorter than it had ever been. Elsevier saw it too. It prompted him to be direct. He reached into the crate and picked up a newly printed copy of the Dialogue.

"Few men enjoy a legacy," he said handing the copy to Galileo. "This will stand longer than everyone in this room." He looked at Famke and Maria Celeste, "And their children. You have endured the injustice of lesser minds and character, Maestro. It is one thing to be a genius. It is quite another to be brave enough to sustain it. I am humbled by you and grateful to be allowed to help send your words into the world."

Galileo looked at the book. He ran a thin hand over it. It was a strange thing to hold a tangible representation of one's mind and soul.

He looked around the room at the artwork on the walls. Drawings of the phases of the moon and tidal charts in correspondence, calculations and the heavenly representation of Orion's belt, and more. They were all images that had begun inside his head. Now they populated the interior of a room. It occurred to him that this small chamber in a domicile had become the universe of his own mind.

He felt quite humbled.

"I have to tell you," said Elsevier. "Your work, it has broken free from those that would have constrained it. If I have contributed to that, then my own life has been well spent. The *Dialogue*. It is a triumph. Everyone agrees, your scientific method, it is changing the world. I think, though, there is something you have underestimated in your own writing."

"What is that?" said Galileo.

Elsevier was a smart man. Galileo had already conceded that, and so his opinion was important. He shrugged.

"A small thing the way you present it, but I suspect it might be an even greater principle than all your other observations."

"Oh?" said Galileo.

"That bodies remain in motion despite opposition, by their nature."

"Yes," said Galileo. "I haven't proven it, and I likely will not. I suppose I'll leave it to some child perhaps not yet born," he smiled.

The old man was wearing down, but Elsevier had one last thing he wanted to say.

"You have conquered it all and in one great work. Atomics, mechanics, the translation of forces. We can't keep up with the demand for the *Dialogue*. It's in every library in Europe. Your principles have won over every thinking person on the continent."

Galileo smiled and waited a moment before responding, "So, nowhere near the majority then."

Elsevier smiled, but it didn't prevail, and he looked at the others with concern. It was clear that he saw the decline coming and as a publisher, as one who took some responsibility for making sure the truth made transitioned to the world, the coming loss of such a source was painful. Sister Maria Celeste saw it on his face and nodded.

Elsevier turned back toward Galileo and patted his hand.

"We must let you rest," he said.

"I believe the time for that is not far off," said Galileo with an understated whimsy.

The allusion to death was not nearly as funny to the rest of them, and Famke, who was affected with a tender heart, leaned closer and said, "It has been a great honor."

The air coming through the window had dropped several degrees in just that short time, and not so terribly far away, a roll of thunder announced what was coming.

"The rainy season," declared Galileo. "Be careful on the road."

The guests stood and walked out of the room. Once outside they climbed into the coach. Elsevier had planned to spend more time in Florence, to perhaps even coax another work from the old genius, but having seen his current state, he now knew that would never be possible.

"What shall we do, Father?" asked Famke.

Elsevier looked out of the coach. To the north a cold front had turned the sky an ominous dark gray and blue. Galileo was right. The stormy season was at hand, in more ways than one. There were stories of changes taking place in England, of clashes stirred by Catholics and Protestants. They were calling it the Reformation, but it seemed far more inclined to dissolution. In an effort at control, authors were required by the government to obtain official approval before they could publish, much as the Church had done in Italy. Ironically, that was good for Elsevier. To protect the integrity of their work, many writers had sought his house, where no such censorship would apply. Of course, such an act would not go unpunished, and in a strange correlation to the very story of the man he had just visited, Elsevier had seen a number of them flee their country as soon as their books were published.

This was why he was heading back to Holland. A war of words was at hand and a new generation would need to carry it forward. Besides, there was one author that he wanted under his imprint. One that he had a feeling was going to be critical to championing thought.

He thumped the roof of the carriage. The driver responded by snapping the reins. A second later the carriage lurched forward and they were on their way.

In the study, Maria Celeste leaned over her father searching his face, a concerned look on her own.

"What is it?" she asked.

Galileo smiled, but it was just a façade of pleasantry.

"First, could you help me to the window? Viviani? Torricelli? I would like to feel the breeze."

The two scholars leaped to his aid and helped him sit up. Then gently they supported him in the short walk to the chair in front of the desk. The gentle wind was blowing steadily, carrying with its cool tonic, a smell of rain. Thunder sounded again, and Galileo closed his eyes and took a long cleansing breath.

"I think you might fetch the physician after all," he said.

Maria Celeste rushed over and put her hands on his thin shoulders.

"What is wrong?" she asked as the other two looked on with alarm.

"It seems I am blind," he said simply.

•

The cause was not apparent. Upon examination, the doctor, noted again the irregularity of his heart, but when he suggested another round of bleeding, Galileo waved him off with disgust.

"I am almost a husk as it is," he said wryly.

With nothing more to offer than some additional tortures, the doctor conceded, but at the door he allowed to Maria Celeste that the malady that was taking down Galileo by increments was not far from getting him entirely. Whatever time left, while certainly short, could not be specifically predicted.

One thing was certain. Had he been forced to read the psalms on his own, this would have happened sooner. Now she would serve as his eyes entirely. In the next few months his decline accelerated. A hernia kept him from rising from the bed without great pain, and when he did stand, or sit upright, the failing mechanics of his heart would give him bouts of mild apoplexy and dizziness.

Whenever that happened, he would jokingly point out that finally, he was feeling the earth move and only wished he could share the experience with his former enemies.

"He is preparing to go, I fear," said an affected Viviani.

Maria Celeste nodded, and when the portly scholar began to weep with the same intensity that he would have for his own father, she put a consoling arm around his shoulders. The world with Galileo in it was coming to an end, but there was one more extraordinary moment still in store. A final last salvo.

It was at the end of a painful week, and almost as if the world sensed it was going to lose him, a torrent of mail requesting interviews and permission to visit had poured in. As Maria Celeste sorted through them, one caught her eye, and the answer to the correspondent she could safely assume would be in the affirmative. Writing the response for her father, she had added a postscript of her own.

The visitor should hurry.

•

The guard at the front door of the Galileo home had long since ceased anything even remotely close to a serious police function. He had in a strange way become almost a part of the household. At the very least he had transformed to a much more benign fixture, so much so that Maria Celeste had placed a chair outside the door so that he could sit under the eave of the roof and avoid the hot sun and weather.

Now, he leaned back as a smattering of rain fell. It wasn't going to last long. Beyond the rapidly moving clouds, he could see the bright blue of a sunny sky. He had just to outlast it.

He was thinking of that when a splendidly apportioned carriage rounded the corner at the end of the street and approached. The guard had seen no end of fancy conveyance pull up in his time protecting the world from Galileo Galilei. There had been papal carriages, elaborate livery carrying civil authorities and nobility, but none of those could compare with the one that stopped in front of him just then.

The molding on the outside was extremely ornate and had been painted a light gold as a perfect accompaniment to the overall coat of royal blue. The window covers were not the usual leather, but velvet, and a deep purple to indicate some sense of status and greater luxury for the passenger inside. As the guard took it in, it occurred to him that if carriages could be equated to birds of plumage, this one was a peacock.

A moment later, the carriage driver, with an elegant purple umbrella in hand, jumped down and opened the door. Another dramatic second passed and then a foot extended, like one from an ecdysiast revealing from behind a stage curtain. It was clad in a red velvet slipper from which rose a white stocking that tucked into a pair of matching red silk knee britches. As the driver extended a hand to assist, it was grasped by a slim, almost feminine hand of milky white complexion.

Leaning out, the occupant could still not be immediately identified by the guard as a man or woman and only as he got closer did the fascinated sentry note the fine mustache of the same auburn hue as the long hair descending to the man's shoulders.

Throughout their progress, the driver carefully held the rain cover so that not a single drop made contact as the stylish young man walked to the door. As to his demeanor, he seemed extremely casual, almost fey like a member of royalty, or one so accomplished or acknowledged that he had outdistanced even that strata.

At the door he stopped and announced himself in perfect Italian, "John Milton is here to see the *Doctore*."

John Milton was a star, and like Galileo, already something of an intellectual outlaw. Disinherited by his own Catholic father for having been found reading a Protestant prayer book as a teen, he had gone on to meteoric success as a poet, pamphleteer and social commentator. Though not without his own scars from his time in the academic world, he had been mockingly known as the "Lady of Christ's College" for his very feminine appearance. Like so many of his ilk, he had left England because of the increasing censorship. Ever the politically astute player, though, he had made certain for it not to appear that he had fled so that he could work without submission to a repressive reformist movement in his native land. Under the guise of a lecture and performance tour, he had made his way to Florence, where in almost all matters and mannerisms he had found a place that spoke to his soul. Everything from the style and sensibility of this part of the world felt like a perfect match for his mindset. Now, he was going to indulge it once more by meeting with the one man whose work, life and history provided an inspiration and a correlation to his own.

The front door opened just then, and Maria Celeste smiled genuinely as she stepped back for him to enter. The guard had no idea who he really was, but the carriage, his deportment and now the Sister's response told him enough.

He bowed slightly as the ethereal Milton walked inside.

"*Signor* Milton," said Maria Celeste.

"*Sorella*. Sister," he replied again with a perfect Italian inflection.

She liked that and smiled again before leading him to the door of the study, where she paused.

"He has been looking forward to this," she said.

"As have I," said Milton.

Galileo had been clear. He would not receive someone he regarded like Milton as an invalid. Granted he could not actually see him; the world had been reduced to a useless amalgam of blurry shades, but he was determined that he would present himself with as much dignity as possible.

He turned at the sound of them entering.

"Your guest has arrived," said Maria Celeste.

As a poet, Milton was a sensitive man and seeing the vaunted Galileo in such a state, his eyes welled up. He immediately walked over and deferentially knelt next to the bed.

"*Professore* Galilei. My joy."

Galileo stretched out his hand. Milton took it gently and leaned down to kiss it as he would a prince.

"I am a big fan of your writing," said Galileo.

"And I yours," said Milton.

"Then again, I have an excellent reader," he said indicating Maria Celeste.

She nodded her acceptance of the compliment.

"It is necessary these days, I'm afraid, but please, sit," he said. "We can flatter each other."

"I know," said Maria Celeste, as he was about to say more. "A good wine is in order."

Milton gave her a smile as Galileo grinned appreciatively.

"I worry that someday soon, she will realize she has learned far more than I could ever teach. "He leaned in closer and whispered, "She's quite an intellect."

"And I have excellent hearing," she said from the kitchen.

Milton looked around at the drawings and the devices like so many brilliant decorations in the office. He seemed dazzled and was out of his chair taking a closer look at the drawings of the moon's surface when Maria Celeste returned with the wine. She poured a glass for each of them and placed one in her father's hand.

"To honored guests," said Galileo.

They toasted and had their affirming sip just as Viviani and Torricelli walked in.

"Ah said Galileo. "That must be my associates."

"I know who you are," said Milton. "*Professore*s, an honor."

As they nodded acknowledging their flattery, Maria Celeste stood up.

"And with that, I must take my leave. There is an outbreak of dysentery among the children. We are caring for them at the convent."

At the mention of it, Milton started. He reached into his coat and withdrew a bulging sack of coins.

"For the Poor Clares," he said. "That they may warrant the name a little less."

She smiled and took the sack.

"*Grazie*. It will certainly help."

Then she turned and walked away.

"So," said Galileo, "how long will you be in Florence?"

The way he said it carried a tone of awareness, of the greater social reason for his travel outside England.

"I am here for the summer," said Milton.

"How nice," chuckled Galileo and then he added dryly, "I am not sure that I am,".

Milton smiled despite the genuine alarm the words inspired in Galileo's two colleagues. One had to admire his defiant humor in the face of impending darkness. He certainly knew how valuable that was.

"And what is it that brings you here?" Galileo was being discreet. He knew enough but did not want to pry.

"The wit," said Milton lightly.

"And here I thought it was the beauty," smiled Galileo.

"Well, beauty too," said Milton looking around at the devices and artwork in the room. "I have copies of those drawings of the moon," he added.

Galileo nodded.

"Yes, they were the beginning of many problems," he said. Then rethinking added, "Well actually, it began the awareness. The facts were there all along. I just admitted to them."

"And all hell broke loose," said Milton.

It was the first time the phrase had been uttered in the history of the world.

"I like that," chuckled Galileo. "If you believe the charges against me, then I suppose it did."

"I heard a story, that the Spanish navy tried to apply your longitudes to a helmet apparatus," said Milton.

"It's true. Of course, I didn't design that. Someone who didn't understand what I was saying did it." He considered the fiasco for a moment. "They almost destroyed their entire fleet."

Milton chuckled.

"If only Queen Elizabeth had access to you when the armada attacked."

"Not everyone who knows the truth knows how to use it," affirmed Galileo." He leaned forward intimately. "The concept was sound, but alas it did not translate. It was a generally bad idea." He smiled and added, "If you promise not share this with anyone...I have them occasionally."

Milton laughed. "Of course not. The way I see it, you've been punished enough for your good ones."

Galileo thought on that for a moment.

"Legitimate thought will always suffer the blows of the ignorant and those who reason well will always be greatly outnumbered by those who reason badly."

Milton chuckled again then studied the old genius.

"You want to know the real reason, I wanted to meet you?"

Galileo tilted his head questioningly.

"*The Divine Comedy*," said Milton seriously.

Galileo's eyebrows went up in surprise.

"I didn't write that," he said flatly.

"No, but you did apply mathematics to map the volume and area of each of Dante's levels of hell."

Now Galileo chuckled. "Of all the things I have done. That one always comes up. Well, as I was condemned to go there, I thought I would determine how much room I would have, so I'd know how many of my possessions I could bring."

A quick intimacy had been established and Milton decided to share the idea that Galileo's work had inspired.

"You might be interested. Your little exercise, it has given me an idea. A story, of original sin, a fall from grace," he said.

"Adam and Eve?" asked Galileo.

"More original than that even, an act of defiance in heaven and its penalty," said Milton.

Then Galileo understood. "Ah Lucifer. I always found him more interesting than prohibitive. And so, Dante's hell?"

"Yes. Your assessment. Science, mathematics applied to the theological."

Galileo frowned, searching his memory. "The first level was much larger. I suppose because it was for the less sinfully accomplished." He grinned. "Apparently, even in the afterlife mediocrity constitutes the largest demographic."

Even Viviani and Torricelli had to grin at that.

"For a potential heretic like myself, there is much less room," said Galileo teasingly. "On the plus side, the heretics are guarded by demons, so at least I'll have had someone to regale."

"Maestro," said Viviani nervously.

"Of course, as I have recanted, my destination is not quite so assured," he laughed, then another thought sobered him. "Aren't you a little concerned that your own work may lead to the same fate as mine?"

Before Milton could answer, a sudden clap of thunder sounded nearby.

"An admonition, perhaps," chuckled Galileo nodding into the cool breeze.

The rain began falling harder now. Galileo listened and took a sip of wine. His obvious, simple pleasure in the elemental struck Milton as impressive.

"A good sign, rain," he said at last. "This time of year, it helps the vine. It's laying by. Of course, too much, too early or late weakens a grape."

"Is that a scientific observation or an artistic one?" asked Milton.

"I am a tired old man. I think I shall leave the art to you. Science is what I know." He suddenly, really did sound quite tired.

Milton could read the unspoken message and with a look of decorum said gently, "Oh, of course. You must be weary. Forgive me for my enthusiasm."

Galileo reacted.

"Not at all. I have enjoyed this. You must visit me again when you have finished your tale of the heavenly fall." With a half-smile he added, "But I beg you...write swiftly."

Milton stood and took Galileo by the hand.

"Of course, Maestro," he said.

He handed his glass to Viviani and started for the door. Just before he exited, though, he paused and said, "Forgive me for asking, but I must know."

"Yes?" said Galileo.

"If you had it to do over again. Would you still your pen? Save yourself such pain?"

Mary Celeste's head popped up. It was the defining question. She looked at her father poignantly.

Galileo smiled. "Of course, the truth demanded it. Regardless of the cost of its declaration, denying it would have impoverished my soul. God placed the evidence before me. I could not turn my face away from it any more than I could from him. What the Inquisition never understood was that I was and still am, a devout man."

Milton smiled as Galileo nodded toward the window and continued.

"How then could I avoid reading His open book of the heavens?"

"Even though the Church attempted to geld you, to silence you? To cut off any chance for the offspring of your intelligence and creativity?" asked Milton.

It was a remarkably similar statement to what Father Ferrero had said in making his case that Galileo recant. Instead of showing alarm though, Galileo smiled.

"Well, it really was no surprise. I mean, is there anyone that wants to castrate an intellectual more than a holy man?" grinned Galileo.

Milton laughed.

"Good-bye, *Doctore*," he said.

"Good-bye," said Galileo.

•

That day when Sister Maria Celeste left for the convent was the last day any of them would see her alive. The outbreak was cholera, though in that era precious little was known about how it happened and even less was known about how it spread. The majority of the afflicted that had been brought into the convent that morning were children. By midday their parents were presenting. By the evening, the illness was also affecting the stretcher bearers and the sanitarians that carried the chamber pots. The disease swept through them all, sapping strength as the alimentary canal issued the life-sustaining fluid of the body in a torrent of rice water that no amount of oral replacement could match. As night fell, Maria Celeste was running a fever. The next morning, she was dead.

It was Vincenzio that brought his father the news, along with a declaration that he should not worry for care and gave him his word that he would see to his well-being in the years to come. One look at the grief on his father's face, though, and it was obvious that he would not be obligated for nearly that long. Between the decline of his body, new pains and the further failing of his sight, Galileo was no longer eating, because he told his beloved Viviani and Torricelli, he just didn't see the value in rewarding a body that was serving him so poorly.

The truth was that the loss of his daughter, confidant and most kindred spirit was a crippling and decisive blow.

In the end, all he wanted was for them to place him in his chair at the table in front of the open window. He turned his face toward it just as he had when he could see the heavens or alternatively, the restorative view of the vineyards.

Now the cool breeze rewarded him, parting his long beard and lifting his gray hair to whisper around his ears. It was a message he was still interpreting when he took his final breath.

•

Matteo Zanconi was a mediocre thief on a good day. He was nowhere near that good when he was drunk, and as the cretinous guard led him down the jail corridor that night, he was still considerably intoxicated. He did sober considerably, however, when a rat ran past his feet as the guard unlocked the cell door.

"This place is not fit for an animal," he said.

"And yet too good for the likes of you," said the guard before pushing him inside.

The interior was depressing, dank – and with the cloud covering the moon outside the very narrow window – almost completely dark.

Matteo sat down on the small hard bed and groused at his situation. He was still thinking about it when the clouds parted, and something on the far wall caught his eye.

He leaned forward and squinted. There really was something there and it looked like writing. He got up and walked across the room.

Just then, another wave of clouds covered the moon and the lettering disappeared. Matteo was curious now. He ran his hand over the deeply cut letters, but he couldn't quite determine their meaning just by touch.

He was at a complete loss and about to give up when the clouds parted suddenly again, and the lettering stood out in stark relief. Matteo blinked and frowned, grasping at the inaccessibility of the words. Try as he might, though, he couldn't make sense of the message. In the end, he was left with the mystery of the simple phrase, etched in stone like some immutable rebuttal that simply read – *And Yet It Moves.*

THE END

....

A natural philosopher, astronomer, and mathematician, Galileo established the sciences of motion, astronomy, strength of materials and the development of the modern scientific method.

Known as the "father of physics" his work influenced and inspired the efforts of Newton, Einstein, and Stephen Hawking.

His words prevail.

About the Author

Matthew Minson, MD is a screenwriter, author, and director whose work has been recognized by Faulkner-Wisdom, Writer's Digest, Goldberg, and the Nicholl Fellowship at the Academy of Motion Picture Arts and Sciences. His novel, *Sun City*, is the 2022 Best Indie Book Award winner for humor. He has published numerous short stories, most notably one that he adapted and cowrote as the award-winning short film *New Soul*, which received the Encore Award at Cinequest in 2015. His 2019 directorial debut, *You Have Arrived*, was a selection and best short nominee at numerous festivals. An internationally recognized Public Health expert, Dr. Minson is the creator of the healthcare app *Minson's Guide to Specialty Hospitals* and his *Prepare to Defend Yourself* series of healthcare and social advocacy books published by Texas A&M University press have received numerous awards including a "Best of the Year" selection by Library Journal. His artistic interests are focused on greater issues of humanity and social conditions which are often explored by the interactions of his characters. In particular, he is interested in the effects of social media, environment and their threat to the individual, though he maintains a sustained optimism bolstered by the influence of his wife and two dogs.

www.writerminson.com

Acknowledgments

Thanks for reading! If you like the book, please add a short review on Amazon or your favourite bookseller website and let me know what you thought!

www.ingramcontent.com/pod-product-compliance
Lightning Source LLC
Chambersburg PA
CBHW070628260626
47161CB00007B/2625
* 9 7 9 8 9 8 5 4 7 1 7 2 4 *